The stirring story of the life and times of Richard Bolitho is told in Alexander Kent's bestselling novels, all available in Arrow.

By the same author

Midshipman Bolitho
Stand Into Danger
In Gallant Company
Sloop of War
To Glory We Steer
Command A King's Ship
Passage to Mutiny
Enemy in Sight!
The Flag Captain
Signal – Close Action!
The Inshore Squadron
A Tradition of Victory
Success to the Brave
Colours Aloft!

FORM LINE OF BATTLE!

Alexander Kent

ARROW

First published by Arrow Books in 1970

© Alexander Kent 1969

Alexander Kent has asserted his
right under the Copyright, Designs and Patents Act, 1988
to be identified as the author of this work

First published in the United Kingdom by
Hutchinson in 1969
Random House, 20 Vauxhall Bridge Road, London SW1V 2SA

Random House Australia (Pty) Limited
20 Alfred Street, Milsons Point, Sydney,
New South Wales 2061, Australia

Random House New Zealand Limited
18 Poland Road, Glenfield
Auckland 10, New Zealand

Random House South Africa (Pty) Limited
PO Box 337, Bergvlei, South Africa

Random House UK Limited Reg. No. 954009

A CIP catalogue record for this book
is available from the British Library

ISBN 0 09 908850 9

Printed and bound in Germany by
Elsnerdruck, Berlin

Contents

The thundering line of battle stands,
    And in the air Death moans and sings:
But Day shall clasp him with strong hands,
    And Night shall fold him in strong wings.

JULIAN GRENFELL

1

The Old *Hyperion*

The frigate *Harvester*, nine days outward bound from
Spithead, turned easily into the gentle offshore breeze and
dropped anchor, the echoes of her gun salute reverb-
erating and grumbling around the towering wall of Gibraltar's unchanging Rock. Her young captain let his eye
rest a moment longer on the busy activity below the
quarterdeck as his men threw themselves into the work of
swaying out boats, urged on by sharp commands and
more than one cuff from an impatient petty officer. Entering harbour was always a tense moment, and the captain knew that he was not the only one aboard who was
aware of the big ships of the line anchored nearby, the
largest of which wore a vice-admiral's flag at the fore,
and no doubt there were several telescopes already
trained on his small command ready to reprimand or
criticise.

With a final glance he strode aft and crossed to the starboard side where a tall, solitary figure leaned against the
hammock nettings.

'Shall I signal for a boat, sir? Or would one of mine
be sufficient?'

Captain Richard Bolitho pulled himself from his
thoughts and turned to face the other man.

'Thank you, Captain Leach, I will take yours. It will
save time.' He imagined he saw a touch of relief in the
man's eyes, and realised that it could not have been easy

7

for so young and junior a captain, who had not yet attained the coveted post rank, to carry him from England as a passenger.

He relaxed slightly and added, 'You have a fine ship. We made a quick passage.' He shivered in spite of the early-morning sunlight and saw Leach watching him with new interest. But what could he understand of Bolitho's feelings? While the frigate had beaten down the English Channel and round Brest, where once more the British squadrons rode out all weathers to watch over a blockaded French fleet, Bolitho's thoughts had reached far beyond the plunging bowsprit to this moment only. Down across the Bay, with its blustering winds and savage currents, and still further south until the coast of Portugal loomed like a blue mist far abeam. He had had plenty of time to think of what lay ahead, of his new command, and all that she might come to mean to him. In his solitary walks on the frigate's spray-dashed quarterdeck he had been conscious of his role as a mere passenger, and more than once had had to check himself from interfering in the running of the ship.

Now, beneath the Rock's great shadow, he must push such thoughts out of his mind. He was no longer a frigate captain with all the independence and dash that post entailed. Within minutes he would take command of a ship of the line, one of those which swung so calmly and so confidently above their reflections just two cables distant. He made himself look squarely at the one which lay astern of the flagship. A two-decker, one of the seventy-four-gun ships which made up the backbone of England's far-stretched squadrons. The frigate beneath his feet moved restlessly even within the calm waters of the anchorage, her tapered topmasts spiralling against the washed-out blue sky, her rigging humming as if from impatience at the very necessity of being near her heavier consorts. By comparison the two-decker looked squat and unmoving, her towering masts and yards, her double line of ports, adding to her appearance of ponderous power, around which the busy harbour craft scurried like so many water-beetles.

The other man watched the gig being rowed round to the entry port and saw Bolitho's coxswain standing beside a pile of personal luggage like a thickset dog guarding his master's most prized possessions.

He said, 'You've a good man there, sir.'

Bolitho followed his glance and smiled. 'Allday has been with me since . . .' His mind went back over the years without effort, as if every thought and each memory was always lying in wait like a half-forgotten picture. He said abruptly, 'My first coxswain was killed at the Saintes in '82. Allday has been with me ever since.' Just a few words of explanation, yet how much more they meant to Bolitho, just as Allday's familiar shape was a constant reminder. Now the Saintes and the frigate *Phalarope* were eleven years in the past, and England was at war again.

Leach watched Bolitho's grave face and wondered. During the uneventful voyage from Spithead he had wanted to confide with him, but something had stopped him. He had brought plenty of other passengers to Gibraltar and usually they made a pleasant diversion in the daily routine. Officers for the garrison, couriers and replacements for men killed by accident or design in a war which was already spreading in every direction. But something in Bolitho's impassive, almost withdrawn manner had deterred him from close contact. He looked at him now with a mixture of interest and envy. Bolitho was a senior captain and about to take a step which with

9

any luck at all would place him on the list for flag rank within a few years, maybe only months.

From what Bolitho had said he guessed him to be in his middle or late thirties. He was tall and surprisingly slim, and when he smiled his face became equally youthful. It was said that Bolitho had been away for several years between the wars in the Great South Sea and had come back half dead with fever. It was probably true, he decided. There were deep lines at the corners of his mouth, and beneath the even tan there was a certain fineness to the skin and cheekbones which betrayed such an illness. But the hair which was pulled back to the nape of his neck was black, without even a touch of grey, and the one lock which curled down above his right eye added to his appearance of controlled recklessness.

A lieutenant touched his hat. 'Boat's ready, sir.'

Bolitho held out his hand. 'Well, goodbye for the present, Leach. No doubt we will meet again directly.'

The frigate's captain smiled for the first time. 'I hope so, sir.' He snapped his fingers with sudden irritation. 'I almost forgot! There is a midshipman aboard who is also appointed to your ship. Will he go across with you?'

He spoke carelessly, as if he were discussing a piece of unwanted baggage, and Bolitho grinned in spite of his inner anxiety. 'We were all midshipmen once, Leach.' He nodded. 'He can come with me.'

Bolitho climbed down the ladder to the entry port where the bosun's mates and marines were assembled to see him over the side. His boxes had already vanished, and Allday was waiting by the bulwark, his eyes watching Bolitho as he knuckled his forehead and reported, 'All stowed, Captain.'

Bolitho nodded. There was something very reassuring about Allday. He was no longer the lithe topman he had

10

once been. He had filled out now, so that in his blue jacket and wide duck trousers he looked muscular and unbreakable, like a rock. But his eyes were still the same. Half thoughtful, half amused. Yes, it was good to have him here today.

Then Bolitho saw the midshipman. He got a quick impression of a pale, delicate face and a thin, gangling body which did not seem able to hold still. It was odd that he had not seen him before within the close world of the frigate, he thought.

As if reading his mind Leach said shortly, 'He's been seasick for most of the voyage.'

Bolitho asked kindly, 'What is your name, boy?'

The midshipman began, 'S-S-Seton, sir.' Then he lapsed into blushing silence.

Leach said unfeelingly, 'He stutters, too. I suppose we must take all kinds in times like these.'

Bolitho hid a smile. 'Quite so.' He waited a moment and then added, 'Well, Mr. Seton, you go down into the boat first, if you please.' He saw the boy's mind wrestling with this early complication in his new career and then said, 'Carry on, Allday.'

He hardly heard the twitter of pipes or the harsh bark of commands, and only when the gig had moved clear of the frigate's hull and the oars sent her skimming across the unbroken water did he permit himself another glance at his new ship.

Allday followed his stare and said quietly, 'Well there she is, Captain. The old *Hyperion*.'

As the little gig pulled steadily over the blue water Bolitho concentrated his full attention on the anchored

11

Hyperion. Allday had perhaps made his comment without thought, yet his words seemed to jar another chord in Bolitho's mind as if to rule out this further meeting as mere coincidence.

Hyperion was an old ship, for it was twenty-one years since her keel had first tasted salt water, and Bolitho's rational mind told him that it was inevitable he should see her from time to time as his service carried him from one part of the world to the next. Yet whenever his mind and body had been tried to the limit it now seemed as if this old ship of the line had somehow been close by. At the bloody battles of the Chesapeake, and again at the Saintes, when his own beloved frigate had almost been pounded into submission, he had seen her blunt bows thrusting through the thickest of the smoke, her sides flashing with gunfire and sails pockmarked with holes as she fought to hold her place in the line.

He narrowed his grey eyes as the sunlight lanced up from the water and threw a pattern of dancing reflections across the ship's tall side. He knew that she had been in steady commission now for over three years and had returned home from the West Indies with high hopes for a quick pay-off and well-earned rest both for herself and her company.

But while *Hyperion* had sailed serenely on her peacetime affairs in the Caribbean sunlight and Bolitho had fought wretchedly against a consuming fever in his house at Falmouth, the clouds of war had gathered once more across Europe. The bloody revolution which had seized France from coast to coast had at first been viewed with nervous excitement from across the English Channel, a human reaction of people who watch an old enemy weakened from within without cost to themselves, but as the fury spread and the stories filtered back to England of a new, even more powerful nation emerging from the din of execution squads and mob carnage, those who had known danger and fear in the past accepted the inevitability of yet another war.

Followed by an anxious and protesting Allday, Bolitho had left his bed and had made his way to London. He had always detested the false gaiety of the town, with its sprawling, dirty streets and the contrasting splendour of its great houses, but he had made up his mind that if necessary he would bend his knee and plead for a new ship.

After weeks of fretting and fruitless interviews he had been given the task of recruiting unwilling inhabitants of the Medway towns to fill the ships which were at last being called into commission.

To the senior powers of the Admiralty whose immediate duty it was to expand and equip a depleted fleet Bolitho was a clever choice for the work of recruitment. His exploits as a young frigate captain were still well remembered, and when war came his was the kind of leadership which might win men from the land for the uncertainties and hardships of a life at sea. Unfortunately Bolitho did not view his appointment with the same enthusiasm. It was somehow characteristic of his make-up that he saw it as a lack of confidence and trust by his superiors whom he suspected of thinking the worst about his recent illness. A sick captain could be a danger. Not just to himself and his ship, but to the vital chain of command, which once weakened could bring disaster and defeat.

The following January England had reeled from the news that the King of France had been beheaded by his own people, and before their minds could adjust to the shock the new French National Convention declared war.

It was as if the fury of the whole French nation had shaken the country from the course of reason. Even Spain and Holland, old allies from the past, had received the same declaration, and now, like England, stood awaiting the first real onslaught.

And so the old *Hyperion* had sailed again with hardly a pause in harbour. To Brest and the inevitable lot of the Channel Squadron to blockade and watch over the French ships sheltering beneath the guns of the shore batteries.

Bolitho had continued with his task, his despair at not being given an immediate command only helping to play fresh havoc with his health.

Then as winter gave way to spring he had received his orders to proceed to Spithead and take passage for Gibraltar. As he sat in the stern of the gig he could feel the heavy envelope in his breast pocket, the authority to control and command this ship which now towered above him and reduced all else to insignificance.

Already he could hear the twitter of pipes, the stampede of bare feet and the clatter of muskets as she prepared to receive him. He wondered briefly how long they had awaited his appearance, whether or not his arrival would be greeted with pleasure or misgivings.

It was one thing to take command from another captain who was leaving for promotion or retirement, quite another to step into a dead man's shoes.

The gig rounded the high bows and Bolitho stared up at the bright overhanging figurehead. Like the rest of the paintwork the figurehead's gilt looked fresh and clean, which was one small sign of a well-run ship. Hyperion the Sun God carried an out-thrust trident and was crowned with the rising sun itself. Only a pair of staring blue eyes broke the sheen of gold, and Bolitho found time to wonder how many of the King's enemies had seen that gilt face through the smoke and had died-minutes later.

He looked round as he heard something like a gasp and saw the thin midshipman staring up at the towering masts and furled sails. His face seemed full of dread, and the hand which gripped the boat's gunwale was stiff like a claw. Bolitho asked quietly, 'How old are you, Mr. Seton?'

The boy tore his eyes from the ship and muttered, 'S-Sixteen, sir.'

Bolitho nodded gravely. 'Well, I was about your age when I joined a ship very like this one. That was the year *Hyperion* was built.' He gave a wry smile. 'And as you see, Mr. Seton, we are both still here!'

He saw the emotions chasing each other across the midshipman's pale face and was glad he had omitted to add that the occasion he had described had been his second ship. At that time, and from the age of twelve, he had been constantly at sea. He wondered why Seton's father had left it so late before sending him into the Navy.

He straightened his back as the boat shot forward towards the entry port and a voice rang out. 'Boat ahoy?'

Allday cupped his hands and yelled, '*Hyperion!*'

If doubt there had been, there was none now. Every man aboard would know that the straight-backed figure in the gold-laced hat was his new master, the man who, next to God, held complete sway over every life in his ship. One who could flog or hang, just as he could equally reward and recognise the faults or efforts of everybody under his hand.

As the oars were tossed and the bowman hooked on to the main chains it took all of Bolitho's self-control to hold himself motionless in the sternsheets. Strangely, it was the seasick midshipman who broke the spell. He made to scramble towards the side, but Allday growled, 'Not

15

yet, my young gentleman!' He pulled him back to his seat and added, 'Seniors are last in the boat but *first* out, got it?'

Bolitho stared at each of them and then forgot them. Pulling his sword against his thigh, for once he had witnessed a new captain falling headlong backwards into his barge, he climbed stiffly up through the carved and gilded entry port.

As he removed his hat he was almost overwhelmed by the immediate response which seemed to come from every side, from above and below his bared head. The greeting which had started with the shrill scream of pipes as his face had appeared over the side burst into a wild crescendo of noise which at first his mind had difficulty in sorting out. The drums and fifes of a small marine band, the slap and snap of muskets being brought to the present and the swish of swords completing the general salute.

He felt hemmed in by the scarlet ranks of marines, the blue and white of assembled officers, and, above all, the packed faces and pigtailed heads of the men who had been hurriedly called from their duties throughout the ship.

He should have been ready, but in his heart he knew he had been so long in frigates that this sudden upsurge of figures had caught him entirely off guard. As his mind accepted this and his eye moved quickly over the nearest rank of shining guns, the freshly holystoned planking and the taut web of rigging and shrouds, he became aware, perhaps for the first time, of his new responsibility.

Up to this instant he had been considering the *Hyperion* only as a different way of life. Now, as the band fell into sudden silence and a tall, grave-faced lieutenant stepped forward to meet him, he understood his real purpose. The realisation both surprised and humbled him. Here within her fat, one-hundred-and-eighty-foot hull the *Hyperion* contained a whole new world. A strange imprisoned existence in which some six hundred officers and men lived, worked and, if required, died together, yet stayed apart in their own segments of discipline and seniority. It was hardly surprising that many captains of such ships as *Hyperion* were overwhelmed by their sense of power and self-importance.

He realised that the tall officer was watching him intently, his face set in an expressionless mould. He said, 'Lieutenant Quarme, sir. I am the senior aboard.'

Bolitho nodded. 'Thank you, Mr. Quarme.' He reached inside his coat and drew out his commission. The noise and sudden excitement had left him feeling faint. After the weeks of waiting and fretting all at once he needed to find the privacy of his new quarters. This Quarme looked a competent enough officer, he thought. He had a sudden picture of Herrick, his old first lieutenant in the *Phalarope* and the *Tempest*, and wished with all his heart that he and not Quarme had stepped forward to greet him.

Quarme moved quietly along the rank of officers, murmuring names and adding small additions about their duties. Bolitho kept his face quite impassive. It was far too early for smiles and general acknowledgements. The real men would emerge later from behind these stiff, respectful faces. But they seemed a general enough collection, he decided vaguely, but so many of them after a frigate. He walked along the rank, past the lieutenants and senior warrant officers to where the midshipmen waited with fascinated attention. He thought of young Seton and wondered what he was thinking of this awesome spectacle. Terrified, most likely.

17

Two marine officers stood rigidly before the scarlet ranks with their white crossbelts and silver buttons, and across the main press of figures beyond were the other warrant officers, the professionals who decided whether a ship would live or die. The boatswain and the carpenter, the cooper and all the rest.

He felt the sun very warm across his cheek and hurriedly opened his papers. He saw the watching figures crowd forward to hear and see better, and others dropped their eyes as he looked towards them, as if afraid of making a bad impression at such an early moment.

He read the commission briskly and without emotion. It was addressed to Richard Bolitho, Esquire, from Samuel Hood, Admiral of the Red, and required him to take upon him the charge and command of captain in His Britannic Majesty's ship *Hyperion*. Most of the men had heard such commissions read before, some no doubt many times, yet as he read through the neat, formal phrases he was conscious of the silence. As if the whole ship were holding her breath.

Bolitho rolled up the papers and returned them to his pocket. From one corner of his eye he saw Allday move slightly aft towards the quarterdeck ladder. As always he was ready to mark the way for his retreat from formality and discomfort.

In spite of the sun across the tops of the hammock nettings he felt light-headed and suddenly chilled. But he gritted his teeth and forced himself to remain quite motionless in front of the marines. This was a crucial moment in his life. His impression on his men might later decide their fate as well as his own. He had a sudden, sickening picture of himself falling in a fresh bout of fever with every eye watching his disgrace and humiliation, and surprisingly the mental scene helped to steady him.

He raised his voice. 'I will not keep you long from your duties, as there is much to do. The water lighters will be alongside directly, for I intend to hold this favourable wind and make sail this afternoon.' He saw two of the lieutenants exchange quick glances and added in a harder note, 'My orders require me to take this ship and join Lord Hood's squadron off Toulon without delay. Once there. we will make every effort to contain the enemy within his harbours, but if possible, and *whenever* possible, we will seek him out and destroy him.'

A slight murmur moved through the packed seamen, and Bolitho guessed that even up to the last moment when the ship was detached from the Brest blockade and ordered to Gibraltar to receive a new captain many hopeful souls aboard had retained the belief that the *Hyperion* would be returning home. His words, his new commission, had killed that hope stone dead. Now, with the first fragment of spread canvas and the merest puff of wind, every mile which dragged beneath the weed-covered keel would carry them further and further away from England. For many it might be a one-way journey.

He added more calmly, 'England is at war with a tyrant. We need every ship and every loyal man to overthrow him. See to it that each one of you does his best. In my part I will do mine.'

He turned on his heel and nodded curtly. 'Carry on, Mr. Quarme. Detail water parties and make sure the purser has plenty of fresh fruit aboard.' He stared across the mist-shrouded bay towards Algeciras. 'With Spain our new *ally* it should not be too difficult.'

The first lieutenant touched his hat. Then he called. 'Three cheers for King George!'

Bolitho walked slowly aft, feeling drained and ice cold. The answering cheers were ready enough, but more from duty than feeling.

He climbed the ladder and walked across the spacious quarterdeck. As he lowered his head beneath the poop Allday said quietly, 'No need to duck here, sir.' He was grinning. 'Plenty of room for you now.'

Bolitho did not even hear him. Ignoring the rigid marine sentry he stepped over the coaming and into his wide stern cabin. His private world. He was still thinking of the ship as Allday closed the door and began to unpack one of his boxes.

.   .   .   .

Richard Bolitho pushed some of the litter of papers across his desk and sat back to rest his eyes. When he examined his pocket watch he realised with a start that he had been poring over the ship's books and records for almost six hours without respite, his busy mind conscious the whole time of the noises beyond the closed door and across the deck above.

More than once he had almost broken his concentration to go out into the sunlight, if only to satisfy himself that the ship's routine was functioning normally, but each time he had forced himself to sit still and to carry on with his study of the Hyperion's affairs.

Time and experience would show him the real strength and weakness of his new command, but with just a few hours alone in his quarters he had already built up a working picture in his mind. From what he had read and examined it seemed as if the Hyperion under the command of the late Captain Turner had been the essence of normality. The punishment book, which Bolitho had inspected first, and which he always considered to be the safest measure of a ship's captain if not the performance of his command, showed the usual list of petty offenders, with the punishments of flogging and disrating no more or less than one might expect. On the West Indies station there had been various deaths reported from fever and careless shipboard accidents, and the daily log books showed nothing out of the ordinary.

Bolitho leaned back still further in his chair and frowned. It was all so normal, even dull, for a ship of the *Hyperion*'s past and record that it sensed of indifference.

Again he looked around his new quarters, as if to glean some small picture of its late occupant. It was a spacious, even elegant place, he decided, and after the close confines of a frigate seemed palatial.

The day cabin where he was sitting ran the whole width of the stern, over thirty feet from side to side, and the tall stern windows below which was stationed the handsome carved desk shone in the afternoon sunlight and threw the wide harbour and its anchored shipping across his vision in a colourful panorama.

There was an equally large dining cabin, and on either beam a smaller separate compartment, one for sleeping and the other for the charts.

On a sudden impulse he stood up and walked to the mahogany dining table. It contained six additional leaves, so it seemed that Turner had been a lavish entertainer. All the chairs, as well as the long bench seat below the stern windows, were of finely tooled green leather, and lying across the normal deck covering of black and white squared canvas was a rich carpet, the price of which Bolitho imagined could have paid a frigate's company of seamen for several months.

He tried to relax his tired mind, to tell himself that it

21

was a lack of self-confidence rather than a true cause for concern which left him so apprehensive.

He stared at himself in a bulkhead mirror, noting the frown which creased his forehead, the patches of sweat across his shirt. Unconsciously he brushed at the lock of black hair above his eye, his fingers touching the deep diagonal scar beneath it and which ran upwards into his hairline. It was odd to think that when the wildly swinging cutlass had cut him down and left him marked for life the *Hyperion* had even then been sailing within a few miles of where the fight had occurred.

There was a nervous tap at the door, and before Bolitho could speak it swung open to reveal a narrow-shouldered man in a plain blue coat who was carrying a silver tray.

Bolitho glared at him. 'Well?'

The man swallowed hard. 'Gimlett, sir. I'm yer servant, sir.' He had a piping voice, and with each syllable displayed a set of large, protruding teeth, like a frightened rabbit's.

Bolitho saw the man's eyes swivel towards a small side table upon which was laid his lunch untouched and, unknown to the wretched Gimlett, unseen till this moment.

Bolitho's anger at being disturbed softened slightly. The fear on the man's face was quite genuine. It had been known for an irate captain to have his servant flogged for merely spilling a cup of coffee.

Gimlett said, 'If it wasn't to yer liking, sir, I'll . . .'

'I was not hungry.' The lie was a suitable compromise. 'But thank you, Gimlett, for the thought.' He looked at the servant with sudden interest. 'Did you serve Captain Turner for long?'

'Yessir.' Gimlett shuffled from one foot to the other.

'He was a fine master to me, sir. Very considerate indeed.'

Bolitho smiled slightly. 'I take it you're a Devon man?'

'Aye, sir. I was chief ostler at the Golden Lion at Plymouth but came away with Cap'n Turner to serve my country the better.' His eyes suddenly fell on the pile of papers on Bolitho's desk and he added hastily, 'Well, I was in a bit of trouble with one of the chambermaids, sir. It seemed the best thing to do all round.'

Bolitho smiled more broadly. Gimlett was apparently under the impression that his late master might have left some written record of his real reason for quitting the land. He said, 'So you were only with Captain Turner while the ship was in the Indies? You did not actually go ashore to his home?' The last question was an effort to clear the look of complete incomprehension from the man's worried features.

'That's right, sir.' He looked around the wide cabin. 'This was his home, sir. He had no family. Just the ship.' He swallowed again, as if afraid he had said too much. 'Can I clear away, sir?'

Bolitho nodded thoughtfully and walked back to the windows. That was the best explanation so far. Under Turner the ship had become a home, a way of life rather than a ship of war. And her company, away from England for three years with neither combat nor hardship to trouble them, would have become equally unprepared for the challenge of blockade and war.

Twice during the day Quarme, the first lieutenant, had visited Bolitho to report on progress. Under Bolitho's casual questioning he too had more or less admitted that Turner was a fair captain but inimaginative, even lethargic.

But it was hard to assess Quarme's true feelings. He

23

was twenty-eight years old, with calm but uncompromising features, and gave the impression of a man who was just biding his time for better things. As well he might with ships being commissioned on every hand and gaps already left by death and injury. If he stayed out of trouble he might have a small command of his own within the year. The fact that Turner had made no recommendation had at first made Bolitho suspicious. Now as he built up a mental picture of his predecessor he began to realise that Turner probably wanted the ship and everything aboard, including his officers, to remain the same. It was a reasonable, if selfish, explanation, he thought.

There was one further factor in Turner's make-up which still left him feeling troubled. In his private papers which Quarme had opened after his death he had left what amounted to a will. There were a few small bequests to some distant relatives, but the part which caught Bolitho's attention was the neatly written addition at the end.

. . . and to the next captain of this ship I leave and bequest all my furniture and fittings, my wines and my personal belongings, with the true and sincere hope that he will continue to retain them for his own uses and the well-being of the ship.

It was an unusual bequest indeed.

At first Bolitho had intended to have Allday pack up everything and send it ashore to the Rock garrison. But he had left England in a hurry, so great was his eagerness to join the *Hyperion*. Apart from his uniforms and a few personal items he had come with little to ease the life of a captain in a ship of the line. Now as he looked round the great cabin he had second thoughts. It was as if by agreeing to Turner's eccentric desires he had allowed the man to remain aboard also. Dead and buried he might be, but in the captain's quarters his memory seemed to hang like a presence.

There was another tap at the door, but this time it was Quarme. He had his hat beneath his arm, and in the reflected sunlight his face looked guarded.

'I have mustered the officers in the wardroom as you ordered, sir.'

As he spoke, four bells of the afternoon watch chimed overhead, and Bolitho guessed he had been waiting for the exact moment of entry.

'Very well, Mr. Quarme. I am ready.' He pulled his uniform coat from a chair back and readjusted his neckcloth. 'I have completed reading the log, you may take it with you.'

Quarme said nothing. Instead he looked at the old sword which hung on the polished bulkhead. It had almost been Allday's first action to hang it there, and as Bolitho followed Quarme's stare he thought of his father and his father before him. Even in the sunlight it looked tarnished and old. But he knew that if he had brought nothing else from Falmouth but that sword it would have been worth more to him than all the rest of his possessions.

He half expected Quarme to comment. As Herrick would have done. He shook himself angrily. It was useless to continue with these pointless comparisons.

He said coldly, 'Lead the way if you please.'

Since his first-ever command, that of the tiny sloop *Sparrow*, Bolitho had always made a point of meeting his officers informally on the first possible moment. Now as he followed Quarme out on to the quarterdeck and down a wide ladder to the maindeck he found himself wondering about his new subordinates. He could never rid himself of the feeling of nervousness, although time and time again he had told himself that it was their part to be the more apprehensive.

The wardroom was directly beneath his own cabin, with the same set of wide windows across the stern. But the sides were lined with tiny cabins, and the corners jammed with sea-chests and the litter of personal equipment. Two of the ship's upper battery of twelve-pounders were also present, and Bolitho was briefly gratified that unlike the wardroom his own cabin would be spared the chaos and damage when the ship cleared for action.

The wardroom was crowded with standing figures, for apart from the five lieutenants and marine officers Bolitho had made sure that the midshipmen and senior warrant officers were also present. These latter were the true link between poop and forecastle, as he knew from hard experience.

He seated himself at the head of the long table and placed his hat beside a rolled chart. 'Seat yourselves, gentlemen, or stand if you desire. I would not wish you to change your habits for my temporary convenience.' There was some polite laughter. The captain was, after all, merely a guest in a wardroom, although Bolitho had often wondered what might happen if such a privilege be denied. He opened the chart slowly, knowing that their eyes were still on him rather than it.

'As you are now aware, we sail to join Lord Hood. It is understood that in Toulon there are certain forces who, although French, are firmly against the present Revolutionary Government, and with help may well be the tools to overthrow it. By showing our strength and using every opportunity to harass the enemy's shipping we may have the chance to aid that state of affairs.' He looked up and caught sight of young Seton's face framed between the shoulders of the two marines.

He continued evenly, 'By the middle of July, Lord Hood will have such a force available as to make all this possible. Every ship will be needed. It is therefore essential that each officer does his utmost to ensure there is no wastage in effort or training.' He looked around their intent faces. 'We may not be free to return here or to any other supply base for some time to come, is that understood?'

Quarme said quietly, 'I think the second lieutenant has a question, sir.'

Bolitho glanced across to where a languid, bored-looking young officer was sitting on one of the chests. He said, 'I forget your name for the moment.'

The lieutenant eyed him coolly. 'Sir Philip Rooke, sir.'

There was nothing insolent in his tone but Bolitho could see it in the man's pale eyes like a challenge.

'Well, *Mr.* Rooke, and what is the question?' Bolitho's voice was equally calm.

Rooke said in the same flat tone, 'We have been in commission for three years. The ship's bottom is as green as grass and she is as slow as an old cow.' There were a few murmurs which might have been agreement and he continued: 'Captain Turner was assured that we would be relieved of our station at Brest and that we should return to Portsmouth within the month.'

Bolitho watched him thoughtfully. So far Rooke was the first to emerge from behind his mask.

He said at length, 'Captain Turner is dead. But I am sure he would not have wished his ship to miss the chance to perform her duty.'

Rowlstone, the surgeon, a small, unhealthy-looking man with crumpled features like uncooked suet, jumped

27

to his feet. 'I did what I could, sir! He died of a bad heart.' He looked round the wardroom wildly. 'Sitting at his desk he was. He was past my help, I tell you!'

Rooke glared at him. 'What would *you* know about it, man? You're more used to a butcher's knife than any sort of medicine!'

Ashby, the captain of marines, pulled in his stomach and flipped a fragment of dust from his glove-tight uniform. 'He was a good man. We all miss him, y'know.' He stared hard at Bolitho. 'But I agree with you, sir. This is war. The fight's the thing, eh?'

Bolitho smiled dryly. 'Thank you, Ashby. That is very reassuring.'

Then he looked across at Gossett, the ship's master. He was a great barrel of a man, and although seated at the table his head was almost level with that of the miserable-looking surgeon. 'And you, Mr. Gossett? What is your opinion?'

Gossett placed his fists on the polished wood and stared hard at them. As well he might. They were like two huge pieces of meat.

He said deeply, 'We've a good set of spare spars an' canvas, sir. Th' ship's old right enough, but she can still fetch up with better an' younger craft.' He grinned so that his small bright eyes receded into his tanned face. 'I once sailed an old seventy-four out of battle with only one mast an' the lower gundeck awash!' He chuckled as if it was one great joke. 'The Frogs'll find us ready enough if they gives us the measure, sir.'

Bolitho stood up. He had started the pot boiling. The next few days would tell him more of these men.

He said shortly, 'Very well, gentlemen. The wind is still fresh from the nor'-west. We will make sail within the hour.' He glanced at Quarme's set face. 'Call all

28

hands in thirty minutes and prepare to break out the anchor. We have nine hundred miles ahead of us before we sight the squadron. Be sure you make good use of them.' He looked round at the others. '*All* of you.'

As they parted across the door he strode quickly out of the wardroom and up to the sun-drenched quarterdeck. He did not know why, but it had been a bad beginning. Perhaps he was still suffering from the fever, or maybe he was too tired from waiting and worrying. Then again it was entirely possible he was unready for a ship such as *Hyperion*.

He stood a moment longer and stared up at the towering masts and at the tiny figures working aloft like careless monkeys.

Allday moved across the deck and said, 'I've told Gimlett to lay out your seagoing gear, Captain.' He breathed in deeply then added, 'I'll be glad to get to sea in my own ship again. I was a mite sick of the hills and the same old sights each day.'

Bolitho swung round and then checked himself. It was too easy to take out his tiredness and anger on Allday.

'At least the women in Falmouth will get a rest from your visits, Allday!'

The coxswain watched Bolitho until he vanished beneath the poop and then grinned broadly. Aloud he muttered, 'You've no need to worry, Captain. You've not changed, and nothing'll change you either!'

Then he leaned on the nettings and stared across at the anchored ships in the bay.

2

A Show of Confidence

Bolitho left his cabin and walked quickly towards the quarterdeck. Below the shelter of the poop the two pig-tailed helmsmen stiffened beside the big double wheel, but Bolitho paused only long enough to peer at the compass. North-east by north. It seemed as if the card had been riveted in that direction for days. For eight long days since the *Hyperion* had left Gibraltar the progress had been slow and painful, with the ship only able to maintain an average three knots. Twice they had been becalmed, and since weighing anchor had logged a mere five hundred and twenty miles all told.

But as he stepped out into the bright midday sunlight Bolitho could see as well as feel the difference. A few minutes earlier a breathless midshipman had run into his quarters to announce that the light, passive breeze was at last freshening, and when he looked up at the masthead pendant he saw it whipping out abeam, and the freshly set sails were filling and booming with renewed purpose.

Quarme turned back from the quarterdeck rail and touched his hat. 'I've set the t'gallants, sir. Let us hope this wind keeps up.' He looked strained.

'It will, Mr. Quarme.' Bolitho was wearing neither coat nor hat, and felt someting like sensuous pleasure as the wind ruffled his shirt and cooled the dryness of his lips. 'We'll get the royals on her directly.'

He leaned his hands on the sun-dried rail and stared down at the maindeck. The starboard battery of sixteen guns was run out as if for action, and the crews, stripped to the waist and sweating, were completing yet another exercise. Below from the lower gundeck he could hear the squeal and rumble of trucks as the heavy twenty-four-pounders followed their example, and without looking up he said, 'Fifteen minutes to clear for action today, Mr. Quarme. It is not good enough.'

'The men are tired, sir.' Quarme was careful to keep his reply non-committal. 'But there is some improvement today, I think.'

Bolitho grunted. With the ship so long in commission with the same company the general seamanship and sail drill were good. There was a slickness to setting and shortening sail which to a landsman might appear almost casual. Bolitho knew from past experience that the average warship put to sea for the first time with her people composed more of pressed and awkward landsmen than trained hands, and for that he was grateful. But a ship of the line was no frigate. Her sailing qualities were normally confined to keeping station and closing the enemy rather than any subtle manœuvres. It was only when she drew abeam of that enemy, where she would stay until victorious or vanquished, that her true worth could be counted. And whatever Quarme really thought, Bolitho knew that the *Hyperion*'s gunnery was appalling.

Every day and all day he had exercised the guns through every possible eventuality which he could imagine. From the main armament to the stubby carronades, from the quarterdeck twelve-pounders to the marines in their musketry, he had worked every weapon and man without respite. If as Quarme insisted there had been some improvement it was still far from satisfactory.

He said at length, 'We will exercise the starboard battery again. Pass the word.'

He made himself cross to the weather side as Quarme

shouted his instructions to the maindeck. With the ship on the starboard tack and heeling ponderously to the freshening breeze the guns would have to be manhandled back against the tilting deck before the drill could begin, and Bolitho saw some of the less arduously employed hands pause in their work to watch.

There was Buckle, the grey-haired sailmaker, squatting with his mates checking and repairing the last of the heavy-weather canvas which the ship had used off Brest, the needles and palms pausing as they turned to stare. Even Gossett, the master, a sextant shining in one huge fist like a child's toy, halted in the patient instruction of two deceptively interested midshipmen and frowned as Lieutenant Rooke's voice echoed around the listless gunners.

'Now *pay attention*! Withdraw guns and prepare to load!' He was standing on the starboard gangway which ran above the battery and linked quarterdeck with forecastle and was staring angrily at his men, his face blotchy with heat and impatience. 'The next man to drop a rammer or fall over his feet will dance at the gratings!' He pulled a watch from his pocket.'Now begin!'

Grunting and slipping on the sanded planking, the men threw themselves against the guns, their bodies shining with sweat as they levered and spiked the long muzzles back from the open ports until they stood at the full extent of their tackles.

Bolitho had watched Rooke closely in the last eight days. He seemed to carry out his work efficiently enough, but his manner was unpleasant, and he appeared to have difficulty in containing his temper. Only the previous day Bolitho had arranged a contest between both of the maindeck batteries, and the larboard side had won by three minutes. Rooke had been nearly beside himself. Now as his men crouched beside their guns Bolitho could feel the tension like a physical force.

Rooke yelled, 'Load!'

There was a wild scramble, each crew being driven and harangued by its gun-captain as practise cartridges and imaginary balls were cradled into muzzles while the heavier seamen gripped the falls and waited to race their guns for the waiting ports.

Quarme muttered, 'Better this time, sir.'

Bolitho did not answer. But it was certainly smoother, in spite of the over-eagerness on the part of some of the younger men. He saw Rooke gripping the rail as if willing his men to move faster, and knew he was well aware of his captain's presence on the quarterdeck.

Rooke shouted, 'Run out!'

Obediently the trucks squealed across the worn planking, and as each gun-captain feverishly sprinted to prime his vent there was a sharp clatter and three of the furthest gunners went sprawling. Every other gun-captain had his hand in the air, but at the leading weapon there was complete confusion.

Rooke screamed, 'What the hell! What the bloody *hell*!'

Some of the upper-deck idlers were openly grinning, and when Bolitho turned he saw that Lieutenant Fowler, the officer of the watch, was staring at his feet his mouth stifled with his handkerchief.

Rooke strode along the gangway until he was above the offending gun. 'Bell, I'll see your backbones for this! I'll have you flogged till . . .'

The gun-captain stared up at him his hands spread helplessly. 'T'worn't me, sir! T'were the young gennelman 'ere!' He pointed at Midshipman Seton who was struggling from between two dazed sailors beside the gun.

' 'E fell over 'is dirk, sir, an' t'other two went atop of 'im!'

'Hold your tongue!' Rooke seemed to realise that everyone was staring at him. He said in a more controlled voice, 'And what did you do wrong this time, *Mr*. Seton?'

The boy picked up his hat and looked round like a trapped animal. 'Sir, I-I . . .' The words would not come for several seconds. 'I tried t-to help with the f-falls, sir.'

Rooke sounded quite calm again. '*Did* you?' He wiped his mouth with his hand. 'Well, don't stand there slavering! Pay attention when I address you!'

Bolitho turned away. It was unbearable to see Seton suffering like this, but to interfere now would only undermine Rooke's authority in front of the men.

Rooke persisted loudly, 'Why in God's name did your mother and father send you to sea, Mr. Seton? Surely there was some other work you could bring confusion to?'

Some of the men laughed, and then Seton said in a strangled voice, 'I-I have none, sir. M-My p-parents a-are . . .' He could not go on.

Rooke stared down at him, his hands on his hips. 'No father or mother, Mr. Seton? Then you must be a bigger bastard than I imagined!'

Bolitho swung round. 'Mr. Quarme, please fall out the crews and secure guns.' He glanced quickly aloft. 'The wind is holding well. You may set the royals now.' He made himself wait a few minutes as the pipes passed his order and the topmen swarmed up the ratlines in a tight mass, their bodies black against the clear sky. 'And have Mr. Rooke lay aft.'

Bolitho walked to the weather side and thrust his hands behind his back. He could see the growing breeze ruffling the blue water and breaking it here and there into short,

34

lively whitecaps. The noon position was estimated at some thirty miles south-east of Tarragona, but to all intents and purposes the sea was endless and empty. But his calculations had already been verified by the mainmast lookout swaying on his precarious perch almost two hundred feet above the deck. He alone had seen the distant mountains of Spain. His eyes were their only contact with the land. Bolitho was glad he had decided to stand well out to sea to avoid the opposing offshore current. His decision had given him the best of the wind too, and if it held they would find Hood's ships all the sooner.

'You sent for me, sir?' Rooke was watching him, his chest heaving with exertion.

'I did.' Bolitho eyed him calmly. 'Your men did quite well. With practice they will improve still further.'

He saw a slight glimmer in Rooke's eyes which might have been amusement or contempt. He added slowly, 'In future I hope you will refrain from that sort of treatment which you just gave Mr. Seton.'

Rooke's face was wooden. 'He needs discipline, sir. They all do.'

'I agree entirely. But bullying is another matter, Mr. Rooke.' There was an edge to his tone. 'It does not help discipline to insult and humiliate a midshipman in front of men who may depend on him in battle!'

'Is that all, sir?' Rooke's hands were trembling against his sides.

'For the present.' Bolitho looked up as the last of the royals flapped and then hardened to contain the wind. Against the sky the full set of sails gleamed like white pyramids. He added, 'You'll get better results by setting a good example, Mr. Rooke.' He watched the lieutenant walk stiffly towards the gangway and frowned. He had made an enemy of Rooke, but it seemed unlikely that a

35

man of his nature would make friends with anyone.

Quarme hovered nearby. 'I am sorry about all that, sir. He is a bit outspoken at times.'

Bolitho faced him. 'It is a pity *you* are not more outspoken, Mr. Quarme. I should not have to do your work for you!'

Quarme looked as if he had received a slap in the face. 'My work, sir?'

'Yes. I do not expect to have to interfere amongst the officers.' He let his words sink in. 'Now let that be the last of it.'

But as he walked to the opposite side of the deck and began to pace slowly back and forth he knew in his heart that it was not the end of it at all.

! ! ! ! !

The next four days were much as those which had gone before, with sail and gun drill taking precedence over all other routine. As the *Hyperion* tacked round the last jutting corner of the Spanish mainland and steered northeast across the Golfe du Lion there was little to ease the weary monotony or to smooth the atmosphere of irritation and resentment.

During his daily walks on the poop or quarterdeck Bolitho was conscious of his own isolation and the barrier which he had made between himself and his officers. It was necessary, he was more sure of that then ever now. They could resent, even hate, him if they wished, but they had to be drawn together, woven into a weapon which he could use when the time came.

He was still puzzled by Quarme's attitude to Rooke. When they were together Quarme seemed nervous and unsure of himself, although in all matters of duty he was efficient and hard-working. Perhaps he was awed by Rooke's noble upbringing. It was not uncommon for quite senior officers, let alone aspiring first lieutenants, to be impressed to the point of servility with a subordinate who might have influence at Court or in Parliament, and who could perhaps be the means of quick advancement. But that seemed unlikely here. They had been too long in the same ship. Surely something would have happened by now.

Bolitho sat at his desk and toyed unwillingly with another of Gimlett's meals. Through the stern windows he could see the crisp whiteness of the ship's short wake, and heard the thump and creak of the steering gear as she butted along in the steady, unswerving wind. In the afternoon sunlight the sea threw back a million dancing reflections, and the endless stretch of small, restless whitecaps made him more aware of his loneliness.

There was a knock at the door and Piper, one of the midshipmen, stepped carefully into the cabin. With a full press of sail the *Hyperion* seemed to stay steady and immovable at one angle, so that against the open door Piper's scraggy body appeared to be leaning over as if in a strong wind.

'Mr.—Mr. Inch's respects, sir, and he thinks we have just sighted the squadron!' His eyes followed Bolitho across the cabin, never leaving him as he pulled on his coat.

'He thinks?' Bolitho felt strangely relieved. At last something might happen to break the apathy.

'Sir?'

Bolitho smiled. Lieutenant Inch was the ship's junior lieutenant, an eager if unsure young man. He would, of course, never commit himself to an actual statement.

He asked, 'How is Mr. Seton settling down?'

Piper screwed up his face so that he looked like a wizened monkey. 'He's a bit sick, sir.' He sighed. 'He's not used to it all yet.'

Bolitho hid a smile. Piper was also sixteen, yet spoke with the assurance of an admiral.

He walked past the marine sentry and on to the quarter-deck. The wind was still very fresh, but as he glanced forward across the leaping bowsprit he caught sight of a growing grey wedge of land. They had been following it all day, losing it as they ploughed through some open bay and picking it up again near the next headland.

Quarme said formally, 'Masthead reports six sail of the line to the north, sir.'

Bolitho saw Inch's long face watching him across the first lieutenant's shoulder. He was nodding vacantly in time with Quarme's words.

'Very well. Alter course two points to larboard to intercept.'

He crossed the deck and watched the men pouring up from below as the bosun's mates yelled, 'Hands to the braces there!'

Gossett stood stolidly near the wheel his lower lip between his teeth as the great yards began to swing round. To the helmsmen he growled, ''Old 'er, man! Full an' bye!' Then he glanced aloft at the thundering sails and gave a slow smile. Bolitho had seen that smile before and knew that Gossett was satisfied.

Bolitho took his glass and steadied his legs against the pitch and roll of the deck. With the wind sweeping down across the bow and the ship sailing as close as she was able to it the motion was uneven and more pronounced.

He heard Quarme snap, 'Aloft with you, Mr. Piper, and be sure you make a proper report!'

Bolitho saw the tall pyramids of sails evenly spaced

and shining like polished shells in the sunlight. Even from the deck there was no mistaking them.

He said to the quarterdeck at large, 'Stand by to report all signals.'

Then, carried by the wind like a flute he heard Piper calling from the mainmast. 'Six ships of the line, sir! The leading one wears the admiral's flag!'

The six ships were running on the opposite tack, and as Bolitho studied them through his glass he saw them growing in size and detail until the leading one, a huge three-decker with the admiral's flag at the main, filled his lens so that he could see the hull shining with thrown spray, the red and gold of her figurehead.

As he strained his eye to watch her he saw the tiny black balls streaking up the yards and breaking out like coloured metal in the wind.

Inch shouted, 'Flagship's signalling, sir!' He was hopping with excitement, as if he personally had spirited the squadron over the horizon.

Caswell, the signal midshipman, had already perched himself in the mizzen shrouds his big telescope steadied like a gun.

'She's flying our pendant, sir!' His lips moved slowly. Then he called, 'Victory to Hyperion, "Take station to windward!"'

Quarme said quickly, 'The admiral'll be wanting you to go across, sir.'

'I imagine so.' Bolitho pushed his hands behind him to hide his excitement. 'Tack the ship and then call my boat's crew and prepare for lowering.'

Quarme nodded. Then he raised his speaking trumpet. 'Stand by to go about!'

From beside the wheel Gossett bellowed, 'Ready ho!'

Then as the seamen ran to the braces he snapped, 'Helm a'lee!'

The hands up forward let go the headsail sheets and the *Hyperion* swung slowly into the wind, every block and sail flapping and banging as if outraged at this sudden change of direction.

From the maindeck came a yelp of pain, followed by a sharp, 'Lively, you awkward bugger! Lord 'Ood is watchin' you!'

Breathless and groaning, the men at the braces dug in their toes and hauled the great yards round, further and further, until with the jubilant roar of thunder the sails billowed and then filled, taut and bulging, while the ship beneath them heeled over to the wind.

Bolitho saw Gossett grinning and said, 'She handles well, Mr. Gossett. Slow but *very* determined.' He added, 'We will have the royals off her, Mr. Quarme.'

The fresh orders sent more men clambering aloft, and as the sails grew smaller and then vanished at the hands of the topmen Midshipman Caswell, who had run frantically to the opposite side of the quarterdeck, shouted, 'Flag to *Hyperion*, "Captain repair on board forthwith!"'

Bolitho snapped. 'Acknowledge!' He looked down at his shabby seagoing uniform. There was no time to change now. From any admiral 'forthwith' meant immediately, if not sooner. 'Call away my barge!'

As the six other ships drew closer the *Hyperion* turned once more into the wind, sails thundering in protest and every shroud and stay vibrating like some mad musical instrument.

The barge was already swayed out, and as Bolitho took his sword from an anxious Gimlett, Allday shouted, 'Lower away!' By the time Bolitho had reached the entry port the boat was dipping and plunging alongside, the white oars raised like twin lines of polished bones.

He almost missed his footing, but as the barge squeaked heavily against the *Hyperion*'s fat flank he jumped out and down, praying that he had not misjudged it.

Allday breathed out. 'Out oars! Give way together!' Then he thrust the tiller hard over, and by the time Bolitho had regained his wind the *Hyperion* was already dropping fast astern.

She was swinging round once more to keep station on the flagship, and Bolitho felt a touch of pride as he watched the sails filling and the sluice of spray breaking back from her counter. He had been aboard her for twelve days only, yet already he could hardly remember what had gone before.

•   •   •   •   •

No sooner had Bolitho made another precarious climb from his barge to the flagship's entry port than he was met by her captain, and with hardly more than a curt greeting was led aft to the great stern cabin. If Bolitho's quarters in *Hyperion* were spacious, those of Admiral Hood were even grander on every scale.

Hood was seated on the bench below the stern window with one leg propped comfortably on a stool and his massive head in silhouette as he stared out at the ships which followed slowly in *Victory*'s wake. He made no effort to stand but waved his hand towards a chair beside his writing table.

'I am very pleased to see you here, Bolitho. You appear to have carried the years well.'

Bolitho seated himself carefully and studied his

41

superior with interest and admiration. He knew that Hood was nearing seventy, yet apart from a certain looseness around the jowl and the slowness of his speech he appeared to have changed little in the eleven years since their last meeting. The heavy brows and large beaked nose were the same. And the eyes which now swung to study him across the table were as clear and bright as a young man's.

The admiral asked suddenly, 'How do you like your ship, eh? Good enough for you?'

'I am well satisfied, sir.' Bolitho knew that Hood rarely wasted much time on unnecessary conversation and was taken slightly off guard. Perhaps, after all, Hood was feeling his years. But for the war he would now be enjoying a more restful life well away from the burden of commanding a fleet.

Hood continued abruptly, 'I remember you well. You did good work at the Saintes.' He sighed. 'I wish I had my old flagship, the *Barfleur*, here with me today, but she is with Lord Howe in the Channel Fleet.' He heaved himself from the seat and moved heavily across the cabin. Over his shoulder he said, 'You've read all the intelligence reports, I suppose.' He hurried on without waiting for a reply. It was safe to assume that any captain joining his command would have made himself fully familiar with every available detail if he wished to stay a captain. 'Just over yonder the French have at least twenty sail of the line bottled up in Toulon. I intend to see that they stay there until I decide what next action to pursue.'

Bolitho digested this information carefully. With a growing British squadron daily patrolling the French coastline it would be madness for the enemy to expect their own ships to enter or leave Toulon, or Marseilles either for that matter.

Hood added sharply, 'In a week or so I shall have twenty-one ships under my flag, and by that time I will know what to do. Compte Trogoff commands the French ships at Toulon, and our agents there have already reported that he is ready to negotiate terms with us. He was loyal to his king, like many more in Toulon. But his position is dangerous. Unless he can be sure of real support from his own people he will never allow us to land our men and take over the port.'

Bolitho said carefully, 'I would think that he has little time left to make up his mind, sir.'

Lord Hood gave what passed for a smile. 'You are right there, by God! There are reports that the French General Carteau is already marching south. I am hoping that such information is also available to Trogoff, for either way I am afraid his days will be numbered unless he obtains our assistance.' He drew one hand across his throat. 'He would not be the first French admiral to die on the scaffold. Not even one of the first dozen!'

Bolitho tried to imagine himself in the position of the wretched Admiral Trogoff. His was a difficult decision indeed. Beyond the sealed door the giant hundred-gun flagship murmured with life, the creak of spars and rigging, the muffled shout of orders. Across in his own ship Quarme and the others would be watching and wondering. Like himself.

Pipes shrilled from the upper deck and there was more stamping and shouting. Another captain from one of the ships astern no doubt.

The admiral said calmly, 'What this campaign needs is a show of confidence. We cannot afford a failure at this early stage.' He looked hard at Bolitho. 'Have you heard of Cozar Island?'

Bolitho tore his mind back from the crowded possibilities of a full-scale invasion with the *Hyperion* in the van of the attack.

'Er, yes, sir.' He saw the glint of impatience in Hood's eyes and added, 'We passed it to seaward on the night of the sixth.'

'And I take it that is all you know of it?' Hood's question was sharp.

'It lies off the French coast, sir, but is actually Spanish.'

'Well, that is slightly better,' said Hood dryly. 'In fact, Cozar was given by the late King Louis to Spain in exchange for some concession in the Caribbean. It lies about one hundred and twenty-five miles west-south-west from the chair you're sitting on. It is a miserable, sun-scorched place, and until recently was used by the Spaniards as a penal settlement. With their usual contempt for human life they realised that only convicts and scorpions could live there.'

He stood quite still, looking down at Bolitho as he continued, 'But Cozar has one important asset. It has a magnificent harbour, and no other landing places at all. There is a fort of some kind at either end, and a well-sited battery could keep a whole fleet at bay for as long as necessary.'

Bolitho nodded. 'So close to the French coast it could be used like a stone frigate. Our ships would be safe for replenishing stores and sheltering from bad weather, and could dash out and attack any coastal shipping without warning.'

Hood said nothing and Bolitho realised with sudden clarity what the admiral had implied about his 'show of confidence'. He said quietly, 'Also we could launch a second invasion from there should the Toulon venture prove successful.'

Hood eyed him grimly. 'You get there in the end,

Bolitho. Well done!' He walked back to the windows. 'Unfortunately the French may have realised Cozar's importance already. I sent the sloop *Fairfax* to investigate a week ago. Nothing has been seen of her since.' He slapped his hands together violently. 'Spain is our new ally, but under real pressure who can say how long such allegiance will last?'

There was a nervous tap at the door and a flag-lieutenant peered in at them.

Hood glared at him. 'Get *out*, damn you!' In a calmer voice he continued, 'I have a Spanish squadron with me now. If we are to seize and occupy Cozar then the Spanish must *outwardly* be the main cause of the victory.' His eyebrows lifted slightly. 'It will clinch our relationship and will show the French that we are united not merely from fear but out of mutual respect.' He smiled grimly. 'Well, that is how it should look, eh?'

Bolitho rubbed his chin thoughtfully. 'And you want the *Hyperion* to take part, sir?'

'I do. Of all the captains under my command I think you are possibly the best suited. I seem to recall that you carried out some very successful raids in the Caribbean. That sort of initiative and imagination is what we need at the moment.' He looked away. 'You will accompany two Spanish ships of the line, of course, but the operation will be under the overall command of Vice-Admiral Sir William Moresby, d'you know him?'

Bolitho shook his head, his mind still mulling over Hood's words. After coming so far with the hope of taking part in the real campaign, and now this. *Hyperion* would go about and sail back again, with nothing but some local skirmish at the end of it. Once ensconced on their own territory the Spanish would be quick to rid themselves of *Hyperion*, Vice-Admiral Moresby or not.

Hood eyed him gravely. 'He's a good flag officer. He knows what to do.'

Bolitho stood up, knowing the interview was over. He turned as Hood said suddenly, 'I sent for you personally because I want you to realise the importance of this mission. Whatever happens, and I mean just that, I want that island taken without delay. If the French have time to garrison it properly they will be in a position to harry my supply ships and spy on everything I do. My fleet is stretched to the limit already. I cannot afford to send more ships to watch Cozar for the rest of time. Do I make myself clear?'

The door opened a few inches and the flag-lieutenant said desperately, 'I beg your pardon, my lord, but the captain of the *Agamemnon* has come aboard and wishes to have an audience with you.'

Instead of flying into a rage Hood gave a rare smile. 'That's young Captain Nelson, a contemporary of yours, Bolitho. Well, he's going to be disappointed this time.' His hooded eyes glinted with amusement. 'He'll have heard about the Cozar business, and like you he is a man who prefers to act on his own sometimes!'

Bolitho toyed with the idea of suggesting a change of orders when Hood added briefly, 'But his *Agamemnon* is a fast ship. I'll need her here if things go against us.'

'Yes, sir.' He thought of Rooke's contemptuous words, 'She's as slow as an old cow!' and added, '*Hyperion* will show her ability when the time comes.'

The admiral stared at him. 'I never doubted it, my boy.' He chuckled as Bolitho walked towards the door. 'I doubt that the war will end tomorrow. There will be plenty of opportunities yet!'

Bolitho walked out of the door and almost cannoned into the harassed flag-lieutenant who immediately thrust a large sealed envelope into his hand and muttered, 'Your orders, sir. Vice-Admiral Sir William Moresby will be shifting his flag to *Hyperion* from the *Cadmus* within the hour. May I suggest you make haste back to your ship, sir? Sir William is, er, rather rigid in his requirements about being properly greeted.'

Bolitho grunted and hurried towards the entry port, his mind buzzing with the swift turn of events. *Cadmus* was a big three-decker. No doubt Lord Hood needed *her* too, he decided bitterly.

The flagship's captain was waiting with the side party and gave Bolitho a worried smile. It could not be easy to serve in the same ship as Lord Hood.

But as Bolitho clambered down into his waiting barge he forgot him and turned his mind to the problems of turning *Hyperion* into a flagship. She was no three-decker, and Sir William might find it somewhat crowded.

The barge pulled clear, and Bolitho saw Allday watching him anxiously from the tiller. Then he looked back at the towering side of the *Victory* and guessed that already his short visit had also been forgotten.

Then as he glanced up at the flagship's great quarterdeck he saw a slight, even frail, figure leaning on the nettings and watching him. His uniform was more faded then Bolitho's, and his hair was tied back in a stiff, unfashionable queue. As the barge crew pulled lustily around the *Victory*'s quarter Bolitho saw the other man raise his hand in what might be a salute or a gesture of resignation.

Bolitho lifted his hand to his hat in reply. It must be Nelson of the *Agamemnon*, he thought. Such a fragile figure for a captain of a ship of the line, and on the *Victory*'s quarterdeck he looked dejected and lost.

Bolitho settled himself grimly in the sternsheets and

stared across at his own command. Well, this Nelson had nothing to be jealous about, he thought angrily. He could *have* the Cozar operation and welcome!

Allday lowered his head and asked softly, 'Good news, Captain? Are we staying with the fleet?'

Bolitho glared at him. 'Attend to your steering! This barge is swaying like a Portsmouth whore!'

Allday watched the back of Bolitho's shoulders and smiled to himself. For months he had worried about Bolitho's health. Opposition from above was better than any medicine, he thought cheerfully. But heaven help the French!

3

Decision for Sir William

Bolitho waited beneath the poop just long enough to accustom his eyes to the gloom and then strode out on to the quarterdeck. At first glance there was little to show that the dawn hovered just below the invisible horizon, but as he looked up through the dark tracery of rigging and beyond the ghostlike outlines of the sails he noticed that the stars were paler and the sky, instead of being like black velvet, now held that strange purple hue which never failed to fill him with pleasure.

A shadow loomed from the quarterdeck rail and Quarme said, 'The dawn'll be up within thirty minutes, sir. I had the hands called an hour early as you ordered, and they have all been fed.'

Bolitho nodded. 'Very good.' His vision was improving, or was the light already strengthening? He heard the splash and sizzle of embers alongside and knew that the cooks were throwing the remains of the galley fire overboard, also in accordance with his instructions. He suddenly felt stiff and cramped, and wished he had taken the time for another mug of coffee.

With Vice-Admiral Moresby occupying his quarters Bolitho had been sleeping in a makeshift cot in the chartroom. Most captains would have taken over their first lieutenants' cabins under such circumstances, but Bolitho found the cramped privacy of the tiny chartroom more suitable for his present mood of uncertainty and doubt.

For nearly three days the *Hyperion* with two Spanish ships in company had headed for the island of Cozar. Days of irritations and maddening conferences between Moresby and the Spanish admiral, which had uncovered little but the intention of each man to have his own way. Now the two other ships were miles astern, having hove to for the night with the usual Spanish indifference for urgency and timing.

Bolitho said suddenly, 'Hands aloft, Mr. Quarme. Get the topgallants and courses in, if you please. Tops'ls and jib will suffice for our purposes.' He heard Quarme passing his orders and saw the immediate air of activity across the maindeck.

According to his careful calculations the island now lay some four miles off the starboard bow, and with the sun soon to rise astern of her, *Hyperion* would be less visible to a drowsy sentry if stripped down to minimum canvas. In the light airs the slower speed would be an additional advantage.

All his inbuilt caution might be proved as empty as the Spanish admiral had outspokenly declared on the previous afternoon when he and his two captains had been rowed across to the *Hyperion* for another long conference. Cozar might indeed still be in Spanish hands, and his preparations, his stealthy approach under cover of night, might show as a waste of time. But Bolitho respected the French as much as he disliked them. They would be foolish to overlook the possibilities presented by such a formidable fortress.

The Spanish admiral, Don Francisco Anduaga, was a tall, disdainful autocrat who had made no bones right from the start about what he thought of serving under Moresby's overall command. Moresby was a thickset, aggressive little man who showed little interest in Anduaga's more sensitive feelings, and ploughed through the planned arrangements with the stubbornness of a bull terrier. And the arrangements about which they could agree were few indeed. An acceptance of British signals, a rough plan of approach, but little more beside.

But Anduaga had brought one useful addition on his last visit. A swarthy lieutenant who had actually served at Cozar Island when it was used as a penal settlement. His facts were impressive, but only to those who actually controlled the island from within.

Barely five miles from end to end, it sounded the most inhospitable place on earth. Surrounded by steep, dangerous cliffs and scattered rocks it was only accessible by way of the great natural harbour on its southern side, and then by one landing place below the battery of a strong hill fortress. There was a smaller hill at the other end of the island with an ancient Moorish castle and a lesser battery to forestall anyone foolhardy enough to attempt to storm the cliffs by day or night. And between the two hills was one central one which rose to over a thousand feet, and from which even a half-blind lookout could see an approaching ship before it topped the horizon.

The lieutenant had rolled his eyes sadly. 'It is a terrible place, Captain. Not fit for beasts.'

Bolitho had persisted, 'What about fresh water? Have they good supplies?'

'Alas, no. They depend on a rainfall to fill a man-made reservoir. Apart from that they bring it by sea.' He had dropped his eyes with sudden embarrassment. 'From the port of St. Clar, but of course that was when we were allied with France, you understand.'

Moresby had interrupted angrily, 'If you are thinking of cutting off the water supply, Bolitho, you can think again. We have no time for a blockade, and in any case we don't know what supplies they have at their disposal.'

Anduaga had watched them with obvious irritation. 'But why are you all so concerned?' He had a smooth, silky voice which matched his air of complete superiority over the rest of them. 'My eighty-gun *Marte* will pound them to fragments! But I can assure you that there will be no problems.' His eyes had become suddenly cruel. 'The Spanish garrison would have me to reckon with if they were foolish enough to surrender to a lot of peasant soldiers!'

A voice broke into Bolitho's brooding thoughts. 'Land! Land on the weather bow!'

He moved restlessly. 'Alter course a point to starboard, Mr. Gossett.' Then to Quarme he added, 'Clear for action, if you please, but do not have the guns loaded or run out.'

Again the pipes shrilled, and as the darkened decks filled and surged with running figures Quarme asked quietly, 'Will you tell the admiral, sir?'

Bolitho listened to the thuds and bangs below decks as

51

the screens were hastily torn down and anything which might hamper the gunners was dragged below the water-line.

'I fancy Sir William will know already, Mr. Quarme.' he replied dryly.

He had hardly finished speaking when a midshipman burst from the poop and gasped, 'The admiral's respects, and, and . . .' He faltered, aware that the men around him were all listening.

Bolitho said abruptly, 'Well, what *exactly* did he say, boy?'

The wretched midshipman stammered, 'He asked what the hell do you think you're playing at?'

Bolitho kept his voice even. 'My compliments to Sir William. Be so good as to inform him that we have just cleared for action.' He looked across at Quarme and added coldly, 'But I see that it still took over ten minutes!'

He saw Quarme's tall frame stiffen, but continued, 'Give me my glass.' Then while the others stared after him he pulled himself on to the mizzen shrouds and began to climb. The coarse ratlines felt damp and unsteady beneath his shoes, and he found he was gripping them tighter than necessary as he made his way slowly aloft to the mizzen top. He hated heights, and had done so since he had first gone aloft as a twelve-year-old midshipman. He knew it was anger as well as pride which made him do this sort of thing, and the realisation made him even more irritated.

He threw his leg over the wooden barricade and opened his glass. As he glanced down at the pale deck far below he realised he could already pick out details more clearly. The black breeches of the guns below the gangways, Captain Ashby's square of marines formed up abaft the foremast, their scarlet uniforms appearing black in the

52

strange light, and even aft by the taffrail he could see the faint glow of a lantern from the cabin skylight. Sir William was now fully awake. He would grumble and mutter about not being kept informed, but Bolitho knew already that Moresby would be much quicker to accuse him of negligence if he overlooked anything.

Bolitho forgot all of them as he trained his glass over the barricade, his feet taking and allowing for the ship's gentle roll and the steady shiver of the mast itself.

There it was right enough. They were approaching the island from the south-east, close-hauled on the larboard tack, so that the three hills overlapped against the dull-coloured sky to make what looked for all the world like a giant, battered cocked hat.

There was a clang of metal from the maindeck followed by a snarl of anger from an invisible petty officer. Bolitho closed his glass and climbed swiftly back to the quarterdeck. In his haste he even forgot his fear of heights.

'Keep those hands quiet, Mr. Quarme! We are less than three miles offshore. If they are still asleep over there I would like them to remain so!'

'They were *my* sentiments, Bolitho.'

He turned and saw Moresby's figure framed against the poop like a pale ghost. Then he realised that the admiral had thrown a coat over his white nightshirt, and on his head he still wore a red sleeping cap like a candle-snuffer.

Bolitho kept his tone formal. 'I must beg your pardon, sir. But it seemed wiser to be prepared.'

The admiral glared at him. 'So *you* say!'

Gimlett appeared hovering nervously behind the admiral with a tray and two glasses. For Moresby this was a morning ritual. One glass contained a raw egg. The other was half filled with brandy.

Bolitho looked away, sickened, as the admiral gulped down his strange mixture.

Moresby smacked his lips and said dourly, 'Sky's brightening at last.' He swung round so that the tassel of his cap bounced in the breeze like a pendant. 'Where are those damn Dons?'

'It'll take 'em hours to catch up, sir.' Bolitho tried to hide his eagerness. 'Perhaps we should close the shore still further? The bottom shelves very steeply hereabouts to over eighty fathoms.'

The admiral grunted. 'It seems quiet enough. Maybe Don Anduaga was right, after all.' He scowled. 'I hope he is!'

Bolitho persisted, 'I have detailed a full landing party, sir. Ninety marines and one hundred picked seamen. We could drop the boats within a cable of the entrance before the garrison knew what was happening.'

Moresby sighed. 'Hold your horses, damn you! I dislike this business as much as you do, but Lord Hood's orders were explicit. We let the Dons go in first.' He walked back to the poop. 'Anyway, you'd look a damn fool if the Spaniards arrived a day late and there *was* trouble. You heard what that lieutenant said about the defences. They'd massacre your men before they got out of the boats!'

Bolitho dropped his voice. 'But not this early, sir. Surprise is the thing. As soon as the fortress garrison has seen us we'll never get another chance.'

'I'm going to get dressed.' Moresby sounded dangerously calm. 'My God, you frigate captains are all the same. No sense of responsibility or risk!' He stalked away with Gimlett trotting in his wake.

Bolitho walked twice up and down the quarterdeck to

settle his mind. Moresby was old for his rank and was probably over-cautious.

Gossett intoned, 'Island's abeam, sir.' He was squinting at the tightly braced yards.

Bolitho nodded. He had allowed his taut nerves to distract him. He had not really expected Moresby to fly in the face of Hood's orders, but he had still hoped. He said wearily, 'Very well. Wear ship and lay her on the opposite tack, Mr. Gossett.'

The *Hyperion* nudged steeply into the offshore swell and swung dutifully across the wind, her sails drawing immediately as the cool breeze sent a gentle ripple across the water alongside.

'Lay her on the starboard tack, Mr. Gossett.' Bolitho pictured the chart in his mind. 'There is a long ridge of rock jutting out from the astern end of the harbour entrance. There may be a sentry there.'

He thought of the men by the guns, of his officers waiting and wondering throughout the ship. They would be smiling now, he thought bitterly. Thinking that their new captain was more nervous than vigilant. All the drills and preparations would be wasted if his inbuilt caution had proved him wrong.

He looked up at the masthead pendant and saw that it was touched with pale gold like spun silk. And when he peered across the bows he realised that the horizon had appeared, a dark line between sky and sea. How quickly the dawn came up here, he thought. The realisation only depressed him further. With it would come the blazing heat, the air of motionless and helpless inactivity while the ship wallowed above her mirrored twin barely making headway.

'Deck there! Two ships on the lee bow!'

Quarme muttered, 'The Dons did not sleep long, after all, sir.'

'Maybe they mistrusted our admiral.' Bolitho stared at the glassy, undulating swell alongside. 'My respects to Sir William. Inform him of their approach.'

Quarme waited. 'Shall I fall out the men from quarters, sir?'

'Just do you are told!' Bolitho regretted his outburst immediately, but made himself stay by the rail as Quarme hurried away with his message.

The sun, blood-red and angry, lifted above the sharp horizon to paint a widening path across the empty expanse of water. Then Bolitho saw the topsails of the two Spanish ships. In the strange light they too looked fiery and unreal.

He turned as Moresby reappeared on deck. He was fully dressed in his gold-laced coat and hat, and was wearing his best presentation sword as if for a review.

The admiral breathed in deeply. 'A fine day, Bolitho.' He snapped his fingers and took a glass from the signal midshipman and then trained it on the other ships for several minutes.

He sighed. 'Make a signal to the *Marte*. Tell her to take station astern.' He blinked in the sunlight and added, 'You will then wear ship and lead the line back across the southern approaches. If nothing happens we will enter harbour.' He tossed the glass to the midshipman. 'Don Anduaga can have this damn island with pleasure.' Then he walked aft and stood in silence watching the flags soaring up the *Hyperion*'s yards.

As the sun climbed steadily above a glittering horizon

the dawn opened up the sea in every direction, like a curtain being ripped from a window. Here there was no drowsy period of half-light, no chance to adjust. One minute it was night. And the next . . . Bolitho pulled his mind away from such meaningless comparisons and walked aft to watch the two Spanish ships. With the sunlight astern of them they made a splendid sight. Both had shortened sail, but their masts and yards were so decked with gay flags and resplendent banners it was impossible to determine whether they were making signals or merely preparing to celebrate a bloodless victory.

Anduaga's flagship, the *Marte*, was like something from a child's picture book. From her garish figurehead to her tall, sloping poopdeck she was alive with colour and movement, and crammed in cheerful confusion on her upper deck Bolitho could see her cargo of Spanish soldiers who were to make up the largest proportion of the landing force.

He deliberately turned his back and moved his glass across to the island. In the bright sunlight it did not appear half so threatening. The hills which he had thought to be grey were covered with tiny, stunted bushes and sun-dried scrub, and only the wide round tower of the fortress remained to add a touch of uncertainty. There was no sign of life but the the line of writhing surf at the foot of the cliffs, and the natural harbour was still hidden in deep shadow so that not even the keen-eyed masthead lookouts could see any sort of activity within.

Moresby said flatly, 'Very well, Bolitho. Fire a gun. This is close enough.' His voice seemed loud in the tense silence.

Bolitho waved one hand towards the maindeck and saw Pearse, the gunner, move aside as the forward twelve-pounder lurched back with a loud bang, the sound of the single detonation echoing and booming around the high cliff and sending the gulls screaming skyward in violent protest.

Bolitho kept his glass trained on the hairline above the fortress, and as he held his breath he saw a flag jerking hastily upward to the truck, and after a second's hesitation it broke out gaily in the offshore breeze. He lowered his glass and looked at the admiral. Moresby was smiling grimly. Even without a glass it was easy to see the flag. The bright red and yellow of Spain.

Moresby made up his mind. 'Signal the *Marte*. His ships will tack in succession and enter harbour.' He eyed Bolitho coldly. 'You will continue on this course and then tack to follow suit.'

Bolitho saw Midshipman Caswell scribbling hastily on his slate and then said. 'I think we should send a boat in first, sir. One of the cutters perhaps?'

Moresby watched the flags rise from the deck and then beckoned him across to the rail. 'I've wasted enough time, Bolitho! Do you think I want the Dons telling everyone that we are too frightened to believe our own eyes?' He stuck out his jaw. 'Remember that this is supposed to *inspire* confidence!'

Caswell bleated, '*Marte* has acknowledged, I think, sir!'

The Spanish flagship was spreading out more sail, and as they watched they could see her shape lengthening as she heeled round towards the island.

The *Princesa*, a smaller vessel of sixty-four guns, dropped out of formation, her sails flapping in confusion as she endeavoured to tack round after her consort.

Gossett growled. 'Didn't see the signal, most like!' He watched the ships with obvious contempt. 'They'll all be drunk by nightfall!'

Moresby said, 'May I suggest you release your men from quarters, Bolitho. Secure guns and ports before you tack.' He seemed suddenly angry. 'There has been enough foolishness for one day!'

Bolitho clenched his fists and crossed to the weather side. 'Did you hear that, Mr. Quarme?' He saw the first lieutenant nod, his face as immobile as before. 'Carry on then!'

'Deck there! I can see the topmasts of a ship well up th' harbour!'

Several people looked up at the lookout's tiny silhouette, but most were still staring glumly at the glittering Spanish ships astern.

Bolitho snatched the speaking trumpet from Quarme. 'What is she, man?'

'Nothin' much, sir!' The man seemed to realise he was speaking with his captain and added firmly, 'She be a sloop, sir!'

Bolitho walked to the rail and shouted at the men by the guns who were already replacing the extra lashing on the twelve-pounders and bolting the ports. 'Belay that order!'

He looked at Moresby and said, 'That sloop, sir. It might be the *Fairfax* which Lord Hood sent out for news from here.' He waited, gripping his hands behind him as he watched the uncertainty growing on the admiral's features. He added stubbornly, 'If it is our ship then . . .'

Moresby looked away, 'God, man! If you're right!' He made an effort to control his voice as he snapped, 'Make a signal to the *Marte*! Tell her to withdraw and take station astern. Then make the same signal to the *Princesa*!'

But the Spanish flagship had completed her turn, and with the fresh morning breeze across her larboard bow was heading straight for the smooth waters of the harbour entrance.

Moresby said, 'Fire a gun, dammit! Make him see our signal!'

But the gun crews were still caught in the confusion of countermanded orders and it was a full three minutes before the forward gun boomed another blank charge.

Caswell said breathlessly, 'No acknowledgement, sir!'

Lieutenant Inch, who had taken no part in the general discussion said suddenly, 'I can see smoke, sir!'

Bolitho lifted his glass, seeing the rough grey stone of the fortress suddenly stark in the harsh sunlight. As he steadied the telescope he saw the growing haze beyond the lower walls and heard Inch add doubtfully, 'Well, it wasn't gunfire.'

Bolitho looked at Moresby and saw the dismay on his face. The admiral said thickly, 'Furnace smoke! They're heating shot, by God!'

Another cry from the masthead brought every glass round once more. In the twinkling of an eye the flag above the fortress had vanished. It was replaced instantly by a new one, and as it broke out to the sunlight Bolitho heard the admiral give a low murmur of disbelief, as if he had still been hanging on to some small hope, when there was none.

Bolitho closed his glass with a snap. The white flag with its new tricolour in one corner swept away all past uncertainty.

He looked at Gossett. 'Wear ship, if you please. Steer east by north.' To Moresby he added quietly, 'Well, sir?'

The admiral tore his eyes from the *Marte*. It was evident that Anduaga had seen the French flag, and it was equally obvious he could do nothing about it. The harbour entrance was less than a mile across, and the French commander had timed it so that the *Marte*'s great shadow had passed between the fortress and the long headland on the opposite side before he showed his true colours.

The *Marte* heeled slightly, her yards bracing round as she sailed closer to the fortress side. Anduaga probably hoped to go about inside the wider expanse of the harbour and sail straight out of the opening in one swift manœuvre.

Even a fast frigate would have found it difficult. *Marte*'s men were hampered by the packed soldiers, and order of any sort gave way to complete confusion as the first gun opened fire from the battery walls. In addition the *Marte*'s captain had failed to allow for the sheltering wall of the headland. His sails flapped aimlessly, and for a few long minutes the ship was all aback.

Moresby said tightly, 'Close the harbour entrance, Bolitho! We must support Anduaga!' He turned as the air trembled to a full salvo from the battery. Tall waterspouts were rising beyond the Spanish flagship, but still Anduaga had not fired one shot in reply.

Bolitho said harshly, 'Alter course two points to larboard, Mr. Gossett.' He looked across at Quarme. 'Have the guns loaded and run out.' He was surprised that his voice remained so calm. Inwardly his whole being wanted to scream with desperation at Moresby's latest order. It was useless to follow the *Marte*. It had been pointless from the moment the flag had been hoisted. No ship was a match for a carefully sited shore battery. And heated shot into the bargain. Bolitho looked up bitterly at the *Hyperion*'s yards as they squeaked round obediently to the braces. Every shroud and spar, every plank above her waterline was as dry as tinder.

He called, 'Bucket parties ready, Mr. Quarme! If one

heated ball has more than a minute in the timbers you know what to expect!'

Moresby lowered his glass. 'Signal the *Princesa* to take station astern.' Across the water he could hear the beat of drums, and as he watched saw the sixty-four running out her guns.

Bolitho could not contain himself. 'Too late!'

The admiral did not face him. 'The *Marte* might still be able to withdraw. If we give her full support . . .' He broke off and stared transfixed as a great tongue of flame soared up the flagship's side. It was so vast that it made the *Marte* seem tiny by comparison. She had at last run out her guns, but even as her upper battery exploded in a ragged salvo the searing wall of flames engulfed the whole larboard side, so that the flapping sails and cheerful banners vanished in seconds, like ashes in a strong wind.

A fog of brown smoke drifted from the stone walls above the cliff, and every few seconds one or more of the big guns added to the holocaust below.

Somehow the *Marte*'s jib and foresail survived, so that the breeze swung her round, the lazy movement carrying the flames leaping across her upper deck. Within minutes she was ablaze from bow to quarterdeck, and from the crowded poop tiny, pitiful figures were dropping overboard to join the struggling bodies who already sought safety in the glittering water.

Bolitho made himself concentrate on the slanting hillside as it pointed down towards the *Hyperion*'s bowsprit. 'Steady! Starboard a point!' He heard Caswell sucking breath between his teeth, and in the grim silence he could listen to the burning ship like a man in some sort of nightmare.

Closer and closer, until mercifully the overhanging headland had crept down to hide the dying *Marte* from sight. But above the hill he saw the pall of black smoke and the great drifting curtain of blown sparks as the battery hammered the stricken ship into blazing ruins.

His mouth was bone dry, but he must not think about it. The *Marte* had a company of seven hundred men. She had in addition upwards of two hundred soldiers aboard and a hundred terrified horses.

There was a direct orange flash from the hillside and then a loud slap overhead. Bolitho looked at the smoking hole in the mizzen topsail and then at the admiral.

Moresby gritted his teeth as he said, 'We *must* attack, Bolitho! What else can we do?'

Bolitho looked away as another ball screamed past the mainyard and ricocheted across the water like a crazed serpent.

He said, 'We must withdraw, sir. With all respect, this move is lost to us.' Again he was amazed at his own calmness. Yet every second carried his ship nearer and nearer to the entrance. Fifteen more minutes and he would have to tack. One way or the other. He added doggedly, 'The Frogs can pound us to fragments, sir. Even if we reach the other part of the harbour they'll be waiting for our boats to try and land.'

He saw Moresby's features twisting with doubts and fears he could only guess at. Whatever he did now he would see his future in ruins. An eighty-gun ship destroyed and her company burned or captured, and above all the French flag over Cozar, untouched and unreachable. Then he pushed the feelings of pity from his mind and said harshly, 'For God's sake, sir! We cannot fight those guns!'

Then Moresby looked up at his flag rippling from the foremast and said with his old abruptness, 'Handle your ship as you will, Bolitho! But we'll not give in to those treacherous dogs!' He glared. 'Not now! Not ever!'

Bolitho eyed him squarely and coldly, then walked to the rail. 'Larboard batteries to full elevation, Mr. Quarme! We will engage as we round the headland!' He glanced up quickly as a shoulder of hillside lifted to blind the enemy gunners. But respite was only temporary. Once round the point and at least seven big guns would bear on the *Hyperion*.

He listened to the bosun's mates piping his orders between decks and heard the scrape of metal as the double line of guns pointed their muzzles skyward.

Then as the ship threw her shadow almost to the foot of the cliffs a great silence fell over the decks, unbroken even by distant gunfire.

Ashby's marines had clumped aft and now lined the quarterdeck and poop nettings, their muskets loaded and ready. Lieutenant Shanks, Ashby's second-in-command, stood by the poop rail, his heavy curved hanger still in its scabbard, as if to condemn the hopelessness of muskets against stone and heated shot.

Caswell called, 'Sir! The *Princesa*'s hauled off!'

It was true. Horrified or fearful at the sight of the *Hyperion* driving right inshore to the foot of the cliffs, the other Spanish captain had obviously decided to use his own discretion rather than obey Moresby's last desperate signal.

Moresby said thickly, 'That cowardly dog! I'll see him in chains for this!'

Bolitho ignored him. It was easy to do with death so close at hand. His usual fear of mutilation and agony under the surgeon's knife at the approach of battle gave way to a dull acceptance. It was strange that but for his own singlemindedness he would still be in Kent. He thought of Moresby's determination and felt violently

64

angry. To think that such eager men, and others swept up by an impartial Press, should trust their lives to men like him! When all else failed, when he was proved wrong, all he could think of was dying bravely! And when *Hyperion*'s old timbers lay rotting beside those of the Spaniard's the French flag would still be there.

A shaft of sunlight lanced across the quarterdeck and with something like shock he realised that his ship was already moving into the calmer waters of the harbour approach. There across the bow was the far side of the opening, an unfinished stone jetty shining in the sun like giant's teeth. He could see the small sloop anchored around a bend in the steep hills which surrounded the protected bay like a green wall. There were some tiny figures rowing a longboat across the sloop's bows, untroubled by the horror below the fortress.

They were so confident that as the *Hyperion*'s bowsprit crossed the opening they ceased rowing, and one man even stood up to watch.

Bolitho grasped the quarterdeck rail, feeling his heart against his ribs like drum beats. 'Mr. Rooke!' He saw the lieutenant turn his face up from the maindeck, shading his eyes against the glare. 'You will control the firing! I want the guns fired in succession, two by two as they bear! Aim for the parapet and fire on the uproll!' He saw Rooke nod and then turn back to his crouching gunners.

Hyperion was cutting the entrance more finely than the carefree *Marte* had done, so the French battery would have to wait a moment longer. As the ship glided slowly past an out-thrust spit of rocks Bolitho heard cries of shocked despair from the tops, and when he leaned over the nettings he saw what was left of Anduaga's flagship.

She was still burning fiercely, but some internal explo

sion must have blasted out her bottom, so that she lay like a flaming pyre across a ridge of hard sand, her masts all gone, her hull gutted almost to the lower gundeck. She was surrounded by a drifting carpet of ashes and charred woodwork, amongst which the wounded and flayed survivors jostled each other, splashing and screaming, clutching even at the many corpses which moved with them in a macabre dance.

Rooke's voice was crisp. 'Open fire!'

The broadside rippled unhurriedly down the *Hyperion*'s side, each upper gun firing in unison with its larger consort on the lower deck.

Bolitho felt the ship quiver as if being shaken by a jagged reef. He watched narrowly as the balls struck the top of the stone walls below the smoking muzzles and saw a few chips fly in the air like pebbles. As if from far off he heard his gun captains yelling like madmen, 'Reload! Run out!', and the trucks squealing again like pigs as they raced each other for the open ports.

Then the first two guns fired from the battery. One ball whipped overhead and crashed into the far side of the harbour. The second hit the ship hard below the quarterdeck, the shock vibrating up through the planking even as the men ran with their buckets to quench the eager twist of smoke from the embedded iron.

'Fire!' Again the guns lurched back on the tilting deck, their own smoke eddying back through the ports, acrid and blinding, as the gunners feverishly sponged out the hot muzzles and rammed home their charges.

They were past the entrance now. More guns joined in from the battery, and Bolitho's iced mind recorded at least two more hits below decks. Somewhere a man was screaming, the noise going on and on, so that some of the boys running from the magazine with powder seemed terrified by its persistent discord.

'Larboard a point, Mr. Gossett!' Bolitho watched the helm going over and saw the seaman nearest him gripping the worn spokes with all his strength.

A solitary horseman cantered over the crest of the hill and paused to open his telescope. He seemed to stare down at the ship like a bored spectator, and Lieutenant Shanks snarled, 'A guinea for the first man to bring him down!' The marines responded eagerly, each man glad to be doing something at last, although everyone knew that the muskets would not reach half that distance. But the horse shied and the mounted soldier hurriedly withdrew. The marines cheered and grinned at each other through the smoke, as if they had vanquished an army.

Bolitho turned away as another ball screamed down from the battery and hammered into his ship. But this one passed through a gunport and clanged against the metal of a twenty-four pounder before smashing into the press of men on the opposite side. He could hear the desperate shouts of the officers and the awful screams from the wounded, but when he looked at Moresby the latter was staring straight ahead, one hand resting on his sheathed sword, the other tapping a tattoo against his thigh.

'Fire on the lower gundeck, sir!' Midshipman Piper skidded to a halt, his monkey face black with smoke. 'Ten men wounded, too!' He swallowed hard. 'There's a bloody gruel down there, sir!'

Bolitho found time to marvel at the boy's calm. Later he would break. If he lived long enough.

'Detail more fire parties, Mr. Quarme!' He tore his eyes from the thin plume of smoke from the forehatch. 'Lively there!'

It was hopeless. As the ship moved further into the harbour so she made a better target. Bolitho could see the landing place now, and that too was crammed with soldiers and the glint of weapons. Here and there a musket flashed, and he knew they were shooting at some of the *Marte*'s men who had been strong enough to swim that far.

A kind of throbbing madness pulsed through Bolitho's head, so that he felt half dazed. He could stand no more of it. To throw his ship and his men away for nothing.

He swung round to face Moresby, but as he turned he felt something akin to a hot, sandy wind pass his face, and as he opened his mouth to cry a warning the ball struck the nearest gun and exploded in a screech of splinters. Three marines fell writhing from the nettings, and the helmsman whom Bolitho had noticed earlier dropped gasping to his knees, his fingers tearing at his stomach as if to contain the entrails which spewed out on to the planking.

Quarme was yelling, 'The admiral is hit!' He ran from the rail and stooped down beside him calling, 'Fetch the surgeon! *Hurry*, man!'

Bolitho crossed the deck in two strides. 'Return to your station, Mr. Quarme!' From the corner of his eye he saw Gossett pushing the agonised man from the wheel and guiding another through the smoke. He heard cries all around him, but as the smoke eddied and swirled over the bulwarks his world was momentarily contained on this small patch of sunlit quarterdeck. And all the time Moresby was staring up at him, unable to speak, for a splinter had gouged into his throat, tearing it away like a blow from a great talon.

Midshipman Caswell faltered, swallowing hard to control his nausea, then forcing himself from the bulwark dropped down to support the admiral's head on his lap.

Still looking at Moresby's stricken face Bolitho rapped, 'Stand by to go about, Mr. Gossett!'

Some sort of understanding showed on Moresby's face, and he feebly tried to move, so that the blood poured from his wound and across his white waistcoat.

Bolitho shouted, 'Now! Helm alee!' Down in the smoke he could hear men cursing and struggling, and disembodied above the fog the yards began to swing round. The guns were still firing, and as a freak down-draught cleared the smoke from the bows Bolitho saw the fortress swinging across the forecastle as if on a pivot. He felt a sudden prick of pride for this tired old ship. She was answering well in spite of the fools who manned her.

He knelt at Moresby's side and saw the man's tongue bobbing as if to tear itself free. Over his head Caswell's face was torn with fear and pity as his tears ran unheeded, making pale lines through the grime of gunsmoke.

Moresby whispered, 'You were right, Bolitho, damn you!' He shook as a ball whimpered above the poop and severed a backstay like thread. 'I should have seen—should have realised . . .' He was choking in his own blood.

Bolitho said quietly, 'Rest easy, sir. I am taking the ship away from this.'

Moresby closed his eyes. 'Running from them!' He groaned. 'In all my years I've never run . . .'

Bolitho wanted to go back to his ship, but his sudden compassion for Moresby made him stay. He said, 'Not running, sir. We will come back and take that battery for you!'

A gunner's mate ran to the quarterdeck his eyes wild. 'Captain, sir!' He stopped dead as he saw the admiral and then continued in a calmer voice, 'The fire's out, sir!'

Moresby seemed to hear him and muttered, 'Of course, you are a Cornishman, Bolitho. Never did like 'em. Too damn independent, too—too . . .' The blood gushed across his chest and neck and his head lolled against Caswell for the last time.

Bolitho stood up. 'Are we clear?' He saw Gossett staring at him. '*Well?*'

The master licked his lips and then nodded. 'Look, sir!'

The entrance was gliding past once more. Abeam lay the burning hulk of the *Marte* and her attendant corpses. Dead men and horses floated across the *Hyperion*'s bows and unwillingly parted to let her through.

Only a few shots followed her out, for the gunsmoke and that of the burning flagship made a very effective screen. Or maybe the French gunners were too jubilant to care. As well they might be, Bolitho thought bitterly.

He said, 'Wear ship, Mr. Gossett. Steer due east once you clear the approaches.' To the quarterdeck at large he added coldly. 'I told the admiral we will return.'

He caught sight of the unharmed *Princesa* still hove to and standing far out from the battery's reach. He heard himself say, 'Signal the *Princesa*. I want her captain aboard within the hour.' He looked around the stained deck, at the protesting wounded who were being dragged below to meet the surgeon's knife. At the splintered deck where Moresby had fallen, and at the admiral himself. He said aloud, 'If the Spanish captain refuses to obey my orders I will open fire on *him*!'

Gossett saw his face and turned away. He knew Bolitho meant what he said. There was no relief on the captain's face as he might have expected. He had saved his ship and had shown honour in the face of stupidity. But in his eyes there was a wildness which Gossett in all his experience had not seen before. Like that in the eyes of an injured animal. In his heart he knew the look would stay there until *Hyperion* lay at anchor in the harbour and the battery's guns were made harmless.

Bolitho heard some of the men cheering and snapped, 'Secure the guns, Mr. Quarme, and report to me on all damage and casualties. There will be time for cheering later perhaps.' He stared astern towards the drifting bank of smoke which followed the ship like a curtain. 'But now there is work to do.'

Quarme mopped his sweating face with the back of his sleeve. 'Will we be returning to the squadron, sir?' He faltered as Bolitho eyed him coldly then hurried on, 'I mean, sir, both admirals are dead and . . .'

Bolitho turned away. 'Then we will just have to manage on our own, won't we, Mr. Quarme?'

4

Plan of Attack

Lieutenant Ernest Quarme tucked his hat beneath his arm and stepped into the captain's cabin, squinting his eyes against the fierce glare which was thrown upwards through the stern windows to paint the deckhead and furniture in a strange green light.

'You sent for me, sir?'

Bolitho was leaning out over the sill staring down at the *Hyperion*'s tiny wake as it bubbled sluggishly from the weed-encrusted rudder. For a moment his eyes were blinded by the darkened cabin, then he sat down on the bench seat and gestured towards a nearby chair. He knew the first lieutenant was watching him intently, his features betraying nothing of his inner thoughts, and Bolitho hoped that his own face was equally devoid of expression.

Around the cabin the ship creaked and murmured as she wallowed heavily on a slow south-easterly course, her sails hardly filling, and showing more use as shelter from the sun for the men working about her decks. Like muffled drumbeats he could hear the thud of hammers and the occasional rasp of saws as Cuppage, the carpenter, and his mates completed the repairs and hid the last remaining scars left from the brief and savage action.

Bolitho rubbed his eyes and tried to clear the tiredness from his mind. If only the other scars were as easily erased. But the anger and relief, the jubilation of escape and the excitement of battle had soon given way to gloom and depression, which hung over the ship like a storm-cloud. For that short, one-sided fight had been two long days ago. Two days of monotonous tacking and patrolling back and forth, with the island and its mocking flag a constant reminder of their failure.

Bolitho had searched his mind again and again for some method of attack, so that as the hours drew into days each plan became more dangerous and every hope of success more doubtful.

Then this morning the final blow had fallen. The dawn light had found the *Hyperion* some seven miles to the south-west of the island, an area which he had selected as the most suitable for making a quick dash down on the protected harbour, making use of the prevailing off shore winds.

He had placed the Spanish sixty-four, *Princesa*, on the other side of the island, where she had the best chance of catching the captured sloop *Fairfax* should she try and escape by that route.

And the sloop was yet another essential link in the overall plan. The French garrison had no other ship available to carry the news of Moresby's attack and the patrolling British squadron, and unless some sort of storeship was sent from the mainland they would remain in a state of siege. Bolitho had toyed with the idea of a cutting-out operation, but had instantly rejected it. He knew in his heart that it was more as a balm to his hurt pride than a plan with any true value. Moresby's attack had cost *Hyperion* more than enough already. Eight killed and sixteen wounded. The damage to morale was beyond measure.

Then as the morning light had strengthened the news had broken. The lookout at the mainmast head had reported no sign of the *Fairfax*. She had somehow slipped out during the night, and now, as the midday sun beat down relentlessly on the dried decks, she was probably entering St. Clar and screaming the news abroad. The defences would be alerted, but even worse, the French would now know the strength of the vanquished squadron. It was more than likely that along the French coast in inlets and harbours there were ships of the line just waiting the chance to dash out and avenge the indignity of Hood's blockade. Several such ships were known to have slipped past the British patrols, and others were probably in the vicinity already.

Bolitho blamed himself bitterly for the sloop's escape, although he knew well enough it was what he had expected. No ship of the line was fast enough to find her in the dark, and the hill-top battery made sure that the *Hyperion* stayed clear during daylight.

He looked across at Quarme and asked slowly, 'How is the visibility now?'

Quarme shrugged. 'It varies by the hour, sir. But just now it was less than two miles.'

Bolitho nodded. From first light the wind had dropped more and more, so that now the sea's milky surface was hardly ruffled by pitifully light airs which hardly gave the ship steerage way. And as the day drew on a strange mist had gathered, ebbing and writhing like steam, and even the island was lost from sight for quite long periods. Not that it mattered now, he thought heavily. The garrison knew they were there just the same. And the sloop had escaped. Quarme said suddenly, 'May I ask what you intend to do, sir?'

Bolitho faced him and replied, 'Do you wish to make a suggestion?'

The other man dropped his eyes. 'It is hardly my place, sir, but I believe it would be prudent to inform Lord Hood of what has happened.' He seemed to expect an interruption, but then continued, 'You could not be blamed for what occurred. By delaying your despatch to the admiral you might, however, incur his real displeasure.'

'Thank you, Mr. Quarme. I have already thought of that.' Bolitho stood up and walked across the carpet. For a moment he stared hard at his sword hanging by the doorway and then added, 'But we have only two ships. If I send the *Princesa* there is no saying what story will be laid before the admiral, in spite of whatever written despatch from me. And if we leave this station do you really think the Spaniard can deal with some sudden attack from the mainland?' He saw Quarme shuffle his feet uneasily and smiled. 'You think perhaps that I was too hard on the *Princesa*'s captain?'

Without difficulty he could see the unhappy Spaniard sitting where Quarme now sat. He was a sullen, resentful man who at first had pretended to know little English. But Bolitho's scathing words had made his eyes flash with anger and then shame as he had given him his verdict on the *Princesa*'s failure to join the battle.

At one point the Spaniard had leapt to his feet, his mouth twisted in anger. 'I must protest! I could not reach the entrance in time. I will complain to Admiral Hood of your accusations.' Then more loftily he had added, 'I am not unknown in high government circles!'

Bolitho had watched him coldly. Seeing again the death agonies of the Spanish flagship, the burned and butchered remains floating across the *Hyperion*'s bows.

'You will be even better known, Captain, when I have placed you under arrest for cowardice! Admiral Moresby invested full command in me before he died.' It was surprising how easily the lie had come to his lips. 'And nothing you have said so far has persuaded me that you are fit even to remain alive!'

Bolitho hated to see any man humiliated, and he had had to force himself to watch the other captain's misery and fear. But that was two days ago, when there had still been a slight chance of reversing their mutual defeat. By now the Spaniard might have ideas of his own.

Quarme said, 'I still think that you should inform Lord Hood, sir. Whatever the Spanish captain did or did not do will make little difference as far as the future is concerned.'

Bolitho turned away, angry with himself. Angry with Quarme because he knew he was right. Yet in the back of his mind he seemed to hear Hood's words. 'I want that island taken without delay!' Without delay. Right at this moment aboard the *Victory* the admiral would be in the middle of his own problems. The internal politics of Toulon, the show of confidence he had so carefully described. And all the time the French army would be moving south towards the coast.

Bolitho said calmly, 'You and I seem to disagree about several things. You disapproved of my burying Sir William Moresby at sea with the other dead seamen.'

Quarme was disconcerted by this new tack. 'Well, I thought that under the circumstances . . .'

'Admiral Moresby died in battle, Mr. Quarme. I see no point in drawing a line between his sacrifice and those of the men who gave their lives for him.' His voice was still calm but cold. 'Sir William is as safe now as he would have been in some graveyard.' He made himself return to the stern windows. 'Our people have lost heart. It is never good for men to lose a first battle. So much depends on their trust when next they face a broadside.' He added wearily, 'They died with their admiral. They will share his grave as well as his privilege!'

Quarme opened his mouth and looked round startled as a distant voice entered the quiet cabin.

'Deck there! Sail to the sou'west!'

Bolitho stared at Quarme and then snapped, 'Come with me. Maybe the French are out already!'

On the quarterdeck the sun greeted his shoulders like heat from a furnace, but Bolitho hardly noticed it as he looked first towards the island and then to the masthead. Of Cozar there was still no sign. But to seaward the mist was thinner and more fragile above the blinding water, and as he took a telescope from Midshipman Caswell he asked, 'Can the lookout make her out yet?'

In the glass he could see little more, but for a splinter of white sail barely making a break on the sea's edge.

The lookout called, 'She's a small ship, sir! On 'er own an' steering due east!'

Bolitho said, 'Get up there, Mr. Quarme, and tell me what you see.' He knew the others were watching him and had to control the urge to go aloft himself.

Lieutenant Rooke was officer of the watch, and stood by the quarterdeck rail, a glass beneath his arm, his hat tilted against the glare. As always he was faultlessly dressed, and beside the other men in their stained shirts, or as most were stripped to the waist, he looked like a London dandy.

Bolitho ignored all of them and tried not to stare up at Quarme's tall figure as he climbed swiftly towards the crosstrees. Rooke would be enjoying all this, he thought grimly. No doubt he would be quick to enlarge on his captain's failure once they rejoined the squadron. Bolitho told himself he was being unfair. Maybe his dislike for Rooke hinged on his more general aversion to privileged aristocrats within the Navy. Titles given as rewards for valour and true achievement were one thing, but so often they became intolerable burdens for the eager offsprings. Bolitho had found plenty of them on his visits to London. Spoiled, self-important little upstarts who owed their appointments to birth and financial power, and knew little of the Navy but for the uniforms they wore with such dash and conceit.

Quarme shouted suddenly, 'I can see her right enough, sir! Sloop of war by the look of her! She's holding her course to the east'rd!'

Rooke spoke for all of them. 'She'll be from Gibraltar. Despatches and mail for the fleet.'

Bolitho looked across at Gossett's massive figure. 'You have served in these waters before, Mr. Gossett. Will this weather hold?'

The master frowned, his eyes vanishing into his brown face. 'Not long, sir. These light airs come an' go, but I reckon the wind'll get up afore eight bells.' He was not boasting, he was giving a statement born of long experience.

Bolitho nodded. 'Very well, Mr. Gossett. Call all hands and prepare to wear ship. We will alter course and intercept that sloop immediately.'

Quarme arrived at his side breathing heavily. 'We could signal her to close *us*, sir.' He sounded almost shocked that a line-of-battle ship should make allowances for such a tiny unit of the fleet.

Bolitho eyed him gravely. 'As soon as we are within range have a signal sent on, if you please. I don't want to lose her now.'

Quarme was mystified. 'Signal, sir?'

Below on the maindeck the men pulled themselves from their dulled torpor as the pipes drove them to their stations for wearing ship.

Bolitho said quietly, 'Tell her to heave to and await my orders.'

'I see, sir.' Then Quarme said, 'So you have decided to send despatches to Lord Hood, after all.' He bit his lip and nodded slowly. 'It is the best decision, in my opinion. No one will blame you, sir.'

Bolitho watched the marines clumping aft like soldiers to man the mizzen braces with their usual unseamanlike precision. Then he dragged his mind back to Quarme's remark and said flatly, 'I have no intention of sending a report to Lord Hood, Mr. Quarme. Not until there *is* something to report!'

It took the best part of two hours to close the other vessel within hailing distance, but by six bells of the afternoon watch both ships had gone about and were heading due south, away from the mist-shrouded island.

Then Bolitho signalled for the sloop's captain to come aboard, and as both ships shortened sail he returned to his cabin and sent for Quarme.

'I want all officers assembled in this cabin fifteen minutes after the sloop's commander, Mr. Quarme.' He ignored the mystified expression on the other man's face and continued crisply, 'And all warrant officers not employed in working the ship, right?'

'Aye, aye, sir.' Quarme's eyes moved to the quarter windows where the little sloop rode easily in the *Hyperion*'s lee. 'Can I ask what you intend, sir?'

Bolitho eyed him impassively. 'Fifteen minutes, Mr. Quarme.'

He controlled his gnawing impatience as the sounds of a boat coming alongside and the shrill of pipes announced the new arrival. But by the time an equally mystified Lieutenant Bellamy, commander of H.M. Sloop *Chanticleer*, arrived in his cabin he was, outwardly at least, quite composed again.

Bellamy was a young, gangling officer with troubled eyes and an air of sad apprehension about him.

Bolitho got straight to the point. 'I am sorry to summon you aboard in this way, Bellamy, but as senior officer of this squadron I have need of your ready assistance.'

Bellamy digested the beginning without much show of excitement. But he did not question Bolitho's right of stopping him either, and Bolitho considered the use of the title 'senior officer' had already been of some value.

He continued, 'Over yonder lies Cozar, which as you may know is now in enemy hands. It is my intention to

79

reverse that arrangement, and at once.' He eyed the lieutenant searchingly. 'But only with your help, you understand?'

Bellamy obviously did not. If a seventy-four was powerless to act it hardly seemed likely that his frail-timbered sloop could add much to the proceedings. But he nodded nevertheless. Maybe only to humour Bolitho, a squadron commander who had to all appearances but one ship at his disposal.

Bolitho smiled. 'Very well then, I will tell you what I intend.'

Fifteen minutes later Quarme opened the door and stood aside as the *Hyperion*'s officers filed silently into the cabin, their eyes at first busy on these sacred quarters, and then finally settling on the gangling lieutenant.

Bolitho faced them calmly. 'Well, gentlemen, at last we have a plan.'

The eyes shifted to him and stayed there.

'In an hour or so we will alter course to the north and beat back towards the mainland. There is not much time, and a great deal to do. Now, it seems to me that the French will not attempt to return to Cozar during the night. For one thing it is a mite dangerous, and the other is that they might run against us or the *Princesa*.' He unrolled a chart on the table. 'By dawn tomorrow I intend to be in this position to the nor'west of the island, and as soon as we are sighted by the garrison then Lieutenant Bellamy will take his ship straight into the harbour.'

If he had announced a visitation from God his words could not have had a greater effect. Some of the officers stared incredulously at Bellamy for explanation or confirmation, but the latter merely looked at his feet. Others exchanged baffled glances and threw strange stares at

Bolitho, as if to reassure themselves that he had not gone raving mad.

Bolitho smiled slightly and continued, 'In the next hour I want one of our carronades taken across to the *Chanticleer*.' He tightened his jaw, hearing his own words committing himself and every man present. 'In addition she will carry one hundred of our seamen and all the marines.'

Captain Ashby could contain himself no longer. 'But what will happen, sir? I-I mean, dammit, sir . . .' He trailed away into helpless silence as Rooke's drawling voice broke in from the side of the cabin.

'So you want the Frogs to think that the sloop is the *Fairfax* returning to harbour, sir?'

Bolitho nodded silently. Rooke was sharp enough anyway, and well ahead of the rest.

'Exactly.'

There was a great buzz of murmurs and questions, and then Quarme asked doggedly, 'What chance is there of success, sir? I mean to say, the *Chanticleer is* a sloop, but she's nothing like the *Fairfax*. She's older and smaller!' There were several nods around him.

'A good point, Mr. Quarme.' Bolitho thrust his hands behind him. 'However, I have found from experience that men usually see what they expect to see.' He looked around their faces very slowly. 'And the enemy will see a sloop being chased back into harbour by the *Hyperion*. They will open fire on *this* ship to cover her escape. By the time they realise what has happened we will be inside the harbour and too close to the landing place for the French to depress their guns.'

He had every man's full attention now. Even the midshipmen were craning forward to listen.

He said, 'But it has to be quick, gentlemen. At any moment from now on the French might be sending other

81

ships. Then again some keen-eyed lookout might see the difference in sloops before we can enter harbour. But the garrison will be soldiers. Need I say more?'

Surprisingly, several of them actually laughed. It was a small beginning.

Bolitho looked round. 'Do we have a French flag? One of the new ones?'

Several heads were shaken.

Bolitho sought out the grey-haired sailmaker. 'Well, Mr. Buckle, you have thirty minutes to make one, so get to it!'

He did not wait for the man to reply but turned to the *Hyperion*'s gunner. 'Mr. Pearse, you can get the carronade swayed across as soon as you like. Select a good crew for it, and use whatever boat you require.'

He watched him follow the sailmaker and then added evenly, 'When we made our last attack on the harbour we were hidden from the battery for a few moments by a shoulder of land. If this ship keeps on that same course as before the enemy might move some of the other guns across to hit us better. They will be very confident by that time, and will know that we would never attempt to sail directly into a trap. If they do that the sloop will have an even better chance.'

There was a murmur of excitement. It was a plan at last. There was still a lot to be sorted out and explained. But it was a plan.

'Very well, gentlemen, you may go. Attend to your duties. I will be on deck directly to deal with the next phase.'

As they left the cabin Bolitho turned once more to Lieutenant Bellamy. He had expected some comment, even protest, but Bellamy had said nothing at all, and

Bolitho was not sure he had understood half of what was expected of him.

He said, 'Thank you, Bellamy, that was most helpful.'

The lieutenant stared at him and swallowed hard. 'It was?' He gulped again. 'Er, thank you, sir.'

Bolitho followed him on deck and watched him walk unsteadily towards the entry port. Then he breathed out very slowly. He had failed to inform Lord Hood of the failure to take Cozar. He had assumed overall command of an operation which might end in real disaster and a great loss of life. He had even waylaid a sloop with its despatches and mail, and would possibly destroy the little ship for good measure.

He looked up at the masthead and saw the pendant lifting and stirring itself in a growing breeze. But if there had been any excuse for avoiding action before, there was none now. The consequences for what he had already done had made that impossible.

Then pushing the doubt from his mind he crossed to the weather side of the quarterdeck and began to pace up and down with steady concentration.

Bolitho awoke with a violent start and for several seconds stared at Allday's stooping shape and the heavy jug which he carried in one hand.

Allday said quietly, 'Sorry to wake you, Captain, but it's getting a mite lighter on deck.' He held out a mug and began to pour a hot drink while Bolitho gathered his thoughts and peered around the sloop's tiny cabin.

Above the chair in which he had fallen into an exhausted sleep he could see a pale rectangle of light from the quarterdeck skylight, and the sudden realisation of

83

what lay ahead held him rigidly in his seat, like a man emerging from a nightmare only to find it is real.

The hot coffee tasted bitter, but he felt it exploring his insides and was grateful for it.

'How is the wind?'

Allday shrugged. 'Light but steady, Captain. Still from the nor'-west.'

'Good.' He stood up quickly and let out a curse as his head struck the low deck beams.

Allday controlled the impulse to grin. 'Not much of a ship, is she, Captain?'

Bolitho rubbed his arms to restore the circulation and replied coldly, 'My first command was a sloop of war, Allday. Very like this one.' Then he smiled ruefully. 'But you are right. Such craft are for the very young, or the very small!'

The door opened a few inches and Lieutenant Bellamy bobbed his head inside. 'Ah, sir, I see you have been called.' He showed his teeth, 'A fine day for it!'

Bolitho eyed him with surprise. It was amazing how Bellamy had thrown himself into the scheme of things. If anything went wrong he would have much to explain. In the Navy it was not always sufficient to hold on to the excuse that you were only obeying someone else's orders.

Bent almost double, Bolitho followed him up a short ladder and on to the sloop's quarterdeck. It felt very cool, and in the pale light he could see patches of broken cloud and a few catspaws of tossing water. He shivered and wished he was wearing his coat. But like the rest he had discarded anything which might be seen and recognised by a vigilant sentry.

Bellamy was pointing across the larboard bow. 'Cozar is about five miles over yonder, sir. It'll not be long now.'

Bolitho walked aft to the taffrail and strained his eyes astern. The breeze was steady on his skin, but of the *Hyperion* there was no sign. He walked slowly back past the unprotected wheel, his shoes sounding strangely loud in the silence.

Once again he pushed his mind back over the past hectic hours, seeking any flaw or mistake in his plans. He recalled Quarme's brief show of dismay when he had told him that he was to be left in charge of the ship. Even Bolitho's patient explanation had done little to change things.

If the French were not deceived, or the sloop was overcome before she could be laid alongside the landing place, nobody in the attacking force would survive.

It was Bolitho's plan. He would take the risk. But he could sympathise with Quarme all the same. He had learned that Quarme was a career officer with little money or influence to back his progress. His sort depended on being given charge of a cutting-out operation, or a scatter-brained scheme like this one. Others climbed the slippery ladder to promotion by way of the deaths or advancements of their superiors, and maybe Quarme had already hoped that Captain Turner's sudden demise would see him on his way.

But if all failed in Cozar the *Hyperion* needed a good, level-headed man in command, no matter how temporary, and Quarme had proved that he was more than able to run the ship.

Bellamy said anxiously, 'The horizon's clearing, sir.' He was dragging at his watch. 'God, this waiting!'

It was certainly brighter. Bolitho could see the sloop's full upper deck and the black finger of her bowsprit against the paling sky beyond. But for the small ship's sluggish response to helm and wind it was hard to imagine that crammed below decks were all of Ashby's marines, as well as fifty of *Hyperion*'s seamen, with another fifty uncomfortably hidden beneath a tarpaulin on the maindeck itself. It was fortunate that Bellamy was already sailing shorthanded, but nevertheless it took every piece of hold space as well as the berth deck to cram them inside the sloop's hull.

The *Chanticleer*'s own seamen were sitting or lounging around the bulwarks, saying little, and waiting to spread every stitch of canvas as soon as the order was given.

Bolitho's mind strayed to the awful possibility of Quarme's failure to reach the rendezvous in time. All night the sloop had hurried on ahead, just in case some snooping fishing boat or coasting craft should see them sailing in company and kill the only possible chance of success before they had even started.

He looked along the starboard battery of guns. The sloop was armed with eighteen tiny cannon, the whole broadside of which would hardly make a scar on that imposing fortress.

'Ah!' Bellamy let out a gasp as the golden rim of sunlight lanced brightly over the edge of the sea.

And there was the island. Maybe four miles clear, with its humped hills and the fortress square and black against the growing sunlight. Approaching from the west gave the island a different shape, Bolitho thought, but as he lifted his glass he could see the white breakers at the foot of the headland, and realised how tall and formidable the cliff looked by comparison.

He shivered again and was instantly reminded of the months he had lain in his bed at Falmouth. Without effort he could picture the big grey house, the view of the anchorage and Pendennis Castle he had seen from his window between bouts of dizziness and oblivion. The house with its great dark portraits of all the past Bolithos who had lived and died by the sea. It was full of memories, but empty of warmth. For he was the last of the line, with no one to carry on the family tradition.

He thought too of Nancy, his youngest sister. She had watched over him during his illness, and with Allday had nursed him through one agony after another. She adored him, he knew that well enough, and had tried to mother him whenever she got the chance.

Bolitho studied the slow-moving clouds impassively. If he was to die this morning, Nancy would have the old house. She was married to a Falmouth farmer and land-owner, a County man who lived only for blood sports and good fare. He also had a ready eye for Bolitho's house, and would be more than ready to move in.

Allday whispered, 'Your sword, Captain.'

Bolitho lifted his arms automatically and felt the firm clasp of the belt about his waist as Allday adjusted the buckle.

Allday muttered, 'It's a mite loose from the last time you wore it, Captain.' He shook his head. 'You need some good Cornish lamb inside you!'

'Don't fuss, damn you!' Bolitho dropped his hand and ran it over the worn hilt. He should have left the old sword hanging in his cabin aboard *Hyperion*. But the thought of leaving it to fall into someone else's hands, or worse, for it to go to Nancy's husband, was unbearable. That man would stick it on his wall amongst his fox masks and deer heads like one more shabby souvenir.

He tried to recall exactly the moment when his father had given it to him, but he could no longer obtain a clear picture of the proud old man, with his single arm and thick greying hair.

87

He lifted the sword a few inches in its scabbard and saw the razor-edged blade glimmer in the frail sunlight. It was old, but it was as true as ever. He snapped it down and swung round as Bellamy muttered thankfully, 'There she is, by God!'

The *Hyperion*'s hull was still deep in shadow, but her topsails and courses were clear and white in the sunlight, like those of a phantom ship. Even as he watched he saw the top-gallants appear as if by magic, and the sudden lift of spray around her beakhead as the land breeze found her and heeled her slightly in a tired curtsy.

Allday said, 'She's altering course. She's seen us!'

There was a sudden flash from the *Hyperion*'s fore-castle, followed within seconds by a dull bang. Every-one on the sloop's deck ducked with alarm as a ball screamed overhead and smashed hissing into the sea be-yond.

Bellamy gasped, 'I *say*, that was close!'

Bolitho could feel the same cold excitement that he had known so often in the past, and felt a grin frozen to his face like a mask. 'It was meant to be! This has to look right!' He seized the outraged Bellamy's arm. 'Come on then! Jump to it!'

The lieutenant cupped his hands and yelled, 'Hands aloft! Loose courses and foretops'l!' He ran to the op-posite rail as his men broke into sudden activity. 'Run up the colours, damn you!' But even he seemed surprised as the makeshift French flag broke from the gaff and whipped defiantly in the wind.

The sloop was responding well, and caught in a lazy offshore swell she threw back the spray from her stem in great white streamers.

The *Chanticleer*'s only other officer joined in the con-fusion. 'Hands to quarters! Have the guns run out!'

Bolitho watched the ports jerking open and the slim muzzles sniffing above the creaming water alongside. There, lashed like some snub-nosed beast was the *Hyperion*'s second carronade. It was already loaded and had been doubly checked while Bolitho had slept in his cramped chair.

Such a weapon threw a giant sixty-eight-pound shot which burst on impact. It was crammed with grape, and at short range was murderous in its performance. Today it might be the margin between success and failure.

Another twelve-pound ball whimpered overhead and threw a tall waterspout within half a cable of the sloop's bows.

Bolitho turned as Rooke appeared beside him, his slight figure wrapped in a borrowed pea-jacket. Even like that he somehow looked smart and well turned out.

Rooke said tightly, 'That'll be Mr. Pearse, the gunner. He'll fire each shot himself, if I'm not mistaken, sir.' He tightened his jaw as a third ball slammed hard alongside and deluged the sloop's own gunners with spray.

'He certainly has a good eye.' Bellamy sounded anxious.

Bolitho lifted his glass as a distant trumpet call echoed above the moan of rigging and hiss of spray. He saw the flag rising above the fortress, the gleam of sunlight on a telescope or weapon by the battery wall.

He snapped, 'Alter course, Bellamy! Remember what I told you, and cut as close as you dare to the headland!'

He left Bellamy to his work as the *Hyperion* changed her tack and swung round menacingly to run almost parallel with the sloop. She was a good mile away, but under her great press of canvas and with the wind under her stern she was moving fast and well. Any observer from the shore would certainly assume she was making a desperate effort to overreach the sloop and catch her before she could tack and enter the safety of the harbour.

There was an echoing roar from the cliff, and they all heard the high-pitched whine as the ball passed high overhead.

Rooke said, 'I didn't see anything!'

Bolitho bit his lip. Through his glass he had seen a hole appear right in the belly of the *Hyperion*'s main course. It was a very good shot indeed.

He said, 'At least they are concentrating on Quarme for the moment!' But the humour was only in his voice. In the growing light *Hyperion* held a kind of beauty which he found hard to explain. He could see the angry figurehead, the gleam of reflected water in her tall side, and felt something like pain as another gun fired from the battery to throw a waterspout right alongside the old ship's poop.

That one could possibly have ricocheted into the hull timbers, he thought grimly. When he looked up at the fortress again he saw that there was still no furnace smoke above the ramparts. But it would not take them long to fan the overnight embers awake, and then any such shot could turn the *Hyperion* into an inferno.

Quarme was too close inshore. Maybe he had misjudged it, or perhaps he wanted it to look extra realistic.

He heard Rooke snarl, 'Tell that fool to hide himself!'

A pair of horny bare feet were protruding from beneath the spread tarpaulins, but they vanished with a yelp as a petty officer lashed out with his rattan.

Bellamy was more concerned with his own ship than the *Hyperion*'s danger. He was beside the wheel watching both binnacle and sails as the dark-sided headland crept out as if to meet the *Chanticleer*'s bows head on.

He dropped his hand. 'Braces there! Lively, you idle bastards!'

Groaning and protesting the sloop quivered and then heeled over to the thrust of wind and rudder. One snag-toothed rock seemed almost to graze the hull as she surged around the headland to where the flat water of the harbour greeted her like a placid trap.

Bolitho said quietly, 'Shorten sail now, Mr. Bellamy. And pass the word to the men below.' His hand against the sword hilt felt clammy with sweat.

He turned to watch the *Hyperion*'s shape shorten as she started to tack closer inshore. She too had reduced sail, and he held his breath as two more waterspouts lifted within feet of her side. The French were firing more rapidly now, and it seemed likely that they had acted just as he had anticipated by moving more of the guns to the seaward side of the battery.

He swung round to face forward, unable to watch the *Hyperion*'s dangerous manœuvres. He saw that some of the sloop's men were clustered by the forecastle, watching the widening approaches of the harbour. He shouted angrily, 'Look *astern*, you idiots! If you were Frogs you'd be more afraid of the *Hyperion* than your own anchorage!'

His words steadied them and helped to break the tension of his own thoughts.

Rooke said, 'There's the landing place, sir!'

Bolitho nodded. It was a little more than a wooden pier below a rough, narrow road which twisted away between a great cleft in the hillside beyond. There were many figures already there, and he could just make out the muzzle of an old field-piece crouching between its two massive iron wheels.

'Steady now, Mr. Bellamy.' He had to lick the dryness from his lips. 'Make for the anchorage beyond the pier. But when we are within a cable of the landing place get the sails off her and steer for the pier! You'll be in the lee of the hill by then, the ship's own way should take her in!'

Bellamy tore his eyes from the bows. 'It won't do my timbers any good, sir!' But he grinned. 'My God, this is better than running the fleet mails!'

Bolitho caught a glimpse of Inch, the *Hyperion's* horse-faced junior lieutenant, his head framed in an open hatch, and knew that the rest of the landing party were packed behind him like peas in a barrel. It must be worse for them, he thought vaguely. Crammed in the sloop's small hull in complete darkness, with nothing but fear and the sounds of gunfire to keep them company.

He snapped, 'Wave to the soldiers on the pier!' Some of the sailors gaped at him. '*Wave!* You've just escaped the bloody English!'

He sounded so wild and angry that several of the men actually yelled with insane laughter and capered like madmen as the figures on the pier began to wave back.

Bolitho wiped his forehead with his shirt sleeve and then said quietly, 'When you are ready, Mr. Bellamy.'

When he glanced briefly astern the harbour mouth was already sealed by the outflung wedge of headland. Above it he could see the *Hyperion's* upper yards and felt an overwhelming relief as he realised that she was already going about and heading for the safety of the open sea.

Then Bellamy barked, 'Now! Helm alee!'

When he faced forward again, Bolitho saw that the bowsprit was pointing straight towards the cleft in the hillside. Very deliberately he drew his sword from its scabbard and began to walk towards the carronade.

5

Short and Sharp

With the sails whisked from her yards the *Chanticleer*
continued to glide steadily towards the rough wooden
pier where some thirty or so French soldiers had gathered
to watch her approach. Slightly to one side of the chat-
tering soldiers a disdainful, moustached officer sat stiffly
on his horse, only his hands and feet moving to calm his
mount as the battery guns continued to fire after the invisible *Hyperion*.

Then, as the sloop swung drunkenly towards them, the
men nearest the water's edge seemed to realise that
something was wrong. In the next few seconds everything
happened at once.

From right forward in the bows a whistle shrilled, and
as the last gunport was raised and the carronade
trundled into full view the deck tarpaulin was hauled
aside, and from beneath it and from every hatch the sloop
became alive with swarming seamen and marines.

Too late the soldiers tried to press back towards the
safety of the narrow road, but behind them there were
others trying to push further forward on to the pier, and
here and there a man still cheered and waved towards the
sloop's topmasts and the flapping French flag.

The carronade's roar was like a thunderclap. Penned
in by the cliffs, the explosion was so great that it started
several tiny avalanches of loose stones, whilst high against
the sky hundreds of terrified seabirds wheeled and
screamed in protest.

The great ball cleaved through the packed troops and

struck the iron-wheeled cannon beyond. There was another great flash, and as the smoke swirled back across the sloop's tilting deck Bolitho saw the soldiers falling and dying, their ranks carved apart in bright scarlet channels.

He waved his sword. 'Fire!'

This time it was the turn of the small deck guns. They were already loaded with canister, and as their whiplike cracks momentarily overcame the screams and terrified shouts on the shore the contents of their little muzzles sprayed across the remaining survivors, cutting them down like grass before a scythe.

Bolitho hurled himself over the bulwark, his shoes skidding on blood and torn flesh, while at his back the seamen surged to follow, their eyes blank, as if dazed by the slaughter around them.

Grapnels dug into the pier, and with a final lurching groan of protest the *Chanticleer* came to a halt, her deck trembling as marines and sailors tumbled ashore to be held and checked into some sort of order by their officers.

A mere handful of Frenchmen were running back up the road, followed by musket shots from eager marines and jeers from the seamen who were armed mainly with pikes and cutlasses.

Bolitho grabbed Ashby's arm. 'You know what to do! Keep your squads well apart. I want it to look as if you've got double the men available.' Ashby was nodding violently, his face scarlet from shouting and running.

It took a good deal more yelling to get the maddened marines to fall in on the road, their uniforms clashing with the grisly remains and writhing wounded about them.

It was only then that Bolitho realised the French officer and his horse had somehow escaped the onslaught of grape and canister unscathed. A sailor ran to catch the horse's bridle, but in one swift movement the officer raised his sabre and cut him down. The man fell without a sound, and something like a sigh rose from the motionless marines.

There was a single pistol-shot, and dignified to the end, the French officer toppled from his saddle to lie beside the landing party's first casualty.

Lieutenant Shanks handed the smoking pistol to his orderly. 'Reload,' he said curtly. Then to Ashby he added formally, 'I think *you* should take the horse, sir.'

Ashby swung himself gratefully into the saddle and looked down at Bolitho. 'I will go along this road, sir. It should take about twenty minutes to reach the fortress, I imagine.' He twisted round to watch with detached professional interest as his first squad of marines broke off in a trot to disperse as scouts on either hillside, their coats shining in the scrub like ripe fruit.

Two drummers and two fifers took up their positions at the head of the main force, and behind them Lieutenant Inch with seventy seamen formed into some semblance of order.

Ashby doffed his hat. Seated on his captured horse he made a very soldierly figure, Bolitho thought.

The marine roared, 'Fix bayonets!'

Bolitho turned his back to stare along the steep cliff towards the headland. From this point he could not even see the battery ramparts. His own party of seamen was waiting at the end of the pier with Rooke and a midshipman in charge.

Ashby shouted, 'Right turn! By the left, quick *march*!'

It was like part of a crazy dream, Bolitho thought. Ashby on the grey horse at the head of his men. The glitter of bayonets and clink of equipment, and the steady thud of boots as they squelched indifferently through the bloody carnage left by the sloop's savage onslaught.

And to add to the unreality the drums and fifes had broken into a jaunty march, 'The Gay Dragoon', and Bolitho found time to wonder how the bandsmen could remember the tune at a time like this.

He walked stiffly across to Rooke. 'We must make a move right away.' He pointed down to the fallen rocks which lined the foot of the headland like a broken necklace. 'We will have to climb along there until we get beneath the battery. It is a good two cables, so we must be quick before the garrison recover their wits.'

Rooke grimaced. 'When the Frogs see Ashby's army approaching their main gate they'll think the end of the world has come!'

Bolitho nodded. 'I hope so. Otherwise we'll get more than loose stones dropped on our heads!'

Slipping and gasping the line of seamen struggled along the base of the cliff. They could hear the big guns firing again, and Bolitho guessed that Quarme was approaching for another mock attack. By now the garrison would know of the landing, but there was little they could do but sit firm and wait for the assault. When, as Rooke had remarked, they saw Ashby's confident approach along the island's only road they should assume it was coming from that direction.

Bolitho had studied every available item of information about the fortress, and prayed that there had been no outstanding changes in its general construction. The circular keep was surrounded by a great octagonal curtain wall in which there were deep gun embrasures at regular intervals. On the inland sides of the ramparts was a deep ditch crossed by a single bridge below the fortress gates. But to seaward, and above the cliff itself there was only the curtain wall. Whoever designed the fortifications had assumed it improbable that anyone would get past the harbour entrance, and if so would be equally unlikely to climb the one-hundred-foot cliff.

Bolitho slipped and fell waist deep in water. It was very cold, despite the sun, and the shock helped to steady him.

They struggled on. The pace was already slowing, for cramped shipboard life was no training for this sort of exercise.

Rooke gasped, 'The fort could be harder to take than we thought, sir. It may still fall to Ashby to make a frontal attack.'

Bolitho glanced at him. 'Like most old fortifications, I suspect that this one was built on the assumption that any attacks would come from the sea. Nobody ever seems to allow for rot from within.'

He ignored the uncertainty on Rooke's narrow features. Almost unconsciously he was thinking of Pendennis Castle, by which he had grown up as a boy, had watched from his window on countless occasions.

That too had been constructed to defend Falmouth from the sea. Then during the Civil War it had been made to change its rolè, and the old castle had turned its defences inwards to withstand the attacking troops of Cromwell, to defend the last bastion of King Charles.

One of the old portraits in Bolitho's house showed the siege as a background for Captain Julius Bolitho, the man who had tried to lift the blockade by forcing his shipload of stores through to the beleaguered castle. But in vain. He had died from a musket ball, which had saved him from the more degrading end by hanging. And the castle had fallen just the same.

Bolitho groped his way along the top of a sea-smoothed rock and stared up at the cliff. 'I think this is the point.' His heart was pounding against his ribs, and his shirt was moulded to his body with sweat.

It looked very steep indeed, but if he had correctly estimated the distance, they should be directly below the rounded top of the headland where the rampart came to within feet of the edge.

'Mr. Tomlin, are you ready?'

Tomlin was the *Hyperion*'s boatswain. He was short, squat and extremely hairy, and a man of great strength. But in spite of his formidable carriage and muscular power, Bolitho had never seen him strike a man in anger.

Now he was standing on a rock, a heavy grapnel in his hand like a huge claw. 'Ready, sir!' When he opened his mouth he revealed a large gap left by the loss of two front teeth, this too added to his strange appearance by giving him a terrible maniac grin.

Bolitho glanced round at his small party. They were soaked in spray and sea-slime, and looked wild-eyed and desperate.

He spoke slowly but crisply. There was no time left for mistakes. 'Mr. Tomlin will go first and secure the grapnel. You will then follow me, two men on the line at a time, understood?' Several nodded dumbly and he continued, 'No one will make a sound or do anything until I say the word. If we are seen before we can cross the wall there will be no time to escape back down here.' He eyed them grimly. 'Just do as I do, and stay together.'

He had to stifle the sudden compassion he felt for these weary, trusting seamen. They *must* trust him. It was the only way.

Bolitho nodded curtly. 'Very well, Mr. Tomlin, let us see the strength of those arms, if you please!'

Tomlin made the steep ascent appear easy, and in spite of the crumbling cliff face he swarmed upward with the agility of a young and nimble maintopman. Within fifteen feet of the cliff edge was a narrow ledge, and as soon as Tomlin had reached this point he made use of the heavy grapnel for the first time, driving it deep into a clump of jutting rocks, his stocky body outlined against the sky like a grotesque gargoyle. Then he tossed down the stout line and peered at the faces upturned from the rocks below.

Bolitho tested the line and then began to climb. The cliff face was rougher than he had thought, and the sparse footholds were slippery with gull droppings, so that by the time he reached the ledge and Tomlin heaved him unceremoniously up beside him, he was gasping for breath.

The bosun grinned, his remaining teeth shining like fangs. 'Very quick, sir!' He gestured with a thick thumb. 'T'others'll follow now.'

Bolitho could not reply. He staggered to his feet and gauged the next and final part of the climb. Over the lip of the cliff he could see the top of the rampart and a drifting haze of gunsmoke from the battery. There were two embrasures, but both were empty, and he guessed that the guns had been manhandled to the other rampart so as to concentrate on the *Hyperion*.

A few stones splashed far below, and he knew that the first of his men were swarming up behind him. But he dared not look down. The agony of suspense and the actual effort of climbing had taken their toll.

He said between his teeth, 'Very well, I will go up now.' He looked enviously at Tomlin's ugly features and wondered how he could appear so calm and self-assured. 'See that they stay quiet!'

99

Tomlin grinned. 'I'll throw the first bugger down the cliff who utters a whisper, sir!' And he meant it.

Bolitho began to drag himself up the sloping rock face, suddenly conscious of the sun against his neck and hands, the rough touch of gorse beneath his clawing fingers. His whole world was concentrated on a small patch of cliff, and even time seemed to have lost meaning and reality.

From one corner of his eye he could see the sea, blue and clear like glass, with an horizon so bright that it stung his vision. Of the ship there was no sign, but as the cliff shook to the muffled rumble of gunfire he knew that she was still close by.

Then he raised his head and saw the rampart. It was so near that he could see the tufts of grass and tiny blue flowers which grew unconcerned between the weathered stones, and the bright scars beside the embrasures made by the *Hyperion*'s first attack.

As he hauled himself over the edge and crawled quickly to the foot of the rampart he felt naked in the sun's glare, and expected a sudden challenge, or the terrible agony of a musket-ball in his back.

The nearest embrasure was only a few feet from the ground, and hardly daring to breathe he rose slowly on to his knees and peered over the rim. For a moment he forgot his own danger and the responsibility for what lay ahead. He felt strangely detached, like a mere spectator separated from reality and pain by distance and time.

The octagonal wall which surrounded the central fortress had been built regardless of foundation, so that it was moulded to the slopes and humps of hillside, as if nothing would ever dislodge it. Bolitho's embrasure was one of the highest points on the wall, and through it he could see past the sturdy tower to the twin gates on the far side of the battery. He could even see the road as it dipped down between the hills to vanish below the gates, and the busy figures of stripped and panting soldiers as they carried fresh balls towards the waiting guns which overlooked the sea.

Even in the sun's glare the balls shone with heat, and although each one was carried by a pair of soldiers in a strange iron cradle, the men were straining away from its furnace glow as they loped across the hard-packed ground.

Bolitho heard his men scrambling over the edge at his back, Rooke's whispered threats and commands as they fanned out on each side of him. But he did not turn to watch. He was studying the shallow earth mound below the fortress wall, into which the shot-carriers came and went like busy moles. The magazine and furnace, no doubt. Protected by a heavy earthwork just in case a lucky shot from some enemy cannon should reach this far.

Rooke said tersely, 'All here, sir.' There was a cut on his cheek and his eyes were blazing from either exertion or suppressed tension.

'Good.' Bolitho stiffened and pressed his face against the warm stone as his ear picked up the far-off beat of drums and the faint sounds of Ashby's fifes. He almost forgot his own danger as he watched the distant scarlet column wheel around a bend of the road with the grey horse trotting importantly at the head. The marines' red coats appeared to remain motionless, but the white legs moved in perfect unison, so that the twisting column looked for all the world like a bright caterpillar with a back of shiny steel spines. Ashby had done well. The squads were spaced apart as he had ordered, and gave the impression of a much larger force.

Now he could see the rest of the column, Inch's sea-men, a swaying, distorted mass of white and blue, their feet churning up a pall of dust to add to their formidable appearance.

Rooke asked, 'How many Frogs are there, sir?'

Bolitho narrowed his eyes, watching the French gun-ners as they became aware of the approaching column for the first time. There were about fifty soldiers within the battery walls, he thought. Inside the fortress itself there could be double, or treble that number, but he doubted it. He could see just a few heads outlined against the sky, and another small group on a watchtower beside the double gates.

'Enough for their purposes, Mr. Rooke.' He had also seen the defences beyond the wall, across which Ashby's men would have to attack should his own plan fail. Two steep embankments, one freshly dug, and although he could not see inside them he guessed that they would be strewn with sharpened stakes and other hazards. Any at-tacking troops would be cut down by grape- and musket-shot before they had even reached the main ditch below the wall.

Ashby was making a great show of his approach. Marines were wheeling and re-forming in squads and single lines, and others tramped away on either flank, probably as mystified by their orders as the French were in watching them.

Bolitho said quietly. 'We've only a few minutes. The French'll soon realise that this is a bluff.' He ducked in-voluntarily as a single gun roared from the other wall, then added meaningly, '*Hyperion* cannot keep up her slow feints and withdrawals either. One of those balls would set her ablaze if it hit somewhere that our people could not reach in time.'

Rooke drew his sword and then checked the pistols at his belt. 'I'm ready,' he said flatly. 'But I am still of the opinion we should make for the main gates. If we could reach them before the Frogs realise we are here, we could open the way for Ashby's frontal attack.'

Bolitho replied evenly, 'And if we failed? They would kill us piecemeal and Ashby would be destroyed at their leisure.' He licked his lips and lowered himself from the embrasure.

The seamen were all watching him, trying to gauge their own future in his eyes.

He said, 'When I give the word we will cross the rampart by way of these two embrasures.' He was conscious of the precious seconds ticking away, but these men had to understand exactly what was required of them. 'We have about seventy-five yards to cross before we reach the entrance of the fortress. At present it is open, but if they see us too soon it will be slammed shut in our faces!' He forced himself to smile. 'So run like the devil himself is after you. If we take the fortress the men at the battery will surrender. They cannot survive on their own.'

With a start he realised that one of the watching faces belonged to Midshipman Seton. Rooke saw his surprise and said offhandedly, 'I thought it right he should come, sir. We will need all our experienced hands later.'

Bolitho looked at him coldly. 'Lieutenants are not immune from cold steel either, Mr. Rooke!'

Tomlin said gruffly. 'The battery's opened fire agin, sir. They'm not worried about Captain Ashby, it seems!'

Bolitho drew his sword and brushed the lock of hair from his eyes. 'Then over we go, lads! Not a sound out of anyone, or I will see him flogged!'

Even the most fearful man present knew that such a threat was quite empty. If the French saw them now, flogging would be the very least of their troubles.

He stood up slowly and threw his leg over the edge of the embrasure. The wall was very thick, but he felt a steadying hand under his arm and knew that Allday was close at his back. It was strange that he had forgotten all about his coxswain during the slow approach along the cliffs. Perhaps because he had relied on him for so long and could take his loyalty and courage for granted. He said suddenly, 'If I fall, Allday, go on with Mr. Rooke. He will need all the help he can get.'

Allday studied him calmly. 'Aye, aye, Captain.' Then he hefted a great boarding axe over his shoulder and added, 'But it's more likely that the Frogs will be aiming at *him*.' He was actually grinning. 'With all due respect, Captain, you look too ragged to be worth shooting at!'

Bolitho met his eyes and then said quietly, 'One day you'll go too far, my lad!'

Then, as Rooke appeared at the head of the second party and began to climb through his embrasure, Bolitho leapt down on to the ground and sprinted towards the round tower.

Unimportant things appeared with stark clarity as he pounded across the open ground. Small white stone chippings and a discarded shirt. A crude stool and an earthenware jug of red wine, they all flashed past as he ran with his shadow towards the fortress wall.

He reached it gasping and pressed his shoulders against the great stone blocks as he waited for the others to join him. It was quite incredible, but they had not been seen. And from this side of the tower it seemed as if they were in sole possession, for guns and gates, ditches and men were all hidden by its massive bulk.

He signalled with his sword and began to move along the wall. The doorway was completely concealed by the sweep of the tower's curving side, and when he eventually reached it he was almost as surprised as the two men who leaned on their muskets beside it. One soldier dropped on one knee and threw his musket to his shoulder, while the other, more quick-witted or less brave, turned and fled through the narrow entrance.

Bolitho parried the musket aside and charged after him, his mind blank to a terrible scream as a cutlass cut the sentry down before he could fire. For an instant he was half-blinded as he plunged into the tower's cool darkness, but as he hesitated to gain his bearings he saw a steep, winding stairway and heard the loud cries of alarm from the floor above.

He shouted, 'Mr. Tomlin, bar the door!' He was almost knocked from his feet by the rush of sailors. 'Then search the lower deck!' He turned and ran for the stairway, half-dazed by the echoing shouts and wild cries as the men's first fear gave way to something like madness.

There was an explosion from a curve in the stairs and a man screamed right at his side before falling back on top of those behind. A small door opened on to a narrow passage, and Bolitho caught sight of a French soldier running towards him, his bayonet levelled like a pike as he charged straight for the press of figures on the stairway. Bolitho could move neither up nor down, but as the bayonet seemed almost within reach of his heart Allday's axe flashed through the gloom and the soldier tumbled headfirst after the dead seaman.

Bolitho stared with sudden revulsion at the broken musket by his feet. A severed hand still gripped the stock as if alive in spite of Allday's savage stroke.

He said thickly, 'Come on, lads! Two more flights of stairs!' He waved his sword, his mind reeling with the same crazed infection as that which gripped his men.

But at the top of the final curve they were confronted by a tight line of soldiers, their muskets unwavering, the fixed bayonets giving a lethal glitter as they faced the on-coming mob of seamen. Someone yelled an order and the whole world exploded in musket-fire. Bolitho was hurled aside by falling bodies, his ears ringing with screams and curses as the soldiers dropped to their knees and a second line of men fired at point-blank range.

The stone steps were slippery with blood, and on all sides his men were struggling to escape the sudden slaughter. Bolitho knew that the impetus of attack was breaking. The mad exultation of reaching the fortress un-seen was giving way to panic and confusion. He saw the soldiers standing shoulder to shoulder, moving down the stairway towards him, their bayonets ready to complete the final phase of destruction.

With something like a sob of despair he hurled him-self up the last few steps, his sword striking aside the first two bayonets as they lunged at his torn shirt, and with all his strength struck at the men in the second rank. The shocked soldiers were too closely packed to move their long muskets, and he saw one man's face open up in a great scarlet gash as the sword slashed him aside like a puppet. He could feel their bodies reeling and kicking at him, even the heat of their sweat against his bruised limbs as they staggered across the steep stairway in a living tide.

Someone struck him in the spine with a musket, and through a haze of pain he saw a hatless officer trying to aim a pistol at someone below him, his face a mask of frantic concentration. With one last effort Bolitho lifted his sword clear of the struggling figures around him and struck out for the officer. The force of the blow jarred his arm to its socket, and as more and more men surged

106

into the fight he saw the officer's mouth opened in sound-less agony as the blade cut through epaulette and collar to lay open his artery like some hideous flower.

He could feel himself falling backwards, yet someone was holding him and yelling his name. Then he was be-ing forced forward, his feet stumbling over corpses and pleading wounded as the British sailors charged towards the rectangle of sunlight at the top of the stairs.

As if in a wild dream he saw Rooke thrust his sword into a man beside the doorway and hurry on without even breaking his stride. A tall, pigtailed seaman charged up to the dying Frenchman and drove his boarding axe into his shoulders with such force that he had to stand on the man's buttocks to tear it free.

Allday was holding him upright, the big axe swinging like a reaper's hook whenever any survivor from the wild attack tried to break down the stairs as an only way of escape.

Bolitho forced the pain and nausea to the back of his mind as he realised that unless he did something at once his victorious men would kill every Frenchman left in the fortress.

He pushed Allday aside and followed the others out into the sunlight. To Rooke he snapped, 'The *flag*! Get it down, man!'

Rooke swung round, his eyes wild. Then he saw Bolitho and seemed to come to his senses. He croaked, 'Did you hear that? Then jump to it, you dolt!' A sea-man beside him was trying to throttle a wounded soldier with his bare hands, but released him with a gasp of pain as Rooke struck his shoulder with the flat of his sword.

Allday waited until the French flag lay on the stone-work, then he unwrapped the ensign from about his body and handed it to the breathless seaman.

107

'Get this up, lad!' Allday shouldered his axe and watched as the flag lifted and then broke in the warm breeze. 'That'll give 'em something to bite on!'

Bolitho moved across to the rampart and leaned heavily against the worn stones. Below him, inside the battery wall, the French gunners were staring with dismay at the British ensign above the tower, and the *Hyperion* which even now was going about and preparing to tack towards the harbour entrance.

He felt sick and desperately tired, yet he knew that so much had still to be done. Wearily he made himself turn and look around at the breathless victors. There seemed to be very few left of the twenty-five he had brought with him. He said, 'Take these French soldiers and lock them up.' He looked round as Tomlin appeared at the open doorway. 'Well?'

The bosun knuckled his forehead. 'I have a French officer 'ere, sir. 'E's in charge of the guns.' The fangs gleamed with pleasure. ''E 'as surrendered, sir!'

'Very well.' He could not face the Frenchman now. The look of hurt and humiliation always carried by the vanquished. Not now. He said, 'Mr. Rooke, go below and disarm the battery. Then open the gates and welcome Captain Ashby with my compliments for a job well done.'

Rooke hurried away, and Bolitho heard distant cheering. From the ship or Ashby's marines, he neither knew nor cared.

Allday's face swam across his vision, anxious and questioning. 'Are you all right, Captain? I think you should rest awhile.'

Bolitho shook his head. 'Leave me to think. *I must think!*' He turned and saw Seton staring down pale-faced with horror at a wounded French soldier by his feet.

The man had been stabbed in the stomach, and there was blood pouring freely from his open mouth. But he still hung on to life, pathetic and desperate as his words choked in his own blood. Perhaps in these last seconds he saw Seton as some sort of saviour.

Bolitho said, 'Help him, lad. He can do no harm now.'

But the boy hung back, his lip trembling as the man touched his shoe with one bloodied hand. He was shaking uncontrollably, and Bolitho saw that his dirk was still in its scabbard. He must have gone through hell a dozen times, he thought vaguely. But he said, 'He's not an enemy now. At least let him die with somebody at his side!' He turned away, unable to watch as the terrified midshipman dropped on his knees beside the gasping, bubbling thing which clutched his hand as if it was the most precious object in the whole world.

Allday said quietly, 'He'll be all right, Captain. Given time, he'll learn.'

Bolitho eyed him emptily. 'It's not a *game*, Allday. And it never was.'

Ashby clumped up the stairs, his face split in a great, beaming smile. 'By God, sir! I just heard what you did!' He banged his hands together. 'I say, sir, I mean, it really was splendid, what?'

Bolitho looked towards the *Hyperion*. She was settled on her final course towards the entrance now, and he could see men swarming across the boats and preparing them for lowering.

He said, 'I will want you to march across the island to the other fortification, Ashby. They will surrender quickly enough, I imagine, when you inform their commander they are alone now.'

But Ashby refused to move. His scarlet face and uniform seemed to blot out everything, and his voice filled Bolitho's mind like echoes in a cave.

'A *splendid* victory, sir! Just what we needed! Really *splendid*!'

Bolitho replied, 'If you say so, Ashby. Now please go and do as I say.' Thankfully he watched the marine march through the doorway, still muttering with excitement.

Had he really known what he was doing when he had thrown himself against the French bayonets? Or had it been a fighting madness coupled with the mounting fear of defeat and shame?

Down on the battery the ramparts were alive with shouting marines, and he saw two of the seamen astride Ashby's horse, grinning and whooping like children as they cantered amongst the dazed prisoners.

Allday said, 'He is right, Captain. They were done for when you acted as you did.' He shook his head. 'Quite like old times it was. Short an' sharp, with a few bloody noses at the end of it!'

Bolitho looked down at Seton. He was still sitting beside the French soldier, grasping the bloody hand and staring at the man's face with terrible concentration.

Allday followed his glance and then said, 'He's dead, Mr. Seton. You can leave him now.'

Bolitho shuddered. It was over. He said, 'I shall want a message taken down to the *Chanticleer*. Bellamy must sail at once and inform the *Princesa* that we have taken the island.'

He swung round, realising that Seton was standing beside him. His lip was still trembling, and there were tears running down his pale face.

But his voice was steadier now and strangely determined. 'I w-will go for you, sir, if you th-think I can do it.'

110

Bolitho laid one hand on his shoulder and studied him for several seconds. Allday's words seemed to linger in his mind like an epitaph. 'Given time, he'll learn.'

He said slowly, 'Very well, Mr. Seton. I am quite sure you can do it.'

He watched the boy walk stiffly towards the doorway, his arms hanging at his sides, his face turned away from the staring corpses and moaning wounded. That could have been me, he thought dully. Twenty years ago I nearly broke and someone helped me to survive with words. He screwed up his eyes against the sunlight. But try as he might he could not remember the words, or the man who had saved his sanity when, like Seton, his boy's world had crumbled about him. He straightened his back and thrust the sword back into its scabbard.

Then he said, 'Follow me, Allday. Let us go and see what we have captured.'

6

Parley

Bolitho stepped quickly into the stern cabin and slammed the door behind him. For a few moments he stood gratefully in the welcoming shade, knowing it to be merely an illusion after the relentless heat of the quarterdeck, where he had just witnessed a flogging before the assembled ship's company.

Gimlett, his servant, shuffled nervously across his vision and stared at him with something like awe as he

111

removed his hat and coat and tore open the front of his shirt before unbuckling his sword. Without a word he dropped them into Gimlett's arms and walked wearily towards the open stern windows.

The scene which greeted his eyes never changed. The flat, glaring water of the anchorage and the barren hills of Cozar Island shimmering in a heat haze above the sheer-sided cliffs. Even the ship felt unmoving and lifeless. But that was no illusion, for she was moored both fore and aft just inside the arms of the harbour entrance, so that she could present a whole broadside to any would-be attacker who might scorn the hill-top battery as he had once done.

His eye fell on a glass decanter and goblet which Gimlett had placed on his desk. Almost automatically he poured a full measure and drank it straight down. It was some of the coarse red wine which they had found in plenty in the captured fortress. It gave a brief impression of freshness for a matter of minutes, but like a constant spectre the thirst was soon back again.

Bolitho threw himself on to the bench seat below the windows and listened to the patter of feet across the quarterdeck as the last of the assembled men dismissed below. They needed no goading now. It was close on noon, and in spite of the awnings and the canvas air ducts rigged above every hatch and companion, the ship was already like an oven.

It was strange that after all these years as a sea officer he had never hardened himself completely against flogging. There was always something which touched his nerve, or some unexpected incident to add to the slow misery of the proceedings.

Frowning, he poured another glass of wine. The man who had just been punished at the gratings was one of

112

those flaws in the pattern of discipline and routine, and he felt strangely troubled, even though it was over and the victim was somewhere in the bowels of the ship receiving the surgeon's rough attention to his lacerated back.

The man in question had been thirsty. It had been as simple as that. In the dead of night he had attempted to broach one of the rancid water casks in the hold and had been caught in the act by the ship's corporal.

Two dozen lashes sounded lenient enough by lower deck standards. In the Service, discipline was harsh and instant. If a man took liberties he might just get away with it. But if not, he knew what to expect.

This man had somehow avoided trouble before, in spite of long service in a dozen ships. Maybe he had been more fearful of losing his pride than of agony under the lash, but after the first five strokes he had begun to scream, while his naked body had writhed against the blood-spattered gratings like a man being crucified.

Bolitho stared with distaste at the empty glass. The ship was quiet now. No shouts, no plaintive notes from some forecastle fiddler, no skylarking amongst the midshipmen. There was no spark left of that unexpected victory, no lasting exultation to ease the sullenness and brooding which hung over the ship like a bad omen.

He ground his teeth with sudden fury. *Three weeks*. Three long weeks since they had stormed up the fortress steps and hauled down the French flag, and with each dragging day the tension and bitterness mounted.

There was a nervous tap at the door and then Whiting, the purser, peered apprehensively into the cabin. 'You sent for me, sir?'

He was sweating freely for he was extremely fat, with layer upon layer of chins which wobbled above his chest

113

with each step that he took towards the desk. Normally he laughed a good deal, but like most of his trade he retained a pair of sharp, unblinking eyes, and it was said that he knew the extent of the ship's stores down to the last rind of cheese. As he stood shifting from one foot to the other, Bolitho was reminded of a giant codfish.

'I did, Whiting.' He tapped the papers on his desk. 'Have you checked the water again?'

The purser hung his head as if he was in some way to blame. 'Aye, sir. Cut down to a pint a day per man we can hold out for one more week.' His lower lip pouted doubtfully. 'Even then they'll be drinking maggots for the most part, sir.'

Bolitho stood up and leaned his palms against the warm sill. Below him the water was so clear that he could see small fish darting above their shadows across the hard sandy bottom of the anchorage. What must he do? What *could* he do? For three weeks he had waited for the sloop *Chanticleer* to return with help from the fleet. He had written a full report for Lord Hood, and had expected a supply ship at the very least within the first few days. But nothing broke the horizon for two whole weeks. At the beginning of the third one the lookouts on the fortress had reported a French frigate approaching from the north-west. For an hour or so the enemy sail had shown itself like a feather above the horizon and had then withdrawn. And the French could afford to wait, he thought savagely. Their island garrison had been awaiting a fresh supply of drinking water within days of the *Hyperion*'s attack. Now the shallow reservoir was filled with dust, and beneath a pitiless sun the English sailors and marines lolled about like corpses with a mere pint per day to hold back the agonies of thirst.

He thought of the last flogging. There would be others soon, he decided bleakly.

He pushed himself away from the sill and crossed to the quarter windows. At the far end of the little bay he could see the Spanish *Princesa* floating calmly above her reflection like a carved model. Perhaps he had ordered the *Hyperion* to be moored across the entrance because of her and not for fear of a seaward attack, he thought. From the moment the other ship had dropped anchor there had been friction, mounting in some cases to open fighting, between seamen from the *Hyperion* and those of the Spaniard.

After the first week of fruitless waiting the Spanish captain had come aboard to see him. He had got straight to the point. There were nearly a hundred French prisoners on the island. One hundred more bellies to be filled with food and fresh water.

'We must destroy them.' Captain Latorre had sounded eager. 'They are useless to us!'

His lust for blood had been another reason for Bolitho's decision to keep control of the main fortress in his own grasp. Ashby's marines had it to themselves, while the Spanish soldiers from the *Princesa* had to content themselves with the old Moorish fort at the other end of the island.

Latorre had been furious, both with Bolitho's refusal to butcher the prisoners and with his equally firm refusal to allow the Spanish flag to fly above the battery.

The purser broke into his thoughts. 'Them Spaniards have got plenty of water, sir. I'm sure of it.' He scowled. 'Damn them!'

Bolitho eyed him calmly. 'Maybe, Mr. Whiting. I suspect you are right. But if *Hyperion* were not anchored here with her guns bared I think the gallant Captain

Latorre would have already gone. To demand to inspect his ship's stores would be inviting disaster. And I do recall that we are supposed to be allies in this venture!'

The sarcasm was lost on the purser. 'Dons or Frogs, you can't trust none o' them!'

There was a further interruption as Quarme poked his head inside the door.

'Well, Mr. Quarme?' Bolitho saw Whiting sigh, as if relieved that the weight had been lifted from his fat shoulders.

Quarme looked tired. 'Signal from the battery, sir. That French frigate was just sighted to the nor'-west, though God knows what he is using for wind.' He wiped his face. 'I wish to heaven we were out there with him!'

Bolitho nodded to the purser. 'Carry on, Mr. Whiting, but make sure that the casks are guarded watch by watch.' As the door closed he continued, 'That frigate will be keeping an eye on our topmasts, or the flag above the battery.'

Quarme shrugged. 'It is a waste of time. Even with Ashby's small force we can hold the island against a fleet!'

Bolitho eyed him narrowly. It was strange that Quarme had so little imagination. 'Let me remove any doubts, Mr. Quarme. If we do not get water within the week we will have to leave this place. Evacuate it!' He turned away angrily. 'The French know about the water, just as they must know we have not been sent any relief.' He shaded his eyes and stared across at the tall cliffs. Below in the placid water the charred remains of the Spanish flagship *Marte* shone in the sunlight like black bones. 'And without a favourable wind we might even then be too late. Our people are in a bad state already for want of water.'

116

'Help may be on its way, sir.' Quarme watched him pacing the cabin. 'Lord Hood *must* have received your report.'

'Must he?' Bolitho paused in his stride, suddenly angry with Quarme's empty trust and his own inability to find a solution. 'I am glad to hear it. Damn it, man, the *Chanticleer* could have foundered! There might be fire or mutiny aboard her right this minute!'

Quarme tried to smile. 'I think that unlikely . . .'

Bolitho stared at him coldly. 'So you believe that we should just wait and see, is that it?'

Quarme's smile froze. 'I was only meaning that we could not be expected to know this would happen, sir. We took the island as instructed, we carried out our orders to the best of our ability!'

Bolitho felt suddenly calm. 'Obeying orders is not always the final solution, Mr. Quarme. In the King's service you may have many victories and triumphs. But make one mistake and the value is wiped away.' He tugged the shirt away from his damp skin. 'It is not always enough to have tried.'

He made himself sit down again. 'Face the facts. We have no water to speak of, but against that we have ample stores of spirits and wine. Sooner or later some hotheads are going to run wild, and when that happens we will lose more than this damned island!' He gestured towards the cliff. 'Without Ashby's marines aboard how long do you imagine we could control a company of drink-maddened seamen?'

Quarme stared at him. 'I have served in this ship for several years, sir. I know most of our people well. They would never betray . . .'

Bolitho waved his hand. 'I do not know whether to admire your faith or to pity you your ignorance!' He

117

ignored the sudden flush of anger on Quarme's cheeks. 'I have seen mutiny at close quarters. It is an ugly thing. A terrible thing.' He stared out at the mocking water. 'But they were just ordinary men. No better or worse than these. Men do not change. Only situations.'

Quarme swallowed hard. 'If you say so, sir.'

Bolitho twisted on the bench seat as Allday opened the door a few inches.

'Yes?'

Allday darted a brief glance at the first lieutenant and then said evenly, 'Begging your pardon, but a marine has just come aboard with a message from Captain Ashby.' He eased himself into the cabin. 'He sends his respects, Captain, and would you be prepared to receive the senior French officer in audience?'

Bolitho dragged his mind away from the mental picture of the empty water casks. 'For what reason, Allday?'

The big coxswain shrugged. 'Private reasons, Captain. He'll only speak with you.'

Quarme scowled. 'Bloody impudence! I suppose because you stopped the Dons from cutting their throats the French prisoners think you'll grant any damn thing they ask!'

Bolitho looked past him. 'My compliments to Captain Ashby. Tell him to send the man across without delay. I will see him.'

Quarme clenched his fists. 'Will you require me here, sir?'

Bolitho stood up, his face thoughtful. 'When I send for you, Mr. Quarme.' He watched him stalk towards the door and added slowly, 'In war we must change with the wind, Mr. Quarme. No breeze can be ignored when you are drifting on a lee shore!'

The senior surviving officer of the Cozar garrison was an elderly lieutenant of artillery named Charlois. He was a heavily built man with a crumpled, melancholy face and a drooping moustache, and in his ill-fitting uniform and heavy boots presented anything but a military appearance.

Bolitho dismissed Lieutenant Shanks, who had brought the prisoner from the fortress, and then asked the Frenchman to sit down beside the desk. He saw his eyes watching him as he poured two glasses of wine, but was not deceived by this officer's unprepossessing appearance. For he had commanded the island's main battery. Under his care and knowledge the big but outdated guns had pounded the Spanish eighty-gun flagship into a blazing inferno in a matter of minutes, so that when her magazines had finally exploded the savage victory had been complete. Of the thousand or so ship's company and soldiers crammed aboard, less than a dozen had survived the ordeal. The latter had been carried by the sluggish current to the opposite side of the anchorage, and this fact alone had saved them from the final slaughter by the French sharp-shooters below the cliffs.

Charlois raised his glass and said haltingly, 'Your health, Captain.' Then he drained the wine in one quick gulp.

Bolitho eyed him gravely. 'You speak good English.' He hated this waste of time spent in idle remarks, but knew it to be necessary as each summed up the other's strength and weakness.

The officer spread his thick hands. 'I was a prisoner in England in the last war. I was in a castle at Deal.'

'And why do you wish to see me, Lieutenant? Is there some trouble amongst your men?'

The Frenchman bit his lip and glanced quickly around

119

the cabin. Then he lowered his voice and said, 'I have been thinking about our plight, Captain.' He seemed to come to a decision. 'Yours and mine. You have no water for your ships and men. You cannot hold out much longer, is that not so?'

Bolitho kept his face impassive. 'If you came out here to tell me this then you have had a wasted journey, m'sieu!'

Charlois shook his head. 'I regret that I have offended you, Captain. But I am getting old now, and I have outgrown the natural caution of a serving officer.' He smiled at some secret thought. 'But I must rely on your word at a gentleman to repeat nothing of what I am about to say. I have a wife and family in St. Clar and have no wish for them to suffer on my account.'

Before Bolitho could speak he continued quickly, 'I think maybe that you do not realise that my soldiers are not of the true army, eh? They are militia, recruited for the most part from St. Clar itself. We have all grown up together. We are simple folk who did not ask for war and revolution, but had to make, as you say, the best of it. The garrison commandant was different, he was a true professional.' He shrugged wearily. 'But he died in the fighting.'

Bolitho slid his hands below the desk and gripped his fingers together to control his rising impatience. He asked quietly, 'What are you trying to tell me?'

Charlois dropped his eyes. 'It is said that your Lord 'Ood intends to attack Toulon. There is much feeling there because of the King and his death under the revolution.' He took a deep breath. 'Well, Captain, in my small town there is the same feeling!'

Bolitho stood up and walked towards the charts which were spread across the dining table. He knew what the

120

outspoken confession had cost the French officer, what it would mean to his future if it leaked out that he had betrayed his country with words to an English captain.

He said at length, 'How can you be so sure of all this?'

'I have seen the signs.' Charlois sounded sad. 'St. Clar is a small town, no different from a hundred others. We have a few vineyards, a little fishing and coastal trade. Before the Revolution we were slow but content. But this unrest in Toulon and to the east has made compromise impossible. Even now the government is sending an army to crush these idealists for all time. And when that happens they will go further. To fight a war with England our government cannot allow even a small chance of an uprising happening again.'

Bolitho turned and studied him gravely. 'They will come to St. Clar too, is that it?'

Charlois nodded heavily. 'There will be killings and reprisals. Old scores will be paid off in blood. It will be the end for us.'

Bolitho could feel the excitement churning at his insides as he turned the Frenchman's words over in his mind. After all, Lord Hood had indeed implied that the main purpose of taking Cozar was to give an impression of a multi-pronged attack on the French mainland. But even he had not suspected that such an invasion might be welcomed.

Charlois watched him anxiously. 'We could arrange a parley. I know the mayor very well. He is married to my cousin. It would not be difficult.'

'It sounds *too* easy, m'sieu. My ship would be in danger of attack should your words prove false.' He watched closely for some sign of guilt, but there was only desperation in the man's eyes.

'I have thought about it for many days. You have all

121

my men as prisoners. In St. Clar they have the crew of your sloop *Fairfax* which we took as a prize here in Cozar. You could parley for an exchange. That is not uncommon, eh? Then if the signs were favourable we could explore the possibility of joining Toulon's fight against the King's murderers!' He was sweating badly, and not merely because of the heat.

Bolitho bit his lip until the pain steadied his racing thoughts. 'Very well.' He shot Charlois a hard glance. 'I would also want water in exchange for the prisoners.'

Charlois staggered to his feet, obviously relieved to be free of his inner burden. 'That would be simple, Captain. This island was to be fully garrisoned in a month or so, and the water lighters are already at St. Clar.'

Bolitho crossed to the door. 'Pass the word for the first lieutenant.' Then he walked back to the desk and eyed the French officer for several seconds.

He said quietly, 'If you have tried to deceive me, m'sieu, you will regret it.'

Quarme entered the cabin. 'Sir?'

'I want all the French prisoners stowed aboard within the hour. By that time I will have drafted fresh orders for Captain Ashby, for we will have to sail without him.'

Quarme stared at him. '*Sail*, sir?'

Bolitho signalled for the waiting guards to escort Charlois from the cabin then he said calmly, 'I want all the boats swung out forthwith. Our people can warp the ship from the anchorage. With luck we will take advantage of some offshore breeze to get under way again.'

Quarme still did not seem able to grasp what was happening.

'But, sir, the hands are too parched and exhausted for that sort of task! Some of them are lying below like dead men!'

122

'Then stir them, Mr. Quarme, *stir* them!' He looked through the windows towards the haze-covered hills. 'Break out every last drop of water for them. I want this ship at *sea*, do you understand? By tonight I intend to close St. Clar and arrange a parley.' He watched his words causing consternation on Quarme's face.

Almost gently he added, 'It may be the *breeze* I was telling you about earlier.' Overhead he heard the shrill of pipes and the sounds of the guardboat being pulled clear of the side. 'Before we see another day dawn, Mr. Quarme, we may have had some small achievement. We will either have paved the way for future operations on the mainland, or we will all be prisoners of war.' He smiled openly at Quarme's rigid features. 'Either way we will have water to drink!'

Bolitho walked slowly across the quarterdeck and held his watch close against the shaded binnacle lamp. In the dim glow he saw that the time was exactly half past three in the morning, and less than fifteen minutes since he had last allowed himself a glance at his watch.

He recrossed the deck with the same slow tread, every step a concentrated effort to control his rising sense of urgency and despair. It had been two full hours since the *Hyperion* had hove to and dropped her jolly boat in the black, undulating water alongside. Two hours of waiting and fretting while the *Hyperion* had sailed slowly back and forth with the great wedge of land barely two miles abeam. Soon it would be getting lighter, although for the moment the night was as dark as ever. Only the stars remained bright and unmoving, and as he stared upwards through the black tracery of shrouds and rigging it seemed as if some were within feet of the gently spiralling topmasts. They cast a small glow across the topsails, so that against the night sky they appeared ghost-white and vulnerable.

The offshore breeze was holding steady and felt ice cool after the heat of the day, and although the ship was cleared for action most of the gun crews still lolled beside their weapons, exhausted from the agonising haul out of Cozar. In relays they had pulled on their oars, blinded with sweat, their hands raw and blistered as like beasts of burden the ship's boats had warped the *Hyperion* clear of the anchorage and out to the open water beyond.

Once it had seemed as if the *Hyperion* was only intent on destroying herself on the shoals by the harbour entrance, and only the extra efforts of the oarsmen, urged on by blows and curses from their petty officers, had pulled her clear. But even that had not been enough. The dazed and gasping seamen had stared hopefully astern, their eyes watching the sails for some sign of life. But the canvas had mocked them, hanging from the yards limp and flat, so that it seemed as if the wind would never come.

Sun-dried, exhausted men were barely a team to combat the *Hyperion*'s bulk at the best of times. Her one thousand six hundred-odd tons seemed to play with the puny boats which tugged at her massive bows like so many beetles. And then, even as one of the cutters had fallen away from her station, the oarsmen drooping at their thwarts indifferent to both blows and threats from a frantic midshipman, the sails had given one violent shiver, and as the men had stared wearily with disbelief, the water around their boats had come alive with small, whipping catspaws.

For the rest of the daylight and deep into the night hours the ship had regained her power from the growing north-westerly and had driven up and around the distant coastline.

Then, as soon as night had closed in around them, they had shortened sail and beaten nearer and nearer to that great slab of deeper darkness, beyond which lay the sheltered port of St. Clar.

Now it was over there abeam, lost beneath the stars and below the rolling bank of hills beyond. There was not a light or beacon, and more than once a nervous look-out had reported small craft approaching the ship, only to discover they were shadows or some trick of current to pluck the nerves of every man aboard.

Bolitho laid his hands on the quarterdeck rail and stared fixedly into the darkness. He was unable to stop himself going over and over what he had done, and as the minutes dragged past he felt the rising tension of despair adding to his uncertainties.

He had allowed the French officer, Charlois, to go ashore in the jolly boat to make contact with his friends in St. Clar. The chance of the rough plan succeeding had always been thin, but Bolitho still tortured himself with doubts of what he could have done, of what he should have done to give the scheme even a small hope of success. It was no consolation to know that he still had all the French prisoners aboard. Without water he might just as well surrender to St. Clar, or scuttle the ship within reach of the shore.

He thought too of Lieutenant Inch's excited horse-face when he had told him that he was to take charge of the jolly boat's small party. Inch was a keen enough officer, but he lacked experience for this sort of thing, and Bolitho knew that deep in his heart he had chosen him more because he was the junior lieutenant and therefore the least loss if Charlois chose treachery rather than any desire to parley.

He thought suddenly of Midshipman Seton. It was strange that he had volunteered to go with Inch, and stranger too that Bolitho felt such a sense of loss now that he was gone from the ship. But if Seton had a terrible stammer, he could do something better than anyone else aboard. He could speak fluent French.

Quarme murmured at his side, 'Any orders, sir?'

Bolitho squinted his eyes at the distant hump of land and tried to memorise the picture of the chart in his mind. 'Lay her on the larboard tack, Mr. Quarme. Full and bye.'

Quarme hesitated. 'That will bring us very close inshore, sir.'

Bolitho looked past him. 'Put two good leadsmen in the chains. We must give the jolly boat every chance.'

He heard the men stirring at the braces and the gentle slap of water around the rudder as the helm went over. What was the point? If Inch was already a prisoner he was only prolonging the agony. With the morning sun would come disaster. The end of everything.

From forward came a splash followed by the leadsman's droning chant, 'By th' mark twenty!'

A small figure moved below the nettings, and he saw Midshipman Piper's monkey-like shape standing on tiptoe to peer at the land. It was strange how close he and Seton had become. The cheeky, devil-may-care Piper and the nervous, stammering Seton. But as Bolitho watched the boy's apprehensive movements he knew just how firm the friendship had become.

'. . . and a quarter less fifteen!' The chant floated back

to mock him further. Once around this slab of headland and the water shoaled considerably.

The big wheel creaked at his back and the helmsman intoned, 'Nor' by west, sir! Full an' bye!'

Quarme crossed to his side again. 'If this wind drops away, sir, we'll not be able to beat clear of the headland on the far side of the bay.' He sounded very much on edge.

'I'm as much aware of that as you, Mr. Quarme.' He faced him in the darkness. 'More so, I expect, since it is my responsibility.'

Quarme looked away. 'I'm sorry, sir, but I just thought . . .'

He broke off as the leadsman called tonelessly, 'By the mark ten!'

Bolitho rubbed his chin. 'Shoaling.' Just one word, yet it seemed to mark the failure like a crude signature.

He heard himself say, 'We will continue deeper into the bay. By the time we reach the other side the sky will be brightening, and by then . . .'

He swung round as a voice yelled, 'Boats on the larboard quarter, sir!' As he ran to the nettings the lookout added sharply, 'Three, no four on 'em, sir!'

Bolitho snatched a telescope and swung it across the nettings, his mind aching with concentration as he stared over the heaving pattern of dark water and reflected stars. Then he saw them, low black shapes outlined by a disturbed pattern of white splashes.

He heard Rooke snap, 'They're under oars, my God! Big sweeps too by the look of 'em!'

Bolitho shut the glass and handed it to Midshipman Caswell. But before he could speak he heard Quarme's voice right by his ear, sharp and insistent, and only barely controlled.

'Boats under sweeps, sir! They'll be oared galleys. My God, I've seen them in the Indies. A big gun right in the bow and able to row round under a ship's counter and pound her to boxwood without her being able to turn fast enough to hit back!'

His voice must have carried to the other side of the quarterdeck and Bolitho saw several faces turned towards him and heard a sudden buzz of alarm.

'Control your voice, Mr. Quarme! Do you want our people to panic?'

But Quarme seemed unable to stop himself. 'I knew this would happen! You wouldn't listen! You don't care about anything but your own glory!' He was sobbing now, as if he neither knew nor cared what he was saying.

Bolitho said harshly, 'Keep silent, man! Get a grip on yourself!'

Rooke's voice cut through the darkness like a knife. 'I heard that, sir!' He seemed to have forgotten about the approaching boats. About everything but the fact that by speaking up he had killed Quarme's career as surely as if he had shot him with a pistol.

Quarme turned and stared at him, his body suddenly limp and swaying with the deck like a drunken man.

It was a tableau. An unmoving collection of statues, none of whom could control events any more.

Gossett, massive and unmoving beside the wheel. The gunners by the quarterdeck nine-pounders, crouching and watchful like disturbed animals. Caswell and Piper too shocked to move or speak, and Rooke by the rail, hands on hips, head on one side, his face pale against the night sky.

As if from the sea itself a voice suddenly shattered the silence. '*Hyperion* ahoy! Permission to board!'

Bolitho looked away. It was Lieutenant Inch. Quietly he said, 'Heave to, if you please, and signal Mr. Inch's boat alongside. Open the boarding nets for him, but watch the other craft in case of tricks.'

Quarme broke from his trance and made as if to carry out the orders, his movements automatic, the products of discipline and training.

Bolitho's words halted him in his tracks. 'You are relieved, Mr. Quarme. Go to your quarters.' To Rooke he added, 'Carry on, if you please.'

Quarme said, 'I only meant to say . . .' Then he turned on his heel and walked to the ladder, the men parting to let him pass. Ashamed for him, yet unable to take their eyes from his misery.

Bolitho walked aft to the poop ladder and stood for several long minutes while his anger and disappointment gave way to dull acceptance. If Rooke had stayed quiet he might have been able to overlook Quarme's insubordination. If Quarme had retained his self-control for just a moment longer, Inch's unexpected return might have saved him. But in his heart he also knew that he would never have been able to trust Quarme again, no matter what Rooke had said or done. Quarme had been afraid, and later his fear might have cost lives other than his own. Bolitho knew that every man but an idiot was afraid. But showing it was unforgivable.

Lieutenant Inch clattered up the quarterdeck ladder and groped his way breathlessly past the silent onlookers. 'I'm back, sir!' His long face was split in an excited grin. 'We found the mayor of St. Clar. He's coming up the side now.'

'And those other boats, Mr. Inch, what are they?'

Inch became aware of the heaviness in Bolitho's tone and of the tension around him. He swallowed hard. 'I brought the water lighters, sir. I thought it would save time.'

Bolitho stared at him impassively. 'Save time?' He thought of Quarme below in his private prison. Of Rooke and all the others who depended on him, right or wrong.

Inch nodded awkwardly. 'Aye, sir. They were all jolly decent about it really . . .' He looked down aghast as something long and dark fell from his coat and rolled to Bolitho's feet.

'And what is that, Mr. Inch?' Bolitho could feel the tension of his mind like a vice.

Inch said in a small voice. 'A loaf of fresh bread, sir.'

From the darkness a voice broke into a helpless burst of laugher. It was taken up by the midshipmen and by the men at the guns, some of whom had not heard a word. It was relief, despair and gratitude all mixed together.

Bolitho said slowly, 'Very well, Mr. Inch. You have done a good piece of work tonight.' He felt the same nervous excitement plucking his words like strings. 'Now pick up your loaf and attend to your duties.'

As Inch fled past the chuckling seamen he added, 'Prepare to anchor, Mr. Rooke. As the fifth lieutenant has just told us, it will save time!'

He turned on his heel adding, 'Pass the word for Lieutenant Charlois and his mayor. I will see them in my cabin.'

As he ducked his head unnecessarily beneath the poop he allowed his guard to drop. Nothing which happened now could or would surprise him. Taking on water within gunshot of an enemy port. A loaf of bread on the quarterdeck. And an officer who broke, not under fire, but under the pressure of his own doubts.

He heard the clatter of blocks and the flapping protest

of canvas as the ship heeled heavily into the wind to drop anchor.

He found Allday waiting beside his desk, a glass of brandy poured and ready.

'What are you gaping at, Allday?' He glared angrily at his own reflection in the stern windows. Even in the poor light from the two swinging lanterns he looked strained to the point of exhaustion.

'Are you all right, Captain?' Allday watched him gravely.

'It's not my body which is sick this time!' He sat down wearily on the bench seat and stared at the hilt of his sword.

The coxswain nodded. 'It will come right in the end, Captain.' He swung round angrily as feet clattered in the passageway beyond the door. 'Shall I send them away?'

Bolitho looked at him with sudden affection. 'No, Allday. If it is all to come right, as you predict, then we must help it along a little!'

Midshipman Piper stepped briskly into Bolitho's cabin and then faltered as he saw his captain staring astern through the great windows.

'Mr. Rooke's respects, sir.' Piper's eyes dropped hopefully towards an untouched tray of food on the table. 'The masthead lookout has just sighted Cozar on the lee bow.'

Bolitho did not turn. 'Thank you.' Half to himself he added, 'We will enter harbour in about three hours, all being well.'

Piper seemed surprised by this display of confidence and nodded with sudden gravity. 'Aye, sir, with the

131

t'gallants and royals drawing so well we shall have no difficulty.'

Bolitho turned and eyed him emptily. 'There is something you can do for me, Mr. Piper.' He had not even heard the boy's comment. 'Would you go below and tell Mr. Quarme to join me right away.'

'Aye, aye, sir.' Piper scurried away, his mind busy as to how he would describe his intimate conversation with the captain to the less informed members of the gunroom.

Bolitho slumped down on the bench seat and stared at his untouched meal with something like nausea. He was hungry, yet the thought of food sickened him.

It was strange that after all that had happened he could find no joy, no sense of achievement. In the fresh northwesterly the ship seemed to be ploughing across the whitecapped sea with new life, and even the harsh sunlight lacked its earlier feeling of danger and foreboding. With all sails set and every shroud and stay humming like part of a finely tuned instrument, the *Hyperion* sounded as if she was pleased with herself, even grateful for her fresh chance. There were other shipboard noises too which should have given him confidence. Some of the men were singing and calling to one another as they worked high aloft on the swaying yards, their cares momentarily dispersed by the knowledge that there was fresh water in plenty to drink, that the sailor's terror of thirst was moved back in time to become merely another possibility.

Bolitho stared at the frothing wake and at the handful of swooping gulls which had followed the ship all the way from St. Clar. Even now it was hard to believe what had happened. The furtive boats, and alien French voices in the darkness. Inch's excitement, and the interview with Lieutenant Charlois and the mayor of St. Clar. The latter had been a small, leathery man in a velvet coat, a vital little being of quick gestures and a disarming laugh.

While every man had worked with a will to sway the fresh water casks aboard, the mayor, whose name was Labouret, had further confirmed everything that Charlois had described. The people of St. Clar had no love for the English, but then as Labouret had remarked, they did not really *know* them! But the Revolution they did know. What it had done, and what it would do if allowed to continue.

Bolitho had listened to them with hardly a word of interruption. In his mind he had seen the Revolution through new eyes, and had sensed the same feeling of uncleanness he had endured when his men in the frigate *Phalarope* had mutinied. That mutiny had been caused by other men's deeds. and had occurred in spite of everything he had done to prevent it and all he had tried to put right. And when it had come it had been as swift and as terrible as if he had provoked it himself.

And as he had listened closely to the two Frenchmen he had felt deeply for them. To them St. Clar might seem the centre of the whole world, but Bolitho knew that their cause was already lost. They had not caused the Revolution, but like a mutiny it had happened none the less.

Charlois had said finally, 'I kept my word, Captain. You have water and the crew of the sloop *Fairfax*.' He had smiled with something like embarrassment. 'We must keep the sloop for the present, you understand? It would not be well to show our hand completely, eh?'

Bolitho understood well enough. If Lord Hood shied away from the idea of a further attack on the mainland, the sloop might be the only token of loyalty for the men of St. Clar to show to a revengeful Revolutionary Court.

In the dawn's clear light the *Hyperion* had weighed and

butted out into the freshening wind. Apart from the returned company of the sloop and the water, the French had even supplied fresh new casks to replace the *Hyperion*'s rotten and much-used ones. They had made their gesture, and had even sent horsemen to the headlands to make sure that the *Hyperion*'s presence remained undetected and safe.

In the early light, as the water boats had cast off, Rooke had remarked, 'I doubt the Frogs will keep their mouths shut for long! Some damn fisherman will be off up the coast to sell information to the nearest French garrison!'

Bolitho had replied coldly, 'Such deceit may have been your own experience, Mr. Rooke. In Cornwall it is not unknown for towns and villages to have that kind of loyalty.'

Rooke had said nothing. Perhaps in the dawn's pale light he had seen the warning in the captain's eyes.

Bolitho stared moodily at the written report on his desk. Just a few more lines and it would be done. If he could get Lord Hood's advice and backing a full invasion would still be possible. Either way St. Clar might become a battleground.

He reached out and touched the unfinished report. Again his mind clouded with the one thing which had tainted everything else. Maybe if he told Quarme to hold his tongue he could arrange for him to return to England. With the country once more gripped in a war it was unlikely that many would notice the faults of a mere lieutenant. Quarme might start again. By taking it upon himself to send him away, Bolitho knew that he might be able to save him from a court martial, even if he risked one for himself. There was only Rooke, he bit his lip and frowned. But first of all it depended on Quarme and how he felt after his enforced privacy with his thoughts.

There was a knock at the door, but when he looked up it was not Quarme but the master.

'I am sorry, Mr. Gossett, but unless it is an urgent matter it will have to keep.'

Gossett watched him sadly, his great body swaying with the ship like a tree. 'I just saw young Mr. Piper, sir. 'E was upset, so I thought I'd better bring the news meself.'

Bolitho stared at him, suddenly ice cold.

Gossett nodded slowly, 'Mr. Quarme is dead, sir. 'Anged 'imself in 'is cabin.'

'I see.' Bolitho turned away to hide his stricken face.

The master cleared his throat noisily. 'Poor man, 'e's been very worried of late.'

Bolitho turned and met the other man's eyes. 'When I took Cozar with the *Chanticleer* I had occasion to watch *Hyperion* making those mock attacks to draw the battery's fire. It was superb seamanship.' He let his words hang in the air and saw Gossett's eyes flicker with sudden alarm. 'Seamanship gained from many years in every sort of vessel, and *under fire*.'

Gossett shifted his feet. 'I suppose so, sir.'

'*You* sailed the *Hyperion* that day, did you not? I want the truth!'

The master lifted his head with something like defiance. 'I did, sir. 'E was a good officer. But if you'll pardon the liberty, 'e was 'aving a lot o' trouble with 'is wife. She comes o' good stock and likes to live well.' He shrugged wearily. 'Mr. Quarme was a lieutenant an' nothing more, sir.'

'You mean that he had no money?' Bolitho's voice was toneless.

'That's right, sir.' The master's tanned face became

135

angry. 'Then there was all this filthy talk about 'im pinching some money that was in 'is keeping . . .'

Bolitho held up his hand. 'Why wasn't I told about this?'

Gossett looked away. 'We all knew 'e would never steal from 'is own ship, sir. Not like some as I could mention. 'E was going to 'ave it out with Cap'n Turner, 'e even told me as 'ow Cap'n Turner 'ad found out the true thief.'

Bolitho said quietly, 'But Turner died of a heart attack.' He thought of the surgeon's guilty outburst at the first conference in the wardroom and Rooke's scathing attack on him.

Gosset said gruffly, 'I'm sorry I let you down, sir, after all you've done for us an' the ship. But I felt I owed it to 'im y'see.'

'I see.' Bolitho rested his fingers on the waiting report. 'It is no excuse, Mr. Gossett. Your loyalty must always be to the ship, not to individuals.' He eyed the master levelly. 'But thank you for telling me. I expect I would have done the same.'

Then he said, 'This is just between ourselves, Mr. Gossett.'

The master nodded firmly. 'Then so it will remain, sir.'

For a long while after Gossett had left the cabin Bolitho sat quite motionless by the windows. Then he picked up his pen and wrote swiftly across the bottom of his report '—this gallant officer whom as I earlier reported handled the ship with great courage under constant enemy fire with no regard for his personal safety, later took his own life under tragic circumstances. He was, I am convinced, a sick man, and but for his failure to consider his own welfare before the security of his ship, would have lived to make a place for himself in the Navy where his name would be long remembered.'

He signed the report and stared at it for several minutes.

It was little enough, he thought bitterly, and would do nothing for Quarme. But in England it might bring some small comfort to those who read it and still remembered him as the man Gossett had tried to shield from disaster.

But Bolitho knew that disaster when it came usually attacked from within. From that there was no defence.

7

A Knight of the Bath

With all but her topsails and jib clewed up the *Hyperion* completed her tack and settled sedately on a course towards the harbour entrance. The upper deck and gangways were filled with idlers and unemployed seamen, as with something like awe they stared at the scene which greeted them beyond the fortress and its stark headland. Bolitho raised his glass and moved it slowly from side to side. It was hard to remember this as the same barren anchorage he had vacated the previous day. When the masthead lookout had reported seeing topmasts beyond the cliff he had imagined it might be one of Hood's supply ships, or at most a frigate with despatches and new orders. But as the ship glided slowly across the dancing water towards the humped hills he realised there was far more to it than that.

Anchored in the centre of the natural harbour was a tall three-decker, a rear-admiral's flag drooping listlessly from the mizzen, and beyond her, close to the pier where the carronade had decimated the French troops, lay another large ship, which from her workmanlike appearance could be nothing else but a supply vessel. In the shallower water on the eastern side was a frigate and a small sloop which he quickly recognised as the *Chanticleer*. The Spanish *Princesa* was exactly as he had last seen her, but if the assembled vessels were both unexpected and impressive, the activity which surrounded them was even more so.

Around the ships and plying back and forth to the pier were boats of every shape and size. Cutters and gigs, launches and jolly boats, they seemed endless, and when Bolitho shifted his glass to the hillside beyond the fortress he saw a widely flung rectangle of pointed tents interspersed with tiny scarlet figures and an occasional camp-fire. It seemed as if the army had arrived, too.

With a start he realised the *Hyperion* was already through the protective arm of the entrance, but when he glanced at Rooke he saw that the lieutenant was still standing rigidly by the quarterdeck rail, his speaking trumpet under his arm as if on parade.

He snapped, 'Wear ship, if you please!'

Rooke flushed angrily and raised the trumpet. 'Hands wear ship! Lee braces there!'

Bolitho compressed his lips tightly. Rooke was a good enough officer when it came to fighting and day-to-day routine, but he seemed to shrink in size when it came to taking charge of the *Hyperion*'s great bulk in confined waters.

Pearse, the gunner, was standing by the foremast shading his eyes as he peered aft towards the quarterdeck.

Bolitho nodded curtly, and with a dull bang the first gun sent the echoes rolling around the cliffs as *Hyperion* paid her respects to the rear-admiral, whoever he was.

Bolitho knew he could ignore the routine of saluting. As the guns crashed out at five-second intervals and the ship crept forward in a cloud of drifting smoke he gauged the distance, his eye and brain noting the unruffled water below the tall cliffs, the slackening vigour of the masthead pendant.

'Tops'l sheets!' Rooke sounded out of breath. 'Tops'l clew lines!'

Bolitho saw the men strung out along the tapered yards, their tanned arms moving in unison, totally unconcerned by their dizzy height above the deck.

'Helm alee!'

With the breeze all but gone the *Hyperion* turned lazily into the wind, her remaining sails vanishing as Bolitho dropped his arm with a slice, and from forward came the shout, 'Let go!'

He half listened to the splash and the attendant rumble of outgoing cable, glad that the saluting guns had finished so that he could think clearly again.

Midshipman Caswell broke the sudden silence. He had kept his glass trained on the flagship, his mind empty of everything but the necessity of being the first to see the flags break from her yards.

'*Tenacious* to *Hyperion*. Captain repair on board in fifteen minutes.'

Bolitho saw Allday waiting by the poop. 'Tell Gimlett to lay out my best uniform immediately. Then call away the barge.'

He saw Gossett staring at the powerful three-decker and asked, 'Do you know her?'

Gossett pouted thoughtfully. 'She was with us off Brest

for a while, sir. Then she went into Plymouth for an over-haul. She weren't carrying any admiral in them days.'

Caswell looked up from his book. '*Tenacious*, ninety guns, sir. Captain Matthew Dash.'

Bolitho formed a small picture in his mind. 'I met him once,' was all he said. But he was more interested in the rear-admiral. A lot would depend on the sort of man he proved to be. Bolitho hurried to his cabin, throwing off his threadbare seagoing coat and tearing at his faded waistcoat.

Gimlett followed him like an anxious shadow as Bolitho pulled on a clean shirt and ran a comb through his hair. Lord Hood might be senior enough to ignore such niceties, he thought grimly, but this rear-admiral obviously considered otherwise. The fifteen minutes' grace spoke for themselves.

He heard the splash of his boat alongside and All-day's strident tones calling to the bargemen.

And all the while his mind was busy with the possi-bilities now presented by the presence of the ninety-gun ship of the line and the newly landed soldiers. Hood must have seen the value of his first report. It seemed as if action was more than just a rough idea now.

He cursed as Gimlett adjusted his neckcloth and fussed around him with his swordbelt. He was like an old woman, he thought despairingly.

Rooke appeared in the open door. 'Barge alongside, sir.' He looked more composed now that the ship had anchored.

Bolitho thrust his arms into the gold-laced coat with its white lapels and said, 'Have all boats lowered, Mr. Rooke. Send the *Fairfax*'s people ashore and then await my instructions.' He picked up his carefully worded re-port and added slowly, 'When next we enter harbour you must try to get the *feel* of the ship, do you understand?'

'I was concerned about the wind, sir.' Rooke eyed him flatly. 'She's got so much weed on her bottom she might do anything.'

Bolitho reached for his hat. 'Until I decide otherwise you will take the responsibilities of first lieutenant. And those include the wind, and any other damn thing in or around this ship, understand?'

Rooke straightened his back. 'Aye, aye, sir.'

'Good.' He strode out into the sunlight, past the side party, and paused by the entry port. 'I see that the *Chanticleer* is flying her mail pendant, Mr. Rooke. I will send over some despatches, and if there are any letters from our people you had better get them across also.' He paused, his eye falling on the stolid line of bosun's mates, their pipes raised in readiness. The side boys with their rough white gloves, and Inch with his telescope. It seemed odd without any marines.

Then he added quietly, 'You had best parcel Mr. Quarme's possessions and send them too.' He watched for some flicker of regret or pity in Rooke's eyes. But he merely touched his hat and then stood aside as with a squeal of pipes Bolitho climbed down to the waiting barge.

. . . . . .

Captain Dash of the *Tenacious* greeted Bolitho warmly. In his middle fifties, he was a square-set, bluff-looking man with a harsh, grating voice but a friendly enough smile. He was one of the Navy's rare products, for he had actually reached his senior post by way of the lower deck, having entered the Navy as a child volunteer and by effort and determination, which Bolitho could only half

141

imagine, had clawed his way to command a ship of the line.

Bolitho followed him to the wide quarterdeck ladder and asked, 'When did you drop anchor?'

Dash grinned. 'This forenoon. It has been all hell here since.' He gestured with a worn thumb towards the big transport. 'She's the *Welland*, an old ex-Indiaman. She's brought five hundred of the 91st Foot an' half of the loudest-voiced sergeants in the British Army by the sound of 'em!'

He became suddenly serious. 'I was at Gibraltar when the sloop came from Lord Hood with my new orders.' He shrugged. 'So now my ship wears a rear-admiral's flag and I have to remember my manners!'

'What is he like?' Bolitho dropped his voice.

'Hard to tell. He has had me on the hop since he came aboard, but he spends most of the time in his cabin. He's waiting for you right now.'

Bolitho smiled. 'I forgot to ask his name.'

Dash pulled himself up the ladder. 'He's only just got his appointment to flag rank, so you probably never heard of him.' He paused, sweating profusely, and then stared at the mizzen truck. 'You are now under the flag of Sir Edmund Pomfret, Knight of the Bath, Rear-Admiral of the Red.' He broke off and peered at Bolitho uncertainly. 'You *do* know him then?'

Bolitho looked away, his mind reeling. Edmund Pomfret, it did not seem possible. He tried to think back to that one and only time he had ever seen him. It had been in the George at Portsmouth, where he had been summoned to receive the news of his new command of the frigate *Phalarope*. Nearly twelve years back in time. On his way from the inn to his new ship he had passed another junior who had been waiting to receive the full wrath of the admiral. That captain had been ordered from the *Phalarope* because of his senseless cruelty, his total indifference to the wellbeing of his men, even to the margin of life and death. And that man, the one who had sown the seeds of the *Phalarope's* mutiny, had been Edmund Pomfret!

Dash paused outside the door of the great cabin where two marines stared unwinkingly from beneath their black shakos. 'You feeling all right, Bolitho? I heard you had been under a fever, and . . .'

Bolitho touched his sleeve. 'I am well enough. It was just an old memory.'

He tapped the door and heard a voice call sharply, 'Enter!'

Pomfret was seated behind a large desk signing a paper held by his flag-lieutenant. He waved to a chair without looking up. 'Be seated, Captain. I must make sure this is drafted correctly.'

The worried-looking lieutenant winced, but Bolitho kept his eye on the seated admiral.

Pomfret had changed a good deal, but there was no mistaking him. Surprisingly, the heavy admiral's coat and gold lace made him appear younger than his forty years, but beneath his gleaming waistcoat his figure had given way to slight corpulence, and his forehead was creased in what appeared to be a permanent frown.

But the mouth was the same, small and petulant, and the eyes, as they skimmed back and forth over the paper, pale and protruding. He had full, reddish hair, and his skin seemed to be that which defied the sun and was blotchy with heat, in spite of the shaded cabin.

He looked up and waved his hand. 'Carry on Fanshawe. But *try* and be quicker next time!' As the lieutenant hurried away he stared fixedly at Bolitho for the first time.

'That man is a fool.' His voice was quiet but sharp, and he sounded angry. 'Well, Bolitho, what have you to say for yourself?'

Bolitho reached for his sealed report. 'I have just returned from St. Clar, sir.'

Pomfret drummed one hand on the desk and said with forced patience, 'I know all about that from your captain of marines. What I want to know is, just what the hell do you think you were doing there at all?'

'I had to obtain water for my ship, sir. No supplies or any sort of news came from the fleet. I had to use my initiative.' Bolitho kept his voice level and formal.

Pomfret pouted his lip. 'And you made a parley with the enemy too, I believe?'

'Yes, sir. One of the prisoners ...'

Pomfret's interruption was smooth and silky. '*Ex*-prisoners, surely?'

'He gave me reason to hope that we might make good use of St. Clar in future, sir.' Bolitho could hear his own breathing, just as he could feel the anger and resentment growing in him like fire.

'I do not believe in obtaining victory by compliance, Bolitho. The French are the enemy. In future you will obey orders, nothing more. We bargain with strength.' His lip curled. 'Not with brotherly love!'

Bolitho continued evenly, 'I have to report the death of my first lieutenant, sir. It is all in the report.'

Pomfret ignored the envelope and said coldly, 'You seem to have a great attraction for death and destruction, Bolitho. Your first lieutenant, the Spanish flagship and Admiral Anduaga, and of course your own commander Sir William Moresby!'

Bolitho flushed angrily. 'That is unfair, sir! When Sir William was killed I *was* obeying orders to the letter!'

Pomfret waved his hand. It was a very gentle gesture. 'Easy, Bolitho! You must learn to control your temper!'

Bolitho relaxed slightly. So this was how it was to be. He recalled his words to Quarme. 'Men do not change.'

He said quietly, 'When we finally took Cozar our losses were very slight, sir.'

'So I hear.' Pomfret leaned back and plucked at his neck-cloth. 'Well, you are under my command now and things will be different in many ways. And since Sir William died aboard your ship, you can blame yourself for that! I stepped into his shoes, Bolitho, just as you did into Captain Turner's.' He smiled briefly. 'So that is that. I was *en route* for New Holland and Botany Bay when I received my new orders at Gibraltar. I was to have assumed governorship there, to have made something out of that disgusting mess of convict settlements and petty-minded idiots who have been given the task of founding a new colony for us.' His cheeks were reddening with barely suppressed rage. 'And God help them!'

Bolitho said slowly, 'Had I know of your coming, sir, I would have waited in Cozar. But the water . . .'

Pomfret nodded sharply. 'Ah yes, the water!' He eyed him bleakly. 'You are just the same, it appears. Too soft by half!' He nodded again. 'Oh yes, I remember you, Bolitho, have no fear of that.'

'Thank you, sir.'

Pomfret half-jumped to his feet. 'Do not be impertinent!' He slumped down again as if totally exhausted by the heat. More calmly he continued, 'Men do not respect weakness, you should have learned that by now.'

Bolitho had a sudden picture of the luckless convicts in Botany Bay. Hundreds were being shipped there, deported for crimes of every kind. Without the American colonies, England had chosen to send her unwanted criminals to the other side of the world, where the survivors of the privations and unknown fever might live to form a new extension of the country which had rejected them. He wondered if they would ever learn how lucky they were to have avoided Pomfret's ideas of discipline and progress.

Pomfret said absently, 'I am sick and tired of hearing about the honour and loyalty of such rubbish. They lie and cheat and carouse, and despise the sea-officer such as you and I. But when the drumbeats and the balls begin to fly they *need* the tradition and the assurance of King and country. They are as weak as water!'

Bolitho was not sure if he was referring to convicts or seamen, or if to Pomfret they were indistinguishable.

He said, 'They are men none the less, sir. I do not despise a man because he does not share my beliefs.'

Pomfret regarded him narrowly. 'Then you are a bigger fool than I took you for.' He leaned forward as if to give his words more impact. 'You are not commanding a frigate now, Bolitho. Under my control you will learn to do your proper duty as befits the captain of a seventy-four, see?'

'Yes, sir.' Bolitho eyed him impassively. 'But I was alone here. I acted as I thought fit. We have the *Fairfax*'s people back, and soon we might regain the sloop.'

Pomfret wiped his face with a silk handkerchief and said, 'Do you have the sloop's officers, too?'

'No, sir. The French had already sent them north for possible exchange.'

'Pity.' Pomfret nodded absently. 'I would have court-martialled the fools for allowing their ship to be taken by such a stupid ruse. However, they are not my im-

146

mediate concern.' He ruffled some papers. 'I will inform Lord Hood of the present situation, and in the meantime we will garrison this macabre and miserable island *properly*.' He glared at Bolitho's grave face. 'It looks like the most useless place on earth!'

'It has a good harbour, sir. There is an old village where the convicts used to be, but it is derelict now. The fortress you have seen, and ...'

Pomfret frowned and said, 'You can take your marines back. The army will control the island now, under me of course.'

Of course, Bolitho thought grimly. 'And my orders, sir?'

Pomfret yawned. 'Fanshawe will give you them immediately, or I'll know the reason. You will sail forthwith for Gibraltar and execute my requirements as they are *written*!' He ignored the surprise on Bolitho's face. 'I was commanding a convict convoy when all this came about. I have detached some of my ships to assist here. You will go and collect them.'

'But St. Clar, sir!' Bolitho felt the cabin closing in on him.

'It will still be there when you return, Bolitho.' It was a rebuke. 'Lord Hood has given me sole command here. A free hand to do whatever is required to make a success of a rather unsatisfactory beginning.'

Bolitho stood up, his muscles taut and stiff. 'These ships, sir. Are they supplies?'

'Some of them. But it is all written in your orders. Do not fail to reach Gibraltar before all the convoy has departed. I would not be at all pleased, I can assure you!'

As he made to leave Pomfret added flatly, 'I did not ask for this command, Bolitho. But now that it is mine I intend it to prosper, or so help me God I will know the

147

reason!' He appeared to be bored with the interview. 'Now I will read your report and assess its value. I suppose you will want a replacement for your dead man?'

'Yes, sir.'

'Well, speak to the senior officer at Gibraltar. You have my authority.'

Bolitho stifled his reply. It was amazing how promotion could change a man's outlook to a point of godlike supremacy.

He replied, 'Then I will leave at once, sir.'

Pomfret's words followed him through the door. 'My orders will be carried out at all times, to the *letter*!'

Captain Dash was waiting on the middle deck beside the entry port, his face alight with questions. 'How did you make out, Bolitho? Is it the man you remembered?'

Bolitho stared across at the *Hyperion*'s tall masts. 'The same.' He looked down into the waiting barge and added, 'I think we may all be in for an interesting time ahead.'

Dash watched him leave and shook his head worriedly. Then he looked up at the admiral's flag again, and wondered.

. . . .

Within an hour of Bolitho's brief meeting with Rear-Admiral Pomfret the *Hyperion* had weighed and thrust her bowsprit once more towards the beckoning horizon. To her company it seemed as if it was some sort of judgement, and that the ship was doomed to sail on and on for ever, until her timbers fell apart and dropped them bodily into the sea.

The gathering of ships at Cozar, the presence too of the military, had aroused new interest, had even given the *Hyperion*'s seamen a strange sense of pride, as if by going alone to St. Clar and anchoring impudently so close to the enemy shore they had in some way started the whole operation in motion.

When the order to get under way was piped and Ashby's marines clumped resentfully aboard from the fortress the new excitement collapsed into bewildered resentment.

The *Hyperion*'s officers were at least spared the task of inventing ways to keep the men occupied on the return voyage to Gibraltar. In spite of a clear sky the wind force increased almost as soon as Cozar had vanished astern. As the old ship clawed her way south-west and around the southern coast of Spain she was at times close-hauled almost into the teeth of the wind, or worse, beating painfully against it to regain a mile or so already lost. Day after day it went on without respite, with the hands no sooner down from aloft for a brief rest below decks than the cry would come again. 'All hands! All hands! Hands aloft to shorten sail!'

Not that there was much relief below decks either. Ports were sealed against the driving spray, and the confined messes were foul with the stench of bilge and the trapped aromas of hastily cooked meals. *Hyperion* was taking the driving ranks of short rollers very badly. The monotonous clank of pumps went on so continuously that it was unnoticed until it stopped for a change of watch.

On the morning of the tenth day the ship drove thankfully into the anchorage below the Rock, her company too weary and dispirited to care about their reasons for coming or even what lay ahead.

Bolitho sat unmoving in a chair beside the cabin table, hating the clinging dampness of his clothes, but too tired to stir himself. It seemed as if he had not left the deck for more than a few minutes at a time during the voyage, and in the cabin's quiet elegance he felt stale and unclean. The ship's four remaining lieutenants had worked well enough, but they lacked the barest experience in handling the ship under such conditions. Bolitho was more convinced than ever that Captain Turner had trusted no one but Quarme and Gossett with the actual sailing of his ship, and the results of his jealous attitude were now painfully obvious.

Rooke entered the door and said tonelessly, 'Signal from the frigate *Harvester*, sir. She has despatches for you.' He swayed and then collected himself under Bolitho's scrutiny. He most of all seemed to feel his own shortcomings, and for once was unable to shift the blame elsewhere.

Bolitho levered himself from the chair and walked to the quarter windows. Through the salt-encrusted glass he could see the anchored frigate, her red ensign making a bright stab of colour against the Rock. It was just as if she had never moved from the time he had left her after his voyage from England. Was it really only two months ago? It seemed like a lifetime.

Barely two cables ahead of the frigate he could see three heavy supply ships and the small bobbing shape of an eighteen-gun sloop.

He thought of Pomfret's orders which he had read and re-read a dozen times, and which stayed in his thoughts even when he had been fighting his ship into the shrieking fury of wind and spray. Well, they would all have to know soon enough, he thought wearily. And with a man like Pomfret it was just as well to get started on the right foot.

Rooke was saying, 'Shall I send a boat across, sir?'

'No.' Bolitho rubbed his eyes with his knuckles. 'Make

a signal to *Harvester* and the sloop *Snipe* and tell their captains to repair on board immediately.'

Rooke eyed him unsurely. 'Are they the rest of our force, sir?'

'They are, Mr. Rooke. And the three supply ships are to be convoyed to Cozar.'

Even as he spoke he was reminded of Pomfret and his flagship. He could just as easily have convoyed the ships himself. A frigate sent on ahead to Cozar, or even the *Chanticleer*, would have been sufficient to break the uncertainty of waiting for word of new orders. But Pomfret had sailed merely with his escorts and a fairly fast troopship, oblivious or indifferent of Bolitho's difficulties and the shortage of fresh water.

When he turned from the window Rooke had gone, and Gimlett stood by the door showing his buck teeth and clasping his hands together with nervous expectancy.

Bolitho said, 'Clean shirt, Gimlett. And lay out another uniform directly as I have some visits to make.' He rubbed his chin and added, 'I will wash and shave before the two captains come aboard.'

By the time Leach, the frigate's captain, and Tudor, the commander of the *Snipe*, were ushered into his cabin Bolitho was to all outward appearances as fresh and alert as a man who spent his days ashore within the comforts of his house. He waited until Gimlett had poured wine for his visitors and then said, 'Welcome aboard, gentlemen. I trust that you are ready to sail at short notice.'

Leach nodded. 'Admiral Pomfret gave us instructions to remain with the supply ships after the other convoy had left Gibraltar. It seems that several attacks have been made on unprotected vessels of that sort in the past few weeks, and I will feel easier with your *Hyperion* to watch over us.' He relaxed slightly. 'It is good to meet with you again, sir. I trust that young Seton has recovered from his seasickness by now?'

Tudor, a heavy-jawed lieutenant, spoke for the first time. Either the wine or Leach's apparent ease with Bolitho had given him more confidence. 'I am not quite sure I understand, sir.' The others looked at him and he added awkwardly, 'The admiral instructed that one of the New Holland ships, the *Justice*, should stay here with us. I realise that the two supply ships are vital for our squadron,' he shrugged helplessly, 'but a convict ship should never be left here unguarded!'

Bolitho watched him gravely. 'It is not staying here.' They put down their glasses in one motion and looked at him with equal surprise. Bolitho continued. 'The *Justice* is to be taken to Cozar with us.'

Leach said, 'But, sir, she is a *convict* ship! God in heaven, there are three hundred of 'em aboard!'

'I know that.' Bolitho looked at his desk where he had locked Pomfret's orders. He could well understand Leach's confusion. Pomfret must have cross-questioned Bellamy of the *Chanticleer* to a considerable extent before making this surprise arrangement. As he had written in his orders, . . . *it would appear that certain fortifications and matters of mutual defence for the island of Cozar's occupying forces are in poor repair, and in many cases quite inadequate. As no additional labour is to hand to rectify these faults, and given the full authority accorded to me by Lord Hood, it is my intention to use a proportion of the convict cargo as carried in the transport* Justice *hereby under my command.* It was as simple as that.

Once again Pomfret had made it quite clear that he regarded human material with less concern than he would the stress of sailcloth or the replenishment of new spars.

152

Leach asked quietly, 'Can he do that, sir?' He shifted under Bolitho's grey eyes. 'I mean, is it legal?'

'There may be questions raised in Parliament, Leach. By then it seems unlikely that anyone will care. Many will take the view that the shipping of criminals is already costing the country too much when we are at war with France again. To have them "work their passage" might seem reasonable.'

Leach asked stubbornly, 'But do you think it so, sir?'

Bolitho locked his fingers together below the table. 'That is not your concern, Leach!' The harshness in his voice was unintentional, and he knew that Leach had uncovered his uncertainty as if he had spoken his thoughts aloud.

Tudor looked at his feet. 'In that case . . .'

Bolitho stood up, suddenly angry. 'In that case, Tudor, we will get on with it, shall we?'

'Shall I inform the *Justice*'s captain, sir?' Leach was trying to ease away the tension. 'He is a difficult man and shows little liking for the Navy.'

'I will tell him.' Bolitho walked to the windows. 'It is a duty I could well do without.'

Leach said suddenly, 'I understand that you are in need of a senior lieutenant, sir? My own is a good officer and well due for advancement.'

Bolitho was staring at the distant convict ship, seeing it as if for the first time. 'Thank you, Leach, that is considerate of you. Both to me and to an officer you are probably unwilling to lose.' He shook his head. 'But it will have to wait a while. The wind is backing all the time and mounting too, I believe. We must make a move soon or ride out the gale in harbour.'

Leach nodded. 'It has been coming in from the Atlantic for several days.' He stood up and reached for his hat.

'I agree we must sail without too much delay.'

Bolitho followed the two officers on deck and watched them depart for their ships. Then he said shortly, 'My barge, if you please! I am going across to the *Justice*.' He saw the officers exchange quick glances and guessed that they knew almost to a word what was to happen. News travelled faster between ships than any signals system yet devised.

Rooke asked, 'Any orders, sir?'

'Get as much fresh fruit as the boats can carry aboard while I'm away. But this ship will sail by eight bells, understood?'

Then he climbed down to the boat and pulled his cloak around his body as if to hide his thoughts from the watching seamen.

Allday growled, 'Shove off! Give way together!'

Over Bolitho's shoulder he said quietly, 'An odd name for a convict ship, Captain. There were some folk transported from Bodmin just for stealing bread. I don't call that *justice*!'

Bolitho bowed his head as spray whipped across his lips like hail. It was strange that Allday and men like him who had once been forcibly pressed into the Service should speak with such compassion, yet showed no pity for others taken from their homes to serve at sea in a King's ship. But like Allday he knew there was a difference, and although he would have to stifle it in his mind, it would always be there for him too.

'Boat ahoy?' A gruff voice yelled down from the ship's weathered side.

Allday replied loudly, 'Captain of His Majesty's Ship *Hyperion* coming aboard!'

Beneath his cloak Bolitho shivered. The *Justice* even smelt of human decay.

154

8

The Passenger

Captain Hoggan of the transport *Justice* stood arms folded in the centre of his littered cabin and watched Bolitho with obvious amusement. He was a muscular man with thick, unkempt hair, and his heavy coat, which would have been more suitable in the North Atlantic, looked as if it had been slept in.

'If you were expecting a protest from me, Bolitho, you can rest easy.' He gestured towards a bottle. 'Will you take a glass before you leave?'

Bolitho looked around the cabin. It was crammed with sea-chests and baggage of every kind, as well as a shining stand of muskets and pistols. What made a professional seaman take work of this sort? he wondered. A ship which plied its trade back and forth carrying one wretched cargo after another. He guessed that the boxes contained personal possessions of some of the convicts who died on passage, and the realisation made him answer coldly, 'No, Captain, I will not take a drink.'

'Suit yourself.' The cabin's close confines filled with the heady aroma of rum as Hoggan slopped a full measure into a glass for himself. Then he said, 'After all, you are ordering me to take this trash to Cozar. After that they're Pomfret's problem.' He winked. 'To me it just means a short trip and back home at the same price. Far better'n month after month at sea with Botany Bay at the end of it all!'

Bolitho shivered in spite of the trapped air. 'Very well. You will sail as soon as I make the signal. Obey all directions from my ship, and keep station at all times.'

Hoggan's face hardened slightly. 'This is no King's ship!'

'It is under my orders, Captain.' Bolitho tried to hide the contempt he felt for the other man. He glanced at his pocket watch. 'Now be so good as to assemble the convicts. I intend to tell them what is happening.'

Hoggan seemed about to protest. Then he grinned and muttered, 'This beats everything! Why bother with the like o' them?'

'Just do as I ask, if you please.' Bolitho looked away. 'They have that right surely.'

Hoggan clumped away, and within minutes could be heard bellowing orders from the poop. Then he reappeared in the doorway and made a mock bow.

'The gentlemen are ready, Captain!' He was grinning broadly. 'I must apologise for their rough appearance, but they wasn't expecting a King's officer to pay 'em a visit!'

Bolitho eyed him coldly and then walked out on to the windswept deck. Overhead the sky was crossed by narrow clouds, and as they scudded above the spiralling masts Bolitho knew that the wind was still mounting.

Then he looked down at the maindeck and saw the great press of upturned faces. The *Justice* was not much bigger than a large frigate, although he knew that her hull was deep and built more for carrying cargo than for making speed. It seemed incredible that all these unkempt, cowed-looking men could live and survive the rigours of the long voyage to New Holland, for the ship carried a full crew and all the additional stores as well which were required for such a journey. His eye moved along the gangways on either side of the upper deck. Unlike a ship of war they were protected as much from inboard as from a possible attacker, and the business-like swivel guns were pointing not to seaward but straight down on to the assembled convicts.

He noted the mixture of dress, too. Ranging from soiled broadcloth to stinking prison rags, while here and there a man stood out in some colourful garb to add to the unreality of their alien presence. Uprooted from their homes through greed or misfortune, they now stood swaying in total silence, their eyes on his face, their expressions ranging from fear to complete despair.

Some of the watchful guards on the gangways carried whips, and Bolitho's mind rebelled as he saw the expert ease with which they flicked them against their shoes as they waited idly for him to speak and then get about his proper business.

Was it possible that men never learned from past events? Senseless brutality had no place in the proper maintenance of order and discipline. It was less than a year since some of the ill-fated *Bounty* mutineers had choked out their lives before the eyes of the fleet at Portsmouth, yet some men still found more satisfaction from administering the punishment rather than finding the cure.

'I will not keep you long.' Bolitho's voice carried easily above the creak of spars and rigging. 'I am not here to judge or condemn you. That has been done already. I have to tell you that your journey to New Holland has been postponed, for how long I cannot at present say.' He had every man's attention now. 'This ship will sail in convoy to the island of Cozar, a distance of some six hundred miles. There you will be put to work in order that you can make a real contribution in the fight against our country's enemies!'

Something like a great groan rose from the packed figures, and when Bolitho looked at Hoggan he said bluntly, 'Some o' them has womenfolk and children with 'em.' He gestured vaguely over the weather rail. 'They've sailed on with the main convoy.'

Bolitho stared down at the prisoners, both stunned by Hoggan's indifference and appalled by what his words really implied. He should have remembered that it was customary to carry men and women in separate ships, and it was a wise precaution. But he had never before visualised these people as being families, but more as faceless individuals.

A voice called suddenly, 'Me wife, sir! Fer pity's sake, what will she do without me?'

Hoggan yelled. 'Keep *silent*, you snivelling pig!'

Bolitho held up his hand. 'Let me try and answer that, Captain.' To the deck at large he added evenly, 'War leaves little choice in these matters. My own people have not set foot ashore for many months, in some cases for several years. Yet they too have families . . .'

He broke off as the voice called out again. 'But she's gone out there, out to . . .' It trailed away as if the speaker was suddenly confronted with the true horror of deportation.

Bolitho said, 'I will do what I can for all of you. If you work well and obey orders, I am sure that such behaviour will weigh heavily in your favour. Remission of sentence is not unknown.' He wanted to get away from this wretched ship, but could not find it in his heart to merely turn his back and leave them to their despair. 'Just remember that whatever else you may or may not be, you are all Englishmen and faced with a common enemy.'

He broke off as Allday said quietly, '*Hyperion*'s boats are returning, Captain. Mr. Rooke must be worried about the wind.'

Bolitho nodded and turned to Hoggan. 'You may prepare to weigh. I will sail directly.' He watched the up-turned faces slowly breaking apart into small, aimless groups. 'Try not to make their lives any harder, Captain.'

Hoggan eyed him with obvious hostility. 'Are you choosing to give me orders, *sir*?'

'Since you put it that way, Captain Hoggan, yes, I am!' Bolitho's eyes were cold and hard. 'I am also holding you personally responsible!' Then he strode after Allday without another word.

As the barge butted manfully into the growing pattern of dancing whitecaps Bolitho stared across at the *Hyperion* and found time to wonder at the change she had seemingly undergone during his short visit to the *Justice*. He knew that the comparison was an illusion, but after the convict ship's air of decay and hopelessness, the *Hyperion* seemed to shine like part of another world. Her tall, spray-covered side and the purposeful movements of figures above and around her upper deck helped to steady him and ease the turmoil in his thoughts.

He climbed swiftly through the entry port and touched his hat briefly to the assembled side party. To Lieutenant Inch he said, 'Secure the boats at once and report when you have done so.' Then it dawned on him that something was wrong. At any other time he would have sensed it immediately, but he had been too busy thinking about the convicts. He saw Inch staring aft, and as he followed his gaze he realised what had caused his expression of apprehension.

Allday had just climbed up through the port and was unable to restrain himself, 'Bless me! A *woman* on the quarterdeck!'

Bolitho asked quietly, 'Would you be so good as to explain the meaning of this, Mr. Inch?' His voice was dangerously calm.

Inch swallowed unhappily. 'She came aboard in one of the boats, sir. From the Rock, and she had this letter . . .'

Bolitho pushed him aside. 'I will deal with it myself, since you seem to have taken leave of your senses!' He strode aft and up the quarterdeck ladder, his sudden anger beating time with his heart.

He got a swift impression of Lieutenant Rooke, his face frowning and apprehensive, and Midshipman Seton, who was surprisingly smiling in spite of Bolitho's bleak expression.

Then he saw the girl. She was dressed in dark green velvet, and by contrast had a wide Spanish sun hat tied round beneath her chin by a length of bright red ribbon. She was endeavouring to hold the hat still in the whipping wind and at the same time trying to keep her long hair from blowing free across her face.

'May I have some sort of explanation?' Bolitho looked from one to the other.

Rooke made to speak, but the girl said calmly, 'I am Cheney Seton, Captain. I have a letter for you from Sir Edmund Pomfret.' She dropped one hand to her dress and withdrew an envelope, all the time keeping her eyes on Bolitho's frowning face. Her eyes were large and blue-green like the sea, and very grave, and like her voice gave nothing away.

Bolitho took the letter and stared at it, his mind grappling with her words. 'Seton did you say?'

'S-Sir, she's m-m-my s-sister.' Midshipman Seton fell silent under Bolitho's flat stare.

The girl said evenly, 'I am sorry to have caused so much distress, Captain.' She gestured towards a small pile of luggage. 'But, as you can see, it is no mistake!'

Bolitho glared. 'Did you know about this, Mr. Seton?'

160

'He did not.' She spoke almost sharply, and had Bolitho been less angry he might have seen past her pretence of easy self-control. 'I was with the convoy for New Holland.' She shrugged as if it was of little importance. 'Now I am to sail with you to this island of yours.'

'Kindly do not interrupt me when I am addressing one of my officers, Miss, er, Seton!' Bolitho was already out of his depth, and from the corner of his eye saw a growing group of watching seamen below the quarterdeck.

She replied just as crisply, 'Then kindly do not discuss me as I was a piece of furniture on your boat, *Captain*!'

Dalby, the third lieutenant, who had been hovering nearby said helpfully, 'Not *boat*, miss! We call her a ship in the Navy!'

Bolitho shouted, 'And who asked you, Mr. Dalby?' He swung round angrily. 'Mr. Rooke, be so good as to call all hands for getting under way, and make a signal accordingly to the convoy!'

Then he turned back to the girl. Her arms were hanging at her sides now and her hair, which he noticed was of a deep chestnut colour, blew in the wind as if she no longer cared.

'If you will come aft, Miss Seton, I will hear this matter more fully.'

With Allday and Gimlett hurrying ahead Bolitho followed the girl below the poop, conscious of her slim figure and the defiant tilt of her head. Damn Pomfret to hell, he thought savagely. Why couldn't he have told him about the girl? The thought of *Hyperion* being despatched to Gibraltar at a time when the chance of real action was no longer a remote supposition was bad enough. To find Seton's sister waiting to be collected like one more piece of personal luggage was almost more than his mind could accept.

She stepped into the cabin and stared round with the same expression of grave interest.

Bolitho said more calmly, 'And now perhaps you could explain?'

'Do you mind if I sit down, Captain?' She eyed him quietly, her mouth set firmly against compromise.

'Please do.' Bolitho tore open the letter and walked to the windows. It was all there right enough. He said at length, 'I still do not understand the purpose of your visit?'

'I am not really sure it concerns *you*, Captain.' She gripped the arms of the chair. 'But since it will soon be generally known, I am going to Cozar to marry Sir Edmund Pomfret.'

Bolitho stared at her. 'I see.'

She leaned back in the chair, the defiance gone out of her. Almost wearily she said, 'I think not. But if you will be kind enough to tell me where I can rest, I will try and keep out of your way.'

Bolitho looked round the cabin helplessly. 'You may keep these quarters. I will have a cot rigged for myself in the chartroom. You will be more than comfortable.'

For a brief instant her eyes filled with quiet amusement. 'If you are *sure*, Captain?'

Bolitho seized Allday's sudden reappearance like a drowning man grasping a straw. 'Take my gear to the chartroom, Allday! I will change into my seagoing clothes immediately.' Damn the girl, too. She was mocking him for making such a fool of himself. 'Then get Gimlett and instruct him on the new arrangements.'

Allday looked quickly at the seated girl. But his face was expressionless as he answered, 'Looks like a fair wind, Captain.' Then he vanished.

Minutes later, when Bolitho strode on to the quarterdeck, all conversation amongst the assembled officers stopped instantly, as if he had shouted some terrible obscenity at them.

Rooke said formally, 'The transports have their cables hove short, sir.' He was very tense, and Bolitho guessed that he was not enjoying the prospect of handling the ship under the glass of every captain anchored in Gibraltar. It gave him a small sense of cruel pleasure.

He snapped, 'Very well, Mr. Rooke. Get the ship under way, if you please.' He saw Gossett watching him, his expression like that of a sad mastiff. 'Lay a course to weather the headland and put two good hands on the wheel.'

Controlling his irritation with real effort he walked to the rail and looked slowly along the length of his command. The men already poised at the capstan bars, the marines at the mizzen braces, the topmen waiting for the order to move.

He said, 'Make to escorts "weigh when ready".' He took a telescope and studied the transports as they prepared to follow suit.

As the flags soared aloft Rooke lifted his speaking trumpet and shouted, 'Ready at the capstan!'

Tomlin, the bosun, showed his two fangs and waved his fist in acknowledgement.

Rooke moistened his lips. 'Loose the heads'ls! Hands aloft and loose tops'ls!'

Bolitho watched in silence as the topmen swarmed up the ratlines in a human tide, the rattans of the petty officers and master's mates urging on the laggards with more than their usual enthusiasm. It was as if they realised their captain's angry mood and were taking no chances.

'Man the braces!'

As the men strained and groaned at the capstan bars and the great anchor tore itself from the silt and sand of the harbour the *Hyperion* bowed heavily to the rising wind. Then as the full force struck her she tilted even further, the men on the yards fighting and kicking to control the great billowing folds of canvas beneath them. Further and further, and then with the wheel hard over and the yards creaking and bending like huge bows the *Hyperion* paid off to the wind and gathered way. As the anchor was seized and catted by the nimble forecastle hands she settled on a course towards the blown waste of broken wave crests, showing the watchers ashore that she at least was an experienced warrior, and as proud as her name.

Caswell called, 'All ships have weighed, sir!'

'Very well. Signal them to take station as ordered.' He tugged his hat firmly across his forehead and stared up at the masthead pendant. It was stiff and pointing like a spear. 'Signal them to make all sail conformable with weather.' It would be as well to keep signals to a minimum, he thought grimly. There would be time enough later for chasing up the laggards.

He watched the tiny sloop *Snipe* spreading her topsails and overhauling the leading transport like a terrier past a bullock. Her station was ahead of the convoy. *Hyperion* and the frigate would stay to windward, in this case astern of the transports, so that they could dash down if required to defend them. He shifted his glass to the *Harvester* and saw her sleek bows lift and crash down, slicing into the first deep-sea roller with the grace of a wild thing.

Hyperion merely lifted a massive shoulder into it and threw the sea back across the blunt bows in a solid sheet. With the wind astern the deck lifted and fell in a steady smashing motion, while overhead the air was filled with noise of whining rigging and the overall beat and roar of straining canvas as the tiny, shortened shapes of the men aloft fought to obey Bolitho's last order and set more sail.

He thought suddenly of the girl below in his cabin and knew she was the cause of his irritation. He saw Gossett's face soften with relief as he added shortly, 'We may have to take in a second reef directly, Mr. Gossett, but we'll use this advantage to clear the land.'

The master nodded. No doubt he understood better than most that there was no point in dismasting the ship merely to relieve a captain's anger.

The wind's force and direction stayed with the little convoy without much variation until the fourth day out from Gibraltar, and by noon of that day they had logged all of four hundred and twenty miles. Nobody aboard the *Hyperion* could recall the ship making such a good speed, and the voyage had proceeded with little interruption or incident.

By dusk of the fourth day the wind veered suddenly to the north-west and lost a little of its power, but as Bolitho stood on the weather side of the quarterdeck watching the glowing beauty of a great copper sunset he could afford to feel satisfied. The ships had held together well, and even now as he turned his eyes ahead of the *Hyperion*'s plunging bows he could see the transports' hulls gleaming in the strange light as if they were of burnished metal. *Erebus*, the largest transport, led the line, followed at a comfortable distance by her consort *Vanessa*. Both were well-handled vessels, and as they basked in the fading sunset they looked for all the world like men-of-war with their imitation painted gunports and taut rigging. Further astern followed the *Justice*, her hull a dull black and already lost in shadow, her hands still working aloft, as like the rest of the ships they shortened sail for the night.

Above the drumming whine of rigging Bolitho heard a sudden gust of laughter, and guessed that his officers were making full use of their time and the unusual opportunity of entertaining a lady in their mess.

Bolitho clasped his hands behind him and resumed his steady pacing back and forth along the weather side. His regular movement was watched by the two helmsmen, as well as by Dalby, the officer of the watch, who stayed discreetly on the lee side of the deck.

It was strange how the girl Cheney Seton had taken the ship by storm. In spite of her brief appearance on the poop there always seemed to be a goodly crowd of spare seamen ready to smile up at her, or merely to watch her spellbound, as if she was some sort of apparition.

Gimlett was, of course, in his element. He fussed over his passenger like a mother hen and guarded her against every possible intruder with more determination than Bolitho imagined he could possess. She had kept her word, too. She had stayed out of Bolitho's way and had done nothing which might outwardly interfere with the running of the ship.

Bolitho quickened his pacing in time to his thoughts as the realisation returned once more to remind him of one true fact. By her very reasonableness she had somehow managed to isolate him more than ever, rather than the other way round. Perhaps it was for that reason he had granted Inch's cautious request to entertain her at dinner that evening. He had half-expected they might invite him too, but it was not to be, and as he paced the darkening deck listening to the sound of his own shoes on the scrubbed planking he half-hoped there might be some emergency or change of wind so that he could call all hands and break up the sounds of gaiety from below.

When he turned into his cramped quarters in the chart-room he still found it difficult to believe that the girl was sleeping within feet of him in his own cot, or eating in his own cabin, while he hid away like a naughty schoolboy. Stranger still was the realisation that he hardly knew anything more about her than the minute she had stepped aboard. What information there was available was third or fourth hand, and all the more maddening because of its incompleteness. The gunroom messman had overheard Midshipman Piper telling Caswell what Seton had confided to him about his sister. The messman had of course informed Gimlett, who with obvious reluctance, but under threat of violence, had disclosed some of his information to Allday. As the coxswain had stood watching Bolitho shaving or had helped him into his heavy coat when the ship had reeled to a sudden squall in the middle of the night, he had casually imparted his news. Bolitho had accepted it equally casually, and had thereby saved both time and face.

Now as he recrossed the deck, his chin sunk into his neck-cloth, he built up a small picture of the girl who was going to be Pomfret's bride. She was twenty-six years old, and had until recently been in Pomfret's London house acting as a sort of housekeeper. Bolitho's first suspicion had been diminished when Allday had informed him that Pomfret had arranged that to their mutual benefit, as she had been nursing her invalid father, who for some reason which Bolitho could not discover, had been allowed to use the house as his own. Her father was now dead, and she had only a brother left in the whole world. Her mother had died in one of the uprisings in Jamaica when some slaves had revolted and had attacked the Seton homestead, more from convenience than for any real purpose.

Bolitho's frown deepened. That was interesting. Pomfret had been attached to a squadron off Jamaica, and it was quite possibly where he had met and made friends with the Seton family. In those days at least the girl's family must have been quite rich and influential. But what had happened since was past his understanding. But one thing was quite clear, her attitude of defiance which he had at first taken for a natural arrogance was merely a defence. It could not have been easy for her to manage alone in London.

Allday had fed him his last titbit of information that forenoon. Midshipman Seton had been made Pomfret's ward. The admiral was obviously very eager to make sure of his position, Bolitho thought.

Lieutenant Dalby crossed the deck and touched his hat in the darkness. 'All lights burning, sir.'

Bolitho paused and glanced ahead at the slow-moving transports. Each carried a single lantern and would be able to retain close contact even at night. It was his own idea and he was already putting it down to over-caution on his part. But during the afternoon the sloop, *Snipe*, far ahead of the convoy like a searching terrier, had signalled that she had sighted an unknown sail to the northwest. Nothing more had been seen of it, but one had to be careful. It was probably a Spanish merchantman, he thought, although the convoy was standing well out to sea, and even now was some sixty miles from the nearest land. But they were in the Gulf of Valencia, and every day took them nearer to the coast of France.

'Very good, Mr. Dalby.' He did not feel much like confiding in the third lieutenant who was inclined to be over-talkative if given the chance.

Dalby said, 'We will be in Cozar within five days if this weather holds, sir.' He banged his hands together noisily for it was already cold after the heat of the day. 'I hope Miss Seton is not disappointed with her new home.'

That was something else which had been nagging Bolitho more than a little. And the fact that Dalby could discuss it so easily made him unreasonably angry.

'Be so good as to attend to your duties, Mr. Dalby! You should call the duty watch and take another pull on the weather forebrace, it sounds like a flapping bellrope!'

He saw Dalby hurry away and sighed to himself. It was not his concern at all, but how could Pomfret let a girl like that go to a sun-bleached hell like Cozar?

From forward he heard the snap of orders and the weary fumblings of the roused seamen as they sought to find some fault where there was none.

There was a movement on the quarterdeck ladder and he saw two shadows climbing up to the lee side. One he saw was the girl, well wrapped in a long cloak with a hood over her hair, and the other was her brother. The latter had been almost a guest of honour at the wardroom dinner, and was probably well pleased with the sudden popularity his sister's presence had given him.

Seton saw Bolitho's solitary figure and said quickly, 'M-Must go! I-I am on w-watch in an hour!'

He scurried below and the girl turned by the massive trunk of the mainmast, her face pale against the sea beyond.

'Good night, Captain.' She lifted one hand very slightly and then steadied herself against the mast as the

169

Hyperion lifted lazily over a steep roller. 'A very pleasant evening.'

She made to head for the poop but Bolitho said hurriedly, 'Er, Miss Seton!' He saw her falter and then turn back, 'I was, er, just wondering if you are quite comfortable?'

In the darkness her teeth shone very white. 'Thank you, Captain, quite comfortable.'

Bolitho felt himself actually flushing and was suddenly enraged by his own stupidity. What, after all, had he expected?

She said calmly, 'I shall be almost sorry to reach Cozar.'

Bolitho made himself walk across the intervening deck and then said, 'I have been thinking about that. Cozar is not exactly a suitable place . . .'

'I know, Captain.' There was no rebuke or hostility in her voice. It might have been sadness. 'But there it is.'

Dalby pattered across the quarterdeck and stood staring at them. 'Forebrace secure and snug for the night, sir!'

Bolitho turned hotly. 'Go *away*, Mr. Dalby!'

When he faced the girl again he saw that she was holding her mouth and shaking with suppressed laughter.

'The poor man! You've frightened him to death!' She recovered quickly. 'I can't imagine why they all seem to like you so much. You really are a terrible bully!'

Bolitho did not know what to say. 'I do not mean . . .' he began, but he sounded so pompous that he broke off and grinned helplessly. 'I am sorry, Miss Seton. I will try to remember that.'

She nodded. 'Now I will go to my cabin, Captain.'

Bolitho took half a pace after her. 'Might we dine together?' He was out of his depth, and worse, he knew it. 'Perhaps before we reach Cozar?'

For a terrible moment he thought she was going to complete her victory by ignoring him. But beside the helmsman she paused and seemed to consider the request.

'I think that would be very pleasant, Captain. I will think about it tomorrow.' Then she was gone.

The eyes of the two helmsmen glowed in the binnacle light like bright marbles as they watched their captain's confusion.

But Bolitho did not care. He was enjoying a new sensation entirely, and was strangely indifferent to what any of his men thought at that particular moment.

*   *   *

The following morning found Bolitho up, dressed and shaved bright and early. This was not unusual for him, because although he was always fascinated by sunsets at sea, he was even more intrigued and strengthened by the early morning. The air felt fresher, and the sea was without malice in the pale sunlight.

He walked to the quarterdeck rail and stood for several minutes watching the hands moving busily across the upper deck, calling cheerfully to each other as they worked with swabs and holystones to the steady accompaniment of salt-water pumps.

Rooke had requested permission to set topgallants and royals while he had been shaving, and now as he looked up at the gleaming white banks of canvas he felt strangely happy and replete. The ship was behaving well, and the men were far happier than they had been for some time, and more so than they had a right to be. When he thought back to the previous night he felt a brief pang of uncertainty. The girl would be leaving the ship very soon. It was to be hoped that this new sense of comradeship did not leave with her.

But he knew he was really exploring his own feelings. The sudden sense of loss gave him an instant answer, if doubts he had. It was of course quite ridiculous. Right or wrong, she would be an admiral's lady, and he had no doubt that Pomfret would soon use his influence to get away from Cozar and hoist his flag in more amenable surroundings.

He heard Gossett murmur a greeting behind him, and when he turned he saw her walking slowly towards the rail, her face turned towards the filtered sunlight. She had been more tanned than was customary to expect when she had come aboard, and now that he knew she had grown up in Jamaica he was not surprised. But after a few days at sea the tan had settled to a beautiful golden brown, and he felt unusually moved as he watched her enjoying the early warmth of the day to come.

He removed his hat and smiled awkwardly. 'Good morning, Miss Seton. I trust you slept well?' His voice was louder than he had intended, and by the nine-pounders a ship's boy froze above his holystone and stared up at him.

She smiled. 'Very well, Captain. Better than for a long time.'

'Er, good.' Bolitho ignored the gaping seamen by the wheel. 'As you see, the convoy is keeping good station and the wind is still behaving as it should.'

She was watching him, her eyes suddenly grave. 'We will be at Cozar on time then?'

He nodded. 'Yes.' He nearly replied, 'I'm afraid so.' He glanced at the masthead pendant to recover himself. 'I have just instructed my carpenter to start work on a

172

few pieces of furniture which might make your home at Cozar more comfortable for you.' She was still watching him, and he could feel the heat rising to his cheeks. 'They wanted to do it,' he added lamely.

She did not speak for a few seconds. Then she nodded slowly, and he saw a sudden brightness in her eyes.

'Thank you, Captain. That was very kind of you.'

The men working around them, the helmsmen and the officer of the watch all seemed to fade as he continued quietly, 'I only wish there was something more I could do.'

She swung towards the sea, her face hidden by her hair, and Bolitho held his breath with something like panic. He had gone too far. She would cut the ground from under him, as he well deserved.

But she said, 'Perhaps we had better not dine together, Captain. It might be better if . . .' She broke off as a voice pealed down from above.

'Deck there! *Snipe*'s going about! She's signalling, sir!'

Bolitho dragged his mind back from the sudden despair her words had given him.

'Get aloft, Mr. Caswell, and see what you can of her!'

Then to the girl he said quietly, 'I am sorry. I did not mean to imply . . .' He struggled helplessly for words.

She faced him again and he saw that there were tears in her eyes. She said, 'It was nothing you did, Captain. Believe me.'

'Deck there! Signal reads, "*Snipe* to *Hyperion*. Strange sail bearing nor'-nor'-west."' Caswell had to shout above the din of booming canvas.

When Bolitho looked again the girl had gone. he said heavily, 'Very well. Make to *Snipe*.' He frowned. Every thought was a physical effort. 'Make, "Investigate immediately." ' As Caswell slithered down a backstay he added, 'Then signal the convoy to reduce sail.'

He walked past the men by the halyards as flag after flag was pulled from the locker to snake its way up the yards. A mile clear on the starboard quarter the frigate *Harvester* heeled slightly in the wind, and a shaft of sunlight played on more than one raised telescope as the signals broke out stiffly with colourful urgency.

He saw Rooke watching him thoughtfully and said, 'Get the royals off her, Mr. Rooke. We will overtake the convoy otherwise.'

Every available glass was trained on the distant feather of white sail as the little sloop tacked round and away towards the horizon. Another false alarm? Bolitho could find neither relief nor apprehension now.

The minutes dragged by. Eight bells struck from forward and the watches changed.

Allday crossed the quarterdeck. 'You have had no breakfast, Captain.' He seemed anxious.

Bolitho shrugged. 'I am not hungry.' He did not even rebuke him for breaking into his thoughts.

A whole hour went by before the sloop's topgallants reappeared on the sharpening horizon.

Caswell climbed high into the mizzen shrouds, his telescope balanced against the ship's easy roll. 'From *Snipe*, sir.' He blinked and rubbed his streaming eye. Then he tried again. 'I can't quite make it out, sir.' He almost fell from the shrouds as some freak roller lifted the far-off sloop simultaneously with the *Hyperion*. He shouted, 'Signal reads, "Enemy in sight", sir!'

Bolitho felt strangely unmoved. 'Very well. General signal to convoy. "Enemy in sight. Prepare for battle." '

Rooke stared at him. 'But, sir, they might not wish to fight!'

Bolitho's tone was scathing. 'They have not come this far to see *you*, Mr. Rooke!' He saw the sudden flurry of activity on the *Justice*'s poop as his signal broke free to the wind. They are after those transports!'

He looked around the watching figures, the decks which were still damp from the swabs and holystones. Like the other ships around him, everyone was waiting to be told what to do.

He said calmly, 'Beat to quarters, Mr. Rooke, and clear for action!'

Two small marine drummers ran to the larboard gangway, pulling on their black shakos and fumbling with their sticks. Then as the ship held her breath they started to beat out their tattoo, their faces tight with concentration as their message was picked up aboard the *Harvester* and the three transports.

Bolitho made himself stand motionless by the rail as his men poured up from below and the marines hurried aft and aloft to the tops, their uniforms shining like blood in the growing sunlight. Below decks he could hear the thuds and bangs of screens being removed, the whole urgent business of changing a ship from a floating home and a way of life to a unified instrument of war.

He looked again at the quiet sea, but found no comfort. The morning was already spoilt for Bolitho even before the *Snipe* had brought her news.

Rooke touched his hat. He was sweating badly. 'Cleared for action, sir.' The words seemed to spark off a memory of that early resentment and he added, 'Less than ten minutes that time!'

Bolitho looked at him gravely. 'Good.'

'Shall I give the order to load, sir?'

'Not yet.' Bolitho thought suddenly of his breakfast and felt a sharp pang of hunger. He knew he would be

175

unable to eat. But he had to do something. He saw the sunlight lancing down between the straining topsails and felt a new sensation of fear. By tonight he could be dead. Or, worse, screaming under the surgeon's knife. He licked his lips and said tightly, 'You have all eaten. I have not. I will be in the chartroom if I am required.' Then he turned and walked slowly towards the poop.

Gossett watched him pass and breathed out admiringly. 'Did you see that, lads? Not a flicker! As cool as an Arctic wind is our cap'n!'

9

Like a Frigate!

Midshipman Piper peered into the chartroom, pausing only to recover his breath. 'Mr. Rooke's respects, sir, and the enemy is now in sight!'

Bolitho deliberately lifted his cup and sipped at his coffee. It was, of course, stone cold.

He asked quietly, 'Well, Mr. Piper? Is there nothing more?'

The boy gulped and tore his eyes from watching his captain's apparent indifference to the sudden proximity of danger.

He said, 'Three sail, sir. Two frigates and one larger ship.'

'I will come up directly.' Bolitho waited until the boy had hurried away and then swept the untouched food from the table. As he peered searchingly at the chart he was again reminded of his complete isolation. If *Snipe* far ahead of the convoy had sighted the ships in any other position there might have been cause for some small optimism. As it was the enemy were well to windward and approaching his ill-assorted convoy on a converging course. They could take their time, choose their moment to sweep in close to attack.

He picked up his hat and walked swiftly to the quarterdeck. The breeze was still fresh, but already the air was much hotter. He made himself walk to the rail and stare down at the upper deck while every nerve in his body seemed to cry out for him to snatch a glass and search out the enemy.

Below the gangways each crew waited silently beside its gun. The decks around them were sanded to give the seamen maximum grip once action was joined, and beside every twelve-pounder stood a freshly filled water-bucket for the swabs or any sudden fire in the tinder-dry woodwork and cordage.

At each hatch was a marine sentry, bayonet fixed, legs braced to the steady roll of the ship, his duty to prevent any frightened seaman from running below if the pace became too hot.

He took a telescope and lifted it over the nettings. The wallowing convict ship swam hugely across the lens, and then it reached out and steadied on a point below the horizon, far away on the leading ship's larboard bow.

Without turning his head he knew that those around him were watching his face. They had already seen the approaching vessels. Now they wanted to see his reactions and thereby gain comfort or find fresh doubt. He clamped his jaws together and tried to keep his face impassive.

As he edged the glass gently back and forth in time

with the *Hyperion*'s movements he saw the two frigates. They were so close together and pointing almost directly towards his glass that they looked for all the world like one giant, ill-designed ship. One was slightly ahead of the other, and he could see that she was making more sail and spreading her topgallants even as he watched. Thirty-six guns at least, and the second frigate only slightly smaller.

But further astern, and close hauled on the starboard tack, was a ship of the line. Like the frigates she wore no colours, but there was no mistaking that beakhead, the graceful rake of her masts. Probably a French two-decker which had broken out from one of the Mediterranean ports to try and test the pressure of Hood's blockade. He lowered his glass and glanced at the transports. They would make a good start, he thought grimly.

He said, 'We will retain this course, Mr. Rooke. There is no point in trying to run south. The enemy has the advantage if he keeps to windward, and there is nothing to the south'rd,' he smiled briefly, 'but Africa.'

Rooke nodded. 'Aye, sir. D'you think they'll try and engage?'

'Within the hour, Mr. Rooke. The wind might drop. I would certainly attack were I in his shoes!'

He pictured the French two-decker as he had seen her in the glass. She was slightly bigger than *Hyperion*, but more to the point would be much faster, having been snug in harbour and able to receive the full attention of dockyard and riggers.

He made up his mind. 'Alter course two points to larboard. We will lay the ship on the convoy's quarter. Signal *Harvester* to take up station to windward of the leading ship immediately.'

'And *Snipe*, sir?' Rooke sounded tense.

'She can retain her present position, I think.' He imagined the havoc and complete destruction which a frigate's broadside could make of the sloop's frail timbers. 'The next move will be made by the enemy very soon now.'

With her yards braced round the *Hyperion* edged slowly across the wake of the other ships in the convoy, while the *Harvester*, her topgallants and royals ballooning with sudden eagerness, sped recklessly past the *Justice*'s stern and then tacked with equal dash towards the leading transport *Erebus*.

Lieutenant Dalby called, 'The frigates have gone about, sir!'

Bolitho shaded his eyes and watched the two ships swinging round and heeling sharply to the wind. When they had completed their manœuvre they would be running parallel with the convoy, some five miles clear. Even without his glass Bolitho could see that their gunports were still closed, each captain no doubt concentrating on laying himself in the most advantageous position.

The two-decker sailed majestically on her original course as if to pass astern of the convoy and ignore it completely. Bolitho bit his lip. Her captain was doing exactly as he would have done. The two frigates would swoop down on the convoy and attack either the *Harvester* or the leading ship, or both together. If *Hyperion* closed to support the *Harvester* it would take some time to beat back and protect the rear of the convoy, and by then the enemy two-decker would have pounced. It was the oldest lesson of war. Divide and conquer.

Gossett intoned, 'Course nor' by east, sir, full an' bye.'

'Very well.' He stared up at the masthead pendant. 'Signal the convoy to make all available sail.' To Rooke he added sharply, 'Get the royals on her again, I want

179

to see what the two-decker intends to do then!'

With all sail set the *Hyperion* gathered way in time with the transports, and the effect on the French ships was instantaneous. The senior captain had no doubt expected Bolitho to close up his convoy and protect them as best he could from a two-pronged attack. Running away was as unlikely as it was impracticable. But with the ships already drawing away from his guns the Frenchman had no alternative but to give chase.

Captain Ashby breathed out slowly. 'There he goes, by God!'

The tall two-decker was already tacking, her topsails flapping wildly as she swung across the wind. So quick was her response to Bolitho's tactics that she seemed to lean right down into the white-capped water until her mainyard appeared to slash at the wavecrests, her lower gunports completely hidden beneath the cream and surge of her own efforts.

Her sail drill was less efficient than *Hyperion*'s, and that was probably because she had spent more time at anchor than at sea, but within fifteen minutes she too had spread her royals and topgallants in one giant pyramid of gleaming canvas.

Rooke said flatly, 'She's overhauling us, sir. She'll be up to us in thirty minutes.'

But Bolitho was staring ahead watching the *Justice*. She was less than a mile away now, and like the other transports was finding the pace too demanding. The two enemy frigates were standing in closer to the lead ships, and as he strained his eyes through the crisscross of rigging he saw a puff of smoke from the leading one and a ripple of bright flashes.

It seemed an age before the dull rumble of gunfire reached back to him, then he said, 'You may load now,

Mr. Rooke. See that the first broadside is double-shotted with a measure of grape for good fortune!' The first aimed salvo was usually the last to be fired with time to spare. After that men fired more from familiarity than anything else. And down on the lower gundeck it would be even worse. With hardly enough room to stand upright, the crews would fight their guns in a crazed world of dense, choking smoke, or semi-darkness and horror which was better unseen.

'*Harvester* has returned fire, sir!'

Bolitho nodded, half-watching the gunners as they cradled the gleaming balls from the racks and rammed them down the gaping muzzles. The more practised gun-captains checked each ball with something like loving care before loading. Some were better rounded than others. They would go with that first order to fire.

'Make a signal to *Harvester*. "You are at liberty to engage the enemy."' He almost smiled at the empty words. 'Not that he has any choice.'

Rooke asked, 'Shall we run out, sir?' He was staring across the larboard quarter watching the French ship cutting away the distance as she drove effortlessly towards the convoy. Her captain was level-headed enough to stay just that much upwind of the slower *Hyperion*. If Bolitho turned away he would present his ship's stern to the French broadside. At close range that would be enough to reduce the between-decks to a slaughterhouse, and probably dismast her into the bargain. If he held his present course it would be a gun-for-gun battle, with the Frenchman holding his advantage and *Hyperion* unable to tack in either direction without receiving crippling damage.

'Not yet, Mr. Rooke.' His voice was quite controlled, but as he watched the other ship's shadow rising and falling across the glittering water he guessed that Rooke probably imagined he was running away, either from fear or from a complete inability to think of a plan to avoid destruction.

He glanced quickly at the masthead again. He hardly dared to look for fear his eye had deceived him. But the pendant was at a different angle. Only very slight, but it was all he had.

To Gossett he said evenly, 'The wind had veered a point, I believe?'

The master stared at him. 'Well, yes, sir. Just a mite.' He sounded surprised that it should matter.

Bolitho controlled the rising tension in his thoughts. He had to use all his will to shut out the distant crash of gunfire as the frigates engaged the solitary *Harvester*, even to crush the lurking fear that he had already misjudged the situation around him.

'Very well, Mr. Rooke. Shorten sail. Get the royals and 'gallants off her.' He gripped his hands behind him as the topmen swarmed along the yards. '*Now* you may run out the larboard battery.'

The *Hyperion* seemed to sink forward into a trough as the power died in her extra sails. The weeds on her bottom acted as a brake, and Bolitho could see the mizzen topgallant shivering like a tree in the wind and felt the vibration transmitting itself through the planks under his shoes.

Then he walked to the larboard side of the quarterdeck and leaned out to watch as the double line of gunports swung upwards, and seconds later he heard the squeal of trucks as the sweating seamen threw themselves against the tackles and hauled their heavy weapons up the canting deck. A shaft of sunlight touched the black muzzles as they poked from the open ports and Rooke called, 'Run out, sir!'

He gave a slight shiver and turned to watch the Frenchman. She was barely a cable's length astern now, and even though she too was shortening sail, would be alongside in minutes. To the French captain it would look as if Bolitho had tried to drive his convey to safety under full sail but had failed and was now falling back to accept full payment for his folly.

Bolitho licked his lips. They felt like dust. To Gossett he said slowly, 'Stand by to wear ship, Mr. Gossett. In two minutes I intend to go about across his bows!' He did not see the stunned look on Gossett's face. He was looking at the other two-decker. She had run out her starboard battery, and on her gangways he could see clumps of figures and the gleam of sunlight on levelled muskets and cutlasses.

'Aye, aye, sir!' Gossett had recovered his voice again.

To Rooke Bolitho added sharply, 'We will sail back on the same course and engage his other side!' He felt a grin spreading on his face and sensed that same madness he had forcibly controlled at Cozar.

Rooke nodded and raised his speaking trumpet. He looked pale beneath his tan, but somehow he got the words out.

'Stand by to go about! Ready ho!'

'Helm alee!' Gossett threw his own weight to help the straining helmsmen.

For a few seconds the ship seemed to go mad, and as the men in the bows let go the headsail sheets and the hull began to answer the savage demands of the rudder, even the distant gunfire was drowned by the thunder of canvas and the agonised whine of stays and rigging.

'Off tacks and sheets!' Rooke was dancing with impatience and despair. 'Mainsail *haul*!'

What the *Hyperion*'s desperate manœuvre looked like to the Frenchman Bolitho could not imagine, but as he stared fixedly at the other two-decker he felt the sweat like ice across his forehead. Perhaps he had after all left it too late. The other ship seemed to tower across the *Hyperion* quarter like a great cliff, so that as the old hull staggered round it seemed as if nothing would prevent the Frenchman from smashing headlong into her larboard side.

'Let go and haul, you bastards!' Rooke was hoarse and almost screaming. But the men at the braces were almost horizontal with the deck as they dug in their toes and tugged like madmen, their ears and minds blank to everything and their eyes filled with the tall, unrushing sails which loomed high above them blotting out all else.

But she was answering, as with a mighty roar of canvas the yards went round, the sails ballooning and cracking with effort while the deck tilted further and still further towards the Frenchman's onrushing bowsprit.

Bolitho gripped the rail and shouted, 'Stand to! Gun-captains fire as you bear! Pass the word to the lower battery!'

He was almost blinded with sweat and was shaking with wild excitement. Somehow the *Hyperion* had answered his impossible demands and had turned into the wind right across the other ship's course. Now as she heeled on an opposite tack she was already charging down the Frenchman's side, a side lined with sealed ports and as yet undefended. He could see the surging chaos on the ship's maindeck as men from the opposite battery ran across to open the ports, probably stunned by the sudden change of roles.

The *Hyperion*'s heeling bows passed the Frenchman's

forecastle, her shadow across the struggling seamen like a cloud of doom.

Inch was running along the guns, and as he dropped his arm the first pair of guns roared out together. Both ships were passing one another so rapidly that the attack was almost a full broadside, rippling down the *Hyperion*'s hull in a double line of darting red flashes.

Bolitho almost fell as the quarterdeck nine-pounders joined in the battle, while around and above him he could hear Ashby's marines yelling and cursing with excitement as they fired their muskets into the mounting wall of smoke which billowed up and across the Frenchman's side hiding the carnage and damage as they passed within twenty yards of those sealed ports.

Bolitho yelled, 'Stop that cheering! Reload and run out!' He had his sword in his hand although he did not recall drawing it. 'Larboard carronade stand by!' He saw the gunners on the forecastle staring back at him from beside the snub-nosed carronade. They were hemmed in by smoke and seemed to be suspended in space. He turned to Gossett. 'Stand by to go about again! We will cross *his* stern now that we have taken the weather-gage!'

'Look, sir! Her foretopmast's falling!'

Bolitho rubbed his streaming eyes and turned to watch as with something like tired dignity the Frenchman's topmast staggered and then began to topple. He could see small figures clinging to the severed yards, and then being shaken off like dead fruit as with a splintering crash the whole spar, compete with rigging and lacerated sails, pitched forward and down into the smoke alongside.

But the *Hyperion* was already reeling round, the men at the braces and sheets coughing and choking as the guns fired yet again, their minds dulled by the din of noise and the blinding fog of battle.

Bolitho hurried across the deck, his eyes on the smoke-shrouded topsails, pockmarked and ragged from his ship's attack, as once more the *Hyperion* went about to cross the enemy's stern. A gust of wind cleared a patch of water, so that he saw the other ship's counter within fifty feet of the bows. He could see the tall windows, the familiar horseshoe-shaped stern so beloved by French designers, and the small figures clustered above her name, *Saphir*. They were firing muskets, and as he watched he saw some of the forecastle hands falling and kicking in the smoke, their cries lost in the bombardment.

But then, as the *Hyperion*'s bowsprit cast a black shadow across the open patch of water the carronade fired. For a brief instant before the smoke eddied across the water once more he saw the whole section of stern windows fly open as if in some maniac wind, and in his mind's eye he pictured the carnage in the *Saphir*'s crowded lower gundeck as the packed charge smashed through the ship from end to end. On Cozar's pier it had been terrible enough. In a confined space filled with dazed seamen who were already unnerved by the *Hyperion*'s swift vengeance it would be like a scene from hell.

He forcibly thrust the picture from his mind and concentrated, instead on the *Hyperion*'s upper deck. As the ship tacked heavily around the Frenchman's stern the larboard battery were only getting off half the shots which they had achieved in the first assault. All the grating apprehension which had gripped the men earlier while the French ships had approached with such confidence had been replaced by a kind of delirious excitement, and as he peered down through the billowing smoke Bolitho saw more than one gunner capering with wild delight, intent on watching the havoc across the narrow strip of water rather than attending to his own duties.

Bolitho cupped his hands and shouted, 'Mr. Inch! Double up the gun crews from the starboard side, and pass the word to the lower deck to do the same!' He saw Inch nodding violently, his hat awry, his long face blackened by the powder smoke.

The *Saphir* had slewed slightly to larboard, the fallen topmast acting as a great sea anchor, so that it took more precious minutes to sail around her counter. Although *Hyperion* was now technically downwind of her adversary once more the earlier advantage had been rendered useless by the damage to the *Saphir*'s spars and sails. As the bowsprit edged purposefully past the Frenchman's high poop and the forward guns belched out with renewed anger, Bolitho saw great fragments of splintered timber flying up from the bulwarks and the flare of sparks as one of the enemy's guns was hurled bodily sideways on to its crew, the screams only urging the British gunners to greater efforts.

Then as both ships ploughed abeam through the smoke the French upper battery fired back for the first time. It was a ragged salvo, the tongues of flame lancing through the drifting fog, the crashing detonations mingling with the *Hyperion*'s broadside as the distance slowly lessened until both ships were less than thirty feet apart.

The *Saphir*'s gunners had fired on the downroll, and Bolitho felt the deck shake under him as ball after ball smashed into his ship's stout hull or shrieked towards the unseen world beyond the smoke. Men were shooting down from the French tops, and he caught a brief glimpse of an officer waving his sword and then pointing at him as if to will the marksmen to bring him down. Musket-balls slapped into the hammock nettings at his side, and he

saw a seaman staring aghast at his hand where a rico-
cheting ball had clipped away a finger with the neatness
of an axe.

Ashby's marines were yelling insults as they returned
the fire, and more than one man hung lifeless on the
French tops as silent witness to their accuracy.

Again a ragged salvo rippled along the *Saphir*'s upper
ports, but still the *Hyperion*'s masts were unscathed. Her
sails were well pitted with holes, but only a few severed
blocks and halyards bounced unheeded on the nets which
he had ordered to be strung across the upper deck to
protect the sweating gunners.

He saw a small ship's boy scurrying across the deck
bowed down with powder from the magazine. A man
was hurled from one of the twelve-pounders to lie writhing and almost disembowelled at the boy's feet. He hesitated, then blindly ran on towards his own gun, too dazed
to care for the thing which turned the planking into a
scarlet pattern with each agonised convulsion.

Up through the smoke Bolitho saw the French ensign
rising at last to the gaff. The white flag with its bright
tricolour looked strangely clean and detached from the
bedlam beneath, and he found time to wonder who had
bothered to take the trouble to hoist it.

Gossett yelled hoarsely, ''Er main tops'l 'as carried
away, sir!' He was shaking one of the helmsmen in time
with his words. 'By God, look at the bugger now!'

Ashby strode across the quarterdeck, his white
breeches splashed with blood and his sword dangling
from his wrist on a gold cord. He touched his hat, ignoring the whining musket-balls and the screams and cries
which came now from both ships.

'If you give the word, sir, we can board her! One good

rush and we can knock the backbones out of 'em!' He was actually grinning.

A marine fell back from the nettings clawing at his face and then dropped motionless to the deck. A musket-ball had smashed his skull almost in two, so that his brains spewed across the planking like porridge.

Bolitho looked away. 'No, Captain. I am afraid that much as I would like to take her as a prize I must think first of the convoy.' He saw a tall French seaman standing up on the nettings a musket trained at him with fierce concentration. He was outlined against the smoke and oblivious of everything but the need to hit and kill the British captain.

It was strange that he could stand and watch, like an onlooker, as the musket flashed brightly, the sound of the shot swallowed by the heavy guns as the *Hyperion* rocked wildly to another broadside. He felt the ball pluck at his sleeve with no more insistence than a man's fingers. He heard a shrill scream at his back and knew without looking that the ball had claimed one victim. But his gaze was held by that unknown marksman. He must be a brave man, or one so crazed with anger by what had happened to his own ship that he no longer cared for his own safety. He was still standing on his precarious perch when a nine-pound shot from the *Hyperion*'s quarterdeck battery smashed him apart, so that as his trunk and flailing arms pitched down into the churning water alongside, his legs still stayed resolute and firm for another few seconds.

The French ship was in bad shape. Her sails were little more than blackened streamers, with only a jib and mizzen course still fully intact. Thin red ribbons of blood trailed from her scuppers and ran unheeded down her battered side, and Bolitho could only guess at the extent of her casualties. It was significant that the enemy's lower gundeck with its big twenty-four-pounders remained silent and impotent, and it was a marvel that the whole ship had not burst into flames.

But he knew from hard experience that such appearances were deceptive. She could still put up a good fight, and one well-aimed salvo could cripple the *Hyperion* long enough to pare away their hard-won advantage.

He shouted, 'Mr. Rooke! T'gallants and royals, if you please!' He saw the seamen below him gaping as if they could not believe that he was going to give up the stricken two-decker. 'Then have the starboard guns run out!'

To Gossett he added firmly, 'Lay a course for the convoy! We will beat to windward and see what there is to be done.'

Petty officers were already driving the battle-drained men to the braces, and even as he looked round he saw that the Frenchman was drifting astern in the smoke. Almost jauntily the *Hyperion* gathered the wind into her pockmarked sails and pushed after the other vessels.

A naked gun-captain, his muscular torso black and shining like a Negro's, leapt on to his carriage and yelled wildly, 'A cheer for th' cap'n, lads!' He was almost beside himself as the men joined in an uncontrolled wave of yelling and cheering. One gunner even left his station on the quarterdeck and danced up and down, his bare feet flapping on the stained deck, his pigtail bobbing crazily in time with his ecstasy.

Ashby grinned. 'Can't blame 'em, sir!' He waved down at the cheering men as if to make up for Bolitho's grim features. 'That was a wonderful thing back there! My God, you handled her like a frigate! Never believed it possible. . . .'

Bolitho eyed him gravely. 'At any other time I would

190

be gratified to hear it, Captain Ashby. Now for God's sake get those men to work!' He walked quickly across to the weather side, his shoes slipping in a shining crescent of blood as he lifted his glass to look for the convoy.

As the *Hyperion* thrust herself clear of the smoke he saw the *Justice*. She was well astern of the other ships and the tumult of battle which surrounded them in another great bank of writhing smoke. Above the smoke he could see the *Harvester's* topgallants still standing, although how that could be was hard to understand. Most of her sails were gone, and the masts of a French frigate appeared to be almost alongside, yardarm to yardarm.

Sickened he saw a growing bank of flame beyond the two frigates, and as a short gust parted the smoke like a curtain he saw the little sloop *Snipe* burning like a torch as she drifted helplessly downwind. She was completely dismasted and already listing badly, but he could see the savage scars along her flush deck, the lolling corpses by her smashed and upended guns, and knew she had after all chosen not to remain an onlooker to the battle.

The transports appeared to be intact and still protected by the embattled *Harvester*, but as the smoke eddied once more the second French frigate thrust her bows clear and tacked purposefully towards the *Vanessa*. The frigate had lost her mizzen topmast, but was more than a match for the heavy merchantman. From her forecastle her two bowchasers had already opened fire, and Bolitho watched coldly as pieces of woodwork flew skyward from the *Vanessa's* ornate stern as if plucked away by the wind.

He said harshly, 'Starboard a point!' He watched the *Hyperion's* bowsprit edge across the distant ships like a relentless pointer and wondered why her disengagement from the *Saphir* had passed unnoticed.

It was only when the frigate had drawn almost across

191

the transport's stern that some sort of alarm became visible. Then it was already too late. She could not withdraw because of the helpless *Vanessa*, and she could not swing around because of the wind. Desperately she spread her courses and with her yards braced almost fore and aft heeled to the fresh breeze, until the watchers on the *Hyperion*'s decks could see the copper on her bottom gleaming like gold in the hazed sunlight.

Straight ahead, with her hard-eyed Titan below the bowsprit staring at the smoke-shrouded transport, the *Hyperion* drove purposefully past the *Vanessa*'s counter.

Bolitho lifted his sword, his voice stilling an eager gun-captain who even now was tugging at his trigger line.

'On the downroll!' The sword gleamed in the sunlight, and to some aboard the struggling frigate it was probably the last sight on earth. 'Now!' The sword flashed down, and as the *Hyperion* eased herself heavily into a trough and the double line of muzzles tilted towards the sea the air split apart in one savage broadside. It was the first time the starboard battery had fired, and the full fury of the double-shotted charges smashed the frigate's unprotected bilge with the force and devastation of an avalanche.

The enemy ship seemed to lift and then stagger upright, her fore and mainmasts falling as one in a thrashing tangle of rigging and brightly splintered spars.

There were just a few minutes before the *Hyperion* was hidden from the frigate by the *Vanessa*, but the gunners needed no more urging. As the bowsprit and flapping headsails passed the transport's mauled stern the whole starboard battery fired again, the hail of balls ripping down the remaining mast and turning the low hull into a floating ruin.

The men were cheering again, and it was taken up by

the men on the *Vanessa*'s poop. The latter had fallen
back when the last broadside had swept past them, and
some must have thought that the *Hyperion*'s rage was so
great she could no longer distinguish between friend and
foe.

By now her seamen were climbing into the weather rigging to wave and cheer as the old two-decker loomed
abeam, and more than one wept uncontrollably as her
seamen cheered them back.

Bolitho gripped his fingers behind him to stop them
shaking. 'Signal the *Justice* to make more sail and resume proper station!'

Caswell was nodding dazedly, but in spite of his
shocked senses was still able to call his men to the halyards.

'Deck there! T'other frigate is haulin' off, sir!' The
masthead lookout sounded as wild as the rest of them.

Caswell lowered his glass and confirmed the news.
'*Harvester* has just signalled, sir. She cannot give chase.
Too much damage aloft.'

Bolitho nodded. It was no wonder. *Harvester*'s captain had given battle to two frigates at once, aided only
by the tiny *Snipe*. He was lucky to be alive.

He said, 'Signal the *Harvester*, Mr. Caswell.' He
frowned with effort to clear his mind and concentrate on
what was needed. It must not sound trite and meaningless. *Harvester*'s people had shown what they could do.
Nothing he could say would ever match their value. He
said slowly, 'Make, "Yours was a fine harvest today.
Well done." '

Caswell was scribbling frantically on his slate as he added, 'And I don't care if you have to spell out every
single word!'

He shaded his eyes as with a sullen hiss the sloop

193

rolled over to her beam ends, the water around her pock-marked with flotsam and burned woodwork.

Gossett said gruffly, 'The *Erebus* 'as lowered boats to look for survivors, sir.'

Bolitho did not answer. Not many seamen ever bothered to learn how to swim. There would be few to recall the sloop's last and greatest fight.

Heavily he said, 'I want a full report of our damage and casualties, Mr. Rooke.'

Rooke was still staring at the enemy ships. The dismasted frigate was yawning uncontrollably, beam on to the steep troughs, and it would be some time before she could be taken in tow. It was more likely she would sink as she lay. The other frigate was closing the battered two-decker, and above the drifting smoke the signal flags were bright and busy.

Bolitho said, 'We must attend to our convoy. Those two will have to wait another day for final reckoning.' He spoke aloud, but it was almost as if he was speaking with his ship.

Caswell shouted, '*Justice* has acknowledged, sir!' He grinned. 'So has *Harvester*.' He looked around at the other strained and grimy faces. 'She says, "Have discontinued the action!"'

Bolitho felt his lips cracking with a smile. The formality of Leach's reply spoke volumes for the man's tenacity. 'Acknowledge.'

He saw one of the surgeon's mates standing below the ladder, his arms bloody to the elbows. He felt the same pang of despair he had known so often in the past. The suffering and the mutilation which made victory so bitter.

'What is it?'

The man looked vaguely around the deck as if surprised it was still intact. Below the waterline, with the ship wilting and shuddering to the broadsides, it was no easy task to deal with screaming wounded.

'Surgeon's respects, zur. Mr. Dalby 'as bin 'it, zur, an' wishes to speak with you.'

Bolitho shook himself. Dalby? The lieutenant's face floated before his eyes as he had last seen it. Then he said, 'How bad is he?'

The man shook his head. 'Matter o' minutes, zur!'

'Take over the deck, Mr. Rooke. Signal the convoy to resume previous order once *Erebus* has recovered her boats.'

Rooke touched his hat as he passed. 'Aye, aye, sir.'

Bolitho climbed down the ladder, suddenly aware of the stiffness in his limbs, the aching tension in his jaw. Beside their smoking guns his men watched him pass. Here and there a braver soul than the rest reached out to touch his coat, and one even called, 'God bless you, Cap'n!'

Bolitho saw and heard none of it. It was taking all his strength to move between them, and he was conscious only of one thing. They had fought and won. It should be left at that. But as always he knew the cost was yet to be measured.

. . .

Bolitho ducked his head beneath the low beams and groped his way through the semi-darkness of the orlop deck. By comparison the air and light of the quarterdeck even at the height of the battle was fresh and clear, for down here deep in the *Hyperion's* hull there was little ventilation, and his stomach rebelled against the mingled stenches of bilge and tar, of neat rum and the more sickly smell of blood.

Rowlstone, the surgeon, had soon found that his tiny sick bay was quite inadequate for the casualties sent down from the decks above, and as Bolitho stepped into a circle of swaying lanterns he saw that the whole area forward of the mainmast's massive trunk was filled with wounded men. *Hyperion* was plunging heavily in a lively quarter sea, so that the lanterns kept up a crazy haphazard motion and threw weird dancing shadows against the curved sides, or picked out small tableaux for just a few seconds at a time like sections of an old and faded painting.

Above the sounds of groaning timbers and the muffled pounding of water against the hull Bolitho heard the confused murmur of voices, mingled with sobbing and an occasional sharp cry of agony. For the most part the wounded lay still, only their eyes moving in the gyrating lanterns as they stared dully at the little group around the heavy scrubbed table, where Rowlstone, his suety face screwed up with concentration, worked on a seaman who was being held down by two of his loblolly boys. Like any badly wounded man the sailor had been well dosed with rum, and as Rowlstone's saw moved relentlessly across his leg he lolled his head from side to side, his cries muffled by the leather strap between his teeth, his frantic protests drowned by both rum and vomit.

Rowlstone worked busily, his fingers as bloody as the heavy apron which covered him from chin to toe. Then he gestured to his assistants and unceremoniously the seaman was hauled from the table and carried into the merciful darkness beyond the lanterns.

The surgeon looked up and saw Bolitho. Surrounded by wounded and mutilated men he seemed suddenly frail and vulnerable.

Bolitho asked quietly, 'How many?'

'Ten dead, sir.' The surgeon wiped his forehead with

his arm, leaving a red smear above his right eye. 'So far.' He glanced round as two of his assistants half-carried another man towards the table. Like so many wounded in a sea action he had been hit by wood splinters, and as the surgeon's mates tore off his stained trousers Bolitho could see the great jagged tooth of wood where it jutted from below his stomach. Rowlstone stared unwinkingly at the man for several seconds. Then he said flatly, 'Some thirty wounded, sir. Half of them might live through it.'

Another man was slopping rum into the wounded seaman's open mouth. He did not seem to be able to drink the neat spirit fast enough, and all the time his eyes were fixed on Rowlstone's hands with the fascination of hope and terror combined.

The surgeon groped for his knife and gestured towards the side. 'Mr. Dalby's over there.' He eyed the man on the table with something like despair and added, 'Like most of the men he got his wound on the lower gundeck.'

Bolitho turned towards the side as the surgeon bent forward across the naked body on the table. The wounded man had gone immediately rigid, and Bolitho could almost feel the first pressure of that knife in his own body.

Dalby was propped in a sitting position with his shoulders against one of the ship's massive ribs. He was naked but for a wide, sodden bandage around his stomach, and with each painful breath the blood was spreading unchecked even by the thick dressing. As officer in charge of the lower battery he had been cut down by the first French broadside, yet in spite of his wound his face seemed almost relaxed as he opened his eyes and stared up at his captain.

Bolitho dropped on his knees. 'Is there anything I can do?'

Dalby swallowed hard, and a few droplets of blood glistened on his lips. 'Wanted to see you, sir!' He gripped the mattress at his sides and held his breath. 'Had to tell you . . .'

'Don't talk, Mr. Dalby.' Bolitho looked round for a clean dressing, but finding none dabbed the lieutenant's mouth with his handkerchief.

But Dalby tried to struggle forward, his eyes suddenly bright. 'It has been driving me mad, sir! That money . . . I took it.' He fell back against the timbers, his mouth slack. 'Quarme had nothing to do with it. I *had* to have it, d'you see? Had to!'

Bolitho watched him sadly. It did not really matter any more who had taken the money. Quarme was dead, and Dalby should by rights have followed him already.

'It is all right, Mr. Dalby. It is over now.'

Dalby shuddered, his chest and arms suddenly running with sweat. Yet when Bolitho touched him his skin was cold and clammy like that of a corpse.

Then he muttered thickly, 'I owed money. Gambled everything.' He stared at Bolitho, but his eyes no longer held a proper focus. 'I would have told him, but . . .'

Behind Bolitho a man screamed. The sound seemed to scrape at the walls of his mind, but he leaned forward trying to hear what Dalby was saying. The blood was running more freely from his mouth, and with sudden despair Bolitho turned and peered beyond the nearest lantern to where a midshipman was stooping over another stripped and bandaged seaman. 'You, lad, bring me a dressing!'

The midshipman turned and hurried towards him, a clean bandage held out ready.

But Bolitho stared up in shocked surprise. 'In the name of God, Miss Seton, what are you doing here?'

The girl did not answer immediately, but dropped beside Dalby and began to dab the blood and spittle from his face and chest. Even in the lantern's yellow glare Bolitho's mistake was not very obvious. In the midshipman's coat and white breeches, and with her thick auburn hair pulled back to the nape of her neck she passed easily as a young boy.

Dalby stared at her and tried to smile. He said, 'Never a boat, miss! We call her a ship in th' . . .' His head lolled to one side and he was dead.

Bolitho said, 'I ordered that you should stay in the midshipmen's berth until I said otherwise!' His sick despair was giving way to something akin to anger. 'This is no place at all for you!' He could see the bloodstains on her coat and across the front of her open-necked shirt.

She faced him gravely, her eyes studying him with sudden concern. 'You do not have to worry on my account. I saw enough of death in Jamaica.' She pushed a strand of her hair from her eyes. 'When the guns started to fire I wanted to help.' She looked down at Dalby. 'I *needed* to help.' When she raised her eyes again they were almost pleading. 'Don't you see that?' She reached out and gripped his sleeve. 'Please do not be angry!'

Bolitho looked slowly around the littered deck. The naked bodies, dead and wounded alike, lay like macabre statuary, and at his table Rowlstone worked on as if nothing else mattered beyond the swaying circle of lanterns.

Then he replied quietly, 'I am not angry. I suppose I was afraid for you. Now I feel ashamed.' He wanted to get to his feet but was unable to move.

She said, 'I listened to the noise and felt the ship shaking about me as if it would tear apart. And all the time I thought of you, out in the open. Unprotected.'

Bolitho did not speak but watched the quick movements of her hands, the rise and fall of her breasts as she relived each terrible moment.

She continued, 'Then I came here to help these men. I thought they would curse me, or abuse me for being alive and unmarked.' She dropped her eyes and Bolitho saw her mouth tremble. 'They cursed and swore well enough, but they never complained, not once!' She met his eyes again, her expression almost proud. 'And when they heard you were coming down they actually tried to cheer!'

Bolitho stood up and helped the girl to her feet. She was crying now, but without tears, and she did not resist as he piloted her through the lanterns towards the companionway.

On deck it seemed unfair that the sun was still so bright, that the ships sailed on without a thought for what lay astern or those whom they carried. Across the quarterdeck with its great red stains and splintered planks. Past the helmsmen who watched the swinging compass and stared up at the set of each pockmarked sail.

At the cabin door Bolitho said quietly. 'Promise me you will lie down.'

She turned and looked up at him her eyes searching. 'Must you go now?' Then she gave a small shrug, or it may have been a shudder. 'That was a foolish thing to say! I know what you must do. It is all out there waiting for you.' The swing of her hand seemed to indicate the whole ship and every man aboard. She touched his arm unsurely and added, 'I saw the look in your eyes and I think I understand you better now.'

A voice called urgently, 'Captain, sir! *Harvester* requests permission to heave to and carry out burials!'

'Very well.' Bolitho still looked down at the girl's face, his mind rebelling against the thousand and one things which awaited his attention.

He said at length, 'You did well today. I will not forget.'

As he turned towards the sunlight he heard her reply softly, 'And neither will I, Captain!'

10

A Good Officer

Sir Edmund Pomfret stood at one side of the great stern windows in his day cabin, being careful to avoid the rectangle of hard sunlight thrown back from the harbour beyond. He had maintained the same stance throughout Bolitho's report, with his feet apart, arms folded across his chest and his back turned so that it was impossible to see his face or gauge his mood.

Hyperion had dropped anchor below the hill fortress in the early morning after waiting until the transports and the battle-scarred *Harvester* had preceded her into the sheltering arms of the natural harbour. Bolitho had half-expected to be summoned aboard the *Tenacious* immediately, but for reasons best known to himself Pomfret had waited until seven bells of the forenoon watch before issuing his curt signal, 'Captain repair on board forthwith.'

Now as he concluded his description of the battle to

defend the convoy Bolitho could feel the tiredness sapping his strength like a drug, and was able to listen to his own words with something like disinterest, as if they concerned someone else entirely.

Pomfret had not asked him to sit down, and he was conscious the whole time of the cabin's other occupant, a florid-faced army colonel whom Pomfret had briefly introduced as Sir Torquil Cobban, the officer commanding the soldiers encamped on Cozar. But Pomfret had remained standing also, and in spite of his straddled legs and unmoving shoulders he seemed edgy and irritable.

The admiral said suddenly, 'So you lost the *Snipe*, did you?'

It sounded like an accusation, but Bolitho replied wearily, 'If I had had another escort things might have been different, sir.'

Pomfret's head bobbed impatiently. 'If, if! That's all I hear these days!' In a calmer tone he added, 'And your own losses?'

'A total of sixteen dead and twenty-six wounded, sir. Most of the latter seem to be holding their own.'

'Hmm.' Pomfret turned slowly and walked to his table where lay a huge coloured chart. He said offhandedly. 'I would have waited a few more days for you, but after that I intended to sail with or without these supplies.' He shot Bolitho a searching glance. 'I have received news from Lord Hood. His forces have landed at Toulon, and my orders are to proceed with the capture of St. Clar.'

'Yes, sir.' Bolitho had been waiting for this news, but now that it had come it seemed like an anticlimax. He knew Pomfret and the colonel were studying him and made an effort to control his thoughts. He asked, 'Do you wish me to make another parley with the town, sir?'

Pomfret frowned. 'Certainly not. I have not been idle while you have been away. Everything is in hand, I can assure you.' He smiled quickly at the soldier. 'The Frogs will have to watch their manners now, eh?'

Colonel Cobban spoke for the first time. He had a thick, resonant voice, and had a habit of tapping his fingers on his impeccable scarlet tunic with each word.

'God, yes! With General Carteau marching on Toulon, our new "allies" in St. Clar have no choice but to support us.' He seemed to be enjoying the idea.

Pomfret nodded. 'Now, Bolitho, I want you to get your ship ready for sea without delay.'

'The repairs are well in hand, sir. In the four days following the battle we have set all the damage to sails and cordage to rights, and most of the internal repairs are almost completed.'

Pomfret was peering at his chart and did not see the sudden change in Bolitho's expression. Four days. In spite of a constant guard it was all coming back to him. He had hoped that the safe return with his transports, the sudden prospect of action, even the efforts to ensure that his ship was ready and able to fight again, all these things would push the memory of those four short days to the back of his mind until time and distance made them too blurred to hurt him. Without effort he could recall the girl's face as she had listened to him talking about his ship, while together at the quarterdeck rail they had watched the seamen and carpenters working to put right the damage and to clean away the scars and stains of battle.

On the second evening just before sunset Bolitho had walked with her along the weather gangway, pointing out something of the complex maze of rigging and halyards, the very sinews of the ship's strength.

Once she had said quietly, 'Thank you for explaining it to me. You have made the ship *live* with your words.'

She had not been bored or amused. She had been really interested, even though he had spoken as he had simply because it was the only thing he knew, the only life he understood.

He had realised at that moment that she had unwittingly touched on the truth. He had replied. 'I am glad you see her like that.' He had gestured to the shadowy guns below the gangway. 'People see a ship like this pass far out to sea, but they rarely think of those who serve and live in her.' He had stared at the deserted forecastle and had found himself wondering about all those other men who had gone before him, and those who might follow. 'Here a man died. There another wrote poetry maybe. Men join ships like these as boys, as wide-eyed infants, and grow to be men beneath the same suits of sails.' He had touched the rail at his side. 'You are right, she is not just *wood*!'

And another evening they had dined together for the first time in the cabin, and again she had drawn him out, had listened to him speaking of his home in Cornwall, of his voyages and the ships he had seen and served.

But as the miles rolled away under the *Hyperion*'s keel they seemed both to sense that the strange feeling of comfort and understanding was becoming something more. Neither spoke of it, yet during the last two days they appeared to draw apart, even to avoid meeting other than in company.

Within minutes of the anchor splashing down a boat had come alongside, and with it Lieutenant Fanshawe,

Pomfret's aide, to collect her. She had come on to the quarterdeck wearing that same green dress as when he had first seen her, and had stared across at the grim fortress and the barren hills beyond.

Bolitho had seen many of his men standing on the gangways or watching from aloft, and had sensed the feeling of sadness which hung over the ship. Even the petty officers seemed unable or unwilling to drive the hands back to work, and had watched with the rest as the girl had bravely shaken hands with the assembled officers and had kissed her brother on the cheek.

Bolitho had kept his voice as formal as he knew how. 'We shall miss you. We *all* will.' He had seen Gossett nodding in agreement. 'I am sorry that you were made to suffer as you did . . .' Then his words had run out.

She had looked at him with something like bewilderment in her eyes, as if the sight of Cozar had at last made her realise that the voyage was at an end. Then she had said, 'Thank you, Captain. You made me very comfortable.' She had looked around the silent faces. 'It is something I will never forget.' Then without another glance she had gone down to the boat.

With a start he realised that Pomfret was saying, '. . . and I trust you will make good the depletions in your company from *Snipe*'s survivors, and any spare hands you can obtain from the transports.'

'Yes, sir.' He forcibly made himself concentrate on the many details yet to be settled. Dalby was dead, and he had promoted Caswell to acting lieutenant to fill the gap in his officers. That was how it went. A man died. Another moved up the ladder.

Some of the more badly wounded must be taken ashore or to one of the transports where they could be properly looked after. There was fresh shot and powder to take on board, and countless other matters as well.

Cobban stood up, his high polished boots squeaking noisily. He was a tall man and on his feet seemed to dwarf Pomfret. He said, 'Well, I'll be off. I must instruct my officers to make final preparations. If we are to take St. Clar on the fifth we must make sure of everything.' He readjusted his sword and frowned. 'But then, September will be a mite cooler for marching, eh? Either way my troops will do as they are told.'

Bolitho, watching the colonel's tight mouth, knew it was unlikely that he would show much concern for his officers, let alone his private soldiers.

Pomfret waited until Cobban had departed and then said irritably, 'Very tiresome having to deal with the military, but I suppose under the circumstances . . .' He touched the chart vaguely and then asked, 'I trust that Miss Seton was in a place of safety during the, er, battle?'

Perhaps it had been uppermost on Bolitho's mind, or maybe his tiredness was playing tricks, but Pomfret sounded on edge, even suspicious.

He replied, 'She was, sir.' He dropped his eyes as the picture of the naked, screaming figures on the orlop, the swinging lanterns, and the girl in her blood-spattered jacket and breeches moved back into his thoughts.

'Good.' Pomfret nodded. 'Very good, I am glad to hear it. I have had her taken to quarters in the fortress. They will suffice until . . .' He did not finish the sentence. He did not have to.

Bolitho said flatly, 'My carpenters have made a few pieces of furniture. I thought that they might help to make the fortress a little more comfortable for Miss Seton.'

Pomfret eyed him for several seconds. 'Considerate. Most considerate. Yes, you can send them over if you

206

wish.' He walked to the windows and added quickly, 'We sail on the first of the month. Just have your ship ready by that time.' He was staring at the black-hulled convict ship which was anchored at the head of the transports. 'Scum! The sweepings of Newgate, I imagine. But they will suffice for what remains to be done here.' Then without turning he said, 'Carry on, Bolitho.'

Bolitho walked out to the dazzling sunlight, realising suddenly that Pomfret had not once congratulated him or his men on saving the precious supply ships and even managing to cripple two of the attackers at the same time. It was typical of the man, he thought bitterly. Pomfret obviously took such efforts for granted. Only if they had failed would he have made any real comment, and he could imagine what that would have been.

In silence he climbed into his barge and settled himself in the sternsheets. As the oars rose and dipped like wings he thought of Dalby and the empty desperation of his last words. Gambling. It was the curse and the despair of many other officers. Confined to their ships for months at a time, thrust on one another's company and separated by rigid discipline from the men they controlled, it was common enough for such men as Dalby to lose everything on the flick of a card. What started out as a safe distraction became real and overwhelming as the losers fought to regain their dwindling money by betting with wealth they did not possess.

Bolitho knew the true dangers of such behaviour. His own brother had broken his father's heart by deserting from the Navy after killing a brother officer in a senseless duel over a gambling debt.

He shook himself from his brooding and said sharply, 'Pull for the transport yonder!'

Allday looked up at him. 'The *Erebus*, Captain?'

Bolitho nodded. 'The survivors of the *Snipe* are aboard her.'

Allday eased the tiller and said nothing. It was hardly a post-captain's task to go looking for a few casual recruits, and there could not be more than a handful who had survived, but he knew from experience that Bolitho was deeply troubled. When he was like that it was better to say nothing at all.

As it happened the captain of the *Erebus* was waiting to receive Bolitho, his tanned features split in a great grin of welcome.

'I wanted to thank you, Captain!' He pumped Bolitho's hand mercilessly. 'You saved my ship, an' I never saw the like! When your old *Hyperion* tacked round under the Frog's bowsprit I thought you were done for!'

Bolitho let him go on for several minutes then said, 'Thank you, Captain. Now I expect you have guessed why I am here?'

He nodded. 'Aye. But I'm afraid there are only six hands and an officer fit enough for you. There are three more besides, but I fear they'll die before the week is out.' He broke off and stared suddenly at Bolitho's face. 'Are you ill, sir?' He took his arm and added, 'You have gone quite pale!'

Bolitho shook himself free, cursing the man's kindness and his own unpreparedness as the old fever stirred like a raw wound, and he felt the deck slanting beneath his feet as if the ship was in a gale instead of a sheltered harbour.

He replied harshly, 'I will return to my ship, Captain. It is nothing . . .' He looked round, searching for Allday, suddenly fearful of collapsing here in front of the other captain and his men.

It was worse than usual. He did not remember it being so bad since he had left Kent to take passage for Gibraltar. His mind seemed to be revolving like his vision, so that even the *Erebus*'s captain appeared to sway as if in a heat haze.

But Allday was here. He could feel his fingers gentle but firm on his arm and allowed himself to be guided to the ladder, his shoes catching on the deck planks like a blind man's.

The other captain called, 'The sloop's officer, sir! Shall I send him across?' It was a question merely to cover his own embarrassment. He knew that if he tried to help Bolitho it would only add to his pain.

Bolitho tried to speak, but he was shivering so badly that the words would not come.

He heard Allday snarl, 'Eyes in the boat there!' and he guessed his barge crew were all watching and probably laughing at him.

Allday looked up at the other captain and said gruffly, 'Send him across, sir. He'll be needed right enough.'

The *Erebus*'s captain nodded. He did not even seem to notice that it was a mere coxswain who was giving him his orders.

Bolitho said faintly, 'Get me to the ship, Allday! For the love of God get me to her *quickly*!'

Allday wrapped the boatcloak around Bolitho's shoulders and cradled him against his arm. But for it he knew Bolitho would fall down to the bottom of the boat like a corpse. He had seen it all before, and he was filled with pity and something like love. He was angry, too. Angry with the admiral who had kept Bolitho waiting when anyone but a blind fool could have seen what the battle had done to his reserves of inner strength.

He barked, 'Shove off! Give way together!' As the

oars rose and fell he added coldly, '*Roundly! Pull like
you've never pulled before!*' He looked down at Bolitho's
strained features and said half to himself, 'That's the
least you can do for *him*!'

* * * *

Bolitho opened his eyes very slowly and stared for a full
minute at the deckhead above his cot. For once the dull
roaring in his ears seemed to have faded, and he was suddenly conscious of the intrusion of shipboard noises and
once more he could hear the steady sluice of water against
the hull and the far-off sounds of voices.

Almost timidly he tried to move his arms and legs
but the layers of blankets held him so tightly that he lay
still and tried to assemble his thoughts into some sort of
order. He could remember leaving the *Erebus* in his
barge, even to the extent that he could still feel the agony
of waiting to reach the safety of this cabin. It had seemed
as if the *Hyperion* would never draw any closer, and all
the while he had fought to stay upright in the tossing boat,
aware vaguely of the sweating oarsmen and Allday's arm
around his shoulders.

But the actual moment of climbing aboard had gone
completely. The memories were all jumbled together in
crude half-pictures of swaying figures and distorted,
meaningless voices around him. The fever had raged like
a tormenting nightmare, with faces sweeping occasionally
above him and hands holding or moving him, over which
he had no control. Some of the time he must have been
dreaming, only to awake shivering and retching uncontrollably with a throat so dry that he felt his tongue swollen to such a degree that he imagined himself choking to
death.

210

Either awake or in an exhausted sleep he had also been aware of a white triangle that bore no relation or meaning to anything he had ever known before. It seemed to come and go like a tiny sail, never close enough to identify, yet in his reeling mind it appeared to hold a magic quality of comfort.

He turned his head slowly, feeling the sweat on his pillow and the clammy embrace of the sheets. Beside the cot, round-shouldered with concentration, Gimlett was watching him, his body appearing to sway back and forth like a human pendulum.

Bolitho asked, 'How long have I been here?' He hardly recognised his own voice.

Gimlett reached out and plucked at the pillow in an effort to make it more comfortable. 'Three days, sir.' He gave a yelp of alarm as Bolitho tried to push the blankets aside.

'*Three days!*' Bolitho stared around the small compartment with disbelief. 'In God's name get me up!'

Allday's figure moved across his vision, his face set in a grim smile of satisfaction. 'Easy, Captain! You've had a bad time.' Then he reached down and tucked the blankets even tighter.

Bolitho felt his eyes clouding with helpless anger. 'Damn you, Allday! Help me up! I am *ordering* you, d'you hear?'

But Allday only stared at him with complete calm. 'I'm sorry, Captain. But the surgeon said that you were to stay until he . . .'

Bolitho suddenly realised that the cot was swinging steadily and both Gimlett and Allday were *really* swaying. As he twisted his head round he saw the red sunlight darting across the deckhead as the ship lifted and plunged in a steady swell.

He murmured thickly, 'My God, we are at sea!' He saw Allday dart a quick glance at Gimlett and added desperately, 'How did Rooke manage to get her out of the harbour?'

Allday stepped closer, his face near enough for Bolitho to see the shadows of strain beneath his eyes. 'It is all right, Captain, *believe* me!' He gestured towards the open window. 'We are anchored to the east'rd of Cozar, below the Moorish fort. We came out this forenoon as smooth as a young girl's belly!'

But Bolitho would not be consoled. For three days while he had lain useless and incapable in his cot the small invasion fleet had been preparing to get under way. Signals must have poured from the flagship to every captain in the harbour, and what Pomfret must be thinking was past consideration.

He said, 'What time is it?'

'Three bells of the First Dog, Captain.' Allday sat down on a stool and stretched his legs. 'The squadron will sail in company tomorrow morning.'

Bolitho said, 'Are there despatches for me?' He tensed, not knowing what to expect.

Allday's reply was even more surprising. 'All taken care of, Captain.' Now that Bolitho was pulling out of the fever's grip he seemed almost cheerful. 'The admiral has sent his orders across, but nobody outside o' this ship knows a thing about your illness, that I can promise!'

Bolitho closed his eyes. It was not difficult to picture Allday and Gimlett watching over him. The weariness on their faces, the obvious pleasure at his recovery spoke volumes. But to keep his wretched fever a secret from the assembled squadron called for much more than the efforts of a coxswain and a buck-toothed steward. He

felt his eyes pricking with sudden emotion at the realisation that his whole ship's company must have made it
possible.

Allday said quietly, 'There is nothing to fear, Captain. You must be strong and well again so that you can
keep us out o' trouble.' He grinned. 'All this harbour
routine is good training for the young gentlemen.' He
watched as Bolitho opened his eyes and added, 'The
officer from *Snipe* has taken charge and has been acting
first lieutenant the whole time. The flagship has approved, Captain.' He controlled the smile on his lips.
'It just awaits your confirmation.'

Bolitho allowed his limbs to fall limp. That explained
it. Rooke could never have coped on his own.

Quietly he said, 'He must be a good officer.'

'Oh, he is!' The grin could no longer be held in check.

Bolitho stared from one to the other with mounting
exasperation. 'Well? What are you so damn happy
about?' The effort of shouting made his head fall back
to the pillow, and he did not even resist as Gimlett wiped
his forehead with a damp cloth.

There was a movement beyond the screen door and
Allday said calmly, 'That'll be him, Captain.' He did not
wait for Bolitho to speak further but stood up and opened
the door.

The *Hyperion* had swung slightly at her cable, so that
the small cabin was thrown momentarily into deep
shadow. But as Bolitho craned his head to stare at the
figure framed in the door he imagined for a few seconds
that he was still gripped in a feverish dream. For there
was the white triangle. But as he strained his eyes and
blinked away the mist he realised that it was no figment
of imagination or part of any nightmare. The lieutenant
had one arm across his body in a white sling, so that

213

against his shadowed figure it indeed gleamed like a small sail.

But Bolitho forgot his fever and his apprehension as the ship swung slowly back again and the filtered sunlight fell full across the man's face. He still could not find the words, and he knew that the other man was gripped by the same emotion.

Then he said, 'For God's sake tell me I am not dreaming!'

Allday laughed with sudden excitement. 'It's him, Captain, Lieutenant Thomas Herrick as ever was!'

Bolitho tugged his hand from the blankets and seized Herrick's across the side of the cot. 'It's *good* to see you, Thomas.' He felt the pressure returned, firm and hard, as he remembered it from the past.

Herrick watched him gravely. 'And I can't tell you how I feel, sir.' He shook his head. 'You've had a bad passage, but things will soon be all right again.'

Bolitho could not release his hand. 'Things *will* get better now, Thomas!'

The excitement and shock of seeing Herrick again had left him suddenly exhausted, but he said, 'Where have you been? What have you been doing?'

Allday interrupted, 'I think you should rest a while, Captain. Later on I can ...'

Bolitho croaked, 'Shut up, damn you! Or I'll have you flogged!'

But Herrick said, 'He is right, sir. You rest and I will tell you all my news, what there is of it.'

Bolitho relaxed and closed his eyes as Herrick continued in the same level tones he remembered so well. Without effort he could see him as the stubborn, idealistic lieutenant aboard the *Phalarope* in the West Indies, and again in the frigate *Tempest* in the vast wilderness of the

214

Great South Sea. Above all else he could see him as what he was, a loyal, trusted friend.

Herrick had changed a little since he had last seen him. His body was more stocky now, and there were streaks of grey in his hair. But his face was still round and competent, and the eyes which watched him over the cot were as bright and blue as on their first meeting.

Herrick was saying quietly, 'When we paid off the *Tempest* in '91 I had every intention of sticking out for another ship with you, sir. I think you knew that.' He sighed. 'But when I got home to Rochester I found my father dead and money too short for anything beyond staying alive. My father had been a clerk and did not even own the house we grew up in. And I was on half pay, so I had no choice but to take what I could get. I shipped out in an East Indiaman, something I swore never to do, and was lucky to get it with the best part of the Navy paid off and kicking their heels on the beach. I thought maybe when I got back to England you'd be fit and well again, but by that time we were at war again.'

Bolitho said slowly, 'I tried to find you, Thomas.' He did not open his eyes but felt Herrick tense beside him.

'You did, sir?'

'I went to Rochester. I met your mother and the sister you have supported all these years. I never knew she was a cripple.'

Herrick sounded stunned. 'She never said you'd been there!'

'I told her to say nothing. You were away at sea, and knowing you of old I guessed you would leave that security if you thought I had a ship to offer. And I did not at that time.'

Herrick sighed again. 'They were difficult days, sir. But I picked up a berth in the *Snipe* and sailed with the

215

convict convoy from Torbay. At Gibraltar we got new orders, and the rest you know.'

Bolitho opened his eyes and studied Herrick's face intently. 'But your captain, Tudor, came aboard at Gibraltar. He knew I wanted a seasoned first lieutenant, and must have told you.'

Herrick looked away. 'He told me. But I deserted you after the *Tempest* paid off. I was not going to use an old friendship to gain me fresh favours.'

Bolitho smiled sadly. 'You've not changed, Thomas! Still the proud one!' He continued, 'The *Snipe*'s loss was a hard blow for you. With the war expanding as it is you would have got command in no time. Post rank would have followed, and you would have what you richly deserve.' He saw the sudden embarrassment on Herrick's face and said, 'When we capture St. Clar they will be wanting a senior lieutenant to command the sloop *Fairfax*, if she's still there!' He tried to struggle up on to his elbows but Herrick forced him back to the pillow. 'You *must* go to Sir Edmund, Thomas! If you stay in this ship you'll never get the chance of commanding that sloop!'

Herrick stood up and fidgeted with his sling. 'I missed my way once, sir. I'd rather stay with you, if you'll have me.' He saw Bolitho twist his face away and added firmly, 'That is how I want it, sir.'

Bolitho turned and studied him, not knowing what to say.

Then Herrick smiled, so that in the half-light he looked almost boyish. 'Besides which, I know I'll stand a better chance of prize-money if I keep with you, sir. And don't forget I was Pomfret's third lieutenant when he commanded *Phalarope*. If there are any favours in the offing he might well be disposed towards me!'

216

Bolitho said quietly, 'You can joke about it, Thomas. I think you have made the wrong decision.' He reached out and gripped his hand again. 'But by God it's good to have you aboard!'

As Herrick moved out of his vision Gimlett said, 'I think you had better take some soup, zur.'

Bolitho answered firmly, 'Take it away! I am getting up directly, if only to get away from your clumsy hands!'

Allday looked across at the steward and winked. Under his breath he said, 'I think the captain *is* feeling better!'

* * * * *

The following day dawned bright and clear, and when Bolitho walked out on to the quarterdeck the salt wind in his face was better than any tonic. Also it had freshened during the night, and when he glanced up at the mast-head pendant he saw that it was whipping out to its full length.

Herrick watched him walk to the quarterdeck rail and then touched his hat. 'Anchor's hove short, sir. Ready to get under way.' His tone was formal, but as their eyes met Bolitho felt something like the excitement of sharing a secret.

'Very good, Mr. Herrick.' He took a telescope and moved it across the other anchored ships. It was a small force, but none the less impressive, and to Bolitho, who was more used to the independence granted a frigate captain, it seemed almost like a fleet.

Tugging at their cables at carefully spaced intervals were the other two line-of-battle ships. The Spanish *Princesa* was less gaily festooned with bunting than before, and Bolitho guessed that Pomfret must have had something to say about the matter for her to present such a

217

sober appearance. The *Tenacious* was closest inshore, and as he watched he saw fresh flags breaking from her yards and a sudden burst of activity on her upper deck.

Midshipman Piper squeaked, 'From *Flag*! Up anchor, sir!'

From the lee side of the quarterdeck Caswell growled, 'You should have seen that signal earlier, Mr. Piper!'

Bolitho hid a smile as the humbled Piper murmured a suitable apology. As an acting lieutenant Caswell was apparently well able to forget that only four days ago he had been doing Piper's work and taking all the kicks, justified or otherwise.

Bolitho said, 'Get the ship under way, if you please. Lay a course to weather the headland.'

Herrick raised his speaking trumpet, his voice and movements unhurried. 'Stand by the capstan! Loose heads'ls!'

Bolitho crossed to the nettings and watched the troopship *Welland* and the two supply vessels he had escorted from Gibraltar going through the orderly confusion of making sail.

Piper said loudly, 'Signal from *Flag*, sir. Make haste!'

Herrick half-turned and then yelled, 'Loose tops'ls!' He was shading his eyes as he followed the desperate activity above the deck, as first one then a second sail billowed out to thunder impatiently against the fresh wind.

'Anchor's aweigh, sir!'

That was Rooke's voice, and Bolitho wondered how he felt about Herrick's arrival as his superior.

Herrick snapped, 'Braces there! You, Mr. Tomlin, drive those idlers aft! Get 'em on the mizzen braces!'

Bolitho shivered, but not from fever. It was the old thrill and excitement coming back to him as strongly as ever. And he need have no fears on Herrick's part. After a clumsy, deep-hulled Indiaman, probably crewed by semi-articulate seamen from a dozen countries, he would find the *Hyperion*'s well-drilled company something of a relief.

Wheeling ponderously like armoured knights the three ships of the line tacked slowly around the island's crumbling headland. With *Tenacious* in the lead and *Hyperion* and *Princesa* following at quarter-mile intervals they made a formidable and splendid picture.

The three transports, their decks crammed with red-coated soldiers, tacked more carefully to leeward, whilst ahead and astern the sloops *Chanticleer* and *Alisma* acted like sheepdogs around a valuable flock.

The battered *Harvester* had remained in harbour to complete her repairs, and until more help arrived would be the island's only guardship.

Pomfret's only other frigate, *Bat*, had sailed two days earlier, and with luck would be sniffing off the French coast in case of last-minute difficulties.

'Another signal from *Flag*, sir!' Piper was hoarse. "Make all sail conformable with weather!"'

Herrick rocked forward on his toes as the *Hyperion* butted into a steep, white-backed roller. 'Lively there! Set the t'gallants!' He leaned over the rail and pointed with his trumpet. 'You there, with the fancy knife, move yourself, my lad, or you'll feel the bosun's displeasure!' Then he grinned as if he was enjoying a private joke.

Gossett intoned, 'Fleet course nor' by west, sir! Full and bye!'

The deck trembled as more and more canvas crept along the vibrating yards, whilst framed against the sunlight the nimble topmen ran heedless of their dizzy perches, racing each other in their efforts to obey the demanding voice from the deck.

Piper gulped, 'Here, Seton, give me a hand, will you? I'm puffed out!'

Bolitho turned, caught off guard as Midshipman Seton ran to help his friend beside the snaking halyards. Then he lifted his glass and trained it on the island, which as he watched was slipping back into the rolling bank of morning haze like a brown shadow. He could just make out the small Moorish fort, and below it, scattered amongst the fallen stonework, he could also see a crowd of silent, watching figures. They were convicts, working already to repair some of the neglected defences. But now they were watching the ships, wondering no doubt if they would ever live to see England or anywhere else again.

But Bolitho was thinking of someone else. Just the mention of the girl's brother had started the nagging pain of uncertainty again, a pain only temporarily dulled by his fever.

Then he saw Herrick watching him, his face shadowed beneath his hat. He tried to ease the girl's memory to the back of his mind. He had at least got Herrick.

But in spite of this consolation he trained his glass again, and was still watching Cozar when the flagship made another signal and together the ships turned and headed towards France.

11

Gesture of Faith

Lieutenant Thomas Herrick hunched his shoulders into
his heavy tarpaulin coat and leaned towards the wind.
His eyes were raw with salt and flying spray, and as he
peered towards the plunging forecastle he found it hard
to believe that the last dog watch had only just commenced, for already it was as dark as night. Grimly he
turned his shoulders against the howling wind and allowed it to push him aft towards the wheel where four
sodden seamen wrestled with the spokes and stared
anxiously at the sparse array of thundering sails as the
ship crashed and rolled almost into the teeth of the gale.
Even stripped down to close-reefed topsails the strain
was obvious, and the sounds of the sea were lost to the
great pandemonium of banging canvas, the demoniac
whine of rigging and shrouds and a melancholy clank of
pumps.

Herrick peered briefly at the swaying compass and saw
that the *Hyperion* was still holding her course, almost due
north, and wondered just how much longer the weather
would stay against them. It was four days since the
squadron had sailed from Cozar, yet it seemed like a
month at least. The first two days had gone quite well
with a lively north-westerly and clear sky, while in response to Pomfret's steady stream of signals the ships had
driven north-east deep into the Golfe du Lion so that any
prowling French ship might think they were making to
join Lord Hood at Toulon rather than heading for
some project of their own. Then as the wind veered

and mounted and the sky became hidden by low, black-bellied clouds, Pomfret's signals had become more irate and demanding as the deep-laden transports fought with diminishing success to remain on station, and the two sloops were thrown about like oared boats in the rising procession of angry rollers.

There was rain, too, but so great was the sea that it was difficult to distinguish between it and the spray which lifted above the weather bulwarks and soaked the struggling seamen to the skin, or clawed at the feet of the men aloft as they fought to control the glistening sails before they tore themselves from the yards like so much paper.

On the third day Pomfret had come to a decision. While the squadron hauled off to the north-east of St. Clar and hove to until the storm had blown its course, *Hyperion* was to be detached and would drive southward to patrol the southern approaches of the small port until the moment of entry. Somewhere to the northern side of the inlet the solitary frigate *Bat* would even now be rolling madly in an effort to cover the opposite extremity.

Herrick cursed angrily as a sheet of spray sighed over the nettings and dashed him full in the face, running instantly down his stomach and legs like ice-rime. The more he allowed himself to think about Pomfret the angrier he became. It was difficult to think of him as he was now, and whenever Herrick tried to examine Pomfret's motives he seemed to see him as he had once been aboard the *Phalarope*. Moody, evasive, and given to sudden fits of blind, unreasoning rage. It was strange how you never seemed to be able to rid yourself of old enemies in the small, monastic world of the Navy, he thought. Yet friends came and went and their paths hardly ever crossed a second time.

On the previous night as the hands had swarmed aloft

yet again to shorten sail, Herrick had confided his thoughts to Bolitho. But he had been unwilling to discuss either the admiral or his motives, and Herrick knew he had been unfair even to mention his own doubts. Bolitho was a true friend, and a man whom Herrick admired more than any other, but he was above all a captain. A man isolated by the weight of his command and unable to discuss either the prowess or the shortcomings of his superior, no matter what he might believe inwardly.

But Herrick firmly persisted in his own belief that Pomfret, whatever skill he might have attained over the years, was a man who never relinquished an old grudge. He was hard and he was ruthless, qualities common enough in the Service, but more than that he had the stubborn, pig-headed conviction that he could never be wrong.

On the voyage out from England Herrick had heard it said that Pomfret was being sent to New Holland more as a punishment than as any sort of reward. It certainly bore thinking about, for it was unlikely with England at war with an overwhelming enemy that anyone of Pomfret's rank and experience would be sent to control a convict settlement, unless it was to keep him out of trouble.

And his present mania for written orders, his signals which allowed little manœuvre or initiative to his subordinates, all these things seemed to point to a man determined to make good once and for all.

He was certainly an excellent organiser, even Herrick had to give him credit for that. While Bolitho had lain racked with fever in his cabin and he had taken over as first lieutenant, he had seen the evidence on every side. The convicts had been set to work repairing the crumbling defences and building a new stone jetty. And the troops, sweating and red-faced, had been put through one drill after another in readiness for landing at St. Clar. He smiled wryly. Right now the soldiers would be too seasick to do anything, and that would certainly put an edge to Pomfret's temper. And tomorrow was the day. Allowing for the weather, the ships would enter the inlet and take possession of the town, and within a week the whole of Europe might know that the British had made one more prod at a powerful enemy and had actually landed on French soil.

There was a step on the wet planking behind him and he saw Bolitho peering towards the weather rail, his hair plastered to his forehead by the spray. It seemed as if he never slept for more than minutes, but Herrick knew him well enough not to take his constant appearance as a lack of trust in his own ability. It was the way he was. He could never change now.

Bolitho shouted above the wind, 'Any sight of land?'

Herrick shook his head. 'No, sir. I altered course as you ordered, but the visibility has fallen to a bare half-mile!'

Bolitho nodded. 'Come to the chartroom.'

After the buffeting confusion of the open deck the small chartroom with its dark polished wood and spiralling lantern seemed quite remote, even peaceful, in spite of the canting beams and creaking furniture.

Bolitho's face was thoughtful as he leaned on his elbows and studied the chart. With the points of the brass dividers he tapped it in time with his words. 'Mr. Gossett is sure that the wind will ease off tomorrow, Thomas. He is rarely wrong.'

Herrick peered dubiously at the chart and the criss-cross of pencilled lines and bearings which showed only too clearly the *Hyperion*'s meandering efforts to patrol up and down the southern approaches to St. Clar.

The inlet where some enterprising fishermen had originally founded St. Clar was like a deep niche cut in the coastline, as if by a giant axe. Guarded to north and south by steep headlands the entrance was about a mile across and afforded a safe and sheltered anchorage to even the largest craft. But further inland it narrowed considerably, until at the innermost extent it petered out by the mouth of a small but powerful river from the hills beyond. The river served little purpose but to cut the town in half, and traffic to north or south had to use a humped stone bridge at the far end of the harbour.

With unwelcoming cliffs and jagged rocks on either side of the headlands the port was the only safe place for a landing of any size, and if opposed it would take a force ten times that which Pomfret commanded, and even then the result might be failure and terrible loss of life.

Bolitho said slowly, 'It is a great pity we did not make this landing earlier, Thomas. It is a month since my parley with the mayor of St. Clar. The first ardour of conspiracy may have dulled a little.'

Herrick grunted. 'Sir Edmund apparently made good sure that the Frogs are willing to help us.'

'Maybe. But the parley was arranged on their part so that we could help *them*, remember that. They will wish to be remembered as patriots and not traitors, no matter how insecure this plan may prove to be.'

Herrick watched him curiously. 'Do you not believe in it then, sir?'

'To help our cause I think it is as good a plan as we could hope for. Lord Hood could never have expected such additional help as this.' He touched the lock of hair with his fingers and frowned. 'But for the mayor and his friends I am afraid it may yet be a fate worse than any defeat.'

225

There was a clatter of feet in the passageway and Midshipman Piper called breathlessly, 'Captain, sir! Mr. Caswell's respects and we have just sighted a small boat!' He faltered under their combined gaze. 'At least we *think* it is, sir!'

Herrick said, 'More likely a floating log. There'll be no small craft at sea in *this*.'

Bolitho smiled briefly. 'It is Mr. Caswell's first sighting report as an acting lieutenant, Thomas. You must learn to be generous!'

Herrick grinned. 'If you say so, sir.'

The wind and rain roared to meet them, and Bolitho clutched at the nettings for support as Caswell shouted against the din and all the while pointed across the larboard bow where the white-toothed waves danced in a profusion of broken rollers as they cruised to meet the *Hyperion*'s challenge.

Herrick called, 'By God, sir, he is right!' He was squinting against the wind, his face and chest streaming as if he had just been hauled from the water.

Bolitho waited for the ship to lift and plunge over the next line of rollers, and as the deck canted steeply beneath him he saw something black against the creaming wavecrests, and for a few moments longer the thrashing triangle of a tan-coloured sail.

Caswell yelled, 'Fishing-boat, sir! He'll capsize unless he beats back to shelter!'

Bolitho replied, 'It is four miles to the nearest land, Mr. Caswell. If he had wanted to find shelter he would not have strayed this far.'

'A light!' A lookout was pointing excitedly. 'He's showing a light!'

Bolitho steadied himself against a nine-pounder. 'Heave to, Mr. Herrick!' He saw the lieutenant's as-

226

tonishment and added sharply, 'That craft is drifting with the wind and offshore current, and there is no hope of launching a boat in time to board her.' He stared up at the booming canvas. 'We will let her drift down to us. Detail a party of men to grapple her alongside. It will be a matter of minutes, so get the people from that boat and then cast off!'

Herrick opened his mouth and then closed it. 'Aye, aye, sir.' He pulled himself to the quarterdeck rail yelling, 'Mr. Tomlin, stand by to take that boat alongside!' His voice was almost lost to the hiss of spray and the persistent clatter of blocks and halyards. 'Stand by to heave to! Main tops'l braces there!'

There was a sound like tearing silk as the fore topsail parted down its belly and exploded into wildly flapping streamers. But rising and falling with ponderous indignation the *Hyperion* edged round into the wind, the sudden change of direction bringing more noise and the instant chorus of orders from petty officers and master's mates.

The small boat was almost finished, and as she idled clumsily towards the ship's side Bolitho could see the water cascading across her narrow hull and churning unchecked around the crouching figures by the tiller.

The *Hyperion* hardly quivered as the boat crashed alongside. Men were cursing and yelling against the wind as with a second shudder the boat's mast snapped like a carrot and the sodden sail was torn free to float across the *Hyperion*'s upper deck like a released spectre.

Herrick yelled, 'Lively, men! We'll be all aback in a moment!'

Two pigtailed sailors were already over the side, swinging painfully on lines like bundles of fruit as they struggled down on to the boat. It was breaking up fast, and as Bolitho watched from the quarterdeck he saw the bows begin to push beneath the *Hyperion*'s rounded hull, so that it took some fifty hands at the grapnels to hold her alongside.

Lieutenant Inch staggered to the foot of the ladder and cupped his hands. 'Sir! They've got 'em off! A man and a boy!' He reeled and fell heavily as the ship yawed through a sudden arc, the masts and spars shaking at their stays as if to tear free from the deck.

Bolitho waved his hand. 'Cast off! Bring her back on course, Mr. Herrick!' He blinked the spray from his eyes as the foretopmen swarmed up the shrouds to secure the remains of the sail. The thought of being up there with them made his head swim.

There was a bang like a pistol-shot from forward as one of the grapnel lines parted under the strain, throwing the hauling seamen back into an untidy heap of thrashing limbs. But the boatswain managed to free the second grapnel, and with a groan like a cry of pain the fishing-boat rolled her gunwale under the eager water and disappeared in the foam.

Against the rising and falling backdrop of sea and cloud Bolitho could see his men clutching the two survivors. One was quite limp and the smaller appeared to be struggling.

He called sharply, 'Bring those men aft, Mr. Tomlin!'

At his back he heard the wheel squeaking and grinding against the weight of the helmsmen's combined strength, and then Gossett's voice calling. 'On course, sir! Nor' by west! Full an' bye!'

Herrick sounded out of breath. 'That was *close*, sir!' He shook the water from his coat like a dog. 'I never thought I'd see a ship of the line behaving like a jolly boat!'

Bolitho did not answer. He was watching the limp figure carried by Tomlin's seamen, and even in the dull light it was possible to see the heavy boots, the sodden uniform and the man's moustache plastered across his face as if it had no right to be there.

Herrick saw him start and asked, 'Who is it, sir?'

Bolitho answered quietly, 'Lieutenant Charlois. The man who arranged the parley.' He called, 'Get the surgeon and take this man to my cabin at once!'

As the seamen gathered up their limp bundle he turned and stared at the boy. He was about Seton's age, but square-shouldered and with hair as black as his own. He asked, 'What happened? Do you speak English, boy?'

The boy muttered under his breath and then spat on the quarterdeck.

Tomlin said calmly, 'That won't do at all, lad.' He cuffed him swiftly across the ear and then stared with horror as the boy collapsed sobbing on the deck at his feet. 'Gawd Almighty!'

Bolitho said, 'Take him below, Bosun. Keep him dry and warm. I will speak with him later. Now I must see Charlois.'

Inch walked straddle-legged up the tilting deck and watched the surgeon hurrying after Bolitho. He said, 'Upon my word, Mr. Herrick! If it's not one thing it's another!'

Herrick bit his lip and watched the sails as the ship swooped dizzily into another wide trough. 'One thing is sure, Mr. Inch. Whatever it is which has brought that man out here, it cannot be good!'

* * *

Bolitho stood in the doorway of his sleeping cabin and watched as Rowlstone clung to the swaying cot and completed his examination of the unconscious Charlois while one of his mates and Allday held extra lanterns above his head.

The surgeon straightened his narrow shoulders and said at length, 'I am sorry, sir.' He shrugged. 'There is a ball lodged beneath his left lung. I do not think I can help him.'

Bolitho moved closer and stared down at the Frenchman's heavy features and the shallow, painful movements of his chest.

Rowlstone added meaningly, 'Had it been earlier, sir, I might have saved him. But this man was shot some while ago. Maybe three days. See that black stain around the wound? It is very bad.'

Bolitho did not have to look close. He could smell it. He asked quietly, 'Gangrene?'

Rowlstone nodded. 'How he has lived this long I cannot imagine.'

'Well, see that he is made as comfortable as possible.' Bolitho half-turned and then looked down again as Charlois' lids flickered and then opened. For several seconds the eyes merely stared, unfocused and without comprehension, as if they did not belong in the man's face, which in the lamplight gleamed like tallow.

'Is it you, Captain?' The salt-dried lips moved very slowly, and Bolitho had to stoop to hear the words, his stomach rebelling against the foul stench of the wound.

Charlois closed his eyes again. *'God be praised!'*

Bolitho asked, 'I am here. Why did you leave St. Clar?' He hated to see the man struggling against his agony to assemble his thoughts, but he had to know.

Charlois said weakly, 'My son? Is he safe?'

Bolitho nodded. 'Safe and well. He was a brave boy to stay alone at the tiller in this storm.'

'A brave son.' Charlois tried to nod. 'But he hates me now. He despises me as a traitor to France!' A tear ran from the corner of his eye but he struggled on, 'He only came with me as a duty to his father, a duty, nothing more!'

The effort of speaking was taking its toll and Rowlstone eyed Bolitho with unspoken warning.

Gently Bolitho persisted, 'But why come out here?'

'I gave you my word, Captain. We made a bargain, you and I. I thought that it would all be over quickly, but your admiral believed otherwise.' He breathed out very slowly. 'Now it is too late. I had to warn you. It was my duty.'

Bolitho said, 'How long have you been at sea?'

Charois sighed. 'Two, three days, I do not remember. When the ship came to St. Clar I knew it was finished, so I tried to find you. But the boat was fired on. I was hit by some . . .' He rolled his head against the rough pillow, his face contorted with pain. 'It is over for us, Captain!'

'*What ship?*' Bolitho touched Charlois' shoulder, feeling the clamminess of the flesh. 'Try and speak, man!'

Charlois muttered brokenly, 'She was running from the storm after being damaged in a fight with one of your ships. She is called *Saphir*.'

Bolitho watched him sadly. It was ironic that the ship which had unexpectedly arrived at St. Clar was the one which *Hyperion* had vanquished in battle.

Charlois' voice seemed suddenly stronger. 'Her captain is a little upstart! He owes his command to the blood of his betters who died by order of the Revolution! He was quick to guess that something was wrong. He sent horsemen to Toulouse. There are many soldiers there.'

His voice was fainter once more and his breathing short, and in the sealed cabin very loud. 'It is over. You must tell your admiral.'

Bolitho looked away, seeing in his mind's eye the great wilderness of tossing water, the enclosing darkness around his ship. Somewhere, far off to the north-east, Pomfret's squadron was riding out the storm. It would take all night to find him. It could take longer. By that time it would be too late. Pomfret would sail into the inlet to be met by the concentrated fire of a moored eighty-gun ship. Probably the coastal battery would fire on the squadron also, for they would see no point in doing otherwise with their cause already lost.

And Pomfret would go on with the attack. Losing ships and men which he could ill afford. His strength was for holding the town, and not taking it against a hostile force who would be expecting reinforcements at any moment from Toulouse. He tried to picture the chart in his mind. It was all of one hundred and twenty miles inland to Toulouse. Horsemen could be there in a day, or allowing for the roads and heavy rain, a day and night, riding hard. And they would ride very hard, he decided grimly. The garrison at Toulouse were professional, fully trained troops, sent there to control the hills and all the roads to the Spanish border. How long would it take them to march on St. Clar? Three days? He thought of French troops landing at Falmouth. How long would it take English soldiers to march against an invader? Very little time at all.

Gossett had assured him that the gale would drop tomorrow. So there would be nothing to stop Pomfret or give him time to find him.

Charlois said, 'They have put a boom across the harbour. Believe me, Captain, they are ready for anything!'

'Thank you, Lieutenant. Rest assured that what you have done will be remembered."

'I think not.' Charlois was dying even as they watched. 'It might have succeeded if only you had got there in time! But there were doubters and those who were afraid. They needed a gesture, you understand? Just a gesture of faith!'

Bolitho stood back. 'Fetch his son. He is going fast.'

As soon as the shivering youth was brought to the cabin Bolitho walked out on to the quarterdeck. The boy hated the English, not his father. It was right that they should be together now, he thought.

Herrick asked, 'Is it true about the attack, sir?'

Bolitho watched the leaping spray and listened to the whine of wind through the rigging. 'It is half-true, Thomas,' he answered quietly. 'The *Saphir* is at St. Clar. If our people try and storm the harbour there will be a massacre.'

Herrick said at length, 'Then we must cruise off the inlet, sir. That way we can meet the squadron and prevent this attack from starting.'

Bolitho seemed to be speaking his thoughts aloud. 'A gesture. That is what they want. A gesture of faith.'

Then he swung round and grasped Herrick's arm, his face close and determined. 'They shall have one! That *Saphir* has escaped me once, Thomas, I'll not let her spoil anything more for us!'

Herrick did not understand. 'Do you mean to attack, sir?'

He nodded firmly. 'I do. Under cover of darkness and as soon as possible!'

He broke off as the French boy walked slowly past, Allday's arm around his shoulders. It was over for Charlois.

233

Bolitho continued harshly, 'There was a brave man, Thomas. I have no time for one who dies for ambition. But a man who dies for a cause, no matter how unlikely, is a man to be remembered!' He gripped his hands behind him and stared at the dark sky. 'Now bring her around two points to larboard and lay a fresh course for the southern headland. We will be more sheltered there, and safe enough in this visibility to remain unseen.'

Herrick said, 'It will go against the admiral's orders, sir.'

Bolitho eyed him for several seconds, as if his mind was only half on what he was saying. Then he replied tersely, 'I am going to walk for a bit, Thomas. Do not disturb me until we are within a mile offshore.'

As the rain and spray lashed the decks and the *Hyperion* clawed her way closer to the hidden land, Bolitho strode restlessly up and down the weather side, his chin sunk in his neckcloth, his hands clasped behind him. He was hatless, yet seemed oblivious to the wind and spray, and conscious of nothing but his thoughts.

Herrick watched him and found time to wonder that he was still able to be surprised by anything Bolitho could do.

The *Hyperion*'s wardroom felt damp and stuffy, and the air around the gyrating lanterns was encircled with thick blue smoke from several pipes as the assembled officers listened in silence to their captain's steady voice. Outside the pitching hull and beyond the shuttered stern windows the sea noises seemed muted, but it was also true that the ship's movements were less violent now that she was closer inshore and the headland was taking the worst of the wind's force.

Bolitho leaned on the spread chart and looked around at the intent faces. The expressions which met his gaze were as mixed as their owners. Some were obviously nervous, others showed an unthinking excitement. There were some like Herrick who were openly dismayed at the prospect of being left out of the actual operation until its final stage.

He said slowly, 'This is a boat action, gentlemen. It has to be if we are to have any chance of a surprise attack.' He glanced down at the chart, not seeing any of the scribbled details, but in order to search his mind's fullest extent to find if he had forgotten, or worse, failed to explain what he expected of each of these men.

He said briskly, 'We will take the launch, the two cutters, gig and jolly boat. All told we will muster a force of ninety officers and men. Cutlasses and pistols, but make sure the latter are only issued to senior hands. I don't want some eager fellow letting off his weapon too soon and giving the game away!'

Gossett said gruffly, 'You say there's a beacon on the northern 'eadland, sir?' He leaned forward and tapped the chart with his long-stemmed pipe. 'According to the chart it's not been lit since war was declared.'

'Quite so.' Bolitho felt his limbs beginning to tremble with suppressed excitement. 'As we know, it was not alight during our other visit. The French take the view that by night nobody would be fool enough to try and sail into the anchorage without it. That, of course, does not apply to us!'

Several smiled, and he marvelled that such reckless comment could be greeted with anything but doubt. The whole scheme might be killed within minutes of starting if they were sighted by a sentry or stumbled on a patrol.

He hurried on, shutting out the picture of these same

attentive officers lying dead or wounded under the angry sky. 'Mr. Herrick, you know what to do. You will cruise off the inlet and await the signal. When the beacon is lit you will enter harbour.' He fixed Herrick's grave eyes across the heads of the others, shutting them out from his words. 'If the signal does not appear you will under no circumstances try to force an entrance. You will seek out the squadron and endeavour to persuade Sir Edmund to stay clear.' He looked around their faces again. 'For if there is no signal, gentlemen, we will have failed!'

Rooke said, 'There will be the devil to pay if that happens, sir!'

Bolitho smiled quietly. 'And maybe if we succeed, too.' He straightened his back, his expression final. 'Any more comments?'

There were none. They were committed, and Bolitho guessed that like himself most of them wanted to get it over with, one way or the other.

As they moved out to the upper deck Herrick paused and said softly, 'I wish I were going, sir.'

'I know.' Bolitho watched the groups of motionless seamen being checked and rechecked by their petty officers, while others under the charge of Mr. Tomlin busied themselves around the tiered boats in readiness for lowering. He said, 'But this ship needs a good master, Thomas. If I fell in action afloat she would be in your hands.' He shrugged. 'If I die tonight the same applies.'

Herrick persisted stubbornly, 'All the same, sir, I would feel better being with you.'

Bolitho touched his sleeve. '*All the same*, you will stay here and carry out my orders, eh?'

The boatswain crossed the crowded deck and touched his forehead. 'All ready, sir!'

'Very good, Mr. Tomlin. Man your boats!'

236

Seconds later at a whispered command from the quarterdeck the ship wallowed round towards the shore and hove to. The noise of yards and canvas, the creak and clatter of tackles and blocks as the boats were swung high above the larboard gangway seemed indescribably loud, yet Bolitho knew that from the land with the encroaching sounds of wind and sea they would not be noticed, with any luck at all.

He said, 'When we have left you will clear for action. You are short of officers now, but still have plenty of hands.'

Herrick tried to grin. 'I have the master and Mr. Caswell. The oldest and the youngest, and of course the bullocks, sir.'

Bolitho held up his arms as Allday buckled the swordbelt around his waist. For a moment longer he touched the worn hilt at his side and then said, 'The ship is yours, Thomas. Take good care of her.' Then he climbed up the gangway and peered down at the boats tethered alongside. They were filling with men, and even in the darkness he could see the checked shirts of the seamen, the gleam of weapons, the occasional darker shape of an officer.

He called, 'Very well, Mr. Rooke! Carry on, if you please!'

He watched intently as the big launch and the first cutter cast off and with their oars already dropping into the rowlocks idled clear of the side. Rooke and a midshipman were in charge, and within seconds both boats were swallowed up in the gloom. Next Inch in the second cutter cast off, and with rather more noise than necessary pulled lustily around the ship's bows. That only left the gig and little jolly boat, in the charge of Fowler, the third lieutenant, and Midshipman Piper.

Bolitho took a deep breath and glanced quickly around

237

the upper deck. He could see Herrick and Gossett watching from the quarterdeck, and Captain Ashby further aft by the poop ladder, the latter no doubt still brooding because his marines were excluded from the raid.

Allday said, 'Ready when you are, Captain!' In the darkness his teeth were very white.

Bolitho nodded and swung himself out and down the main chains, waiting until the jolly boat lifted momentarily in a wavecrest before leaping down beside the others.

He leaned over the gunwhale and waved to the gig. 'Mr. Fowler, keep close astern of me!' To Midshipman Piper who squatted beside him he added, 'Cast off. There's a long pull ahead.'

The jolly boat lolled clear of the *Hyperion*'s shining side, and as the oars bit into the tossing water turned and headed towards the shore. It was a small boat, and with ten seamen in addition to her crew, as well as Allday and the officers, would make heavy going of it.

Bolitho saw Seton crouching by his knees and wondered what he was thinking about. It would be different from his last visit, he thought grimly.

When he looked astern he could hardly see his ship, and apart from a white cream of surf under her beakhead she was already merged with the dark sky.

The gig was pulling strongly in their wake, the oars rising and falling as one, the black heads of the seamen moving like part of a machine. Of the other boats there was no sign, and he found himself willing them to be heading for their proper objectives, with neither panic nor uncertainty to drive them ashore under some French guard post.

He heard Allday bark, 'Get baling there! She'll ship more water than you've ever sailed on otherwise!' Then to Bolitho he added, 'It will take the best part of two hours to get into position, Captain.'

'It will.' Bolitho sat forward and swayed loosely with the pitching boat. 'If what Mr. Inch says is correct, we shall be hearing the church clock chiming as soon as we round the headland.' He lifted his voice so that the oarsmen could hear. 'It will keep us company all the way up the harbour, lads. If you were in England you'd not be out of your beds as late as this.'

He turned away to study the darker shadow of land as some of the men chuckled at his remark. Please God they live to hear that clock in the morning, he thought.

Below his knees he heard Seton retching uncontrollably. He at least had something worse than fear to contend with.

12

Night Action

It took over an hour to reach the more sheltered water between the two headlands, and by then the jolly-boat's oarsmen were gasping from sheer fatigue. The necessity of constant baling and the regular relief of oarsmen by the extra hands made it difficult to maintain a perfect trim, so that it was all Piper could do to keep the boat on a steady course or to stop the stroke from becoming ragged and noisy.

Bolitho peered astern and saw the gig's dark shape keeping within fifty feet of his own boat. Lieutenant Fowler had more oarsmen, but his boat was proportionally heavier, and no doubt he was staring after his captain hoping and praying for a short rest.

But there was still a long way to go, and as the boat swayed and tossed in a sudden surge of offshore currents he wondered how Rooke and his party was getting on. As they had passed between the headlands at the entrance of the inlet he had seen the faint white outline of the beacon standing at the top of the cliff like a portly ghost, and had prayed that Rooke would be able to seize it without raising an alarm. He had also seen Inch in the second cutter for just a few moments before it had vanished into a tiny cove at the foot of the southern headland. The men in the jolly boat had found time and breath to curse and envy the lot of Inch's party. They would at least be able to loll across their oars while the cutter rode to her anchor and Inch waited for his moment to act.

The bowman hissed sharply, 'There it is, Cap'n!' He was pointing with his boathook, his crouching shoulders outlined against the dark water like a figurehead. 'The boom, sir!'

Bolitho snapped. 'Easy, lads! Get ready to hook on!'

Allday lifted the shutter of his lantern for just two seconds and trained it astern, and they heard the gig's muffled oars rise dripping from the sea and fall silent.

Gratefully the two boats glided to the makeshift boom and squeaked against it while the bowmen dropped their grapnels snugly into place. The boom consisted of a massive cable which stretched away in a black crescent on either beam to vanish into the darkness. It was buoyed by great casks at regular intervals, and although hastily constructed would be more than ample to prevent a ship from entering the harbour.

Bolitho climbed across the boated oars, resting his hands on the wheezing seamen as he scrambled forward into the bows. The boom was waterlogged and greasy with sea slime, and as he looked to either beam he could see it bending with the force of the current. It was as he had expected and hoped. The rainfall had been as heavy as it was rare, and the small river must be swollen to twice its size as it poured down from the hills to gush into the inlet towards the waiting sea.

He looked up startled, realising at that moment the rain had stopped. Even the clouds seemed finer and less menacing, and for a few seconds he felt something like panic. Then the distant church clock chimed once. It was either one o'clock or half past the hour, amid the sounds of spray and creaking timbers it was hard to tell which. But it helped to steady him, and without speaking he returned to the sternsheets. There was still plenty of time, and his men had to be rested.

Lieutenant Fowler leaned across the gunwale from the gig and asked in a strained whisper, 'Can we cross it, sir?'

Bolitho nodded. 'We will cross first. You follow as soon as we are clear. That boom is practically submerged between the buoys. It will not be difficult.'

He froze as a man gasped, '*Boat*, sir! Starboard bow!'

They sat quite motionless, the seamen holding the two boats apart to deaden the sounds; while vaguely in the distance and then more insistently they heard the splash and creak of oars.

Bolitho said softly, 'Guardboat.'

Against the water and cruising wavelets it was impossible to see the actual boat, but the regular slice of oars, the low, white moustache around the stem were clear enough. Bolitho heard a man whistling softly, and more

241

unexpected and frightening, a great, satisfied yawn.

Piper whispered, 'They're following the boom, sir.' He was shivering violently, but whether from fear or the fact that he was soaked to the skin, Bolitho could not be sure.

He saw the guardboat's splashing progress drawing across the bows and becoming more indistinct with each stroke. Naturally the French coxswain would try and stay away from the boom itself with this current running. Caught beam-on to that cable it would take a lot of sweat and effort to get back on course, and without harsh supervision no sailor would bother too much, provided the boom was still intact. After all, nothing could get over it, and as it was guarded at either end it would be simple to detect any effort to cut it.

Bolitho relaxed his muscles very slightly as the guardboat vanished into the darkness. It would probably rest awhile on the other side of the inlet before rowing back again. With luck, fifteen minutes at the very least. And by that time . . . He twisted in his seat and snapped, 'Right, lads! Over we go!'

Squeaking and scraping the two boats slithered over the sagging cable, the oars used like flails as the seamen poked and prodded the protesting hulls clear of the snare and into the harbour. Bolitho watched the nearest cask bobbing astern and half-expected a sudden challenge or an alarm flare to show that he was discovered. Nothing happened, and with renewed vigour the men lay back on the oars, and by the time the church clock chimed two they were on their way up the centre of the narrowing inlet, the current opposing them more and more with each dragging minute.

Even in the darkness it was possible to see the pale houses rising on either side of the harbour on tiers, the lower windows of one peering over the roof of the next.

For all the world like a fishing port in his own Cornwall, Bolitho thought. He could without effort picture the tiny, narrow streets linking the tiers of houses, the nets hung to dry, the smell of raw fish and tar.

Allday said hoarsely, 'There she is, Captain! The *Saphir*!'

The anchored two-decker was just a deep shadow, but against the lightless houses her masts and yards stood out like black webbing. Allday eased the tiller very gently, and followed by the gig they edged out further into midstream and away from the sleeping ship.

Bolitho twitched his nostrils as the wind carried the acrid scent of charred wood and burnt paintwork across the choppy water to remind him of that last meeting. It was possible too to see the break in her outline left by her missing topmast. Here and there he could see a shaded lantern or the soft glow of a skylight from the forecastle. But there was no challenge or sudden cry of alarm.

The captured sloop-of-war *Fairfax* was anchored in the shallower water some two cables beyond the Frenchman. She was swinging at her cable, her slim bowsprit pointing inland as she rocked uncomfortably in the current. Bolitho studied her intently as the two boats glided past. His first command had been a sloop, and he felt a sudden compassion for the little *Fairfax*. There was always something very sad about a captured prize, he thought. Stripped of her familiar figures and everyday language, renamed and manned to the requirements of her captors, she was nevertheless the same ship.

Piper said, 'The bridge, sir!'

It was little more than a grey hump, but Bolitho knew they had reached the end of the harbour, and as if to confirm his calculations the church clock chimed three o'clock. When he looked up he saw that there were some breaks in the cloud now, the occasional star to mark the storm's passing.

All at once the moment of decision was on him. His men could pull no longer, and below the bridge he could hear the tide-race of water like a millstream, which removed any hope of rest for his tired and sweating oarsmen.

He glanced swiftly around the boat. 'Right, lads. We can drift with the current as planned. We will take the main chains, and Mr. Fowler will board over the fo'c'sle.' Gently he withdrew his sword and pointed across the gunwale. 'Put her about, Allday. Keep well clear of the gig. Mr. Fowler has enough to do without worrying about us!'

Allday thrust at the tiller, and as the oars were eased quietly inboard he set a course straight for the sloop's narrow outline. Every man held his breath, so that the sounds of lapping water alongside, the scrape of bared steel, seemed terrifyingly loud. Even the slop of trapped water below the bottom boards made more than one man start with alarm.

The *Fairfax* stood out suddenly above them, her masts and furled sails appearing to reach out for the tiny stars, her sealed ports almost close enough to touch.

Then, as Allday thrust the tiller further still and the jolly boat swung clumsily towards the chains a voice shattered the silence from right overhead.

'*Qui va la?*'

Bolitho saw the man's head and shoulders black against the furled mainsail, and in one movement jerked Seton to his feet, squeezing his arm almost savagely as he hissed, 'Go on, boy! *Speak to him!*'

Seton was still weak from seasickness, and in the sudden quiet his voice sounded cracked and uneven, '*Le patrouiller!*' He retched as Bolitho shook him again. '*L'officier de garde!*'

Bolitho felt a maniac grin frozen on his face and said, 'Well done!' From above he heard the man muttering, more aggrieved than uneasy now that he thought all was well.

With a thud the stem struck the hull, and as the grapnels soared over the bulwark Bolitho leapt for the chains, his sword dangling from his wrist as he struggled with the unfamiliar shapes around him and pulled himself up and over the rail.

From the darkness below the bulwark he heard a sharp cry and the sickening sound of a heavy cutlass biting into bone. Then, apart from the heavy breathing of his men as they swarmed aboard, the slap of bare feet on planking, all was silent once more.

He gestured urgently with his sword. 'Allday, take ten men and seize the berth deck! There'll be an anchor watch aboard, and it's likely they're still asleep!'

There was a clatter of oars and a sudden shout of anger from beneath the bows, and as Bolitho hurried along the darkened deck he saw the first of Lieutenant Fowler's men swarm upon to the forecastle to secure the gig's head-rope.

He snapped, 'Keep silent there! What the hell are you trying to do?'

Fowler hauled himself awkwardly over the cathead and gasped, 'Sorry, sir! One of the men fell on top of me!' He sounded dazed. 'Is everything all right?'

Bolitho grinned in spite of his taut nerves. 'It appears so, Mr. Fowler.' He turned as one of his bargemen, a giant Irishman named O'Neil, padded across the deck and knuckled his forehead. 'What is it?'

'The poop cabin is empty, sorr.' He gestured towards

245

the main hatch. 'But Oi think yer cox'n has found some Froggies below.' He balanced his cutlass expertly in his hand. 'Maybe we should put 'em out o' their misery, sorr?'

Bolitho frowned. 'There'll be none of that, O'Neil!' He turned back to Fowler. 'Now get your party to work at once. I want every piece of spare canvas, loose furniture, *anything* which will burn, and I want it stacked below the foremast.'

Fowler shivered slightly and glanced outboard as the sloop swung diagonally towards midstream. 'Aye, aye, sir. I've detailed some men to haul the oil up from the gig. God, the ship'll burn like a torch in this wind!'

Bolitho nodded. 'I know. And I hate to do it.'

'Is there no other way, sir?' Fowler was watching his men darting back and forth from the bows, their arms laden with small kegs of oil.

'This ship is worth less than the lives of our people, Mr. Fowler. Provided the wind does not shift we can cut the cable and let her drift down on the *Saphir* without too much difficulty.' He slid the sword back into its scabbard and added harshly, 'There is nothing like a fireship to cause panic!'

Midshipman Piper peered up at him, his eyes gleaming with agitation. 'Sir! Down below!' He seemed too confused to find the words. 'Allday has found . . .' He broke off as the coxswain strode quickly through the busy seamen followed by a small figure in a flapping shirt and little else.

Bolitho asked sharply, 'What is happening, Allday? Who is this man?'

Allday stared at the growing pile of canvas by the foremast and then replied quietly, 'I think this one is a master's mate left in charge, Captain.' He took a deep

246

breath. 'But that's not the trouble. I've just been below and there are some thirty wounded Frenchmen down there. Young Mr. Seton is talking to 'em, quietening 'em as best he can.'

Bolitho turned his back and stared towards the distant *Saphir*. Then he asked, 'Are they badly wounded?'

'Aye, Captain. Some of the *Saphir*'s company, it seems. Mr. Seton says that they were to sail some time tomorrow to try and slip past the blockade into Marseilles.' He shook his head. 'Some of 'em'll not see the morning, in my opinion.'

Fowler said savagely, 'Well, it cannot be helped! They might have died in the broadsides. Burning is a quick enough death!'

Bolitho tried to control his racing thoughts. Allday's discovery was like a slap in the face . He had planned and allowed for everything humanly possible. He had not discounted that he might have to fight his way aboard, that he could even be driven off by a vigilant anchor watch or sentry. The gig's approach from the opposite side would have taken care of that, or at worst could have taken the survivors to safety or captivity. He stared helplessly at the toiling seamen and felt suddenly sickened.

Fowler was as right about the wounded Frenchmen as *he* had been about the burning sloop. '. . . worth less than the lives of our people,' he had said.

And in his heart he knew the plan would have worked. The sloop, once ablaze, would have drifted down on the sleeping two-decker like a messenger from hell. Locked alongside, nothing would have stopped the *Saphir* from being fired also, and together they would have burned to the waterline, and the menace to Pomfret's landing would have been wiped away. The *Saphir*'s company had proved their skill in battle, but tired men, awakened in a

247

safe port to see their world ablaze and knowing that once the creeping fire reached the magazines they would all be killed or roasted alive, would soon lose the heart to fight such a dreaded and overwhelming enemy.

He thought suddenly of Rooke and the others at the beacon. They must have taken it by now or an alarm would have been raised. Rooke would be watching for the flames, while below the headland Inch and his men were waiting to dash out and sever the boom. His task was to have been the easiest, for no guardboat would wander aimlessly across the harbour entrance when their own ship was being burned before their eyes.

Tonelessly he said, 'I will send no man to a death like that.' He looked at Allday. 'How many are there in the anchor watch?'

Allday replied, 'Seven others, Captain. I've got 'em tied up as you ordered. We only had to club one of 'em.' He added awkwardly, 'No one could blame you, Captain. The chances are they'd roast you alive if the game was reversed!'

Bolitho studied him gravely. 'I cannot find any comfort from that sort of supposition.' He looked at the sky. It was clearing rapidly, and eastward towards the open sea the stars stretched in an endless pattern as far as the horizon. Herrick was cruising out there somewhere, watching and worrying. Searching for the beacon to guide him into the harbour before the dawn left them naked and vulnerable.

He made up his mind and said, 'I want those men brought on deck. This sloop has two boats, and we can use one of our own also.' He was speaking rapidly as if to convince himself. 'Be as gentle as you can, but *hurry*!' He caught Piper's sleeve in the gloom. 'You take charge of swaying out the boats, lad. You've done it often enough in *Hyperion*, but this time you must take care to make no noise at all!'

Piper nodded and hurried away, calling his men by name. Bolitho watched him until his small body was swallowed up in the shadows and felt strangely moved. Then he forcibly controlled his sudden despair and turned to Fowler. There was no point in thinking of the mishipmen as sixteen-year-old boys. They were King's officers. It was not possible or provident to think otherwise.

Fowler said flatly, 'Unless those Frogs are stone-deaf they're bound to guess something is afoot, sir.' He added bitterly, 'Maybe that Charlois was right after all!'

Bolitho looked at him thoughtfully. 'Would you give the order to fire this ship with those helpless men trapped below?'

Fowler shifted his feet and replied, 'If I was ordered to I would, sir.'

'That was not what I asked.' Bolitho's tone was cold. 'Taking orders is always easier than giving them. If you live long enough, Mr. Fowler, you may well remember that when you have a command of your own!'

The lieutenant said humbly, 'I am sorry, sir.'

There was a bump, followed instantly by a shriek of pain as one of the wounded men was hauled bodily through the ship's main hatch. Bolitho could hear Seton's voice, soothing and pleading as he tried to stem the sudden panic amongst the disturbed Frenchmen. He did not understand what was being said, but it seemed to be taking effect, for the man lay quite still below the bulwark as the first boat lifted from its chocks and swung creaking on the tackles.

Piper was dancing with anxiety. 'Easy there! Avast

hoisting!' Then as the boat swayed over the rail he squeaked, 'Lower away handsomely!'

Bolitho said, 'Take the gig and make it fast aft. We will have to send the jolly boat ashore, I am afraid.'

Fowler replied, 'It was overloaded before, sir. With your party as well . . .' He shrugged doubtfully.

Allday ran across the deck. 'Just three more to get up, Captain. One of 'em is dead already, so I've left him in peace.'

The second boat splashed alongside and the *Hyperion*'s seamen began to manhandle the wounded over the rail to their companions below. Standing bound and terrified in a small group the French anchor watch waited by the mainmast, guarded by several armed seamen, with their dead comrade still by the bulwark as a warning to anyone stupid enough to make any protest.

The men worked swiftly and silently, but as the time dragged by the tension became almost unbearable. Bolitho tried not to watch the sky, for the more he looked the lighter it appeared to become.

He said, 'Mr. Seton, tell these French seamen to keep quiet once they are in the boats. One sound and I'll sprinkle 'em with cannister before they cover half a cable!'

Seton nodded. 'Aye, aye, s-sir!' He was swaying with fatigue and shock. 'I-I'm s-sorry about that n-noise, sir.'

Bolitho rested his hand on his shoulder. 'You've done well, lad. I'm proud of you.'

Allday stood aside as Seton hurried past him and said quietly, 'He's got the makings, Captain.'

'So you said before.' Bolitho cocked his head as the clock chimed four. 'It's late, Allday. How many more now?'

The coxswain peered across the deck. 'Just the two by

the bulwark. I'll hurry 'em along.' But as he made to move one of the limp figures rolled on to his side and emitted a shrill scream. It was so sudden and unexpected that for a moment nobody moved, then as Allday threw himself across the deck, his hands groping for the wretched man's mouth, the sound stopped as if cut off by a door.

Allday rolled on top of the body and said hoarsely, 'Dead, Captain!'

Bolitho was watching the anchored *Saphir*. He had seen the sudden movements of lanterns on her quarter-deck, the darting shadows across the poop skylight.

'No matter, Allday,' he replied. 'He has done his work.'

Every man stopped and stared as the strident notes of a trumpet floated across the dark water, followed at once by the steady tap-tap of a drum. On either side of the harbour lights were appearing in windows, and Bolitho could hear dogs barking and the cries from disturbed seabirds.

When he turned he saw that his men were looking at him, and his sudden despair gave way to a consuming and bitter anger. His men had trusted him, had obeyed his demands without a murmur, even in the face of such overwhelming odds. Now they were standing and waiting, while across that narrow strip of water the French ship came to arms and the trumpet blared like a herald from death itself. From the corner of his eye he saw one of his bargemen crossing himself, and another leaning on the bulwark and staring at the land as if for the last time. Something seemed to snap in his mind and when he spoke he hardly recognised his own voice.

'Cast off those boats, Allday!' He swung on Fowler. 'Stand by to break cable, and tell Piper to take charge of the gig's crew!' Fowler still stared at him and he seized

251

his wrist with sudden determination. 'We've not come this far to give in so easily!' He turned on the silent seamen. 'Eh, lads? Will you fight of swim?'

The trance seemed to break as if by some signal, and as the men ran wildly for the forecastle someone called, 'Come on, boys! We'll singe those buggers afore they spits us!'

There was a dull boom and an ill-aimed ball ricocheted across the water fifty yards abeam. Someone aboard the *Saphir* had evidently manned one of the bow-chasers, but as both vessels were swinging heavily with the wind the shot was fired more from anger than with any hope of immediate success.

The last of the French seamen were leaping over the side, and as the boats' lines were cast off Fowler yelled, 'Ready forrard, sir!'

Bolitho shouted, 'Cut it!'

There was a clang of metal, and as the straining cable parted and cracked back over the bows like a whip the little sloop sheered away with the wind, her deck canting violently with her unexpected freedom.

Allday shouted, 'Shall we burn her now, Captain?'

But Bolitho was gripping the rail and leaning out to watch the other ship. He could hear the hoarse bark of commands, the thud of ports, and then the telltale squeak of trucks as some of the guns were run out in readiness to fire.

'Not yet!'

The *Saphir*'s captain probably imagined that this was a cutting-out operation to free the *Fairfax* before she could be taken elsewhere. Whatever the cost later, he must be made to go on believing that.

Allday swallowed hard and took a firm grip on his cutlass. As the wind pushed the sloop sideways with the current he could see the *Saphir*'s double line of ports. Some were open, and others were following suit as more and more men poured to their stations in response to the urgent trumpet.

The whole harbour lit up as if from sheet lightning as the first ragged salvo crashed and echoed between the sides of the inlet. Tall columns spouted skyward on every hand, and Bolitho saw a broken white shape being carried down the sloop's side and heard the screams cut short as the shattered boat capsized and vanished. A ball must have ploughed into one of the *Fairfax*'s own boats and cut it in two even as the released Frenchmen tried to row the wounded to safety.

More guns roared out, their long orange tongues reflected in the swirling water as if from a second battery. Bolitho felt the hull lurch beneath him and heard the splintering crash of torn timbers as the massive balls ploughed through the lower deck, rending the sloop apart and tearing out her heart.

A man screamed, 'Main topmast's comin' down! Heads below there!'

Figures scattered wildly as the splintered spar and yard thundered across the narrow quarterdeck, the broken stays and shrouds clawing at the men and carrying one bodily over the side.

Again the rippling line of flashes, but this time it was nearer and better aimed. The *Fairfax* shook like a mad thing, the timbers and buckled deck beams groaning in agony, as if the ship was cursing the men who stood by and let her perish.

Bolitho clutched the rail as a ball crashed through the starboard bulwark and ploughed into some seamen who were carrying an injured man to safety. He was thankful for the darkness but the night could not completely hide the tangled and writhing remains which seconds before had been men, nor could it mute the screams and pitiful whimpers from those unlucky enough to hang on to life.

He shut the sounds from his mind and yelled, 'Fire the ship!'

A crouching seaman hurled his lantern into the pile of loose canvas and woodwork, and for a few seconds Bolitho saw his face in the small flame, a mask of unbelievable hatred as the unknown man made his own gesture of defiance and revenge.

The distance between the ships had dropped to less than seventy yards, and for a moment Bolitho thought he had left it too late. Already he could see men running along the *Saphir*'s gangway towards the point where both vessels would embrace. He could hear them cheering and shouting, the voices mingled together so that they sounded like animals baying for the final kill.

Then the small flame seemed to dart along the sloop's tilting deck like a lighted fuse, and as it touched the oiled bundles the whole sloop lit up, so that men shielded their eyes and fell back, fascinated and appalled by what they had done.

Another salvo crashed into the hull, and below decks Bolitho heard the sudden inrush of water, the boom and clatter of collapsing compartments where the sea surged to complete its victory.

He coughed violently as the wind swept the smoke back from the bows, and when he wiped the moisture from his eyes he saw the foremast and topsail yard burst into flames like some giant crucifix. The fire was spreading at a fantastic speed, and aboard the *Saphir* the cries of jubilation were already changing to shouts of alarm and terror. Someone jerked the lanyard of a swivel gun, and Bolitho felt the cannister spray past his face and rip into the deck on the far side. A seaman was picked from his feet, his scream caught in mid-air as he fell jerking like a bundle of sodden rags, his blood marking his movements on the planking like spilled paint.

He saw Seton, bowed behind the bulwark, his hand to his mouth as he ran aft, and he had to call his name repeatedly before he showed any sign of understanding.

'Into the gig, Mr. Seton! Clear the ship!' Beyond the flames he saw the two-decker's tall side, every port and bared gun shining as if in bright sunlight as the fireship cruised towards her.

Allday shouted, 'Come *on*, Captain! We'll be alongside in . . .'

Another blast of cannister raked the deck, making the sparks fly from the leaping flames and cutting down more running figures as Fowler drove his men towards the stern.

Seton flung his hand to his shoulder and said faintly, 'I'm hit, sir!' Then he fell, and as a seaman hurried to his side the *Fairfax* drove her charred bowsprit hard through the *Saphir*'s fore rigging like a lance.

Fowler was yelling, 'Come back, sir! Quick, they're boarding us!'

Men were leaping down already on to the sloop's deck, and while some ran towards the flames others groped through the billowing smoke firing pistols or slashing at wounded and living alike.

Bolitho saw a French seaman charging towards him and felt the wind of a ball past his cheek before he could release the pistol from his own belt. The weapon jumped in his hand and he saw the man swerve and scream, fingers clawing at his chest before he fell back into the smoke. He threw the pistol at another shrouded shape and then pulled out his sword. Still more figures appeared on the quarterdeck, their arms groping like blind men as they ran through the drifting curtain of smoke and ashes. Bolitho noticed vaguely that the clock was chiming again, but from a new angle, and realised that both vessels were now drifting together. Someone aboard the French ship had at last succeeded in cutting her cable, but as an extra powerful gust of wind momentarily cleared the smoke he saw tongues of flame leaping up her rigging and knew that it was already too late to save her.

The smoke dropped again in a choking cloud, and he heard the wind urging the flames along the sloop's deck, the sparks hissing skyward beyond the masthead. Around him men were fighting and yelling, their cries punctuated with the harsh clash of steel and the occasional crack of a pistol. He could feel the deck sagging beneath him, the very timbers vibrating as water poured into the listing hull. It was a race between fire and sea, and with her work done the *Fairfax* seemed eager to slide beneath the surface, if only to hide her misery and escape the destruction they had wrought upon her.

Fowler was back at his side, his sword shining in the leaping flames while he parried aside the blades as more Frenchmen appeared through the smoke.

He shouted above the din, 'We must leave the wounded, sir!' He lunged forward and down and a man toppled shrieking towards the bulwark. As he fell the deck at his back seemed to open and more searing flames spurted between the charred planks, so that he twisted like a carcase on a spit, his hair on fire, his cries lost in the terrifying roar of flames forced up from the deck below.

Bolitho stumbled and found that Seton still lay by the rail, his head pillowed on his arm as if asleep. The seaman who should have taken him to the gig had either fled or was already killed, and with something like madness Bolitho stood astride his body, his sword cutting down a charging seaman and swinging back to catch another who was struggling with Allday beside the wheel.

But the odds were mounting. It could not last much longer. It seemed as if the Frenchmen were so maddened by rage and despair that they were more intent on destroying the handful of British sailors than of saving themselves or their own ship.

Fowler dropped his sword and clapped his hands across his face. He cried wildly, 'Oh, Jesus! Oh, my God!' And in the leaping flames the blood which poured across his neck and chest gleamed like black glass.

He dropped choking on his knees, and a French lieutenant, hatless and with his uniform coat scorched almost from his back, lunged forward to strike his unprotected head. Bolitho stepped forward, but caught his foot on a splintered plank and saw the officer's blade change direction, cutting through the air with all his strength. With one last effort Bolitho held his balance and instinctively threw up his left arm to protect himself. He felt the blade jar against his forearm and sensed a numbing agony, as if he had been kicked by a maddened horse. The French lieutenant slithered sideways, thrown almost to the deck by the force of his attack, and in the advancing fires his face shone like a mask, the eyes bright and staring as he watched Bolitho's sword scything above Seton's body, the razor-edged blade holding the flames until the moment of impact. He did not even scream, but hobbled backward, his fingers digging at his belly, his back bowed as if in some grotesque curtsy.

Allday was shouting, 'She's *going*, Captain!'

Bolitho blinked and tried to wipe the sweat from his eyes. But his arm remained at his side, and with a sense

257

of shocked disbelief he saw the blood pouring down his side, soaking his leg and running across the deck at his feet. Dazedly he shook himself and stared towards the bows. The towering bank of flames had shifted to the *Saphir*, and he could see the furled sails and tarred rigging whipping out in fiery streamers, and other, smaller fires leaping aft urged on by the wind and burning everything they touched. Through the abandoned gunports the ship's interior glowed red like an open furnace, and as he watched he saw men leaping blindly over the side, calling to one another or screaming pitifully as they were held and then ground to bloody pulp by the two blazing hulls.

But the sloop's deck was dipping rapidly, and from below he heard the hiss of seawater as it surged in triumph to quench the flames. The foremast had gone completely and he had not even noticed amidst the savagery of destruction and death around him. Corpses lolled down the tilting deck, and a few wounded crawled whimpering away from the flames or made a last effort to reach the poop.

Allday shouted, 'The gig is standing clear! Come, Captain, I'll help you over!'

Bolitho still stared around him, waiting to fight, to beat off another attack. But he was sharing the deck with corpses.

Allday yelled, 'There are no more! You've done for 'em!' Then he saw Bolitho's arm. 'Here, Captain! Take my hand!' They reeled together as the sloop wallowed heavily on to her side, the small deck guns tearing from their lashings to squeak across to the other bulwark or plunge hissing into one of the great fiery craters.

Bolitho spoke between his teeth, his face pouring with sweat as the pain reached up his arm like a pair of white-hot pincers. 'The boy! Get him, Allday!' Jerkily he thrust the sticky blade back into its scabbard and with his good arm pulled himself aft towards the taffrail while Allday picked up the unconscious midshipman and threw him across his shoulder.

He saw O'Neil by the rail, naked to the waist as he wrapped his shirt around Fowler's face while the lieutenant rocked from side to side, his words choking on the cloth and in his blood.

The bargeman said, 'Oi done what Oi could, sorr!' He ducked as one of the sloop's guns exploded in the heat as if fired by some invisible hand. 'The poor man has lost most of his face!'

Bolitho managed to croak, 'There is the gig! We will have to jump for it!'

He hardly remembered falling, but was conscious of the salt rasping in his lungs, the cool air across his face as he broke surface. The gig seemed to tower above him, and there was Piper, his monkey face black with grime as he pointed with his dirk, his voice as shrill as a woman's.

'There's the captain! Hold him, you lads!'

Bolitho caught the gunwale and gasped, 'Help Mr. Fowler and Seton!'

The water was surprisingly cold, he thought vaguely, and when he looked up he saw that above the billowing smoke the sky was pale and devoid of stars, and the gulls which circled angrily high above the harbour were touched with gold. Not from the fires, but from the sun. While men had died and the ships had burned the dawn had crept across the distant horizon. He was even more astonished when he turned his head, for where the church tower should have been was the tall side of a headland and above it, gleaming white below its lantern, stood the beacon.

He bit back the pain as more hands hauled him inboard to lie panting beside Allday and the others. He wanted to close his eyes, to give in to the sweeping curtain of darkness which waited to ease his growing agony. To shut out the sounds of exploding gunpowder and the crash of falling spars as the *Saphir* started to settle down, her gunports already awash, her maindeck ablaze from stem to stern.

'How many have we lost?' He clutched at Allday's knee while Piper struggled to stem the blood on his arm. 'Tell me, man!'

Allday's plain face was shining with frail sunlight and when he looked down at Bolitho he seemed somehow remote and indestructible. He said quietly, 'Never you fear, Captain. Whatever the cost, it was worth it to see this.' Then with Piper's help he lifted Bolitho's shoulders above the smoke-blackened gunwale while the oarsmen rested on their looms and watched his face with a kind of awe.

The *Saphir* was almost gone and there was little left of the once proud ship. With the sloop she had drifted the full length of the harbour, and now gutted and blazing she was hard aground below the captured beacon.

But Bolitho had no eyes for her, nor even for the few pieces of flotsam bobbing on the current to mark the passing of the *Fairfax*'s final remains. In the centre of the channel, with all but her topsails and jib clewed up, his ship, his old *Hyperion* was entering harbour. Her ports were open, and as she edged slightly towards the anchorage the dawn sunlight lanced along her double line of guns and painted her rounded hull with gold.

Bolitho licked his dry lips and tried to smile as he saw Ashby's marines in a tight square across the quarterdeck and heard the faint strains from the ship's small band. It was faint because of the cheering.

Cheering from the men who lined the yards and those who waited to drop the great anchor. From the gunners in their bright head-scarves and the marksmen in the tops.

As the old seventy-four's shadow passed the severed boom he saw Inch standing in his cutter waving his hat, his voice lost in distance, but his pride and relief all the more obvious.

Allday said gently, 'Look yonder, Captain.' He was pointing to the headland where the artillery breastworks of raw earth and stones stood out like scars against the rain-soaked grass.

A flag had risen above the hidden guns, but not the Tricolour. It was pale and fragile and lifted easily in the dying wind, so that the sunlight showed clearly the golden insignia of the fleur-de-lis.

Allday said, 'You gave 'em their gesture, Captain! *There* is your answer!'

Fowler muttered thickly beneath the bloodied shirt. 'My face! Oh Jesus, my *face!*'

But Bolitho was looking once more at his ship as she swung sedately into the wind, her sails flapping like banners as the anchor splashed down within yards of the spot where the *Saphir* had been moored.

Boats were moving cautiously from the land, each with its royalist flag, and every one crowded with waving and cheering townspeople.

Allday said, 'Out oars! Give way together!' And to the boat at large added, 'They are coming to see the captain, lads!' Then he looked down at Bolitho and smiled. 'And so they shall!'

13

Return to Cozar

The barge crew tossed their oars and sat motionless on the thwarts as the boat slid neatly alongside the jetty where it was instantly made fast to the great rusting iron rings.

Bolitho gathered his cloak around him and stepped carefully on to the worn steps, then he stood for a few moments looking back at the crowded harbour. It was evening, and in the purple twilight the anchored ships looked at peace, even gay, with their twinkling lanterns and glowing gunports, the latter thrown open to clear the heat and humidity of the day. The flagship *Tenacious* anchored in the centre of the stream had strings of coloured lanterns along her poop, and as he stood on the old jetty Bolitho could hear some of her people singing one of the sad songs beloved by sailors the world over.

Now, looking round, it was hard to believe so much had happened, that at dawn this very day the *Hyperion* had sailed past the burning *Saphir* to take command of the port. He eased his arm painfully beneath his cloak and felt the stab of agony lance through him like fire. Without effort he could relive the sickening minutes as Rowlstone had cut the coat sleeve and shirt from the gaping wound, the blood pouring afresh as he had pulled the remnants of cloth from the deep slash left by the French lieutenant's blade. Tentatively he moved each finger in turn, gritting his teeth against the immediate pain, but thanking God that the surgeon had not found it necessary to amputate his arm.

Herrick climbed up from the boat and stood beside

him. He said, 'It's difficult to grasp that we're in France, sir. The ships look as if they *belong* here.'

It was true. Within hours of Pomfret's squadron arriving in the inlet the transports had been unloaded, and gratefully the soldiers had formed up in the bright sunlight before marching through the town inland to the hills and to positions abreast the coast road. In addition to Colonel Cobban's infantry and a small detachment of light artillery there had been a thousand Spanish troops and a full squadron of their cavalry. The latter had looked resplendent and proud in their pale yellow tunics. On perfect horses they had cantered through the narrow streets, watched with fascinated awe by crowds of townspeople and cheered by the many children along the route.

But now the town was like a dead place, for as soon as the landing force had cleared the streets Pomfret had ordered a curfew. The narrow lanes, the bridge across the river and most of the main buildings were guarded by some of the two hundred and fifty marines landed by Pomfret's ships, and foot patrols moved constantly about the town to enforce his orders.

The boom across the entrance had not been replaced, but half a dozen guardboats rowed back and forth in regular sweeps, with the gutted hulk of the *Saphir* close by to remind them of the price of negligence and overconfidence.

Bolitho said, 'Carry on back to the ship, Allday. I will signal for the barge when I require it.'

Allday stood in the boat and touched his hat. 'Aye, aye, Captain.'

He sounded worried, and Bolitho added quietly, 'I do not think that this visit will be prolonged.'

It was strange how Allday fretted about him, he

thought. Had he been present aboard the flagship when he had reported to Pomfret he might have been even more disturbed.

The admiral's reception had been cool, to say the least. He had listened in silence to Bolitho's account of the raid and the events leading up to it, his face completely expressionless.

Then he had said shortly, 'You take too much upon yourself! You knew my orders, yet you decided to act entirely on your own.' He had begun to pace the cabin. 'The French might have been trying to play a double game. All this so-called ardour for their dead king could be a mere tactic to delay our own operations!'

Bolitho had remembered Charlois, his desperate determination to warn him.

'Charlois gave his life, sir. I acted as I thought fit to prevent what might have been a military disaster and a great loss of life.'

Pomfret had regarded him searchingly. 'And you entered harbour *first*, Bolitho. Before me *and* the squadron. Very convenient!'

Bolitho had replied, 'I could not contact you in time, sir. I had to do what I did.'

'There is a point when tenacity becomes stupidity!' Pomfret had not proceeded further with the matter for at that moment Captain Dash had entered to announce that the soldiers were ready to disembark.

Bolitho had been too weary, too sick with pain and effort to care about Pomfret's anger. Looking back, it seemed as if the admiral actually suspected he had planned and carried out his attack on the *Saphir* merely to gain favour, to grasp rewards for himself, even at the expense of losing his ship and every man aboard.

He said to Herrick, 'The admiral wishes all his senior

officers to take wine with him. We had better make sure we are on time.'

They walked in silence along a narrow, cobbled lane where the houses on either side seemed to reach towards each other as if to touch.

Herrick said, 'How long will it be before the enemy launch an attack on the port, sir?'

'Who can say? But Cobban has his scouts around the town, and no doubt Sir Edmund intends to keep up his coastal patrols to watch the road from the north.'

He tried to keep his tone casual, but he could not put the feeling of disappointment to the back of his mind. Pomfret seemed to put a blight on everything. This curfew for instance. The townspeople had greeted the ships and soldiers like their own, had thrown flowers to the grinning redcoats, as if to show that they believed in what they had helped to start and would share the cost, no matter how hard it became.

And aboard the *Hyperion* the wild excitement had soon been pushed aside as Pomfret ordered the squadron to disembark troops and stores with a minimum of delay. Just one word from him would have made all the difference. *Hyperion*'s raiding party had lost fifteen killed and missing, with another ten badly wounded. Viewed against what would have happened had they failed to sink the *Saphir* it was a negligible amount. But in the ship's tight community it was still very personal and deeply felt.

Pomfret had shifted his flag ashore almost immediately, and as the two officers walked across a deeply shadowed square it became obvious that the admiral had chosen his new headquarters with no little care. It was the house of a rich wine merchant, a pleasant, wide-fronted building, with a pillared entrance and surrounded by a high wall. Cross-belted marines snapped to attention at the gates, and nervous-looking servants waited at the tall double doors to take the hats and cloaks as various officers arrived from ships and garrison alike.

Herrick watched gravely as Bolitho eased his bandaged arm more comfortably inside his dress-coat, noting the deep lines around his mouth, the dampness of sweat below the rebellious lock of hair.

He said at length, 'You should have sent me, sir. You're not fit yet. Not by a long shot!'

Bolitho grimaced. 'And miss the chance of seeing this fine house? Certainly not!'

Herrick looked at the hanging tapestries, the rich glitter of perfectly matched chandeliers.

'Sir Edmund seems to find luxury adequate, sir.'

There was no hiding the bitterness in his tone, and Bolitho wondered if Herrick hated Pomfret for what he had once been in the past or for what he imagined he was doing now to his captain.

He smiled briefly. 'You will fall over that tongue of yours one day, Thomas!'

A bewigged footman threw open a door and as a British petty officer muttered in his ear called loudly, 'Captaine de vaisseau, M'sieu Boli . . .' He faltered, unable to complete it. The petty officer glared at him threateningly and then bellowed in a voice more suited to addressing foretopmen, 'Cap'n Richard Bolitho! Of 'Is Britannic Majesty's Ship Hyperion!'

Bolitho smiled and stepped into a long, panelled room. It seemed to be full of officers, both military and naval, and the buzz of noisy conversation died as every face turned towards him. Bellamy of the Chanticleer was the first to start clapping, and while Bolitho stood momentarily confused and off guard the clapping became cheering until the noise filled the building and spread to the quiet gardens outside where the sentries craned their heads to listen to the thunderous applause.

Bolitho walked awkwardly between the shouting, grinning faces, only half aware of what was being said and vaguely conscious of Herrick striding at his side, his body used to shield his wounded arm from any over-enthusiastic officer in the swaying mass of blue and scarlet.

Pomfret waited at the far end of the room, resplendent in full dress, his head cocked on one side, his lips compressed in what might be either amusement or irritation. He waited until a footman had placed a goblet in Bolitho's hand then held up his arm for silence.

He said, 'We have already drunk the loyal toast, gentlemen. I will now give you another. Let us drink to victory, and death to the French!'

Bolitho sipped at the wine, his mind dazed by the noise and the excitement around him. The toast was common enough, but not under these particular circumstances, he thought. But as he glanced quickly around the room he saw with surprise there was not a single French officer or leading citizen present.

Pomfret said, 'That was quite a greeting, Bolitho! A hero's welcome, if I may say so.' His face was blotchy with heat and his eyes seemed very bright.

Bolitho said quietly, 'Did none of the French leaders come, sir?'

Pomfret eyed him calmly. 'I did not *ask* any!'

The wound throbbed in time to Bolitho's sudden anger. 'But, sir, this is a common venture! They are equal in their desire to overthrow the Revolutionary Government!'

'Equal?' Pomfret regarded him blankly. 'In the eyes

267

of the Almighty maybe. But in mine they are Frenchmen, and not to be trusted! I told you before, I do not care for compromise. I am in command here, and I will brook no interference from these damn peasants!'

He turned and saw Herrick for the first time. 'Ah, your able lieutenant. I trust that he has accepted there will be no prize-money from this venture? With *Saphir* and *Fairfax* sunk it may be some time before we catch another sizable ship, eh?'

Herrick flushed. 'I've heard no complaints, sir. Saving life is more important than money in my opinion!'

Pomfret smiled coldly. 'I was not aware that I asked for an opinion, *Mr*. Herrick.' He turned his back as Colonel Cobban thrust his heavy frame through the throng of officers. 'Ah, Sir Torquil! Are all your men in position now?'

The soldier grunted and took a goblet from a silver tray. 'Earthworks thrown up. Guns in place.' He showed his teeth. 'We can sit here for ever if needed!'

Bolitho asked, 'Is that wise, sir? It seems unlikely that we will be forced to stay here long. As soon as reinforcements arrive we shall be thrusting further inland if this landing is to be of any use.'

Cobban turned slowly, his eyes suddenly hostile. 'May I ask what the hell it is to do with you, sir?'

Bolitho could almost taste the brandy on Cobban's breath. He must have been drinking steadily since he had got ashore. He said stubbornly, 'It is a lot to do with me! And I see no reason for your attitude.'

Pomfret interrupted, 'Be at ease, Sir Torquil! Captain Bolitho is the one who took the port in the first place. He is naturally keen to see that his efforts are not wasted.' He was smiling gently.

Cobban looked blearily from one to the other. Then he

said harshly, 'I am a soldier, I do not care to be questioned by his sort.'

There was a sudden silence, then Bolitho said calmly, 'That is a great pity, Colonel. It is also a pity that when you purchased your commission you did not purchase the manners to go with it!'

The flush mounted Cobban's face like blood. When he spoke he sounded as if he was being strangled by his high collar. 'You impertinent upstart! How *dare* you speak to me like that?'

Pomfret said coolly, 'That is enough, gentlemen! Quite enough!' He turned his pale eyes on Bolitho and added, 'I know that fighting duels is common enough in your family, Captain, but I will have none of it under *my* flag!'

Cobban muttered angrily, 'If you say so, Sir Edmund. But if I had my way . . .'

Bolitho said, 'You will find me ready enough, Colonel, if you give me occasion!' His head was hammering like an anvil and he could feel the wine churning in his stomach like a fever. But he no longer cared. Pomfret's quiet malice and Cobban's crude stupidity had driven him beyond caution. He saw Herrick's face, anxious and wary, and then looked down with surprise as Pomfret laid one hand on his arm.

Pomfret said, 'Your wound is no doubt troubling you. I will overlook this outburst.' Then he sighed as if it was of no importance. 'You will be sailing tomorrow, Bolitho, back to Cozar.' He glanced idly around the big room, his eyes distant. 'You can take my despatches to the garrison, and upon your return bring Miss Seton back to St. Clar.' He became almost jovial. 'We will show these people that we are here to stay. I think I might even give a reception of some kind, eh?'

Cobban had recovered himself only slightly. 'The wedding, Sir Edmund? Will you have it here?'

Pomfret nodded, his eyes still on Bolitho's unsmiling face. 'Yes. I think that would show a sort of confidence in the future.' He smiled, 'A final touch, very well timed.'

Bolitho swayed. Pomfret was laughing at him. It was too obvious. And *Hyperion* was being ordered to sea yet again. It seemed as if the ship would never be allowed time to rest. Time to recover and heal her wounds.

He said flatly, 'A frigate would be faster, sir.'

Pomfret replied, 'I want *you* to go, Bolitho. It will give you time to recover yourself. And in the meantime we will try to run this war to your personal satisfaction!'

Bolitho said, 'Is that all, sir?'

The admiral seemed to consider the question. 'For the present.'

A footman held out another tray of goblets but Pomfret waved him away, adding, 'Now, if you will excuse me, Bolitho?' Then he turned on his heel and walked towards the curved staircase.

Cobban said, 'I'll not forget what you said, Captain! You'll be sorry, be sure of that!'

Bolitho glanced at Herrick. 'Shall we return to the ship?' Without a glance at Cobban he walked towards the door.

Herrick swallowed his drink and followed him. His mind was still reeling from the controlled exchange of insults. He wanted to shout aloud to the assembled officers, to tell them what Bolitho had done for them, and exactly what each man owed to him.

He caught up with him by the door and saw that he was breathing deeply and staring up at the fresh stars, his face relaxed and strangely sad.

Herrick muttered, 'The admiral *refused* another glass,

270

sir. I can't understand it. He had a great appetite for wine aboard the *Phalarope*!'

Bolitho did not even hear him. He was thinking of the girl. This time it would be more difficult than ever to carry her as a passenger. When *Hyperion* dropped anchor here again Cheney Seton would become a bride.

He hitched up his sword and said absently, 'We will take a drink with M'sieu Labouret and the others before we leave. I have a bad taste in my mouth at present.' Without another word he strode through the gates and down towards the harbour.

$$\cdot \qquad \cdot \qquad \cdot \qquad \cdot \qquad \cdot$$

'Let go!' Herrick's voice echoed across the sheltered water, and as he lowered his speaking trumpet the *Hyperion*'s anchor splashed down, the ripples moving lazily away in widening circles towards the surrounding cliffs. The forenoon watch had hardly begun, yet after the light airs of the open sea the enclosed harbour already felt like an oven.

Bolitho watched in silence as his ship tugged gently at her cable and the usual business of lowering boats and spreading deck awnings got under way. Cozar had not changed, he thought. The only other ship at anchor below the gaunt cliffs was the frigate *Harvester*, and he could see without using his glass that Leach, her captain, had almost completed his repairs.

He walked slowly to the nettings and looked up towards the hill fortress. Beyond the harbour mouth the sea mist which had floated out to greet their slow approach hung across the entrance, blotting out the horizon and curling around the grey stonework of the fortress and battery like a fog. He shivered and moved his bandaged arm away from his ribs. They had sighted the island early the previous day, but because of the poor breeze had been forced to lie to for the night, with the distant fortress rising from its protective mist like some enchanted castle.

Herrick touched his hat and said formally, 'Boats lowered, sir.' He glanced towards the sloping hillside beyond the fortress. 'It looks as if there are plenty more soldiers to carry to St. Clar.'

Bolitho nodded. The sun-scorched hillside was covered with lines of small tents, and occasionally he caught sight of a red-coated figure and the gleam of sunlight on a bayonet. But it was very quiet, as if like the island the heat and the dust had beaten the heart out of the isolated garrison.

Herrick said, 'I passed the word to Mr. Seton, sir. He is ready to go across.' He was watching Bolitho worriedly. 'Is that all right?'

'Yes.' Bolitho saw the retrieved jolly boat pulling clear from the ship's black shadow, two midshipmen sitting together in the sternsheets. It was right that Seton should see his sister alone before the upheaval of getting under way again. The boy had made a remarkable recovery, and if anything seemed to have gained in stature since the struggle aboard the burning *Fairfax*. The ball which had cut him down had burned a savage crease across his shoulder, but apart from shock and loss of blood he had escaped anything serious. An inch or so lower and . . . Bolitho bit his lip as he watched the oarsmen picking up the stroke and heading for the pier.

Had he really been considering Seton's feelings when he had allowed him to visit his sister? Or was it just one more attempt to postpone the inevitable meeting?

He asked quietly, 'How is Mr. Fowler?'

Herrick shook his head. 'The surgeon is worried about

him. His face is a terrible sight. If it were me, I'd rather be dead!'

Bolitho replied, half to himself, 'That is easy to say, Thomas. There have been times before or during a fight that I have prayed for death rather than mutilation. But when Rowlstone cut the sleeve from my arm I was praying just as fervently to stay alive.'

Herrick watched him and asked, 'How is the wound, sir?'

Bolitho shrugged. 'I would rather be without it.' He did not feel like talking, even with Herrick. On the short voyage to Cozar he had stayed aloof and remote from his officers, contenting himself with an occasional walk on the poop, but staying mostly in the privacy of his cabin. He was being unrealistic and stupid, he knew that. The fever had hardly left him when he had been up and in action again. That fact, and the throbbing ache of his wounded arm was the real reason for his depression. Or so he told himself.

He tried to regain interest in the coming offensive from St. Clar but could find little to excite his usual zeal and eagerness for action. And there was no room for personal bitterness, not for a captain of a ship of the line. He must thrust all his misgivings aside and put right the wrongs which Pomfret's indifference had laid upon his ship.

Once during a night watch when he had been driven from his cot by the tormenting agony in his arm, he had walked out to the darkened quarterdeck and had overheard Rooke speaking with Gossett.

Rooke had said angrily, 'Whatever we do is wrong! When we go for the enemy alone we are blamed! Yet when we succeed, someone else always seizes the credit!'

The master had replied gruffly, 'Sometimes it goes hard

273

when old scores are evened at the expense of others, Mr. Rooke. I think the admiral is doing his task well enough. But I cannot forgive him for his manner to our captain.'

Rooke's response had been sharp. 'It's damned unfair that the whole ship should be punished because of their dislike for one another!'

Gossett had said firmly, 'With all respect, Mr. Rooke, it seems to me that the captain has treated *you* more than fairly.'

'What the devil are you implying? I should have been first lieutenant, it was my *right*!'

'We both know we don't mean *that*.' Gossett had sounded very calm. 'Given a better chance under Cap'n Turner you would have been ready enough, that is true.' He had lowered his voice. 'But Cap'n Bolitho said nothing to you about the gambling, did he? Not once did he threaten to take action against you for stripping poor Mr. Quarme of his savings, or driving Dalby to thieving from his own kind!'

Rooke had remained silent as Gossett had finished, 'You can log me if you have a mind for saying this, but I think our cap'n has treated you more than well. Your needs exceed your purse, so you do the one thing, apart from fighting, which you do so excellently!'

As Bolitho watched the little jolly boat make fast to the pier he wondered why he had not confronted Rooke with this new knowledge. Maybe it was because of his own heated exchange with Cobban. Even as he had spoken he had seen himself with new eyes. He was just like his brother after all. Given the opportunity he would have fought a senseless duel, not perhaps over cards or dice, but for reasons no less trivial. It was an unnerving discovery, and more so because Pomfret had seen it, too.

Herrick said, 'No sign of the convicts, sir. I suppose

274

they're working at the other end of the island.'

Bolitho nodded. The *Justice* had sailed back to England. As far as her master was concerned the convicts could all rot in this place.

He said suddenly, 'Call away the barge. I am going ashore directly.' He could no longer contain his restlessness.

Herrick studied him anxiously. 'Look, sir, it is none of my business, but when you were under the fever I did hear some rumours.' He dropped his eyes under Bolitho's steady gaze. 'You know without my saying that I'd do anything for you. That goes beyond question. I'd die here and now for you if needed.' He looked up, his blue eyes defiant. 'I think that gives me the right to speak up.'

Bolitho asked, 'And what is it you wish to tell me?'

'Just this. Sir Edmund Pomfret is a powerful man to oppose, sir. He must have great influence to ride above losing his first command and all the other trouble he has caused. He has risen to flag rank in spite of all these things. He would be quick to use his influence and authority against you if he thought for one minute you were interested in his lady, sir!'

Bolitho's voice was very calm. 'Is that all?'

Herrick nodded. 'Aye, sir. I couldn't stand by and see such a thing happen without saying my piece.'

Bolitho clenched his fingers and felt the pain shoot up his arm like a knife. '*Now* you may call my barge, Mr. Herrick.' He turned away, his face controlled, but inside his mind was boiling like a whirlpool. It was no comfort to realise that Herrick was right. No compensation to weigh what his words must have cost him.

He added coldly, 'You need have no fears on my behalf. But in future I would be pleased if you would refrain from trying to live my life for me!'

He saw Gimlett lounging by the poop ladder and called sharply, 'Lay out my shoregoing uniform!' He turned beside the abandoned wheel and looked back at Herrick's troubled features. 'So let that be the end of the matter!'

Twenty minutes later Bolitho strode to the entry port, his wounded arm strapped against his side and covered by his heavy dress coat. Herrick was waiting with the other officers, and Bolitho was momentarily tempted to take him aside, to kill this stupid rift which had been of his own making. Angry with himself, angrier still that Herrick had seen through his pitiful defences he snapped, 'Carry on!' Then he lifted his hat to the quarterdeck and climbed down to the waiting barge.

The pipes shrilled and died as the boat idled clear of the ship's protective shadow, and when he looked astern he saw that Herrick was watching him, his sturdy figure suddenly small against the *Hyperion*'s towering side.

Allday said softly, 'Is the arm well, Captain?' Then he saw Bolitho's rigid shoulders and pursed his lips. There would be more squalls ahead for someone, he thought. As he steered the barge towards the distant pier he watched cautiously for some sign, some small change in Bolitho's grim expression. He could not recall having seen him like this before, and any sort of change did not fit into Allday's placid acceptance of things. There was a strange tenseness about Bolitho. A nervous expectancy which was completely alien to him.

Allday sighed and shook his head doubtfully. Like Herrick, all he wanted was to protect Bolitho, no matter from whence or from what the danger came. But he could not shield him from himself, and the enormity of this discovery was very worrying.

To his surprise and annoyance Bolitho was greeted at the pier by a very young officer in the red runic and facings of the infantry.

He touched his hat in reply as the boy saluted smartly and said, 'Ensign Cowper, sir, of the 91st Foot.' He swallowed hard beneath Bolitho's unsmiling gaze and added awkwardly, 'I have brought a horse, sir. I-I thought it would make the journey easier.'

Bolitho nodded. 'That was thoughtful.' He had wanted to make the journey to the fortress on foot. To give him time to think. To clear his mind and plan what he was going to say.

The ensign saw his indecision and said helpfully, 'If you cannot ride I will lead the beast by the reins, sir.'

Bolitho studied him coldly and replied, 'A sea officer I may be, Mr. Cowper, but I am also a Cornishman. Horses are not unknown in my county!' With all the dignity he could muster he heaved himself into the saddle of the dozing animal, watched with both admiration and awe by his barge crew and the ensign's orderly.

They trotted slowly up the dirt road, each jolt of the hooves causing fresh agony in Bolitho's bandaged arm. He forced himself to take an interest in the surrounding scenery, if only to take his mind off himself and his discomfort. The road was deserted but for a listless sentry, with nothing left to mark the havoc wrought by the carronade or the jubilant onslaught of Ashby's marines.

As they turned the bend in the road he saw the fortress, and spread away across the bleached hillside the neat rows of military tents.

He said, 'I suppose that you are eager to join the rest of your people in St. Clar?'

The young ensign twisted easily in his saddle and

277

looked at him with surprise. 'I do not quite know what *is* to happen yet, sir.'

Bolitho stared at the fortress. 'Well, I hope your commanding officer is better informed.'

Cowper grinned, unabashed by the sarcasm. 'But, sir, I *am* the commanding officer!'

Bolitho reined the horse to a halt and faced the ensign across the road. 'You are *what*?'

Cowper's grin vanished and he shifted uncomfortably under Bolitho's fierce stare. 'Well, that is to say, sir, I am the only officer here.'

Bolitho pointed at the tents. 'And you command all these men on your own? For God's sake, what are you saying?'

The boy spread his hands. 'Well, actually, sir, there are only twenty men and a sergeant. The tents are there just in case some French frigate comes spying for information.' He sighed. 'I command an empty camp so to speak!'

Bolitho felt the horse swaying beneath him as he grappled with Cowper's crazy explanation. 'No reinforcements for St. Clar? Nothing at all?'

'None, sir. I received word from Lord Hood two days back. A brig came here from Toulon.' He flicked the reins as Bolitho nudged his horse forward again. 'My orders are to stand guard here until further notice. Also to increase and extend the existing camp as much as possible.' He hurried on as if fearful of what Bolitho would say. 'We cut up every piece of canvas we could find. Old sails, matting, anything. My chaps just march about relighting camp-fires and keeping an eye on the convicts.' His slim shoulders drooped slightly. 'It's all very upsetting, sir.'

Bolitho looked at him with sudden compassion. Just a

boy. He could not have been commissioned long enough to have seen active service, yet he was given a task which would have made others, years senior to him, grey before their time.

He said, 'So the war goes badly at Toulon?'

Cowper nodded. 'It seems so. Lord Hood had two regiments with him there, but they cannot do much more than contain the town and hold the forts around it. It appears that many of the French who were thought to be loyal to the Royalist cause have deserted to the other side.'

'And there will be no men to spare for St. Clar.' Bolitho spoke his thoughts aloud. 'But no doubt the matter is in hand.'

Cowper sounded doubtful. 'It is to be hoped so, sir.'

In silence they trotted across the wooden bridge above the steep ditch with its cruel-looking stakes, and on through the open gates of the fortress. A solitary soldier paced the ramparts beside the battery and another ran to take the horses. Apart from them the only other living person to be seen was a half-naked man tied to the wheel of a gun-carriage, his skin raw from the probing sun, his mouth open and twitching piteously in the glare.

Cowper said unhappily, 'A defaulter, sir. My sergeant says that it is the only way to punish him.' He turned away. 'I suppose that discipline must be enforced by such means.'

Bolitho said, 'Field punishment is all very well when you have an army at your back, Mr. Cowper. I suggest you tell your sergeant that even a bad soldier will be more use than a dead one if you are attacked!'

Cowper nodded firmly. 'Thank you, sir. I *will* tell him.'

Once inside the round tower the air was cool, even icy

279

after the furnace heat of the compound, and as Bolitho followed the ensign up the narrow stone stairs he remembered that other time, when this small space had been filled with musket-smoke and the screams and curses of dying men.

The quarters, occupied over the years by one commandant after another, were grim and characterless. The main room which overlooked the headland was curved to the shape of the tower, and its narrow, deepcut windows shone like brightly painted pictures of another world. There were a few rush carpets, and here and there he saw some of the plain but well-shaped furniture made by the *Hyperion*'s carpenters. They were the only real signs of human habitation worth considering.

A small studded door opened to one side and the girl, followed by her brother and Midshipman Piper, entered the room.

Cowper said, 'Captain Bolitho is here to see you, ma'am.' He looked meaningly at the midshipmen. 'If you will accompany me I will show you the rest of the, er, fortress.'

Seton said, 'I am sorry I-I was n-not at the pier t-to meet you, s-sir.'

Bolitho replied vaguely, 'I was not expecting you.'

He watched the girl as she walked to one of the windows. She was wearing a loose white dress, and her rich chestnut hair hung across her shoulders untied and unchecked.

As the others left the room she said quietly, 'You are welcome, Captain.' Her eyes dropped to his empty sleeve. 'I heard from my brother what happened. It must have been horrible.'

Bolitho felt strained. 'He did well, Miss Seton. His own wound was bad enough, even for a seasoned man.'

280

She did not seem to hear. 'When I saw him with his bandaged arm I think I nearly hated you. He's such a boy. He was never meant for this sort of life.' Her eyes flashed in the sunlight and seemed to match the green water below the headland. 'I suppose that is quite natural. But as I listened to him I came to realise that he is changed. Oh how he is changed!' She looked directly into Bolitho's face. 'And all he can talk about is you, did you know that?'

Bolitho did not know what to say. All his carefully rehearsed words had flown as soon as she had entered the room. He said clumsily, 'That, too, is natural. When I was his age I thought much the same of my captain.'

She smiled for the first time. 'I am glad that you at least have not changed, Captain. Sometimes in the cool of an evening I walk along the rampart and think back to that voyage from Gibraltar.' Her eyes were distant. 'I can even smell the ship and hear the thunder of those terrible guns.'

'And now I have come to take you to St. Clar.' The words seemed to stick in his throat. 'But I imagine you were expecting a ship?'

'A ship, yes.' She nodded, the movement of her hair and neck bringing a fresh ache to Bolitho's heart. 'But not *your* ship, Captain.' She stared up at him, her hands clenched. 'Were you ordered to come for me?'

'Aye. It was your, I mean, Sir Edmund's wish.'

She looked away. 'I am sorry it had to be you. I thought we would never meet again, you and I.'

'I know.' He could no longer hide his bitterness. 'I expect that I will be there too when you become Lady Pomfret!'

She stepped back, her face flushing beneath her tan. 'Do you despise me then, Captain? Does your pride never allow you to make a mistake or do anything to spoil your sense of duty?' She held up her hand. 'Do not answer! It is plain on your face what you think!'

Bolitho said quietly. 'I could never despise you. What you do is your choice. I am one of Sir Edmund's officers. I could have been anyone.'

She ran her hand across her face to brush away a loose hair, the gesture both familiar and painful. 'Well, let me tell you something, Captain. When my mother died in the uprising in Jamaica things were bad enough. But shortly afterwards there was a great storm when many ships were lost. Among them were the two owned by my father. The rioters had destroyed most of our crops and all the buildings. My father needed those two ships to reach England with our last full cargo, you understand? He *needed* them!'

Bolitho watched her anger and despair with growing helplessness. 'I heard of that storm.'

'It ruined my father! And with my mother gone his health gave way completely. Sir Edmund came to Jamaica with his ship to crush the rising. He did not have to help us, but he never hesitated. He paid our passage back to England and covered my father's debts. We could never repay him, because my father's mind became as sick as his body.' She gestured helplessly. 'We were even allowed to use his town house as our own, and Sir Edmund paid for Rupert's education and encouraged him to go to sea in a King's ship, *your* ship, Captain.'

'I am sorry.' Bolitho wanted to reach out and touch her, but his limbs felt like stone.

She stared at him searchingly. 'Look at me, Captain. I am twenty-six years old. With Rupert at sea I am completely alone now. I know Sir Edmund does not love me, but he needs me as a wife. I owe him that at least!'

Bolitho said, 'The years pass, and then suddenly you feel that something has escaped you . . .' He broke off as she took a step towards him, her face both shocked and hurt.

'I *told* you, Captain, I am twenty-six already. That does not mean I have to throw my body to the first man who asks! Sir Edmund needs me and that is enough, it *has* to be.'

Bolitho looked at the floor. 'I was speaking of *myself*, not of you!' He did not dare to face her until he had finished. Then he would leave. 'I am ten years older than you, and up to our first meeting I never regretted anything. My home is in Cornwall, even the land itself was just an interval in time. Somewhere to have roots, but not to stay.' He waited for a sudden outburst but she remained silent. 'I cannot offer you the fine living of London and Sir Edmund's way of life, but I can offer you . . .'

His voice trailed away as she asked quietly, 'What can you offer, me, Captain?'

He raised his head and saw her standing very erect, her face in shadow. Only the quick rise and fall of her breasts showed either emotion or anger.

He kept his voice level. 'I can offer you my love. I do not expect it to be returned in the same way, but if you will give me the chance, just the chance, I will try and make you happy and give you the peace you rightly deserve.' He was aware of the great silence around the room, the indistinct sounds of lapping water beyond the windows. Above all the painful beating of his heart.

Then she said, 'I must have time to think.' She walked quickly to a window, hiding her face from him. 'Do you really know what you are doing, Captain? What it could mean?'

'I only know what you mean to me. Whatever you decide, nothing can or will ever change that.' He saw her shoulders quiver and added quietly, 'I would tell Sir Edmund if you decided . . .'

She shook her head. 'No. *I* must decide.' Then almost distantly she added, 'Sir Edmund can be a hard man. It might go badly for you.'

Bolitho's heart gave a quick leap. 'Then you think, I mean, you really believe you might . . .?'

She turned and then laid her hands on his shoulders, her eyes shining so that they seemed to fill her face. 'Was there ever any doubt?' But as he made to hold her with his sound arm she stepped away, her hands held up to his chest. 'Please! Not now! Just leave me alone to think.'

Bolitho stepped backwards towards the door, his mind awhirl with a hundred churning thoughts and ideas. 'But you *will* marry me? Just tell me once, before I go!'

Her lip trembled and he saw a tear splash down across her breast. 'Yes, Richard.' She was smiling in spite of the tears. 'You are all the man my brother worships, and more besides. Yes, I *will* marry you gladly!'

Later, when the barge carried him back to the *Hyperion*, Bolitho could feel nothing but numbness. The officer of the watch made a formal report as he climbed to the quarterdeck, but he neither heard what he said nor did he remember his own reply.

Herrick was standing dejectedly beside the poop ladder, a telescope beneath his arm. Bolitho crossed the deck in quick strides and said, 'I owe you an apology, Thomas.' He waved aside the unspoken protests. 'My attitude was inexcusable, my words nothing more than ridiculous!'

Herrick was watching him anxiously. 'Is your wound troubling you, sir?'

Bolitho stared at him. 'Wound? Of course not!'

Herrick said awkwardly, 'Well, I am sorry too, sir. I could not bear to see you in trouble, not of your own making.' He gave a great sigh. 'But now we can get to sea, and after the wedding all will be well again. And that is as it should be!' He grinned with sudden relief.

Bolitho eyed him cheerfully, undecided whether or not to play with him further. He said, 'The wedding is postponed, Thomas.'

'Postponed, sir?' Herrick looked dazed. 'I do not understand.'

Bolitho massaged his bandaged arm with his fingers. 'I think Falmouth will be a more suitable place, don't you? And you can give the bride away, if you would do that for me?'

Herrick was almost speechless. 'You *didn't*? You couldn't *possibly* have.' His mouth was opening and shutting in confusion. 'Not Miss Seton, sir? The *admiral's lady*?'

Bolitho grinned. 'The very same, Thomas!'

He walked below the poop, and before the cabin door slammed shut Herrick heard him whistling. Something Bolitho had never done before at any time.

Herrick grasped the teak rail. 'Well I'll be damned!' He shook himself like a dog. 'Well, I'll be double-damned!'

14

Burden of Command

The *Hyperion*'s reappearance in St. Clar excited little
attention or interest, and as she lay at her anchor astern
of the flagship it was evident that the townspeople had
more on their minds than the arrival of the ship which
had started a train of events over which they had no
control.

The Monarchist flags still fluttered bravely from buildings and headland, but in the narrow streets the air was
heavy with speculation and apprehension. Occasionally
people halted in their stride or broke off short in conversation as the distant rumble of artillery or the racing
wheels of a gun-carriage reminded them of the sudden
proximity of danger.

Within minutes of anchoring a launch had come alongside and Fanshawe, Pomfret's harassed aide, had arrived
to accompany Cheney Seton ashore.

On the slow beat back from Cozar Bolitho had dis-
cussed only briefly what they should do. He had not
wanted to spoil the peace and new-found happiness, and
when the moment of parting had arrived he had still been
unwilling to allow her to accept the full responsibility of
facing Pomfret alone. But that was the one thing about
which she was quite adamant. As he had watched her
helped down into the boat he had felt something like pain
and it was all he could do to prevent himself from following her.

That was three days ago, and as he threw himself into
the business of assisting with the port's defences he ex-

pected to hear something from Pomfret at every minute of each dragging hour. And there was plenty to do. Men had to be found to crew a hastily commandeered flotilla of fishing boats and luggers to be used to patrol the countless coves and minute beaches around the inlet and prevent any attempt at infiltration or surprise attack from an unseen enemy. Unseen except by Cobban's pickets and the wide-flung sections of Spanish cavalry.

The news was not encouraging. It was said that heavy guns had been sighted along the inland road, and never a day passed without some clash between the patrols. A local school had been taken over as a field hospital, and plans were in hand to introduce food rationing should the enemy presence tighten into a full-scale siege.

Each day when he returned wearily to the sanctuary of his quarters Bolitho waited for news from Pomfret. Then when the ship fell quiet for another night he would take out the one note he had received from the girl and go over it again as if for the first time. She was not staying at Pomfret's headquarters, but had accepted his suggestion to take up residence with the town's mayor and family, at least for the present. She had ended with the words: . . . *from my window I can see your ship. My heart is there with you.*

Bolitho knew that it was right they should not meet just yet. It was likely that the news of what he had done would spread over the whole port soon enough, but there was no point in adding fuel to whatever fire Pomfret chose to make.

On the third day the summons came. 'All captains and officers in charge of troops to report to field headquarters immediately.'

In the afternoon sunlight the house looked less imposing, and Bolitho noticed that the marines at the gates no

287

longer watched passers-by with indifference, but fingered
their bayoneted muskets and stayed close to the guard-
house. It was rumoured that some of the townspeople
had already fled to the hills, either out of fear for their
families' safety or to await a more prudent time to change
their allegiance. Bolitho could not find it in his heart to
blame them. Pomfret had drawn an unwavering line between his own forces and the people of St. Clar. Their
resentment would change to something worse if the news
did not improve soon.

Some of the servants were packing china and glass into
wooden cases as he entered the wide doorway, and he
guessed that the house's rightful owner was making sure
of his possessions before it was too late.

An orderly ushered Bolitho into a darkly panelled
study where the others were already assembled. He recognised the other captain who, apart from the two sloop
commanders, were all present. The sloops were busy
patrolling the northern approaches and keeping a wary
eye on the coast road, down which a full-scale attack
might come.

Pomfret was standing beside a desk listening to
Colonel Cobban and a tall, haughty-looking Spaniard
whom he vaguely recognised as Don Joaquin Salgado,
the senior Allied officer. There were various representa-
tives of the military, and two or three marines. Not
enough to withstand the whole weight of France, he
thought grimly.

Fanshawe whispered across Pomfret's shoulder and he
glanced quickly towards Bolitho. Just a few seconds, and
in that brief exchange Bolitho recognised nothing in the
admiral's pale, protruding eyes. Nothing at all.

Pomfret said crisply, 'Be seated, gentlemen.' He tapped one foot impatiently until the noise and shuffling had

ceased. 'I have received despatches from Cozar, brought by *Hyperion* three days ago.' Again the merest glance. But ice-cold and without recognition. 'It seems that we are not to receive the military reinforcements which were expected.' He allowed the murmur of voices to subside before continuing, 'But they will come, gentlemen, they will *come*.' He waved one hand across his map. 'This campaign in St. Clar would be the making of our stepping-stone to Paris! As more ships and men are made available we will cut the soft underbelly of France until the enemy sues for peace!' His eyes flashed as he looked round the room. 'And we will deny them that privilege! There will be no peace or parley this time. It will be victory, absolute and final!'

Someone said, 'Hear, hear!' But apart from the lone voice the room's atmosphere was completely still.

Bolitho turned to watch the nearest window. The dusty panes were glittering in the sunlight, and he could see large flies buzzing unconcernedly amongst the well-kept flower-beds. Now, in Cornwall, they would be thinking about the coming winter. Laying in fresh logs, and fodder for the animals. In the country winter was an enemy to be held at bay with no less determination than they needed here in St. Clar. He thought suddenly of the girl, as she would look when he showed her around the old grey house below the castle. The house would live again. It would not just be a place for memories, but a home. A real home.

Pomfret was saying, 'Patrols must be maintained at all times, but no attempt to force a major combat will be entertained until we get more troops and artillery, or unless there is no possible alternative.'

He nodded to Cobban and then slumped down in a high-backed gilt chair, his eyes distant and brooding.

Cobban rose to his feet, his boots squeaking in the rich carpet.

'Nothing much to add. My men are ready and eager to fight. We have had a few casualties already, but that was to be expected. Watch and guard is the motto, gentlemen! We will hold this port and make the enemy wish he had never chosen to oppose us!'

Don Salgado did not look up as he remarked casually, 'Fine words, Colonel. But I am unimpressed!' He toyed with the ornate frogging on his yellow tunic, his face apparently deep in thought. 'I am of the cavalry. I am not used to skulking along hedgerows, or being shot at by some ragged marksman I cannot even see!'

Cobban glared down at him, his carefully chosen words broken by the sudden interruption. He said pompously, 'It is not your concern, if I may say so.'

The Spaniard's dark eyes lifted slowly and fixed on Cobban's red face. 'Brave talk! Perhaps you have overlooked one important point? *I* command over half of this force, not you!' His voice seemed to sting. 'It was agreed that I would subordinate my infantry and cavalry to your overall command, *provided*,' the word hung motionless in the air, 'provided the English sent reinforcements!' He gave an eloquent shrug. 'Your Admiral Hood cannot succeed at Toulon with two regiments. So how can you hope to do better with a mere handful of foot soldiers!' He smiled calmly. 'I trust you will remember that when next you decide to tell me *my* duty here!'

Pomfret seemed to come alive from his trance. 'That will do, gentlemen! The town is ringed by the enemy. There will be harder times to come. But I am assured that massive aid is on the way even as you sit here bickering like women!'

Bolitho watched him closely. If Pomfret was lying to

ease away the tension he was doing so very convincingly. He recalled with sudden clarity something Herrick had said of Pomfret's past and of what this whole campaign could mean to him. He had to succeed, and would suffer no interference or uncertainty amongst his small force. He thought too of Sir William Moresby who had died on *Hyperion*'s quarterdeck below the Cozar battery. He had been a different man entirely. Unsure and uncertain of everything but his plain duty. Pomfret at least was single-minded to a point of fanaticism.

The admiral said, 'It seems that everyone has had his say.' The pale eyes flickered around the room. 'Questions?'

Captain Greig of the frigate *Bat* rose to his feet. 'But if the reinforcements do *not* come, sir, I cannot see what . . .'

He got no further. Pomfret must have been holding himself in check for some time, and the young captain's doubts were the last straw.

'For God's sake stop snivelling, man!' His voice cracked into a shout, but he did not seem to care. 'What in the name of the Almighty do you know about it? You young frigate captains are all the same, and see nothing beyond some brief conflict or the lustre of damn prize-money!' He pointed accusingly at Greig, who had gone quite pale. 'It was your ship which allowed the *Saphir* to enter harbour in the first place! If you had seen her, had tried to earn your pay instead of mooning around like some lovesick farmboy, all this might never have happened!'

Greig said thickly, 'I did not leave my station, because I was ordered to remain in the north'rd, sir!'

Pomfret yelled, 'Be *silent*! How dare you question my word! One more squeak out of you, you impertinent

291

maggot, and I'll have you court-martialled, *d'you hear me*?' Sweat was pouring down his face as he swung furiously towards the others. 'I will not tell you again, any of you!' He banged his fist across the map. 'We are here to stay! We have been ordered to hold this port until we can strike inland. And that is exactly what I intend!'

Bolitho watched narrowly and saw the effect of Pomfret's words on the silent officers around him. They seemed stunned by his outburst. Dash of the *Tenacious* even looked embarrassed. Only the Spanish colonel appeared unconcerned. As he stared at his gleaming boots he could have been smiling a little.

Cobban cleared his throat uneasily. 'That will be all, gentlemen.' He started to gather up some papers and then let them fall again.

Pomfret had seated himself in the gilt chair, and as the officers made to leave he picked up a pair of brass dividers and jabbed them in the air. 'I want a word with *you*, Captain Bolitho!'

Bolitho heard the door closing behind him and stood quite still by the desk. Cobban had walked to a window breathing heavily, as if he had just been running.

Pomfret ignored the soldier, but to Fanshawe, who still fiddled nervously with some papers, he snapped, '*Get out!*'

Bolitho kept his voice flat and impersonal. 'Sir?'

The admiral was leaning back in the chair watching Bolitho while the dividers beat a small tattoo on the desktop.

He said, 'Next to Dash you are the senior captain here.' He was very calm again. 'It is not unlikely that the enemy will try and attack us by sea, or at least attempt to cut off our supplies.' Tap, tap, tap went the dividers. 'You will therefore take *Hyperion* to sea at first light tomorrow and carry out a patrol along the northern approaches to the inlet.'

Bolitho watched him steadily. 'Until when, sir?'

'Until I order otherwise!' Pomfret threw the dividers on the desk. 'I need my flagship here in harbour in case some of these spineless fishermen show the same sort of stupidity as that fool Greig.'

'I see, sir.' Bolitho could sense the heat rising in his wounded arm, the sudden dryness in his throat as the impact of Pomfret's words made itself felt.

Pomfret did not leave him a moment to speak further. He said almost casually, 'By the way, now that Miss Seton has informed me of her changed status, I intend that she should be put aboard the first available ship out of port.'

Bolitho said tightly, 'I can understand your feelings, sir, but they can be no cause for putting her to more inconvenience and hardship.'

'Really?' Pomfret dabbed his forehead with a silk handkerchief. 'You may have overlooked the fact that I arranged for her to come here in the first place! As an English citizen she is under my protection.' His voice grew louder. 'And as flag officer in charge here I intend to enforce that protection without delay!'

Bolitho replied, 'Is that your last word, sir?' Any sort of understanding or compassion he might have felt for Pomfret's predicament faded at that moment in time. It could be weeks before any ship was available to carry Cheney Seton to England, or any other port of safety. And all that time, while tension mounted around St. Clar and the siege blossomed into outright war, she would be alone amongst strangers, while he would be isolated aboard his ship, unable to see or help her.

'It is.' Pomfret's eyes were flat and without pity. 'I do not like you, Bolitho, and I dislike anyone who allows his mind to be changed by sentiment. So be warned!' He stood up violently and walked towards the windows. 'You may leave now!'

Bolitho clapped on his hat and pushed through the door, only half-aware of what he was doing. He would see her at once. There was still time to make arrangements.

He halted in his tracks by the main entrance as he saw Seton and Midshipman Piper talking in low tones below the steps.

'What are you doing here?'

Piper touched his hat and replied glumly, 'I brought Seton ashore in my boat, sir.' His monkey face was heavy with misery. 'He is to report here at once, sir.'

Bolitho shifted his eyes to Seton. 'Do you know the reason, boy?'

'Y-Yes, sir. Sir Edmund has o-ordered that I be u-used f-f-for . . .'

He broke off wretchedly as Piper interrupted, 'He is to be seconded to the military for signal purposes, sir.'

Bolitho controlled his cold anger and said quietly, 'When this is all over I will be happy to see you back aboard, Mr. Seton. You have done well, no, *very* well, and I am equally sure you will bring more credit to the ship in your new work.'

Seton blinked rapidly and stammered, 'Th-thank y-you, sir.'

It was not uncommon for midshipmen to be used in this manner, but the fact that Pomfret had failed to mention it made Bolitho even more certain it was no casual appointment. But surely no man, not even Pomfret, would use a boy's life to gain some sort of revenge? He thought of the admiral's sudden rage with Greig and felt a cold chill run up his spine.

He held out his hand and the boy grasped it tightly. 'I will see that your sister is well taken care of.' It was strange, even unnerving, to realise that this frail-looking midshipman would be as close to him as his own brother had been. As he studied the boy's pale face he knew he would be closer still.

Seton said, 'I am so happy about you and my sister, sir.' Then he walked quickly into the building, and it was not until he had reached the square that Bolitho realised the boy had not stuttered once in his last sentence.

As they reached the jetty stairs Piper asked, 'D'you think he will be all right, sir?' He was trotting to keep up with Bolitho's quick strides. 'I mean, sir, he's lost without me to keep an eye on him!'

Bolitho stopped above the nodding boat and looked down at him. 'I'm sure of it, Mr. Piper. He has had a good teacher!'

But as he climbed down into the jolly boat he tried to tell himself that his words were not just a lie.

*   *   *   *   *

At first light the following day the *Hyperion* weighed, and with her yards braced round to catch the limp north-westerly breeze, passed slowly between the protective arms of the headlands.

The town appeared to be sleeping, for apart from the watchmen and a few drowsy marines, the jetty and water-front were quiet and deserted.

Herrick stood by the quarterdeck rail, hands on hips as he stared critically at the men working high above, their bare arms shining like gold in the probing sunlight.

295

Some of the unemployed hands were on the gangways staring at the slow-moving panorama of hills and sheltered houses, and beside the tiered boars he saw Piper standing with the jolly-boat crew as they secured the final lashings before the ship rose to meet the open sea. The midshipman was shading his eyes and staring across the larboard quarter, and Herrick guessed he was still thinking about his friend.

When he turned away from the rail he realised that Bolitho was also looking astern, a telescope trained across the nettings with his sound arm.

He said, 'Anchor catted and ship secured for sea, sir.'

Bolitho lowered the glass. The creeping side of the nearest headland had pushed the town from sight. But he had seen her. For long minutes as his ship had edged unwillingly towards the harbour mouth he had watched her, holding her slim figure in the lens until the last possible moment. She was standing on a small balcony right above the water, her body pale against the open window, her face so clear and close that he almost imagined he could reach out and touch it. When he lowered the glass, houses and anchored ships shrank away and lost individuality and meaning in the twinkling of an eye. The link was already broken.

He turned his face to the wind and shivered slightly as it explored his chest through the open shirt. When he had been awakened before the dawn he had lain motionless in his cot for several minutes after Gimlett had departed. Without effort he could remember her nearness, the touch of her hand, the very smell of her hair as they had made that hasty farewell at Labouret's house. As he lay in his cot the warmth of the sheets had seemed like the closeness of that embrace, and when he had gone to his mirror to shave the feel of his fingers on his face had recalled the caress of her hand.

He said abruptly, 'As soon as we are clear you may get the courses set, Mr. Herrick. We will steer to the nor'-east and take advantage of this offshore wind.'

Herrick nodded. 'When we were in the South Sea I swore I would never pray for winds such as some of those we met there. But even the North Sea in winter is better than this crawling.'

Bolitho looked at him distantly. 'I know. A sharp wind, the icy spray in your teeth can take away the pain of thinking too much, and too deeply.'

Gossett was watching the distant beacon, his eye measuring the drift and bearing without conscious effort. 'Ready to wear ship, sir!'

Herrick asked, 'Is all well, sir?' He faltered. 'Were you able to make your arrangements?'

Bolitho sighed. 'Some, Thomas. Labouret has promised to do all he can, and I have a good ally there in Captain Ashby. For once I am not sorry to leave him behind on land.'

As the ship moved clear of the headland she tilted readily to the waiting swell, the sunlight lancing down through her taut rigging and playing across the Titan's crown below the bowsprit.

Bolitho jerked himself from his brooding thoughts. 'Wear ship, if you please!'

Herrick waited until the order had been repeated and piped along the upper deck before asking, 'Any orders, sir?'

Bolitho suddenly remembered the freshly made coffee in his cabin. He had not been able to face it before. Now he needed it, if only to be alone. He said, 'We will exercise the lower battery at eight bells, Mr. Herrick. I do not want those guns to get rusted through lack of use.'

Herrick smiled and watched him stride beneath the poop. He was making the best of it, he thought. And he was right to throw the ship and her company into a busy routine as of now. *Hyperion*'s masters came and went with the years and she cared little if anything for their personal worries. She had to be sailed and maintained, so then did the men who served her.

He picked up his speaking trumpet and shouted, 'Mr. Pearse, have the lower battery piped to quarters at eight bells! And I'll want two minutes lopped off the time it takes to clear for action!'

He saw the gunner nod, and then began to pace the quarterdeck. I am even beginning to sound like Bolitho, he thought. The realisation cheered him, and he quickened his stride accordingly.

Nightfall found the *Hyperion* some twenty miles north-north-east from St. Clar, her sails almost motionless as she wallowed heavily in a deep offshore swell. In Bolitho's cabin the air was humid and lifeless, and most of the officers present were careful to stay beneath the open skylight, their faces shining damply in the swaying lanterns.

Bolitho stood with his back to the shuttered stern windows watching in silence as Gimlett moved nervously across the cabin filling the officers' glasses and passing round the pipe tobacco. Beyond the bulkhead the ship was unusually quiet, and only the sluice of water around the rudder and the creak of steering tackles intruded, and then only as reminders of the *Hyperion*'s slow progress. Not that it mattered, Bolitho considered bitterly. His patrol area laid little importance on either speed or direction. The ship just had to be there. But the slow pace, the dull regularity of movement left his men with too much time on their hands. Time to brood and consider their wretched lack of purpose. Whatever else happened he had to make sure that they did not suffer because of Pomfret's imposed isolation. He had called his officers to the cabin socially and for no other reason but to start as he would have to continue, if the carefully built up morale was not to crumble before his eyes.

As he looked slowly around their faces it was again brought home to him how his collection of subordinates had dwindled and changed. Quarme and Dalby were dead, the two marines and young Seton back there in St. Clar. The rest, for the most part, looked strained and worn down by the never-ending work. It was the way of nearly every sailor to grumble about his lot, but these, he decided, had good cause. Young Piper, for instance, was sixteen. He had joined the ship at thirteen, and to the present day had hardly set foot ashore but to carry out minor duties, or in his beloved jolly boat. Throughout the labouring hull it was mostly the same. No wonder landsmen feared those sounds of the press gangs, even the sight of a naval uniform, when such heartless conditions were taken for granted. Yet these men, who lived and died beside the guns they saw on every waking day, were unbeatable in battle, just as they were seemingly unbreakable in spirit. Sometimes they were starved by miserly captains, flogged by tyrants, or treated like animals by others. Yet when the call came they rarely failed. It was something which Bolitho never really quite understood. Some said it was out of fear, others that the inbuilt tradition and harsh discipline of the Navy were the real reasons. But he believed it went far deeper. A man-o'-war was a way of life. The Cause and the Flag often came second to the love of the men around her crowded decks. They fought to protect each other, to avenge old comrades lost in forgotten battles. And they fought for their ship.

He said quietly, 'I called you together, gentlemen, in order that you should see clearly the difficulties ahead. It may be weeks before we are relieved. Nobody knows what the French intend to do, or if they are yet able to do it. But with such uncertainty aboard out place is at sea. Whatever victories the enemy obtains in Europe he cannot win an overall conquest just so long as our ships are ready to meet him.'

He saw Herrick nodding soberly and young Caswell biting his lip.

'We will have daily drills as before. But this time we must go further. Try to take the men's minds off themselves. Arrange contests, no matter how trivial or small, and do your best to encourage them all. What has been unnoticed in the past, good or bad, will become an event if the loneliness and boredom seize control from you.' He lifted his glass. 'A toast, gentlemen. "The ship, and God bless her".'

The glasses clinked and the assembled officers waited for Bolitho to continue.

He said more crisply, 'With our number shrinking as it is, I have decided to promote Midshipman Gordon to acting-lieutenant. He will assist Mr. Rooke with the upper battery.'

He paused as the other midshipmen pounded Gordon's shoulders, and his face, a great mass of large freckles, broke into a surprised grin. Bolitho glanced swiftly at Rooke and noticed he was nodding in silent agreement.

It had been a careful choice. Gordon had been with Rooke when he had stormed and taken the St. Clar beacon. They seemed to get on very well together, and he suspected it was because they both came from old and established families. Gordon's uncle was a vice-admiral, and that knowledge might help to keep Rooke's temper in check.

'In addition,' the buzz of voices stilled, 'I think one of the master's mates could stand watches until Mr. Fowler is well again.'

Inch looked up. 'May I suggest Bunce, sir? He is a very reliable man.'

'You may, Mr. Inch. You can attend to it directly.' He saw Inch nod and take another sip at his glass. What a difference in the man. Perhaps him most of all. From the fifth and junior lieutenant he had risen to fourth, but more important he had gained the self-confidence to go with it.

They all looked up at the skylight as a muffled voice yelled, 'Avast there! What the devil do you think you're about?' There was a sound of running feet, and then the same voice bellowed, 'Deck there! Man overboard!'

As the officers rushed to the door Gossett could be heard shouting, 'Back the mizzen tops'l! Call away the quarter boat!'

The quarterdeck was very dark and not a star was visible beyond the unmoving clouds. Figures were rushing down gangways, and from right aft Bolitho heard the crew of the quarter boat falling over each other in desperation, urged on by the voice which had called the alarm.

Bolitho snapped, 'What is it, Mr. Gossett? How did the man fall overboard?'

Bunce, the thickset master's mate whom Inch had just

301

mentioned, pushed through the running men and touched his forehead. 'I saw 'im, sir. I was by the wheel as one of my lads was changin' the binnacle lamp.' He shuddered. 'I looks up, sir, an' threre's this face starin' at me! Gawd, it was awful, an' I pray to my Maker I never sees the like again!'

The ship was swaying drunkenly as the flapping canvas volleyed and thundered against the yards and masts, and from somewhere beyond the high poop Bolitho heard the thrash of oars, the shouted instructions from the boat's coxswain.

Bunce added, 'It was Mr. Fowler, sir. 'E'd took off all his dressin' and was carryin' a mirror in 'is 'and. 'E was cryin' like a baby, sir, and all the time he was lookin' at 'is face.'

An anonymous voice spoke up from the darkness. 'That's roight, sir! Cut from eye to chin it were, an' no nose at all!'

Bolitho walked slowly to the nettings. Poor Fowler. He had been a good-looking lieutenant before the French officer's sword had felled him at his side.

He heard Bunce say to Herrick, 'I tried to stop 'im, sir, but 'e just went mad! 'E was nearly naked, an' I couldn't 'old 'im.' He shuddered again. ''E just kept runnin', and dived clear afore we could reach 'im!'

Bolitho watched the boat dipping and rising on the ebony water, the oars striking bright patterns of phosphorescence which seemed to cling to the blades like ghostly weed.

'Can't see nuthin', sir!' The coxswain was standing upright in his boat.

Bolitho said shortly, 'Recall the boat, Mr. Herrick, and put the ship back on course.'

He walked past the silent, watching figures and saw

302

Inch trying to console Midshipman Lory, who had been a great friend of Fowler's. He said, 'Mr. Inch, you are now *third* lieutenant, it seems. I hope that is the last promotion for some time by these means.'

Then he strode into his cabin and stared round at the discarded wineglasses. He tried to pull the stopper from a decanter but it was stuck fast, and because of his disabled arm he was unable to get any purchase on it, '*Gimlett!*' He banged the decanter down savagely as the servant ran anxiously into the cabin. 'Get me a glass of wine, and *quickly*!'

When he lifted it to his lips he saw that his hand was shaking badly and he could do nothing about it. But it was not fever this time. He could feel the anger and despair rising inside him like a flood, and it was all he could do to prevent himself from hurling the glass at the bulkhead. He was not blaming himself for Fowler's death, but for letting him stay alive. He should have left him to die in the blazing *Fairfax*. At least he would have been spared the agony and the terror, the dragging hours while he fingered his bandages and his shocked mind lingered on what lay beneath.

Fowler would have been remembered as a brave man. Not as a poor, crazed wreck. Why did the dead lack dignity? How could it be that a man you know, someone whose habits were as familiar as your own, could change in seconds to nothing? An empty shell.

He banged down the glass. 'Another!'

And he had just finished telling the others of such events which could prey on the minds of men. Fowler was no longer a man, it seemed, but an *event*!'

He thought of Pomfret and what he was doing to him, to his whole ship. 'Damn you! *Damn you to hell!*' His voice shook with anger, so that Gimlett recoiled like some beaten dog.

Then he took hold of himself with one savage effort. 'It is all right, Gimlett. Have no fear.' He held up his glass against a lantern and waited for the wine to settle and stay motionless in the beam like blood. 'I was not shouting at you. You can leave now.'

Alone once more Bolitho sat down heavily, and after a few moments drew the girl's folded letter from his coat and began to read.

15

The People Come First

If Bolitho had been prepared and ready to bolster his ship's morale in the face of Pomfret's imposed isolation the reality was far worse than even he had expected. As one week followed another the *Hyperion* maintained her seemingly endless patrol, a great, empty rectangle of open sea, broken only occasionally by the distant coast of France or the brooding shadow of Cozar Island.

Twice they met with the sloop *Chanticleer*, but Bolitho learned little to ease his mounting apprehension. The sloop's role was almost as wretched as his own, for the unpredictable Mediterranean weather with its sudden squalls and maddening calms played havoc with so small a vessel. Bellamy, her commander, was as perplexed as he was by the complete lack of news from Pomfret's head-quarters. There was more rumour than fact. It was said the French were bombarding St. Clar with siege guns, that the fighting had moved so close to the town it was hardly safe to walk in the streets.

But aboard *Hyperion* the vague speculation was as unimportant as it was remote, for on her crowded decks the reality was only today, and the day after that. And Bolitho knew that his men had tried hard not to show their disappointment and resentment. They had fallen in with his wishes, and for a full month the ship had been alive with contests and friendly rivalry of every shape and form. Prizes had been given for the best scrimshaw work and carved models, for hornpipes and jigs, even for the countless small objects made with loving care by the older hands. Tiny, delicate snuff-boxes, cut and polished from hardened nuggets of salt beef, combs and brooches, constructed from little more than bones and pieces of glass.

But it could not last. Small arguments flared into fights, complaints grew and fanned through the ship's tight community, and once a petty officer was struck in the face by an enraged seaman. The latter, of course, resulted in a flogging. It was soon followed by others.

And the officers were not immune from the spreading disease of dissatisfaction and unrest. There had been a card game in the wardroom when Rooke had accused the purser of cheating. But for Herrick's firm intervention they might have drawn blood. But even his watchful eye could not see everything.

Bolitho's one ally was the weather. As the weeks dragged by it worsened considerably, and often the seamen were too weary from setting sails and then reefing again within the hour, to have the energy even for eating. Not that there was anything worth eating now. What fresh food Bolitho had obtained from St. Clar had soon

305

vanished, and the whole ship was down to basic rations of salted beef or pork, to weavily biscuit and little else.

On the eleventh week, as the *Hyperion* plunged close-hauled on the southerly leg of her patrol, the sharp gale which had been with them for several days eased and backed, and with the change came the rain.

Bolitho stood at the weather side of the quarterdeck and watched the rain advancing towards and over his ship like a steel curtain. He was wearing neither coat nor hat, and allowed the rain to soak hard across his face and chest until he was completely drenched. After the ship's rancid water the rain felt and tasted like pure wine, and as he stood squinting into the wind he noticed that some of his men working along the upper deck were also standing in the downpour like himself, as if to cleanse themselves of their despair.

Tomlin, the boatswain, stood by the forecastle supervising the hastily spread canvas scoops, while Crane, the cooper, was shouting at his assistants to prepare the empty casks for filling before the rain ceased. So now there would not even be the excuse of gathering fresh water to allow him to return to port, Bolitho thought wryly. How quickly an ally could become an enemy.

Herrick crossed the deck, his hair streaming and plastered across his forehead. 'When this clears we should sight Cozar off the larboard bow, sir.' He grimaced. 'It seems as if I am always saying that.'

He was right. Sighting the island meant nothing more than the end of the leg. The *Hyperion* wheeled round towards the mainland for the next slow haul.

Bolitho leaned out over the rail as the ship heeled heavily to the wind, heedless of the rain and spray across his spine and legs. When the old ship tilted he saw without effort the great streamers of dragging weed floating up from her bilges. It was like a small submarine jungle, he thought bitterly. No wonder *Hyperion* was so slow. There were years of sea growth. Each weed meant a mile or so of ocean under that pitted keel, every barnacle and gnawing fungus a hundred turns of the wheel. He tasted salt between his teeth, and when he looked up he saw that the rain had passed on, ruffling the sharp wave crests as it drove on and away to the east.

'Deck there!' The masthead lookout's voice carried above the wind. 'Sail on the larboard bow!'

Bolitho looked at Herrick. Both had been expecting the man to sight Cozar. A ship was so uncommon as to be a major happening.

Bolitho said quickly, 'Shake out the second reef, Mr. Herrick! We will run down on her and take a look!'

But there was no chance of missing the unexpected ship, for as her topsails lifted brightly in a sudden shaft of watery sunlight she went about and headed for the *Hyperion*.

Piper was already in the mizzen shrouds with his glass when the first flags broke from the other ship's yards. 'She's the *Harvester*, sir!' He spluttered as a burst of spray lifted over the weather bulwark and all but threw him from his perch. He gasped, '*Harvester* to *Hyperion*. Have despatches on board!"'

Bolitho shivered, hardly daring to hope for anything just yet. 'Stand by to heave to, Mr. Herrick! We will let Captain Leach do all the work for us!'

Almost before the *Hyperion* had completed her manœuvre her wet sails cracking like guns in the face of the wind, the graceful frigate was near enough for them to see the great streaks of salt on her hull, the patches of bared wood where the relentless sea had pared away her paint as if with a knife.

Bolitho watched as the frigate's yards swung dizzily in the wind, her sleek deck canting towards him as Leach flung his ship round to ride unsteadily under *Hyperion's* lee.

Herrick said, 'That's odd, sir. He could have drifted the despatches over on a line. It'll be a hard pull for any boat in this wind.'

But *Harvester* was already lowering a boat, and when it eventually managed to clear the frigate's side Bolitho saw that it was no mere midshipman in the sternsheets, but Captain Leach himself.

'It must be important.' Bolitho bit his lip as a savage white-backed wave threw the boat almost beam-on to the sea. 'Tell Mr. Tomlin to have his men ready to take her alongside!'

When Leach finally appeared up the *Hyperion's* side he hardly paused to regain his breath before hurrying aft to the quarterdeck, his dripping hat awry, his eyes red-rimmed with fatigue.

Bolitho strode to meet him. 'Welcome aboard! It is some time since I have witnessed such a fine piece of ship-handling!'

Leach stared at Bolitho's soiled shirt and unruly hair as if he had only just recognised him. But he did not smile. He said, 'Can I see you alone, sir?'

Bolitho turned towards the poop, aware of his watching officers, the sudden wave of commotion the frigate's appearance had caused. In the swaying cabin he made Leach drink a full glass of brandy and then he asked, 'What is it which brings you out here?'

Leach sat down on one of the green leather chairs and swallowed hard. 'I have come to request that you return to St. Clar, sir.' He touched his salt-cracked lips as the neat spirit bit deeply into the flesh.

Bolitho said, 'The despatches. Are they from the admiral?'

Leach looked at the desk, his face lined with worry. 'There *are* no despatches, sir. But I had to give some reason. There is enough trouble as it is without worrying our own people.'

Bolitho sat down. 'Take your time, Leach. Have you come from St. Clar?'

Leach shook his head. 'From Cozar. I have just taken off the last handful of soldiers.' He looked up, his eyes desperate. 'After doing that I was ordered to find you, sir. I have been searching for two days.' He watched Bolitho pouring him another glass. 'I don't know if I am doing rightly, or committing an act of mutiny! It is getting so that I don't even trust my own judgement!'

Bolitho breathed out very slowly, willing his taut muscles to relax. 'St. Clar is in trouble, I take it?'

Leach nodded. 'The French have been hammering the port for weeks. I have been on patrol to the south'rd, but each time I put into harbour it was getting worse. The enemy made a feint attack from the south-west, and somehow managed to lure the Spanish troops from their positions.' He sighed. 'The enemy cavalry cut them to pieces! It was a massacre! Nobody even seemed to realise that the French had any cavalry there. And these were crack troops, dragoons from Toulouse!'

'What does the admiral intend to do, Leach?' Bolitho's voice was calm, but inwardly he was seething as he pictured the scattered infantry running and dying under the pitiless sabres.

Leach stood up suddenly, his face wooden. 'That is just it, sir. Sir Edmund has said nothing! There are no orders, no arrangements for a counter-attack *or* evacuation!' He was watching Bolitho with something like despair. 'Captain Dash seems to be in charge. He asked me to find you and bring you back.'

'Have you seen Sir Edmund?'

'No, sir.' Leach spread his hands helplessly. 'I believe he is ill, but Dash told me very little.' He leaned forward. 'The situation is desperate, sir! There is panic everywhere, and unless something is done soon the whole force will fall to the enemy!'

Bolitho stood up and crossed to the table. 'You say you have the people from Cozar aboard?'

Leach sounded weary. 'There was only some young ensign, and a few foot soldiers, sir.'

'What about the convicts?'

Bolitho turned as Leach replied emptily, 'I had no orders about them. So I left without them.'

Bolitho pressed his lips into a tight line. It was easy enough to condemn Leach as a heartless fool. It was even easier to see the difficulties and anxieties with which he was faced. Dash was the flag captain, but without signed orders from Pomfret he had already laid himself open to court martial and perhaps worse.

He said quietly, 'Thank you for being honest with me. I will return to St. Clar immediately.' He listened to his own words without emotion. By agreeing with Leach's suggestion he was no longer an onlooker but a conspirator. He sharpened his voice. 'But before joining me you will return to Cozar and take off every single convict, do you understand?'

Leach nodded. 'If that it your wish, sir.'

'It is an order! I gave my word to them. They had no part in all this. I'll not make them suffer any more!'

There was a tap on the door and Herrick said, 'Your pardon, sir, but the wind is getting up again. It will soon be too rough for a boat to return to the *Harvester*.'

Bolitho nodded. 'Captain Leach is leaving now.' He met Herrick's enquiring eyes and added, 'As soon as he is gone you will wear ship and lay a course for St. Clar. I want every stitch of canvas she can carry, understand?'

Herrick darted away and Leach said tonelessly, 'Thank you, sir. Whatever happens now I'll not regret my action in coming for you.'

Bolitho grasped his hand. 'I hope neither of us does!'

As the frigate's boat pulled clear from the side the *Hyperion*'s massive yards swung round, and while she laid over to the force of the wind the topmen swarmed aloft to fight the whipping canvas, their bodies bowed against the pressure, and hands like claws as they struggled to keep from falling to the deck or into the creaming water alongside.

Herrick dashed the spray from his eyes and yelled, 'Is there more misfortune in St. Clar, sir?'

Bolitho felt the deck buck beneath his straddled legs. The old ship was taking it hard. He could hear the spars and stays squealing from the imposed strain, but as more and more canvas billowed and filled above the hull he shut their protests from his mind.

'I fear so, Thomas. It seems that the enemy are tightening their hold around the port.'

He walked to the weather rail before Herrick could ask him more. There was no point in telling him that it now looked as if much of St. Clar's agony came from within. Herrick might resent being held at a distance, but if it came to a court martial he at least would be spared from involvement.

Gossett said, 'You'll not be wantin' the royals set, Mr. Herrick?'

Bolitho swung round. 'Well, *I* do, Mr. Gossett!

311

You've boasted enough in the past about what this ship can do! Well, let me see you prove it!'

Gossett opened his mouth as if to protest and then saw the set of Bolitho's shoulders and decided against it.

Herrick said, 'Pipe all hands again. And have the sailmaker standing by to replace any torn canvas.' He turned to watch Bolitho's figure striding back and forth across the tilting deck. He was soaked to the skin and his wounded arm, only recently freed from sutures and dressing, brushed against the nettings as he moved, yet he did not appear to notice it.

He carries us all, he thought. Worries for us at every turn, yet will let none of us help *him*.

He gripped the rail as a long roller lifted beneath the ship's quarter and roared hissing along either beam like breakers around a reef. The pumps were clanking louder than ever, and when he wiped his smarting eyes he saw that the yards were bending with the pressure and the belly of each straining sail looked as hard as beaten steel. But she was answering. God knows how, he wondered, but the old ship seems to understand Bolitho's urgency, when we do not.

.   .   .   .   .

It took another two frustrating days to reach St. Clar, with the ship clawing her way almost into the teeth of the wind, and no rest for anyone aboard. When the hands were not turned to trimming sails or working at the pumps they were faced by a mounting list of repairs to canvas and cordage, patching and splicing as if their lives depended on it, which well they might. For as the wind howled against the straining sails and the *Hyperion* swayed over at a sickening angle with her

312

lower gun-ports awash, Bolitho drove the ship without respite or concession. It was a contest between ship and captain, with the angry sea and wind common enemies to both.

Officers and seamen alike stopped watching the bending yards or listening to the agonised whine of rigging. It had gone beyond that. If they had the time or the strength to wonder at all they saved it for Bolitho as he handled his ship through one crisis after another, marvelling that he could go on with neither break nor sleep.

During the forenoon watch of the second day the *Hyperion* rounded the northern headland and tacked gratefully into the inlet. Any hope of a breathing space was instantly dashed by the scene which greeted her tired company, and there were a few anxious moments until the anchor splashed down in deep water just inside the arms of the entrance. Sheltered from the wind's full force it was easy to hear the threatening rumble of artillery and the occasional crash of falling masonry as a well-aimed ball found a target in the town itself.

Bolitho swung his glass across the inlet, seeing the great pall of smoke beyond the huddled houses, the savage scars and holes in many of the roof-tops. He had been made to anchor in deep water because the outer harbour was filled with other vessels, driven from the sheltered reaches and jetty by the searching cannon-fire. *Tenacious* and the Spanish *Princesa* were nearest the town, and two transports swung to their anchors with hardly enough room to prevent a collision in any unexpected change of wind. He closed his glass with a snap. Driven out. Made to lie in the last available shelter in the face of the enemy. They could not withdraw any more. There was only the sea at their backs.

He said sharply, 'My barge! I am going to the admiral's headquarters!' He had already seen that the *Tenacious* was without Pomfret's flag.

Herrick hurried aft. 'Shall I come with you, sir?'

He shook his head. 'You will remain in command until I return. Keep a careful watch on the cable. I don't want her to drag and run ashore to join her old enemy.' He stared bleakly at the *Saphir*'s charred remains below the beacon. 'It seems as if we have arrived only to witness the final curtain!'

Bolitho watched Allday as he guided the men at the tackles and his barge swung outboard across the lee gangway. He said, 'I will want Mr. Inch and twelve good men. Have them armed and properly turned out. Whatever the truth may be, I don't want our people to look like a lot of rabble.'

Gossett said to nobody in particular, 'I see that the transport *Vanessa* 'as sailed. She's well out of it, if you ask me!'

Bolitho allowed Gimlett to help him on with his coat. The *Vanessa*'s departure was the only break in the clouds, he thought grimly. He had left Ashby instructions to make sure the girl was put aboard the first ship for England. He had given her money and a letter for his sister at Falmouth. Whenever Cheney Seton reached there she would be well looked after.

'Barge ready, sir!' Lieutenant Rooke was watching him closely. 'It looks as if it was all wasted, doesn't it, sir?'

Bolitho pulled his hat firmly over his forehead and replied, 'A calculated risk is never a waste entirely, Mr. Rooke. As a card player you should understand that!'

Then he hurried down to the barge where Inch and his landing party were already jammed together like herrings in a cask.

As the boat pulled steadily past the other ships Bolitho could see their seamen standing at the gangways, or squatting in the tops, watching the town in silence. They probably realised that their ships were quite helpless now. All they could do was watch and wait for the certain finality of retreat.

Another boom had been rigged further up the harbour, but not to prevent ships from entering. Here and there along its length Bolitho saw the broken remains of shattered fishing boats and other small craft, some of which were burned beyond recognition. The boom was there to stop any such wreck from drifting down upon the anchored ships. In that crowded inlet any such fireship would turn them into a tangled inferno.

The bargemen pulled in silence, their eyes moving from side to side as some fresh evidence of disaster moved to meet them. The houses along the northern side of the harbour were worst hit, and more than one was burning fiercely, apparently untended, while others gaped open to the sky, deserted and forlorn in the drifting smoke. By the jetty were the remains of some more boats, and as he reached for the steps Bolitho caught sight of a white upturned face pinned below the clear water, the eyes still staring towards the land of the living.

He snapped, 'Allday, remain here with the crew! I am going into the town.' He loosened his sword at his hip as Inch formed his seamen into a double line on the jetty. 'There may be trouble, so be prepared!'

Allday nodded and drew his cutlass. 'Aye, aye, Captain.' He sniffed at the air like a dog. 'Just call if you need us!'

Bolitho strode quickly up the sloping road, the seamen hurrying close on his heels. It was far worse than he had believed possible. He saw figures crouching like animals in the ruins, unwilling or too frightened to leave the remains of their homes, and more than one corpse in the rubble, already forgotten in the confusion. Above the crackle of flames and the grumbling cannon-fire he heard the occasional shriek of a heavy ball, followed instantly by yet another thudding crash.

Inch panted beside him, the sweat already pouring from beneath his hat. 'Sounds like heavy ordnance, sir! The Frogs must be in the hills to the sou'-west for them to reach this far!' He winced as another crash splintered against a nearby house and brought down an avalanche of broken bricks and dust.

At the corner of the square Bolitho saw a small detachment of grimy marines. They were grouped around a fire and staring in silence at a large black pot which they had hung across it on a piece of curtain rail. With a start he realised that they were some of his own men, and as the marines turned to stare he saw a tall sergeant spring to attention, an upraised mug still grasped in one hand.

Bolitho nodded. 'Sergeant Best! I am glad to see that you are making yourselves comfortable!'

The marine grinned through the dirt on his face. 'Aye, sir. Cap'n Ashby 'as put our lads right round the 'eadquarters.' He gestured towards the house. 'The Frog gunners keep tryin' to lay a broadside on the place, but the church is in the way.' He broke off as a ball sliced through the top of the church and severed the gleaming weathervane so that it fell like a dying bird to the street below. He remarked with nothing more than professional interest, 'Better that time, I think!'

Bolitho grunted and hurried on towards the gates. There were more marines inside the wall. Some were sleeping beside their piled muskets, others stood or squatted along the steps in front of the house, their faces lined with fatigue and strain.

But as Bolitho approached a corporal rasped, '*Hyperion*'s, 'shun!' And like drugged men rising from some kind of trance the dusty marines staggered to attention, their resentment changing to something like joy as they recognised their captain.

A man called, 'Good to see you, sir! When can we get away from here?'

Bolitho brushed past them. 'I thought you were having too easy a time! So I've come to find you some real work!' It was unnerving the way they laughed at his stupid remark. They were so trusting, so completely reassured now that they had seen him, as if his very familiarity and their own sense of belonging to one unit made all the difference. He found Captain Dash sitting behind Pomfret's big desk, his head resting in his hands.

Bolitho said to Inch, 'Wait in the passage and stop the men from straying away.' Then he closed the door behind him and walked over to the desk.

Dash rubbed his eyes and stared at him. 'My God, I thought I was still dreaming!' He made to struggle to his feet. 'I am very glad to see you.'

Bolitho squatted on the edge of the desk. 'I would have been here sooner, but . . .' He shrugged. That was all in the past now. He added, 'How bad is it?'

Dash brushed his hand across the big map, the movement both weary and dispirited. 'It is hopeless, Bolitho! The enemy is getting more reinforcements every day.' He drew one finger around the town. 'Our men are hemmed in tight. We have lost the hills *and* the road. The whole line is falling back. By tomorrow we might be fighting in the streets.' He tapped the southern headland. 'If they push us off there, we're done for. Once the French get

317

their guns on that headland they can pound our ships to boxwood in a matter of hours. We won't even be able to escape if that happens!'

Bolitho watched him closely. Dash had changed in some way, but he could not yet put his finger on it.

He asked quietly, 'What is the admiral doing?'

He saw Dash start and some of the colour drain from his face. Then he replied, 'Sir Edmund is ill. I thought you knew that?'

'I did. Leach told me.' He watched the quick, nervous movements of Dash's hands. 'What is the matter with him?'

Dash stood up and walked to a window. 'A brig brought despatches from Toulon. The whole thing is finished. Lord Hood has ordered us to evacuate the port and destroy any facilities and shipping as we go.' He ducked involuntarily as a nearby explosion brought down a pattern of white dust from the ceiling. He added savagely, 'Not that there'll be much left by then!'

'And Toulon?' Bolitho felt the muscles tightening in his stomach. He already guessed the answer.

Dash shrugged heavily. 'The same there. They are pulling out completely in the next few weeks.'

Bolitho stood up and clasped his hands behind him. 'What did the admiral *say* about it?'

'I thought he was going to have a fit!' Dash turned, his face in shadow. 'He ranted and raved, shouted insults at everybody, including me, and then retired to his room.'

'When was this?' Bolitho was certain he had not yet heard the worst.

'Two weeks ago.'

'*Two weeks!*' Bolitho stared at Dash with undisguised astonishment. 'What in God's name have you been doing?'

Dash flushed. 'You must see it from my side, Bolitho. I'm no aristocrat, as you know. I pulled myself from the lower deck by my fingernails. To tell the truth, I never expected to get this far,' his voice hardened, 'but now that I have, I intend to hold on to what I've gained!'

Bolitho said coldly, 'Like it or not, you are in charge here just as long as Pomfret is sick.' He banged the desk. 'You must act! You have no choice in the matter.'

Dash waved his arms around the room. 'I cannot take the responsibility! What would Sir Edmund think of me? What would they say in England?'

Bolitho studied him for several seconds. In battle, Dash would fear nothing. With his ship in fragments and out-numbered by the enemy he would fight to the bitter end. But this was quite beyond him.

Then he remembered the battered town, the men like Fowler who had made that first victory possible. He said cruelly, 'Do you really think your career, even your life is so important?' He saw Dash recoil as if he had hit him, but continued, 'Think of these people who are depend-ing on you, and then tell me you can still hesitate!'

Dash said tightly, 'I sent for you, I wanted you to know...'

'I know why you needed *me*, Captain Dash!' Bolitho faced him across the dust-covered map. 'You want me to reassure you, to tell you that what you are doing is right.' He turned away, sickened by Dash's uncertainty and the cruelty of his own words.

'I'll not deny that.' Dash was finding it difficult to con-trol his breathing. 'I've always been one to obey orders. Duty has always been enough. That I could understand.' He stared down at the map. 'I'm lost in all this, Bolitho. In God's name *help* me!'

'Very well.' Bolitho wanted to ease the hurt he had

done to the man, but there was no time. No time at all. 'I am going to see Pomfret. While I'm doing that you must call a meeting.' He tried to clear the bitterness from his mind. 'All the senior officers, here, within the hour, can you do that? And fetch Labouret, the mayor, too!'

Dash muttered, 'Are you *sure*, Bolitho? If anything goes wrong now . . .'

Bolitho eyed him gravely. 'You will get the blame. And it will be no consolation to you to know that I am equally charged, I know *that*, too!'

He walked to the door and then added quietly, 'But one thing is sure, Captain Dash. If you sit here and do nothing you will never be able to face yourself again. It would mean that the responsibility you worked a lifetime to achieve was too great for you. That you were failing at the one time it all really mattered!'

Then he turned and pushed through the door. To Inch he snapped, 'Report to Captain Dash. He'll be wanting messengers. See to it at once.' Then he ran up the curving stairway to where a marine stood at attention by one of the doors.

Inside the room it was dark enough to be night, and as Bolitho groped his way towards some curtains he felt something roll under his shoe and clink against the wall. But his nose had already told him the nature of Pomfret's illness, and when he opened the curtains and stared round the room he felt a sudden nausea rising to his throat. Pomfret lay spreadeagled across the big bed, his mouth wide open, his breathing slow and painful. Around the bed and across the rich carpet were empty bottles, broken glasses and various items of clothing and furniture which looked as if they had been torn apart with the admiral's bare hands.

Bolitho tightened his jaw and leaned forward across

the bed. Pomfret's face was unshaven and waxy with sweat. There was vomit on the sheets, and the whole room stank like some filthy hovel. He took his shoulder and shook it, no longer fearing the consequences or caring for Pomfret's anger. It was like shaking a corpse.

'Wake up, damn you!' He shook him harder, and Pomfret emitted a dull groan but nothing more. Then Bolitho's eye fell on the crumpled papers lying on a bed-side table. He could see the official seal, the familiar crest at the head of the neat writing.

He walked round the bed and began to read Pomfret's orders from Toulon. Once he stopped and turned his head to look at Pomfret's distorted features. It was all becoming clear now. Herrick's comments about Pom-fret's *last chance to make good*, the admiral's own deter-mination to force the St. Clar invasion to a victorious con-clusion. And given help and the expected reinforcements he might have succeeded, he thought sadly.

He continued reading, each line adding to his sense of understanding and despair. There had never been any intention of holding St. Clar longer than necessary to produce some diversion away from Toulon. It was a cat's-paw, nothing more. Had the Toulon invasion proved successful, it might not have mattered so much. But with his own complications and pressure to contend with, Lord Hood had no time to spare for Pomfret's worries. The orders gave firm instructions about destroy-ing shipping and facilities before leaving, but Bolitho's eye fastened on the final wording, his heart chilling as he read the cold simplicity of the orders. 'In view of limited vessels and the close proximity of enemy forces, no civilian evacuation from St. Clar will be possible.'

Bolitho sat staring at the neat writing until it danced before his eyes like a mist. Pomfret must have sat here reading his orders, he thought. But he would have seen his own ruin as well amidst the formal list of requirements. He would be remembered as the man who had been forced to leave the St. Clar monarchists to their fate, to murder and retribution which was too terrible to contemplate. Bolitho turned again to stare at Pomfret's face. Aloud he said, 'And it was not your fault! God in heaven, it was never intended to mean anything at all!' With an oath he screwed the papers into a ball and hurled them across the room.

He recalled Herrick's surprise at Pomfret's refusal to take a drink. That, too, had given way. The completeness of Pomfret's collapse became more apparent and more terrible every moment.

And all the while, as men had died and families had been crushed under their shattered homes, two men had remained helpless and unwilling to act. Downstairs Dash had waited for orders to free him from responsibility, and God alone knew what Cobban was doing, or even if he was still alive.

As he stood up Bolitho caught sight of himself in a gilded mirror. He was wild-eyed and there were deep lines of strain around his mouth. He was a stranger.

He said, 'I was the one who started all this, not you!' On the bed Pomfret groaned and some spittle ran down his cheek.

Then Bolitho strode to the door and saw Fanshawe standing aimlessly beside one of the windows. 'Come over here!' The flag-lieutenant swung round as if he had been shot at. Bolitho faced him impassively, and when he spoke his voice was like ice. 'Go to the admiral and get that room cleaned up!'

Fanshawe's eyes darted nervously past the door. 'The servants have all gone, sir.'

Bolitho gripped his sleeve. '*You* do it! When I come back I want to see it as it was. I will send my cox'n to give you a hand, but no one else is to see him, *do you understand*?' He shook his arm violently to drive home his words. 'Our people out there don't know about all this.' He dropped his voice. 'And God help them, they are depending on us!'

Without another word he walked down the stairs, his mind racing, his ears deaf to the menacing rumble of guns outside the town.

He made himself leave the house to walk round the building to clear his mind. He did not remember how many times he circled the house, but when he re-entered the panelled study the others were there waiting for him.

Labouret was sitting in a chair, chin on chest, but as Bolitho came through the door he rose to his feet and without a word grasped his two hands in his own.

Bolitho looked down at him, seeing too plainly the pain and the misery in his dark eyes. He said quietly, 'I know, Labouret! Believe me, I *understand*!'

Labouret nodded dully. 'It could have been a great victory, m'sieu.' He dropped his eyes, but not before Bolitho had seen the tears running unchecked down his face.

Captain Ashby said, 'Glad to see you again, sir.' He was nodding grimly. 'More glad than I can say!'

Bolitho looked past him. 'Where is Colonel Cobban?'

A young infantry captain said quickly, 'He sent *me* sir. He was, er, not able to get here.'

Bolitho eyed him coldly. 'No matter.' He saw the Spanish colonel sitting in the same chair as before, his uniform as fresh as if he had just been on parade. The Spaniard gave him a curt nod and then stared at his boots.

Captain Dash said heavily, 'Er, if you're ready to begin, Bolitho?'

Bolitho turned to face the others. Dash had not made it public that he was handing over his control to him.

He said quietly, 'There is not much time. We are to begin total evacuation at once.' They looked at each other as he spoke. Surprise? Relief? It was hard to tell. He continued, 'We will make a general signal to the squadron for boats. We can start with the wounded. Are there many?'

The soldiers replied crisply, 'Over four hundred, sir.'

'Very well. Get them down to the *Erebus* and the *Welland* without delay. Captain Dash will make all the necessary arrangements for extra help from our own seamen.'

He looked quickly at Dash, half-expecting some argument, some small spark of pride. But he merely nodded and muttered, 'I'll do that right away.'

Bolitho watched him pass. God, he's glad to go, he thought wearily.

Then he forgot Dash as Labouret asked quietly, 'What will I tell my people, Captain? How can I face them now?' It was obvious that he knew or guessed what was in Pomfret's orders.

Bolitho faced him. 'By the time you have enquired how many of your people want to leave with us the boats will have evacuated all the wounded, m'sieu.' He saw the Frenchman's lip quiver as he added, 'All who want to go can get into the boats. I cannot promise you much, my friend. But at least your lives will be safe!'

Labouret stared at him for several seconds, searching his face as if to unlock some inner secret. Then he said thickly, 'We will never forget, Captain! *Never!*' Then he was gone.

Bolitho said, 'The *Harvester* will be here soon with the

convicts. They can be spread amongst the two transports, too.'

The Spanish colonel jerked upright in his seat, his eyes flashing dangerously. '*What* is this you say? Convicts on top of wounded and wretched peasants! What about my horses, Captain? How can I get them aboard two ships?' The infantry captain added uncertainly, 'And the artillery's guns, sir?'

Bolitho looked through the door as a marine showed Allday up the staircase towards Pomfret's room. He said flatly, 'They will have to be left behind, gentlemen. The people come first.' He held their combined stares until they looked away. '*Just this once*, they come first!'

The colonel stood up and walked towards the door. Over his shoulder he said harshly, 'I think you are a fool, Captain! But brave certainly!'

They heard his horse trotting away through the gates, and Bolitho said, 'Now show me where the soldiers are in position, if you will. This operation will have to be smooth and without any sort of panic, if it is to succeed!'

Thirty minutes later he watched the others depart. All except Ashby. 'Well, is there something you need explaining?' Bolitho felt completely drained.

Ashby pulled down his tunic and fumbled with his belt. Then he said, 'I had no time to tell you, sir. But Miss Seton is still here in St. Clar.'

Bolitho stared at him. 'What?'

'I tried to put her aboard the *Vanessa*, sir.' Ashby looked wretched. 'But she insisted on staying. She's been helping at the hospital.' His eyes gleamed in the dusty sunlight. 'She's been an example to everyone, sir.'

Bolitho replied quietly, 'Thank you, Ashby. I will see her myself.' Then he picked up his hat and walked out into the noise.

16

A Face in the Crowd

Bolitho reined his borrowed horse to a halt behind a massive stone barn and lowered himself to the ground. Ashby, who had stayed with him all afternoon, also dismounted and leaned heavily against the wall, his chest heaving with exertion.

It was early evening, but so thick was the drifting smoke that it could have been nightfall, and in the deepening shadows the savage gun-flashes and the sharper pinpoints of musket-fire seemed to ring the small town with an unceasing bombardment.

Ashby said, 'This is as far as we go, sir.' He gestured towards the pale line of the road. 'The French are within a hundred yards of us here.'

Bolitho moved along the wall and ducked behind a rough barricade of wagons and earth-filled barrels. He could see the scattered line of soldiers spreading away on either hand, their movements slow but regulated as they loaded and fired towards the road, their red tunics dark against the dust and loose stones.

A young lieutenant crawled from behind an upended farm cart and ran swiftly to Bolitho's side. Like his men he was bedraggled and filthy, but his voice was quite calm as he pointed towards the deeply shadowed hills beyond the road.

'We've come back about fifty yards in the past hour, sir.' He ducked as a musket-ball whimpered overhead. 'I can't hold on here much longer. I've lost half of my men, and those which are still able to fight are down to their last powder and shot.'

Bolitho opened a small telescope and peered above the barricade. It was already darker, and as he stared towards the bright flashes he saw too the spreadeagled bodies, the white crossbelts which marked every yard of the retreat. Here and there an arm moved, and once in a brief lull he heard a cracked voice calling for water.

He found himself thinking of the makeshift hospital by the jetty. He had seen the girl working beside two army surgeons and the town's solitary doctor, her dress stained with blood, her hair pulled back from her face with a piece of bandage. It was not like the enclosed horror of the *Hyperion*'s orlop, but in some ways it had seemed worse because of its primitive desolation. The crowded ranks of wounded, the stench and the pitiful cries, a never-ending stream of limping figures coming down the street from the firing line, and from the look of the doctors' haggard faces it had seemed to Bolitho that they worked with neither respite nor feeling, their eyes only on the wretched man who happened to be in front of them at any particular time.

Then she had seen him, and for a long moment their eyes had embraced above the bowed heads and agonised figures between them. Bolitho had told the senior surgeon what he intended to do, but all the while he had been looking at the girl. The surgeon had eyed him with something like disbelief. As yet another wounded man had been carried in he had said wearily, 'We'll get 'em to the boats, Captain! If we have to swim with each one on our backs!'

Bolitho had taken the girl aside to a small room, which appeared to have been a children's nursery at some time. Amidst the litter of soiled dressings and torn uniforms

327

there were crude pictures painted and drawn by some of
the children who were now trapped or dying in the beleaguered town.

She had said, 'I knew you would come, Richard. I just
knew!'

He had held her against his chest, feeling the tautness
in her limbs, the sudden pressure of her head on his
shoulder. 'You're exhausted! You should have gone in
the *Vanessa*!'

'Not without seeing you, Richard.' She had lifted her
chin and studied his face. 'I'm all right, now.'

Outside the building the air had vibrated with gunfire
and the sounds of running men. But in those few moments they had been alone, remote from the bitter reality
and suffering around them.

Gently he had prised her hands from his coat. 'Seamen
from the squadron will be here very soon. Everything
will be done to get everyone away from St. Clar. Please
tell me that you will go with the others?' He had searched
her face, holding on to it with his mind. 'That is all I ask.'

She had nodded very slowly. 'Everyone is saying that
you are responsible for the evacuation, Richard. They
speak of nothing else. That you returned against orders
to help us!' Her eyes had been shining with tears. 'I am
glad I stayed behind, if only to see what you are really
like!'

Bolitho had replied, 'We are all in this together. There
was no other way.'

A shake of the head, the gesture so dear in Bolitho's
memory. 'You may say that, Richard, but I know you
better than you think. Sir Edmund did nothing, and while
others waited, all these men died to no purpose!'

'Do not be too hard on the admiral.' It had been
strange to hear his own words. As if in the last few hours

he had seen Pomfret through different eyes, had even understood him a little more. 'He and I wanted the same thing. Only our motives were different.'

Then the first sailors had appeared inside the hospital, their check shirts and clean, purposeful figures alien and unreal in that place of despair and death.

And now, as he crouched beside this pitiful barricade, he could still picture her as he had last seen her. A slim, defiant figure amidst the harvest of war, even managing to smile as he had mounted his horse and ridden to the other end of the town.

A soldier lurched back from a low wall, emitting a shrill scream before pitching headlong beside one of his comrades. The latter did not even turn his head to look at his dead companion, but continued with his loading and firing. Death had become too commonplace to mention. Survival merely a remote possibility.

Bolitho turned and stared behind him. There was the bridge, and below the ridge of earth and scorched grass lay the river. He made up his mind. 'Have you laid the charges, Lieutenant?' He saw the man nod with relief. 'Very well. Fall back across the river and blow the bridge.'

There was a sudden jangle of harness, and as he swung round Bolitho saw the Spanish colonel trotting calmly along the narrow track, and behind him, their breast-plates and helmets glittering in the gun-flashes like silver, came the remnants of his cavalry.

Bolitho ducked and then ran back to the high barn. He snapped, 'What are you doing here, Colonel? I told you to prepare your men for evacuation!'

Don Joaquin Salgado sat quite motionless in his saddle, his teeth very white in the darkness. 'You have much to achieve before tomorrow, Captain. Be so kind as to give me the benefit of knowing *my* profession also.'

'There is nothing beyond this line of men but open ground and the enemy, Colonel!'

The Spaniard nodded. 'And as someone remarked earlier, if the enemy reach the southern headland before you get clear you are all dead men!' He leaned forward slightly, his saddle creaking beneath him. 'I am not leaving my horses to rot, Captain, nor am I going to shoot them. I am a soldier. I am sick and tired of this kind of warfare!' He straightened his back and drew out his curved sabre. 'Good luck, Captain!' Then without another glance he spurred his horse forward and galloped straight for the barricade. The effect on his men was instantaneous. Cheering and whooping like madmen they thundered in pursuit, the flying hoofs skimming past the dazed soldiers by the barricade, their sabres gleaming like fire as they fanned out and headed for the enemy lines.

Bolitho shouted, 'Fall back now, Lieutenant! That fool has given you the chance!' As the soldiers struggled to their feet and retreated towards the bridge Bolitho turned to stare after the charging cavalry. 'And he said *I* was brave!'

In the darkness he heard the screams of wounded horses, the sharp exchange of shots, and above all the sudden blare of a cavalry trumpet. But the enemy barrage had stopped. There was no time to stand and marvel at any man's courage. Not now. But later . . . Bolitho shook himself from his thoughts and ran to his horse.

Ashby yelled, 'None of 'em will live through that, sir! By God, that man must be mad!'

Bolitho nudged the horse towards the bridge. '*Angry*, Captain Ashby! And I cannot find it in my heart to blame him.'

When they reached the waterfront they were greeted

with even greater confusion. Along the jetty there were boats of every shape and size, and pigtailed sailors were passing women and children down from the steps and out to their comrades without pause, as if they had been doing nothing else for years.

Voices called on every side, officers shouting orders to their men, seamen and marines urging or pleading with some of the civilians who seemed determined to take as much furniture and baggage as the boats would hold.

Bolitho saw a petty officer dragging an old woman away from a tethered calf, saying gruffly, 'No, you can't take that one, Mother! There's little enough room as it is!' But the old woman did not understand and was still struggling and weeping as the seamen carried her to a waiting boat. And why should she understand? Bolitho stood watching in silence. The calf was probably all she owned in the whole world.

Lieutenant Inch pushed through the surging crowd and touched his hat. 'The wounded are away, sir!' He was shouting above the din. 'These are the last of the towns-people who want to go!'

Bolitho nodded. 'And the rest?'

'Hiding most likely, sir.' He winced as a sullen explosion rocked the buildings above the jetty. 'What was that?'

'The bridge.' Bolitho walked to the edge of the stonework and watched the boats gliding downstream.

Another lieutenant reported at his side, '*Harvester* has unloaded the, er, convicts, sir.' He seemed stunned by the noise and chaotic activity.

'Very well.' Bolitho tore his eyes from the hurrying figures, the despair and sudden desperation of escape. 'I'll come and speak to them.'

The convicts were herded into a low-beamed shed behind the jetty. Bolitho recognised Captain Poole of the transport *Erebus* as he stood uncertainly looking at his extra passengers.

He said, 'Are they all ready to leave?'

Poole grinned. 'My ship is like nothing on earth, Captain! You can hardly move a belaying pin for people!' He saw the strain on Bolitho's face and added firmly, 'But never fear, I'll get 'em away from here!'

Bolitho mounted a discarded case and looked around the watching faces. Even in the feeble lantern light he could see that most of the convicts looked fitter than when he had last seen them. He had to force his mind back again. How long was that? Could it really be only four months?

He said, 'You are leaving now aboard the *Erebus*. There are no guards or manacles.' He saw the sudden shiver of excitement move through the packed figures below him. 'Captain Poole has written orders from Rear-Admiral Pomfret which he will hand to the senior officer at Gibraltar.' How easy the lie came to him. The orders were sealed with Pomfret's crest, but the signature was his own. 'I have no doubt that many of you will be pardoned, although some may wish to await the next convoy to New Holland to try and carve out a new life in a different country.' He felt dizzy with fatigue but continued, 'You have behaved with dignity, and no little courage. That at least is worth rewarding!'

He turned to leave, but a voice called, 'A moment, Captain Bolitho!' When he faced them again they were all staring at him, their eyes glittering in the lamplight.

The voice said, 'We know what you have done for us, Captain! Don't we, lads?' There was an answering rumble of assent. 'Some would have left us to rot in Cozar, but you had us took off! We just want you to know that you've give us back more than a hope o' freedom, Captain! You've give us back our respect!'

Bolitho walked blindly into the darkness, the great wave of cheering following him like surf roaring on a reef. Poole was grinning openly, but his words were lost in the noise.

Then Bolitho saw Midshipman Seton standing beside the jetty, one hand in a bandage, the other holding an exhausted horse by the bridle.

The boy said, 'May I rejoin the ship, sir?'

Bolitho touched his shoulder. 'Thank God you're safe! I have been searching for you this afternoon.'

Seton looked embarrassed, 'I g-got lost, sir. Actually, the horse bolted, and it t-took me two days to get back through the French lines.'

Bolitho smiled wearily. 'Mr. Piper will be glad to learn of that, he was expecting you to meet with some difficulty on your own!'

He looked back as the convicts poured down the stairs and into the next batch of boats. 'Stay here and help these men, Seton. When they are clear you can come to the admiral's headquarters. I will be there.'

The midshipman asked, 'Is it over, sir?'

'Nearly so.' The words sounded final. 'At dawn tomorrow we will take off the last of the soldiers.' He shrugged. 'It will be a day for you to remember.'

Seton nodded, suddenly grave. 'I saw my sister before she left, sir. She told me e-everything.' He shifted his feet. 'Everything th-that has happened, sir!'

Bolitho saw Ashby waiting by the horses and replied quietly, 'Now then, Mr. Seton, you are starting to stutter again!' As he walked away he saw that the boy was still staring after him.

The square beside Pomfret's headquarters was deserted but for a few marines and a scavenging dog. He noticed that the enemy's bombardment had stopped and there was a great silence over the battered town, as if it was holding its breath for the coming of daylight and the final act of misery.

He entered the house and found the panelled study empty and strangely forlorn, the map lying on the floor beside Pomfret's desk. As he slumped into a chair he saw Allday watching him from the door.

He said, 'The admiral's sleeping, Captain. I've got him cleaned up, and Mr. Fanshawe is up there watching over him.' He added firmly, 'I think you should get a bit of sleep too, Captain. You look worn out, if I may say so.'

'You may not, Allday!' But he could not find the strength to resist as Allday bent to pull off his shoes and unbuckle his swordbelt.

The coxswain added, 'I've got some soup, Captain. That should put a sparkle back inside you.'

He padded away whistling to himself, and Bolitho let his head loll against the chairback, his whole frame suddenly empty of feeling. There was such a lot still to do. He had not yet found Cobban, or arranged for the final destruction of the port's meagre installations.

Bolitho thought of the girl's face and the brightness in her eyes when they had parted. At first light the ships would sail, leaving only men-of-war to watch over the final phase of retreat.

Retreat. The word hung over him like an insult. It was never easy to accept, no matter how valid the reason.

His head drooped, the weariness closing over him like a cloak. But dimly he heard Allday re-enter the room and felt him wrap a blanket around his aching body.

As if from far away he heard Allday mutter, 'That's

right, Captain, you sleep. There's many who'll sleep in safety because of you. I hope to God Almighty they know who saved 'em!'

Bolitho wanted to speak, but nothing came. Seconds later he surrendered to the waiting darkness.

.   .   .   .   ,

Lieutenant Herrick thrust himself away from the quarter-deck rail and rubbed his eyes vigorously. Another second and he knew he would have fallen asleep on his feet. Around him the darkened ship seemed to be sleeping, and apart from the occasional shuffle from one of the watchkeepers or sentries and the gentle moan of wind through the shrouds, a great silence hung over the sheltered inlet.

The sky had clouded during the night, and as he walked slowly towards the poop ladder he felt a brief touch of rain across his cheek. The dawn was not far away, and already there was an uncertain lightening to mark the distant horizon like dull pewter.

He heard Tomlin, the boatswain, speaking angrily in the darkness, and guessed that he had stumbled upon some unfortunate seaman asleep at his station. It was hardly surprising. The men had worked like demons until the fading light had shown the last of the squadron's boats pulling wearily from the town to disperse amongst the anchored ships. What had seemed an impossible and hopeless task had been achieved, but no one really knew how it had been accomplished in such a short time. Men, women and children. Wounded soldiers and hastily recalled troops from beyond the bridge. Somehow they had been crammed aboard the transports, but Herrick doubted if any had been able to sleep. Each gust of offshore wind brought the smell of fire and death to remind them of that which they would soon leave behind.

And somewhere out there beyond the dark edge of land Bolitho was still busy, he thought grimly. Taking upon his own shoulders what others should have done.

There was a step beside him and he saw Gossett's massive shape outlined against the pale deck shrouded in a tarpaulin coat.

The master said quietly, 'Not long now, Mr. 'Errick.'

'So you could not sleep either?' Herrick banged his hands together to restore the circulation. 'God, this has been a long night!'

Gossett grunted. 'I'll not rest easy until our own people are inboard once more.' He held up his hand as a pipe shrilled across the water like a disturbed bird. 'They're callin' the hands aboard the transports. They'll be weighin' very shortly.'

'Good.' Herrick squinted against the cool wind to watch a small lantern moving along one of the transport's decks. When daylight once more laid bare the ruin of St. Clar the little convoy would be clear out to sea. The Spanish *Princesa* was to act as the main escort, with the frigate *Bat* and one of the sloops for additional support as far as Gibraltar.

Gossett seemed to read his thoughts. 'At least we can depend on the *Princesa* this time. She'll be headin' for her own waters and'll need no encouragement to get a move on!' He sounded bitter.

They both started as a voice challenged from the starboard gangway, 'Boat ahoy?'

Back from the gloom came the instant response, 'Aye, aye!'

Gossett murmured, 'That's odd. It looks like the barge, but the cap'n's not aboard 'er.'

Herrick nodded and strode quickly to the ladder. 'He'll not come until everyone else is away, Mr. Gossett.'

The master sighed. 'You do not have to tell me that!'

The barge hooked on to the main chains, and within seconds Allday was pulling himself through the entry port. He saw the lieutenant and knuckled his forehead.

'Captain's compliments, sir.' He peered back into the barge and hissed, 'Hold your noise, damn you!' Then to Herrick he continued, 'Would you give a hand to take the admiral aft, sir?'

Herrick stared at him. 'The *admiral*?' He saw Rowlstone climbing through the port and the smaller shape of Midshipman Piper close behind him.

Allday said calmly, 'The captain's orders are that Sir Edmund is to be put in his sleeping cabin, sir.' He saw Herrick peering round for the master's mate of the watch and added sharply, 'He said there was to be no fuss! Nobody's to see the admiral until he's on his feet again!'

Herrick nodded, the realisation sweeping over him. He knew Allday of old. He had never known him to panic or get his orders confused. If Bolitho wanted Pomfret's transfer kept quiet, there was a very good reason.

He beckoned to Gossett. 'Here, give a hand!'

Like conspirators they manhandled Pomfret's blanketed figure through the entry port and aft to the quarterdeck. The admiral's aide was assisting with the rough stretcher, and from his dragging footsteps Herrick imagined that he too had been awake all night.

Allday watched the small group groping its way beneath the poop before adding, 'The captain is coming off with the rearguard, sir.' He rubbed his hand across his chin with a loud rasping sound. 'It will have to be quick.'

Herrick nodded. 'We will be ready.' He reached out as Allday turned to rejoin his barge crew. 'Tell Captain

337

Bolitho . . .' He broke off, not knowing how to express his true feelings.

Allday grinned in the darkness. 'I don't have to tell him anything, sir. He'll be knowing what you think, I shouldn't wonder.'

Herrick watched the barge as it backed away from the side. The stroke slow and weary, like the men.

Aloud he muttered, 'I expect he will.'

A seaman called, 'Transports is shortenin' their cables, sir! I kin see the old *Erebus* breakin' out 'er foretops'l already!'

'Very well.' Herrick watched the pale patches of sail giving shape and identity to the other ships as one after the other they prepared to weigh anchor. He said, 'Tell Mr. Tomlin to call our people in fifteen minutes, and see that the cooks have got their fires alight.' He shivered slightly. 'It'll be a while before we get another cooked meal, if I'm any judge!'

Gossett rejoined him at the rail. 'What does it all mean, Mr. 'Errick? Why is Sir Edmund aboard us instead o' the flagship?'

Herrick glanced briefly at the anchored *Tenacious* before replying. 'The reasons are not our concern. But at dawn we will hoist Sir Edmund's flag at the mizzen.' He knew Gossett was staring at him. 'The responsibility shifts with the flag, of that I *am* sure!'

*   *   *   *   *   *

As the first sunlight touched the hills and filtered down between the rubble-strewn streets the enemy guns reopened fire. Black columns of smoke poured from the jetty, the bright sparks and drifting ashes marking the last stages of destruction as small groups of soldiers threw oil-soaked rags into the moored fishing boats and storage sheds before setting them ablaze.

Captain Ashby stood grim faced beside his square of marines watching the remaining files of soldiers hurrying back from the firing line, some carrying wounded comrades, others using their muskets as crutches as they headed for the water and the waiting boats.

In the big house Bolitho stood by one of the open windows, his hands resting on the sill while he studied the hills beyond the town. He heard the crunch of boots below him and saw the young infantry officer peering up at him. 'Is everything completed?'

The soldier nodded. 'The last picket is falling back now, sir.' He turned and drew his smoke-blackened figure to attention as a young lieutenant and three armed soldiers marched around a bend in the road, their step measured and correct, as if they were on parade. The lieutenant was carrying the regiment's colour, and as he passed Bolitho saw there were real tears running down his face, cutting through the grime like painted lines.

Bolitho walked back across the room. The house already seemed lost and derelict, with little to show it had once been Pomfret's 'stepping-stone to Paris'.

In the square Ashby greeted him formally. 'The charges are laid, sir. The Frogs will be here at any time now.'

Bolitho nodded, listening to the creeping murmur of heavy guns as the enemy put down a final barrage on the waiting line of redcoats. Without effort he could still see the crouching figures along the edge of the barricades and earthworks, apparently ready and resolved to withstand the last attack. It was almost the worst part of the whole wretched business, he thought. Just before dawn, while the weary troops had crept back from their positions,

Lieutenant Inch and a party of seamen had prepared the last rearguard under his direction.

But when the French ceased their bombardment and entered the town the soldiers would not shoot back, nor would they surrender, for they were already dead. From the field hospital and the battered earthworks the seamen had gathered up their unprotesting bodies, had arranged them with their muskets in a silent array. There was even a flag above their sightless faces, a last grim mockery.

Bolitho shook himself from his brooding. Dead men could not suffer twice. The living had to be saved.

He snapped, 'Carry on, Ashby! Fire the fuses!'

He heard the blare of a bugle and a sudden wave of cheering as the first French soldiers charged down from the coast road. Around him the marines were breaking up into sections, falling back towards the shattered jetty, their bayonets still trained towards the shadowed streets.

There were no signs of the inhabitants who had chosen to remain in St. Clar. They were hiding and holding their breaths, and when the first wave of fury and bloodshed had passed they would come out into the open to make their peace with their countrymen, Bolitho thought. Friends, even relatives would be denounced as proof of loyalty to the Revolution. The reckoning would be harsh and prolonged.

Right now the first French troops would be staring at the dead defenders, possibly wondering at the meaning of this macabre attempt to delay their final victory.

At that instant the first fuse reached its target, and the whole town seemed to rock on its foundations from the force of the explosion.

Ashby said hoarsely, 'That's the main magazine, sir! That'll have caught some of the bastards!' He waved his sword. 'Into the boats!'

As yet another great explosion savaged the town the marines hurled themselves into the boats to follow those already pulling away downstream. A few French sharpshooters must have infiltrated the harbour buildings, and here and there the water spouted with tall feathers of spray as they fired after the retreating boats.

Ashby watched his lieutenant running towards him from the square, hatless, and carrying a smoking slow match.

'All done, Shanks?'

'The last fuse is just going, sir!' Shanks grimaced as a violent detonation brought down a complete house across the entrance of a narrow street, the shockwave almost hurling him bodily into the water.

The barge was hooked on to the jetty piles, and as the last marines clambered down Allday yelled, 'Here come the cavalry, Captain!'

There were about a dozen of them. They burst from a side-street, and as they sighted the barge at the jetty stairs they charged full tilt through the smoke of the last explosion.

Bolitho took a quick look round and then jumped for the gunwale.

As the boat backed clear the crouching seaman in the bows laid his eye against the mounted swivel gun and then stood clear. With a jerk on the lanyard the gun fired, the final shot of the retreat.

Bolitho clutched the gunwale as the tiller went over, and the roofless houses crept out to hide the tangled, bloody remains of horses and riders cut down by the double charge of cannister.

It was all but over. Briefly he found time to wonder about Colonel Cobban, but in his heart could find no pity for him.

During the night, as he had lain sleeping in Pomfret's deserted study, a messenger had burst in to tell him that Cobban had gone under a flag of truce to the French commander. To arrange a 'peace with honour' as he had described it.

Now, in the grim reality of daylight the French would probably see Cobban's pitiful attempt to save his own skin merely as a delaying tactic to cover the British evacuation. It was grotesque to realise that Cobban might even be remembered as a selfless and courageous officer because of it.

The boats were already gliding into the deeper waters of the inlet, and Bolitho levered his aching body upright in the sternsheets as he watched the two ships of the line waiting to receive them. Then he saw Pomfret's flag flapping gaily from the *Hyperion*'s mizzen and knew that Herrick understood, even if he did not agree with what he was doing.

Within half an hour both ships had weighed, and as the wind freshened to drive the smoke seaward from the burning town Bolitho stood by the nettings, hands clasped behind his back, his eyes fixed on the reflected fires inside the harbour.

But when the *Hyperion* spread her sails and heeled towards the wide entrance there was one final act, as if it had been set and timed for this single moment.

A solitary horseman appeared high on the southern headland, his yellow uniform shining in the pale light while he stood watching the departing ships. Bolitho did not need a glass to see that it was the Spanish colonel. No wonder there had been no sudden bombardment from the headland. Salgado's cavalry had done their work well, but the cost was plain because of this one, lonely figure.

Even as he watched he saw the Spaniard fall sideways

from his saddle to lie within feet of the edge. Whether it was from some unheard musket-shot, or from wounds already suffered in battle, no one knew.

Salgado's horse moved towards the edge of the headland, nuzzling its master as if to return him to life. Long after the ships had cleared the land the horse still stood outlined against the clouded sky. Like a monument.

Bolitho looked away. A memorial to all of us, he thought.

Then he glanced at Herrick, his eyes dull and unseeing. 'As soon as *Harvester* and *Chanticleer* are in company we will lay a course to round Cozar, Mr. Herrick.'

Herrick watched him sadly. 'We are rejoining the fleet, sir?'

Bolitho nodded and then turned towards the rolling bank of smoke. 'There is nothing left for us here.'

Ashby waited until Bolitho had left the quarterdeck and then said quietly, 'But by God the French will remember our visit, Mr. Herrick!'

Herrick sighed deeply. 'So will I, Captain Ashby. *So will I!*'

Then he opened his glass and trained it on the *Tenacious*, as obedient to the flag she tacked ponderously to take station astern.

In his cabin Bolitho stood by the stern windows also watching the three-decker, her sails very white in the morning light. He wondered vaguely what Dash would think now, and whether he would remember where his loyalty lay when the aftermath of battle and retreat cooled to investigation or the search for a scapegoat.

He looked round as Inch appeared in the doorway. 'Do you wish to see me?'

Inch was still grimy from the dust and smoke of St. Clar and his horse face was drooping with fatigue. 'I am very sorry, sir.' He fumbled in his pocket. 'But in the heat of the fighting and that terrible work with those dead soldiers,' he brought out something which shone in the reflections from the dancing water, 'I simply forgot to give this to you.'

Bolitho stared, hardly understanding what he saw. Tautly he asked, 'Where did you get this?'

Inch replied, 'It was one of the convicts', sir. Just before the last of 'em went into the boats for the *Erebus*.'

Bolitho took the ring and held it in the palm of his hand.

Inch was watching him curiously. 'This fellow came up to me at the very last second. He gave me the ring and said I was to hand it to you *personally*.' He faltered. 'He said that he wanted you to have it for your, er, bride, sir!'

Bolitho felt the cabin closing in around him. It was not possible.

Inch asked awkwardly, 'Have you seen it before, sir?'

Bolitho did not answer. 'This man. Did you get a good look at him?' He took a pace towards him. 'Well, *did you*?'

Inch recoiled. 'It was dark, sir.' He screwed up his eyes. 'He was very grey, but quite a gentleman I should say ...'

He fell silent as Bolitho pushed past him and ran out to the quarterdeck. He saw Herrick staring at him but did not care. Snatching a glass from a startled midshipman he climbed into the mizzen shrouds, his heart pounding his ribs like a drum.

Then he saw the convoy, far off below the horizon and almost lost from view. In a week or so they would reach Gibraltar and the human cargo would scatter to the winds for ever.

He climbed unsteadily back to the deck and stood looking at the ring. The man had been grey, Inch had said. But then he was getting grey the last time he had seen him. Ten, no eleven years ago. And to think that all these months he must have watched him from amongst the other convicts, while *he* had known nothing, had still believed his brother to be dead.

But if he had known, what could he have done? Hugh must have been on his way to New Holland for some minor crime like the others. One sign of recognition and he would have been seized for what he really was, a deserter from the King's Navy, a traitor to his country. And Bolitho's own life would have been laid in ruins had he lifted a finger to aid his deception.

So Hugh had waited, had bided his time until the last possible moment before sending his own private message, when there was no chance of facing him. The one possession which he knew would mean more than any words.

Herrick crossed to his side and looked down at the ring. 'That is a fine piece of work, sir.'

Bolitho stared through him. 'It belonged to my mother.' Then without another word he walked aft towards his cabin.

17

'The French Are Out!'

As eight bells chimed out to announce the beginning of yet another forenoon watch Bolitho walked from beneath

345

the poop and took his usual position on the weather side of the quarterdeck. The sky was overcast with low, fast-moving clouds, and the wind which came almost directly towards the larboard beam was heavy with a promise of rain.

He wriggled his shoulders inside his coat and turned to study the *Tenacious*. During the night she had shortened sail to avoid running down on her slower consort, and now lay some two miles clear on the starboard quarter. There was no horizon, and against the dull clouds and lead-coloured sea the big three-decker seemed to shine as if held in some unearthly light.

Bolitho gripped the nettings and turned his head once more into the wind. There was Cozar Island about six miles off the larboard beam, its grim outline shrouded in cloud and spray. While he had sat restlessly toying with his breakfast Bolitho had imagined how it would look, had pondered over the hopes and follies the island's name had come to represent to him.

For three days after leaving the smoking ruins of St. Clar he had gone over each detail again and again, trying to see the short campaign with impartial eyes, to assemble the facts as they would be viewed by an historian.

He bit his lip as he stared unwaveringly at the humped outline. Occupied and reoccupied a hundred times. Fought over and discarded, the island lay waiting for the next assault on its isolation. Now it was abandoned and derelict, with only the many dead to guard its barren heritage.

Herrick had joined him at the nettings. He said carefully, 'I wonder if we'll ever see it again, sir?'

Bolitho did not speak. He was watching the sloop *Chanticleer*, her sails and yards clearly etched against the dull cliffs as she drove close inshore. Bellamy must

346

be thinking of his part in the capture of Cozar. The reckless excitement, the very impudence of their attack might seem mockeries to him now.

He realised that Herrick had said something and asked, 'Did you wish to speak about the routine?'

Herrick's face softened slightly. 'Well, sir, as a matter of fact ...'

'Go ahead, Thomas.' Bolitho turned away from the island. 'I have been poor company of late. You must forgive me.' He had in fact hardly spoken to Herrick since leaving St. Clar. His officers must have respected his wishes to be left alone with his brooding, for on his rare walks on the quarterdeck they had been careful to leave the weather side vacant and undisturbed.

Herrick cleared his throat noisily. 'Have you spoken with the admiral this morning, sir?'

Bolitho smiled. The words had come blurting out, and he guessed that Herrick had been planning this interview for days.

'Mr. Rowlstone is with him now, Thomas. Sir Edmund is very ill, that is all I can tell you at the moment.'

Poor Rowlstone, he thought. He was as much out of his depth with Pomfret as any unskilled seaman. The admiral certainly looked a bit better, but where his body was trying to rally, his mind seemed to stay unmoving and remote, blocked off by the shock and realisation which it still refused to accept.

Pomfret was like a living corpse. He allowed Gimlett to shave him and keep him clean. He opened his mouth to receive soup, or carefully cut meat like a child with no understanding, and he never said a word.

Herrick persisted, 'Look, sir, I must speak my mind! In my opinion you owe *nothing* to Sir Edmund, quite the reverse!' He gestured towards the *Tenacious*. 'Why not

347

shift this responsibility to Captain Dash before we sight the fleet? He is the senior officer, it is unfair that you should have to carry him!'

Bolitho sighed. 'You have seen Sir Edmund, have you not?' Herrick nodded as he continued evenly, 'Would you take his last shred of honour and self-respect and stamp on it?' He shook his head. 'When we rejoin the fleet Sir Edmund will at least be under the protection of his flag and not carried to the reckoning like a trussed chicken for the pot!' He gripped his hands behind him. 'No, Thomas, I'll have none of that!'

Herrick had his mouth open to argue, but closed it with a click as Bolitho swung towards the bows, his head on one side like a dog at a scent.

'Listen!' Bolitho seized the quarterdeck rail and leaned forward. 'It was more of a feeling, and yet . . .' He watched Herrick's face until it too showed understanding.

Herrick murmured, 'Thunder?' Their eyes met. 'Or gunfire?'

Bolitho cupped his hands. 'Mr. Inch! Get the royals on her!' He crossed to the binnacle even as the pipes shrilled to break the silence. 'Bring her up a point!' He waited, biting his lip, until the helmsman intoned, 'Course nor' by east, sorr!'

Bolitho said aloud, 'Where is the *Harvester*, for God's sake?'

Herrick was watching the startled seamen scrambling aloft in answer to the call. He said, 'She's away up there on the larboard bow, *somewhere*!'

Bolitho made himself walk slowly to Herrick's side. 'Well, it was no frigate, Thomas. That was heavier metal on the wind!'

When he peered over the quarter he noticed that the

Tenacious was still on the same bearing, in spite of his own ship's extra canvas. He pounded the rail in time with his thoughts. If only they could get the filth and weed off her bottom the old *Hyperion* would soon show them something!

Herrick said suddenly, 'Could be a blockade runner, sir.'

'Unlikely.' Bolitho was staring at the dull streak where the horizon should have been. 'Lord Hood will have too much on his hands with his own evacuation to care much for enforcing a blockade elsewhere. It will be St. Clar multiplied ten thousand times over, Thomas.'

'Deck there! Sail fine on th' weather bow, sir!'

They stared up at the swaying masthead. Then Bolitho said quietly, 'We shall soon know now. Get up there, Thomas, and report the moment you recognise the facts for me.'

Midshipman Piper appeared as if by magic. 'Sir! *Harvester*'s signalling!'

Bolitho took a glass from its rack and peered along Piper's outstretched arm. The frigate was well out on the larboard bow, suddenly clear and sharp in the lens as some freak wind brushed away the wet haze like smoke.

Piper was shouting, '*Ships in sight to the nor'-east!*' He paused and flipped through the pages of his book. '*Estimate six sail of the line!*'

Bolitho looked aloft and abeam, his mind busy as it digested the frigate's information and slotted it into his own knowledge. The ships, whatever they were, were almost directly ahead of his own. They could not possibly be slower than *Hyperion*, so therefore it seemed most likely they were on the opposite tack and heading straight for him.

Herrick called hoarsely, 'Deck there! It's a stern-chase, sir! Maybe five or six sail of the line after one another!'

Bolitho glanced briefly at the *Tenacious*. 'Come down, Mr. Herrick!' He caught Inch's eye and snapped, 'General signal to our ships, Mr. Inch. "Prepare for battle!"'

As the flags soared up the *Hyperion*'s yards Herrick arrived with a thud beside him, by way of a backstay.

Bolitho looked at him gravely. 'Beat to quarters, and clear for action!'

Herrick touched his hat. 'Aye, *aye*, sir!' Then he grinned. 'Do you think we can snatch a prize from right under the noses of those other ships, sir?'

Bolitho did not smile. 'I think you will discover that the ship being chased is one of *ours*, Mr. Herrick!' Across the water he heard the mounting rattle of drums as the *Tenacious* beat to quarters. Dash probably thought he was mad, and like Herrick imagined it impossible for the enemy to be at large already and in such strength.

The *Hyperion*'s drummers took up the call, and as men poured from the hatchways and petty officers hurried to their stations yelling names as they ran, Bolitho looked once more at Pomfret's flag as it flapped briskly from the mizzen.

When the clamour and noise died away Herrick hurried once more to the quarterdeck and reported, 'Cleared for action, sir!'

Bolitho was still looking at the masthead, his eyes thoughtful. Then he said, '*Hyperion* has been on the *fringe* of things for too long, Thomas. That flag will ensure our proper place in affairs this morning!' He met Herrick's anxious stare and added, 'So you see, I could not transfer Sir Edmund to *Tenacious* even if I wanted to!'

350

Piper had climbed up to the maintop to get a better view. 'Deck there! The leading ship is wearing our colours, sir!'

Bolitho banged his palms together. 'Did I not say so, Thomas?' He was trembling inwardly with excitement. 'Have chain slings rigged to the yards immediately, and lower all boats for towing astern! We want no additional woodwork about our ears *this* day, Thomas!'

Herrick passed his order and stood aside as Tomlin's spare hands dashed aft to secure the towing lines. A ball striking a boat while it lay inboard could fill the air with murderous splinters. But, nevertheless, he felt vaguely uneasy as first one and then the rest of the boats were swung outboard and dropped alongside. It was like casting off the last chance of safety, he thought.

Bolitho said distantly, 'Signal *Chanticleer* to take station to lee'rd. I do not want her to follow *Snipe*'s fate.' He too was watching the boats being passed aft until they bobbed astern at the full extent of their lines. 'The sloop can watch the battle and give us some encouragement!'

Herrick stared at him. How could he do it? To be so calm, so utterly indifferent to the approaching danger.

Bolitho did not see Herrick's expression. He was looking along the full length and breadth of his command. Each detail must be checked. Soon there would be no more time.

Every gun was manned, and each captain was busily looking over his crew and equipment, while back and forth to the magazine hatch the little powder monkeys ran with their shot carriers and charges, their faces engrossed and concentrated on their tasks, their only purpose in life to keep those muzzles supplied when the moment came.

The marines lined the nettings, bayonets fixed and mus-

351

kets at the ready. And forward by the carronades he could see Lieutenant Shanks with his own detachment, his back to the enemy as he stared aft to the quarterdeck.

Rooke and young Gordon were pacing together between their lines of guns, and Bolitho wondered momentarily what they were finding to discuss.

He glanced round the quarterdeck. The nerve centre which could decide the fate of every single life aboard. Caswell was by the nine-pounders, but his eyes were on Piper and Seton at the signal halyards. He was remembering his own past, Bolitho decided. It would be better if he thought of his future.

Bolitho could not bear the waiting. He said, 'I am going below, Mr. Herrick. Then I will see the admiral.' He glanced up at the masthead pendant. 'It will be an hour before we close with them.' He listened to the intermittent boom of gunfire. It was indeed like thunder.

Then he turned and climbed down the larboard ladder. The overall picture of preparation seemed to break up as he approached and individual faces stood out to bring back some past event or memory.

A grizzled gun-captain touched his forehead and said, 'Us'll show 'em today, sir!' He laid a horny hand on the breech of his twelve-pounder. 'Old Maggie 'ere is just bidin' 'er time!' The men around him grinned and nodded.

Bolitho paused and looked at them gravely. 'Do your best, lads.' He shook himself to drive away the realisation that before many hours some of these faces would be dead, and others praying for death to receive them. He said abruptly, 'Make sure they have their scarves around their ears. When we reach England I want them to *hear* the welcome they'll get!' It was terrible the way they laughed and cheered as he passed.

Almost blindly he ran down another ladder and stood for a few moments to allow his eyes to recover. On the lower gundeck it seemed like night after the grey light above. But soon now those ports would fly open and the guns would make this low-beamed place shudder with the hammers of hell. Inch was now at his station with the big twenty-four-pounders, and was actually grinning as he strode to meet his captain.

Bolitho said, 'Do not lose contact with the upper battery. And try to prevent your gunners from getting too excited. We are depending on you today!'

Inch nodded. 'Midshipman Lory is with me, sir. He can keep me informed.'

Bolitho saw the double line of guns, the eyes of their crews glittering in the gloom as they peered towards him.

He called briefly, 'Good luck, lads!'

He glanced at the red-painted sides and decks. They might help to hide the blood, but the sights would be bad enough. He saw the midshipman watching him and re-called his own terrible experience in his first ship. Almost thirteen years old, and he had been serving on the lower gundeck of a similar ship to *Hyperion*. Perhaps the very horror had been too unreal to unhinge him, he thought vaguely. There could be no other reason.

Bolitho was grateful to return to the daylight and the damp air, but as he walked aft into his cabin he wondered what he should do with Pomfret. What might it do to his mind if he was shut below in the orlop?

Rowlstone stood by the windows, staring listlessly at the *Tenacious*. He asked, 'Shall I go to my station, sir?'

Bolitho did not answer immediately. He walked to the open door of his sleeping cabin and stared past Fanshawe's drooping figure beside the cot. Pomfret was propped almost to a sitting position, his chest bared in the stuffy air, his eyes moving back and forth in time with a deckhead lantern.

Bolitho spoke very quietly, 'We are about to engage the enemy, sir. Do you have any orders at present?'

The pale eyes stopped and settled on his face.

Fanshawe said helplessly, 'I don't think he understands, sir.'

Bolitho said slowly, 'Sir Edmund, the French are out!' But Pomfret's eyes did not even blink.

From behind him he heard Rowlstone say, 'I'll have him carried to the sickbay, sir. I can keep an eye on him there.'

Bolitho caught his arm. 'A moment!' He was watching Pomfret's hands. Like two claws they had fastened to the sides of the cot, the knuckles bone-white with strain. Then his mouth opened very slightly, but no words came from it.

Bolitho looked straight into Pomfret's eyes, holding them, willing him to speak. For just an instant he saw a small understanding, a kind of defiance, like that of a trapped animal facing an enemy.

He said quietly, 'You stay with him here, Mr. Fanshawe.' Pomfret's fingers relaxed slightly, and he added, 'I will keep the admiral informed whenever I can.' Then he turned on his heel and walked back to the quarterdeck.

The distant firing had stopped, and as he levelled his glass he saw that the ships were clearly visible now. The one being pursued was a seventy-four, like *Hyperion*, and as she tacked slightly to windward he saw that her outline was marred by the loss of her mizzen. But she had managed to rig a crude jurymast, and her ensign was streaming bravely above the pockmarked sails as more flags broke from her yards.

Piper shrilled, 'She's the *Zenith*, seventy-four, Cap'n Stewart, sir!'

Bolitho nodded, but kept his glass trained beyond the battle-scarred ship towards the jumbled mass of white topsails. He counted six enemy vessels before he had to lower the glass to rest his eye. They were in a ragged line, and were already tacking slowly to windward, their hulls leaning over in the pressure.

Herrick lowered his glass and said, 'They have the wind-gage, sir. There's no doubt about it.'

Bolitho looked round the quarterdeck. 'General signal. "Form line of battle ahead and astern of the admiral!"'

He ignored the burst of feverish activity at the halyards. He knew Stewart vaguely. He was a good captain, and was already tacking his ship to face the enemy. Astern, Dash was acknowledging the signal, and in minutes Bolitho saw the yards begin to swing as the *Tenacious* manœuvred comfortably astern of the flagship.

He tried not even to think the word. *Flagship*. Pomfret was incapable of speaking, let alone directing a battle. And it was eleven years since Bolitho had been in a real sea-fight. At the Saintes he had commanded a small frigate, and that great battle had been fought and won against an enemy equal both in strength and experience. He made himself look towards the enemy. Two to one. Even Rooke might consider the odds unfavourable.

Herrick said, 'We will pass larboard to larboard, sir. We cannot hope to tack across their course now.'

Bolitho nodded. To windward lay Cozar, it seemed as if they were doomed by that place, no matter what they did. Now it acted as a barrier to cut their chances of tacking to windward. If they continued as they were the French ships would pass down their larboard side, would pound them to submission before they could turn and fight again.

He snapped, 'General signal. "Shorten sail!"' The *Zenith* had completed her tack and was now leading the line. Through his glass he could see the mauling the enemy bowchasers had given her, the great scars across her poop. He said calmly, 'We will cut the enemy line in half, gentlemen! That way we will take the weather-gage, and give him a moment of alarm!'

He saw Herrick and Ashby exchanging anxious glances and added, 'It will mean facing three broadsides instead of six.'

Bolitho turned as Allday padded from the poop carrying his best coat and hat. The men around the quarter-deck were all watching in silence as he threw his old sea-going coat aside and slipped his arms into the other one. It was something he had always done before a fight. Madness or conceit? He could not be sure. Perhaps, unlike his predecessor in *Hyperion*, he did not wish to leave anything worthwhile behind should he die today. The stupidity of his racing thoughts helped to steady him, and the watching seamen and marines saw him give a small smile.

Allday held out the sword and asked quietly, 'Must I stay with the admiral, Captain?' He looked wretchedly at the crouching gunners. 'My place is *here*.'

'Your place is where I choose, Allday!' Then Bolitho nodded. 'I will know where you are if I need you, never fret!'

'Both ships have acknowledged, sir!' Piper was shouting, his voice very loud in the silence.

'Good. Now bend on another signal, Mr. Piper. but do not hoist it. "*Tack in succession and re-form line of battle!*"' He withdrew his sword and turned it over in

356

his hands. The steel felt like ice. To the deck at large he added, 'There will be one final signal. You will keep it flying until I order otherwise.'

Piper peered up from his slate, his face pinched with strain and concentration. 'I'm ready, sir!'

Bolitho looked evenly towards the approaching ships. Not long now.

He said, 'When we break their line you will hoist "Engage the enemy closer!" '

Then he returned the sword to its scabbard with a snap.

'And now, Mr. Herrick, you may give the order to load and run out.' For a moment longer he held Herrick's gaze. He wanted to grip his hand. To say something personal or trivial. But the moment was already past.

Herrick touched his hat and then raised his speaking trumpet. He had seen the pain in Bolitho's eyes. He did not have to be told anything.

As he shouted his order the deck seemed to come alive. Ports were hauled open, and as one captain after another raised his hand Rooke roared, *'Run out!'* Then he too turned aft and looked towards Bolitho.

A ragged thunder of cannon-fire echoed across the water, and through the taut rigging Herrick saw the spreading wall of gunsmoke drifting down to enfold the *Zenith* like a cloud.

He heard Gossett mutter, 'Make a note in the log. At two bells of th' Forenoon action was joined.' He cleared his throat. 'And God preserve us!'

Waiting for the final clash seemed endless. Bolitho made himself stand motionless by the rail while he watched the battered *Zenith* receiving the full brunt of the enemy broadsides. Barely seventy yards separated the two-decker as she edged past the leading French ship, but as a down-draught of wind cut through the billowing smoke Bolitho saw with cold relief that her masts were still standing and her guns were running out again as she sailed to meet the next adversary. The second ship in the enemy line was a three-decker, and as he watched Bolitho saw her foremost guns belch fire and smoke, the thundering crash of the detonations making him wince. Above the growing bank of smoke he saw the bright flash of colour at the enemy's topmast, the command flag of an admiral.

He shouted, 'Stand by!' He shut the picture of the flashing guns from his mind and concentrated on the leading ship, as like two wooden juggernauts she and *Hyperion* crossed bowsprits, and the men at the foremost guns stared through their ports and saw the hardening line of the enemy's bows.

Rooke yelled, 'Fire as you bear!'

Hyperion staggered drunkenly as the broadside rippled along her side in a double-edged line, the guns hurling themselves inboard against the tackles, their crews choking and cursing as the great fog of acrid smoke funnelled back through the ports, blinding them as they reeled and groped for the next charges.

Bolitho shaded his streaming eyes and stared up at the enemy's foremast as slowly and relentlessly it carved above the smoke until it hung directly above him. Then the Frenchman fired, the gun-flashes stabbing through the dense smoke and painting it with red and orange, so that it seemed to come alive. He felt the balls crashing into the hull, the splintering thunder jarring the planks beneath his straddled legs as if to burst up through the deck itself.

He yelled, '*Again*, lads! Hit 'em again!'

His brain cringed as the nine-pounders at his back

358

joined in the savage onslaught, and through the deafening gunfire he heard muffled cries and shouted orders as the marines opened fire with their muskets, shooting blindly into the all-enveloping smoke.

Something slammed into the rail by his hand, and when he looked down he saw a wood splinter standing on end like a quill pen.

Ashby bellowed, 'The tops! Shoot down those marksmen, you bastards!'

A marine corporal pulled the lanyard of a swivel gun, and before the dense brown smoke blew back across the quarterdeck Bolitho saw some half-dozen men plucked from the enemy's maintop by the scything burst of canister and swept away like so much rubbish.

Rooke dropped his sword. 'Run out! *Fire!*' Again the extended thunder of the two batteries and the answering crash of iron against timber as the full weight of *Hyperion*'s broadside smashed home.

Bolitho wiped his face with his sleeve. The other ship was already past, yet in spite of the hammering he could see little damage around him. He tried to stop the grin from spreading over his face. The *Tenacious* would soon finish off the leading ship, he thought wildly.

He cupped his hands. 'Easy, lads! The next one is the admiral's ship!' He heard the derisive yells from the smoke-shrouded gunners. 'Give him a proper salute!'

Then he ran across to the other side of the deck, straining his eyes to find the *Zenith*. He saw her maintop mast and commission pendant isolated above the smoke and already level with the third enemy ship. Her foremast had gone, but her guns were still firing, and between the savage broadsides he could hear cheering, like men driven beyond caution or sanity.

He shouted, 'Mr. Piper! Hoist that signal!'

He watched the flags jerking up to the yards and then stared anxiously towards the battered *Zenith*. With only one mast in view it was hard to judge her exact position or bearing.

But Piper was ready. 'She's acknowledged, sir!' He was clinging to the shrouds, oblivious of the oncoming three-decker as he peered at the signal.

Bolitho watched, hardly daring to breathe as Captain Stewart tacked his ship round and headed straight towards the enemy. He could see the *Zenith*'s topmast outlined against the braced yards of the fourth ship in the French line. She was already heading into the wind, and Bolitho had to grip the rail to prevent himself from running along the deck to watch as she swung still further, her bows pushing resolutely across the enemy's course, her guns firing from either beam as she struggled to obey Bolitho's last signal.

Herrick yelled, 'She's through! By God, she's cut the line!'

Men were cheering in the smoke, some hardly aware of the reason, but desperately eager to break their own dazed uncertainty.

Bolitho shouted, 'Stand by, Mr. Rooke!' He ran back to the nettings as the French flagship rose above the fog like a cliff, her forecastle rippling with musket-fire, her bow guns already shooting out their long red tongues as the range fell away to fifty yards.

Rooke yelled, 'Fire as you bear!' He was running down the upper deck, stopping for just a few seconds by each gun as captain after captain pulled his lanyard to add to the deafening bombardment.

From astern Bolitho heard the *Tenacious* adding her massive weight to the engagement, but forgot her completely as the deck bucked wildly beneath him and some twenty feet of the larboard gangway careered into the air, hurling men and splintered timbers back into the smoke.

He saw the nets across the upper deck jumping with severed blocks and pieces of ripped sailcloth, but when he stared aft he could still see every mast and yard intact.

Bolitho shouted, 'On the *uproll*, Mr. Rooke!' He peered towards the Frenchman's braced yards, the sudden flurry of colour as a signal broke to the wind. Their admiral obviously intended to try and stop the British attempt to cut the line, he thought wildly. He pulled out his sword and held it above his head. 'When I give the signal, Mr. Rooke!' His throat was raw with shouting and coughing. 'I want that rigging down!'

Another ragged broadside cut through the trapped smoke alongside, and two twelve-pounders were hurled away from the bulwark as if they were scraps of paper. Bolitho tore his eyes from the men trapped beneath the heavy guns and shut their agonised screams from his mind. Those muzzles must be almost red-hot, he thought vaguely.

He dropped his sword. '*Fire!*'

Hyperion was rolling heavily with the wind, and the force of a full broadside threw her even further over as both gundecks roared out together.

With something like sad dignity the Frenchman's foremast began to totter, the stays and shrouds holding it just long enough to give those trapped in the top and along the yards a few seconds of hope. Then with a great sigh the whole mass of rigging and spars pitched forward through the smoke, cleaving into the forecastle gunners before plunging down towards the shrouded water below.

Bolitho groped his way towards the poop until he found Gossett's massive shape beside the wheel. 'Stand by to wear ship!' Bolitho felt a musket-ball whip past his head and hammer into the poop ladder. 'We will turn across the enemy's line when you are ready!'

He did not wait for an answer but hurried back to the quarterdeck rail. The other ship was wallowing downwind, the trailing mass of spars acting like a giant sea-anchor. But over and beyond her snared bows Bolitho could already see the towering sails of the *Tenacious*, and before he wrenched his eyes back to the next ship in the line he saw the three-decker's broadside smashing into the French flagship, bringing down her main topgallant to add to the confusion below.

'*Now!*' Bolitho had to call twice because of the nine-pounders' vicious barking behind him. 'Now, Mr. Gossett!'

He watched narrowly as the big double wheel began to go over, the helmsmen stepping over two dead comrades as they fought to control the spokes.

At the quarterdeck rail Herrick was roaring at the top of his voice, 'Braces there! Let go and haul!'

Through the smoke the third ship was already firing across the narrowing strip of water. Shots hammered into the *Hyperion*'s hull, and others slapped through topsails and spanker, severing halyards and shrouds and hurling pieces of splintered wood high in the air.

But the old ship was answering. As she swung slowly across the enemy's quarter Bolitho saw some French seamen running aft as if to repel boarders, and then as the *Hyperion*'s intention became clear they opened fire with muskets and pistols, urged on by their officers and the fury of battle.

Across the disengaged side Bolitho saw another ship loom through the fog like some phantom vessel, and with something like disbelief he realised that *Hyperion* was

362

cutting the line, her tapered bowsprit and flapping jib already clear of smoke and reaching out beyond the enemy's weather side.

He shouted, 'Stand by to starboard! It's your turn now, lads!'

A man fell back from a nine-pounder, his face smashed to a bloody pulp, and he saw young Caswell, white but determined, waving another to take his place.

The gunners of the starboard battery waited their moment. The smoke hid the bulk of that fourth ship, but the black bowsprit and gleaming figurehead acted better than any aiming mark.

Rooke bellowed, 'Fire as you bear!'

Hyperion was responding to wind and rudder, and as she edged purposefully around the third ship's counter the starboard battery opened fire on her helpless consort. Two by two the guns bellowed and lurched inboard, their whooping crews already sponging and reloading before the broadside had reached as far aft as the quarterdeck.

Pieces of bulwark flew skyward above the haze of smoke, and the luckless ship's sails streamed from her yards like so much shredded waste.

Bolitho watched until the *Tenacious*'s topmasts crept into line. Dash was following, and above the crashing roar of *Hyperion*'s artillery he could hear the deeper thunder of the three-decker's thirty-two-pounders as they continued to hammer the enemy.

When the *Hyperion*'s bow swung gratefully across the wind the smoke cleared from her decks as if drawn away by a giant hand. All at once her scars were laid bare, and Bolitho felt suddenly stunned by the completeness of her misery.

Dead and wounded lay everywhere on the upper deck. The rest, their naked bodies shining with sweat and blackened by powder, worked at their guns with the wild desperation of souls in hell.

The great net above the littered deck was covered with torn canvas and wood splinters, and here and there a wounded man writhed broken and whimpering in the mesh after being shot down from aloft, like dying insects in a web.

The marines kept up a rapid fire from the nettings, hurling insults as they reloaded, and yelling encouragement to their comrades high in the swaying tops.

The larboard battery fired yet again, the balls ripping a bare twenty yards to blast through the enemy's poop and turn her quarterdeck into a bloody shambles.

Bolitho pounded the rail, silently urging his ship to complete her turn. But it could not last like this. Soon the other French ships would recover and fight back to rejoin their line. Before that happened they must settle with the enemy flagship and smash these three leading vessels into submission.

He swung round as Piper yelled, 'Signal from *Zenith*, sir! "Require assistance!" '

Bolitho had already seen the leading two-decker. She was completely dismasted, but for a stump of her main, and had drifted downwind across the French flagship's bows. Where the two vessels embraced men were already locked in hand-to-hand combat, while in the trapped arrowhead of water between them the guns still kept up their relentless bombardment, their blackened muzzles barely feet apart.

He shook his head. 'Make "Inability", Mr. Piper!' He watched the flags soaring aloft and added, 'Now that other signal, Mr. Piper, lively there!'

Bolitho ignored the rippling flashes as his guns bellowed defiance at the nearest ship. The enemy was hardly

364

firing a shot in return, but aboard her battered decks he could see something like panic as the *Tenacious* followed ponderously through the gap in the line, her triple rows of guns gaping straight at the Frenchman's unprotected stern. He gripped Herrick's shoulder, feeling him jump with shock at the sudden contact. Like himself he was probably expecting a musket-ball, he thought grimly.

'*Zenith* is all but done for, Thomas.' He broke off as a ball ploughed through the quarterdeck ladder and smashed into a pile of crouching marines. Sickened, he saw the blood spreading away like paint, until it seemed it would never stop. Amidst the litter of smashed limbs and screaming men he saw a marine's head rolling across the deck, the eyes still open and staring.

He swallowed hard to control the nausea. 'We must take the enemy flagship, Thomas!' He saw understanding flooding across Herrick's begrimed features. 'It is our only chance!'

He looked round abruptly as someone started to cheer. He saw young Caswell waving his hat like a madman and pointing at the last signal.

'Engage the enemy closer!'

Through the swirling smoke another set of red tongues licked across the water and Caswell was dead. He had had one hand across his chest and the ball smashed it through his body, cutting off his cry with the sharpness of a knife.

Bolitho turned towards the towering three-decker. All the anger and hate, the despair and bitterness seemed to overpower him like a frenzy. The sword was in his hand, and as he waved it he felt his hat plucked away by another musket-ball, so that the rebellious lock of hair fell across his eye, shutting out Caswell's broken body and his staring look of disbelief.

'Starboard gunners take station for boarding!' He was almost screaming. 'Come on, lads! England wants a victory, so what do you say?'

He did not hear the answering cheers and yells, but was already running along the larboard gangway. He leapt across the shattered bulwark and above the naked gunners, the sword in his hand and his eyes fastened on that one patch of colour which still flew from the enemy's topmast.

18

In Gallant Company

By the time Bolitho reached the forecastle the *Hyperion*'s bowsprit was already edging across the French flagship's starboard gangway, thrusting through the boarding nets and into the main shrouds like a giant lance.

He stared round at the crouching seamen and marines and yelled, 'Over you go, lads!' Then as both hulls ground together he hurled himself from the cathead, his sword slashing wildly at the nets, his feet kicking to gain some hold above the dark strip of trapped water.

Across the French ship's bows the dismasted and listing *Zenith* was putting up a stiff resistance, but in face of a great wave of boarders the English seamen had fallen back as far as their quarterdeck, the cutlasses and axes flashing dully through the smoke, the air filled with terrible screams and cries as they retreated across the bodies of their comrades already killed in battle.

But as Bolitho's men leapt over the narrowing gap the French attack hesitated, and at the blare of a trumpet many of the successful boarders turned and ran back to their own ship to meet this new threat from astern.

Lieutenant Shanks was pulling himself up the sagging net, his sword dangling from his wrist as he yelled encouragement to his men. A bearded French sailor ran across the gangway, and before Shanks could jump clear thrust upward with a boarding pike, the force of his charge driving the point deep into the marine's stomach. Shanks gave one shrill scream and dropped like a stone.

When Bolitho looked down he saw the lieutenant's white-clad legs kicking above the water, the motion becoming more violent and terrible as the two hulls moved together to hold the pulped corpse firmly between them.

Bolitho slashed through the last of the net and flung himself down to the deck. The same French seaman was already turning to meet him, but a yelling bosun's mate pushed Bolitho aside and slashed the man down with his cutlass, the blow almost cutting him from shoulder to armpit.

As more and more men jumped from the *Hyperion* it was hard to distinguish friend from foe. Bolitho fired his pistol at the wheel and saw the last helmsman fall kicking on the splintered planking. Then he placed his back against the poop ladder and crossed blades with a wild-eyed petty officer, while the fighting surged around him in a panorama of hatred and terror.

Bolitho parried the heavy sword aside and struck out hard for his neck. He felt the shock jerk up his wrist, and swung round to seek out another enemy even as the man pitched across the rail, blood gushing from a great wound in his throat.

He saw a marine drive his bayonet through a shrieking

midshipman, and Tomlin, the boatswain, swinging a huge
boarding axe like a toy as he carved a path for himself
towards the upper deck, his bare shoulders covered with
blood, although whether it was his own or that of his
victims it was impossible to tell.

A French lieutenant threw down his sword, his mouth
slack with terror as he struggled to catch Bolitho's arm.
He wanted to surrender, either himself or the ship, but
it was to no avail. The *Hyperion's* seamen were not yet
ready to consider reason or quarter, for themselves or
the enemy.

The man moaned and held his hands across his face,
and as a cutlass flashed across Bolitho's vision he saw the
blade sever the lieutenant's hands at the wrists and drive
on to smash him bodily to the deck.

Sergeant Best, wielding his half-pike like a club, staggered to join Bolitho above the reeling mass of men, dragging a French officer at his side.

He shouted, 'This 'ere's th' admiral, sir!' He lashed
out savagely, and a seaman already wounded screamed
and fell sideways across an abandoned swivel gun.

Bolitho stared for a few seconds at the small admiral
before recognition and understanding returned to his
shocked mind. He snapped, 'Take him aft, Sergeant!'
He saw the admiral's agonised face relax slightly and
added, 'Get that flag down, for God's sake, and hoist our
colours above it!'

The admiral tried to speak. Maybe he was grateful, or
he could have been making a last protest, but Best hauled
him away like a sack, and Bolitho knew that but for
the marine's strong arm the French admiral would already be dead.

He heard Tomlin roaring like a bull. 'Avast there!
Give 'em quarter!' And as Bolitho kicked a corpse from

the ladder and ran on to the gangway he saw with amazement that the French seamen were throwing down their weapons and falling back towards the bows. From the relieved *Zenith* he could hear wild cheering, and when he looked across at his own ship he saw the gunners standing back from the smoking muzzles to join in.

The sight of the *Hyperion*'s damage helped to steady him. From the three-decker's high gangway it was all too apparent. There were dead and dying everywhere he looked. Her side was smashed almost beyond recognition, but from the lower gundeck more heads poked through the ports to add their voices to the wild cheering and excitement.

A dazed lieutenant gripped his hand and pumped it up and down, his eyes shining with pleasure. 'I'm from *Zenith*, Captain. Oh my God, what a victory!'

Bolitho pushed him roughly aside. 'Take command here, Lieutenant!' He stared across his own ship, his mind ice-cold as he saw the bows of another Frenchman edging downwind towards *Hyperion*'s disengaged quarter.

He yelled, 'To me, *Hyperions*! Fall back to the ship!'

The lieutenant was still following him. 'What shall I do, sir?'

Bolitho watched while his men began to scramble towards their own ship.

The lieutenant persisted, 'Captain Stewart fell when we cut the French line, sir!'

Bolitho turned and studied him gravely. 'Very well. Drive these French seamen below and put guards on the hatches.' He glanced up at the tattered sails. 'I suggest you bring every fit man across from your ship and prepare to take *Zenith* in tow!' He clapped the dazed officer on the shoulder. 'Good experience for you!' Then he turned and followed the last of his men over the side.

He found Herrick at the quarterdeck rail yelling at the men on deck to cast off the grapnels from the other vessel's hull.

He saw Bolitho and gasped, 'Thank God, sir! I lost sight of you back there!'

Bolitho grinned. 'See yonder, Thomas! That must be the fifth ship in the French line!' He pointed with his sword. 'The fourth has drifted downwind. She'll not bother us for a bit with her bowsprit and fore shot away!'

Rooke yelled up from the deck, 'We can't get clear, sir!'

'Damn!' Herrick ran to the nettings and peered across at the captured ship. 'We must have drifted round more than I thought, sir.' He stared across Bolitho's shoulder, his face suddenly tight with alarm. 'By God, he's going about!' He waved to the men at the starboard battery. 'Open fire as you bear! Lively, if you want to see another dawn!'

The captain of the approaching ship had had plenty of time to plan his next move. While *Zenith* and *Hyperion* were locked in close combat, and Dash completed his destruction of the other two ships, he had clawed upwind, his efforts to retake the advantage well hidden in the smoke of battle.

Now, as *Hyperion*'s men ran desperately back to their guns, he tacked slowly to expose his full broadside at a range of about seventy yards. Not for him the uncertainty of close combat, but as the double line of guns belched fire Bolitho knew he was quite near enough to do his work.

It was like a scalding wind, with all sense of direction and feeling swept away in its path as the full weight of the Frenchman's broadside smashed into the *Hyperion*'s after part with the force and devastation of an avalanche.

With it came the choking smoke, and as men screamed and cursed around him Bolitho stared up with numbed dismay as the whole mizzen mast splintered apart less than twenty feet above the poop.

Then his own gunners replied, their salvo ragged and uncertain while they groped in the swirling darkness and slipped on the blood which covered the scarred deck from scupper to scupper.

Bolitho jumped aside as the topsail yard crashed across the quarterdeck and ground amidst the groping figures like a giant axe.

He heard Gossett roar, 'The steerin's gone, sir!' Then a curse. 'Get back to your station, that man!'

The Frenchman was still there, her yards coming round tightly as she closed in for another broadside. In a brief lull Bolitho heard more gunfire, and with astonishment saw the enemy's sails and rigging jerking wildly and more than one spar ripped away to fall alongside. Through the smoke he got a quick glimpse of close-reefed topsails beyond the Frenchman's rigging, and realised that Captain Leach had also been biding his time before throwing his frail *Harvester* to close quarters with the giants.

Axes rang midst the crash and rumble of gunfire, and he heard Tomlin urging his men to greater efforts to hack away the shattered mast from the poop, while others streamed aft through the destruction and horror to help Gossett rig the emergency steering gear. Not that there would be time, he thought dully.

Rooke was almost beside himself as he strode along the starboard battery, his sword beating time to control the shocked and bleeding gunners as they rammed home the charges and hauled the twelve-pounders up the tilting deck for yet another assault. But there were several empty ports, and upended guns and the grisly remains of their crews were strewn in obscene profusion, while above the battered decks the tops and rigging were festooned with dead and dying seamen as a blast of grape moaned through the shrouds like a messenger from hell itself.

Rooke dropped his sword. 'Fire!'

Bolitho staggered as the guns lurched back on their tackles, and then stared sickened as Rooke seemed to lift from his feet and fly back across the deck as if thrown by an invisible hand. One second he was there waving his sword and shouting at his sweating gunners. The next instant he was sprawled against the opposite bulwark, his limbs broken and twisted, the blood already pouring from a dozen wounds. He must have taken a full charge of canister. There was nothing left of the original man at all.

Shots seemed to be coming from every direction at once, and Bolitho guessed that the third ship in the French line, although crippled by the *Tenacious*'s onslaught, was still firing some of her guns. Her men were blinded by smoke, but some of the balls were hitting and cutting across *Hyperion*'s quarter to add to the damage and slaughter.

Bolitho turned and then stopped in his tracks. For a brief moment he thought he had finally cracked under the strain. In the middle of the quarterdeck, his full dress uniform glittering against the shattered planking and the piles of fallen rigging, Pomfret was surveying the terrible scene as if he was totally immune from danger of any kind.

Allday shouted, 'I tried to stop him, Captain!' He jerked aside with a savage oath as Lieutenant Fanshawe received a musket-ball full in the breast and fell against him, his hands clawing wildly at his arm.

Pomfret ignored the dying man. 'How goes the fight, Bolitho?'

Bolitho felt slightly giddy. He replied, 'The French flagship has struck, sir. At least two more are disabled, I think.'

He added quickly, 'If you must stay here, Sir Edmund, I would suggest you walk for a while. The French have sharpshooters aloft, and your uniform is a fair target.'

Pomfret shrugged. 'If you say so.' He began to pace up and down the littered deck with Bolitho at his side.

Bolitho said, 'I am glad to see you are better, sir. '

Pomfret nodded indifferently. 'Just in time it seems.'

He stopped as Piper ran excitedly through the smoke and held up a large flag across his body. He was grinning and weeping with excitement. He did not even touch his hat as he shouted to Pomfret.

'Here, Sir Edmund! The enemy's command flag! I got it for *you*!'

Bolitho smiled in spite of his ragged nerves. 'It is your victory, sir. It will make a good souvenir.'

A musket-ball plucked Pomfret's hat from his head, but as Bolitho stooped to retrieve it he saw the admiral pointing with his hand. For the first time in days he was showing some emotion.

When Bolitho twisted round he saw the reason. Piper was on his knees, the flag still across his small body. Dead in the centre of the flag was a black hole, and as he reached out to catch him he saw Piper's face crumple with agony. Then he fell forward at the admiral's feet.

Seton staggered through the smoke and dropped beside him, but Bolitho pulled him to his feet:

'The signals, Mr. Seton!' He saw the stunned horror on the boy's face and added harshly, 'They're your responsibility now!'

Herrick watched Seton walk away like a blind man, his shoes slipping on the blood-spattered planks, his hands hanging at his sides as if he no longer controlled them.

Then he bent over the dead midshipman, but Pomfret said sharply, 'Leave him there, Mr. Herrick! Get to your duties!' Without looking at either Bolitho or Herrick he rolled Piper's body on to its back and gently covered his face with the captured flag. He murmured, 'A brave youngster! Would that I had had more like him at St. Clar!'

Bolitho tore his eyes away, realising vaguely that the guns had ceased firing. But when he reached the rail he saw that the other ship was already moving downwind, her topgallants spreading from the braced yards as her hull slid deeply into the dense smoke.

All around men started cheering and dancing, and even some of the wounded dragged themselves up to the battered gangways to watch and add their own voices to the tumult.

Seton called, 'Signal from *Tenacious*, sir!' His voice was quite empty of expression. 'Two enemy ships are withdrawing from battle! The rest have struck their colours!'

Bolitho gripped the rail, his arms and legs shaking uncontrollably. It was impossible. But it was true. Through the smoke and wreckage he heard the cheering going on and on, as if it would never stop. Men capered through the carnage to shake each other's hands, or just to grin towards a friend who had somehow survived the savage harvest.

'Captain, sir!'

Bolitho thrust himself clear of the rail, half fearing that his legs might give way. When he turned he stared with disbelief at Rowlstone who was kneeling on the deck beside Pomfret.

The surgeon said shakily, 'He's *dead*, sir!' He had one hand inside the admiral's gold-laced coat, and when he withdrew it, it was shining with blood.

Gossett murmured, 'My God, 'e must 'ave bin wounded earlier, yet 'e said nothin'!' He took off his battered hat and stared as if seeing it for the first time.

Allday said quietly, 'When that Frenchman crossed our quarter, Captain, a ball came in through the chartroom.' He dropped his eyes under Bolitho's flat stare. 'It killed poor Gimlett, and a splinter struck the admiral.' He hung his head miserably. 'He made me swear not to tell you. He forced me to dress him in his best uniform. I'm sorry, Captain, I should've told you.'

Bolitho looked past him. 'It was not your fault, Allday.' So Pomfret would not receive the reward of the battle after all. But he must have understood that it *was* for him. In his broken mind he had found the strength and the will to show his appreciation the only way he knew.

Herrick said thickly, 'He had courage, I'll say that for him!'

Bolitho looked at the two bodies side by side on the broken deck. The admiral and the midshipman.

He said harshly, 'He is in gallant company, Thomas!'

The smoke was drifting clear of the ships to lay bare the destruction to victors and vanquished alike. The last two Frenchmen were already under full sail. Not that their captains need to fear now, Bolitho thought emptily. Apart from the distant *Chanticleer*, there was hardly enough undamaged sail to equip one ship amongst the battered survivors, let alone give chase.

If only the men would stop their cheering. He saw Inch

walking unsteadily along the upper deck. He stopped and stared down at Rooke's body and then gave what might have been a shrug. *He* was still alive. For today that was miracle enough for any man.

Seton called, 'Masthead has reported ships to the nor'-east, sir!'

Bolitho looked at him blankly. His ears were so stunned by the gunfire that he had heard nothing.

Seton said, 'This time they are our ships, sir!' Then he looked down at Piper's body and began to shake.

Herrick watched him sadly. 'Had they been here earlier . . .' He left it unfinished.

Bolitho rested one hand on his arm and replied quietly, 'Bend on another flag, Thomas. This is still Pomfret's ship.' Then he looked away, his eyes suddenly pricking with emotion. 'And make this signal.' He faltered, seeing again all those faces. Caswell and Shanks, Rooke and little Piper. Like so many more they were just part of the past now. In a firmer voice he said, *'Hyperion* to *Flag.* "We are rejoining the squadron."'

Herrick touched his hat and walked past the cheering marines.

A moment later the flags jerked up the remaining yards to replace the signal which Piper had somehow managed to keep flying throughout the battle.

Herrick had taken the telescope from Seton's nerveless hands, and as he trained it on the distant ships his lips moved as if talking to himself.

He turned and looked at Bolitho. Very quietly he said, *'Victory* to *Hyperion.* "Welcome. England is proud of you." ' Then he turned away, unable to watch the distress in Bolitho's eyes.

Gossett walked between the jubilant seamen and reported, 'The steerin' gear is rigged, sir!'

Bolitho swung round and wiped his face with the edge of his sleeve. He said quietly, 'Thank you. Be so good as to get under way, Mr. Gossett.' He ran his fingers along the splintered rail, feeling the old ship's pain like his own.

'There is still a long way to go yet!'

Gossett made to reply, but Herrick shook his head. He more than any other knew that Bolitho was speaking to his ship. And that was something he would share with no one.

Epilogue

The return of summer brought all things to all people. It was the second so far in a war which now seemed as if it would last for ever. In the towns and cities it was greeted with relief by those who had imagined that their island might already have been under the enemy's heel. By others, separated from loved ones, widowed or orphaned by the war's endless demands, it marked just one more milestone of loneliness or despair.

But in Cornwall, and in the seaport of Falmouth in particular, it was hailed as a time of thanksgiving, a just reward for the hardships and dangers of darker days. Inland, the patchwork of lush fields and flowered hedgerows, the rolling hills with their scattered sheep and contented cattle, all were visible evidence of survival, a sure belief in the future.

In the town itself the atmosphere was almost one of celebration, for although Falmouth was small, it drew its heritage from the sea and the ships and men who came and went on the tides. The long generations of sailors, who had seen St. Anthony's Beacon not as a mere welcome but as a first sight of home, had a true understanding of wider affairs and had done much to influence them.

Even the news was better, as if the coming warmth and the clear skies had at last brought a promise, if not a sight, of victory. Only that week the couriers had shouted the tidings in the narrow streets and along the

379

busy waterfront. It was not just a rumour, but something to fire the most doubting heart.

Lord Howe had fought and defeated a French fleet in the Atlantic in a battle already known as 'The Glorious First of June'. It had been like a tonic. After the setbacks and reverses born of unpreparedness and over-confidence in high places, it was exactly what was needed. Even Hood's failure to hold Toulon six months earlier seemed to shrink in importance, as if it too was just one of winter's forgotten hazards.

Whatever had gone before was history as far as the people of Falmouth were concerned. England was ready, and if necessary would fight until the end of time to break the French tyrant once and for all.

New names and fresh ideas were springing up every day to sweep away the old and the hidebound. Names like Saumarez and Hardy, Collingwood and the young Captain Nelson whose deeds had already gripped the imagination of a nation.

But Falmouth did not have to look beyond its own limits to find a name to applaud. And on this particular day many had ridden in from outlying villages and farms, and even some the of small coastal craft had stayed in port instead of earning their keep, so that their masters could join the crowd outside the old grey church of King Charles the Martyr.

It was not just another sea officer, but one of their own sons who was getting married, a man whose family name was as much a part of Falmouth as the stones of the church or the sea at the foot of Pendennis Point. The Bolitho family had always been good for an exciting yarn during the dark winter months, and this much-discussed marriage was as unusual and exciting as anything from their past exploits.

The girl was very beautiful, and had arrived in Falmouth in the middle of a snowstorm. Few had actually seen her, but it was said she regularly walked above the wall of the Bolitho house watching the sea and searching for the one ship which never seemed to come.

Now the waiting was over, and Richard Bolitho was back. Even the taverns emptied as he walked to the church, and people cheered and called his name, although many had never laid eyes on him before.

But he was a symbol, and he was one of their own. That was more than enough.

To the man in question, that particular day passed in a whirl of vague pictures and excited voices. Of last-minute instructions and conflicting advice. Only certain instances stood out with any sort of clarity, and they seemed to be happening to someone else, as if he was just one more of the onlookers.

Like the first moment of real peace when he had sat stiffly in the front pew, knowing that every person in the crowded church was watching him, yet unable to turn and face them. He had felt like a child, lost and confused, and the next second older than time itself. Everything seemed different, and even Herrick had looked like a stranger in his new captain's uniform.

He had wanted to peer at his watch, but had seen Walmsley, the old rector, looking at him severely, and had decided against it.

Poor Herrick. He seemed as surprised at his promotion to captain as he was confused by the new relationship it had presented. Bolitho had seen him glancing nervously at the line of wall plaques near the pulpit, the record of Bolitho's ancestors stretching back in time. The last one was small and plain. It merely stated, 'Lieutenant Hugh Bolitho. Born 1752. Died 1782.' And he found time to wonder what Herrick would say if he knew the truth about his brother. Somewhere on the other side of the world Hugh might be thinking about it, too, even smiling at the macabre joke which life had played on him.

Then Bolitho's thoughts had been scattered by the sudden boom of the organ and the immediate ripple of excitement at his back. When he had turned he had seen many familiar faces amongst the congregation, some of which brought back memories too painful to dwell on. *Hyperion* was lying at Plymouth, still undergoing repairs to the damage of battle and the long voyage home. But Inch was here, and Gossett, even Captain Ashby, who should have known better. He had lost an arm, but nothing, it seemed, could keep him away. In a month or so he would be taking *Hyperion* back to sea, but he would have to rejoin her long before that. There would be new officers and a whole world of fresh, untrained faces to mould into the old ship's way of life. But no Herrick this time, and very few of the others either. He knew Herrick was angry that he had not been promoted also. But it had been Pomfret's victory. It stated so in the *Gazette*, even though every man-jack in the fleet knew better.

Bolitho had forgotten everything as the girl had appeared in the church entrance, her figure outlined against the sunlight, one hand resting on the arm of her brother.

It was strange to see the boy in civilian dress. Stranger still to realise that he was now a man of property and substance. Pomfret's will had made it plain that he wanted him to have everything. His land and his house, and a considerable amount of money to go with them. The only condition was that he should leave the sea. Young Seton had protested, but Bolitho had made him agree. There were men who fought battles and gave all for their country without counting the odds. Bolitho and Herrick were such men. But if England were to survive the war's growing harvest it needed men like Seton to work from within. Men of loyalty and sensitivity, of gentleness and vision. They would build on the ruins when there was no more need to die for a cause.

Bolitho's recollections after that moment became more confused as she reached his side and the actual service commenced. The touch of her hand, the grave understanding of those eyes which shone like the sea. The rector's reedy voice, and Herrick's acknowledgement as he produced the ring. Too loud and somewhat out of place, his 'Aye, aye, sir!' had brought titters from the watching choristers.

Now it was done, and the waters below the headland were deep in purple shadow. The toasting and the back-slapping, the speeches and his sister's tears, all had gone with the closing of the heavy door.

Behind him in the high-ceilinged room he heard her stirring on the bed. She called quietly, 'What is it, Richard?'

He was watching a ship, anchored far out and ready for the morning tide. A man-of-war. Probably a frigate, he thought. It was easy to picture the officers drowsing over their pipes and tankards, the sound of a violin from the forecastle, and the moan of wind through the shrouds as she tugged impatiently at her cable. Sailors often bemoaned leaving the land, but ships rejoiced at it.

He replied, 'All my family have been sailors. I am the same. There will always be ships, out there, waiting.'

Bolitho turned and watched her as she lifted her arms, pale in the darkness.

'I know that, my darling Richard. And each time you

return here to Falmouth *I* will be waiting, too!'

Down in the deserted dining room Allday stared at the litter of empty glasses and discarded plates. After a moment he picked up an unused goblet and poured a full measure of brandy. Then he walked to the other room and stood looking at the sword above the great stone fireplace. Somehow it looked at peace, he thought. He downed the brandy in one gulp and walked slowly out of the door whistling an old tune, the name of which he had long forgotten.